A LOVELY OBSESSION

CORALEE JUNE

A LOVELY
OBSESSION

To all the badass ladies that stay lowkey as hell and fill their souls with positivity and kindness. For the women that find peace in their damage. For the girls that give grace. To the sisters unafraid to lose chairs at their table and eat alone.

To all the women who are unapologetically themselves, this is for you.

Prologue

HUNTER

18 YEARS AGO

Everything hurts. My stomach is empty and sloshing around from the water Mom gave me three hours ago. I can feel how hungry I am.

The stained mattress on my floor has coiled wires poking at my back. It's dark. I'm not sure Mom paid the electricity bill this month. She has other debts that take priority.

But I'm not scared.

I'm not sure how long I've been forgotten. Years, maybe? Maybe since I was born. I guess it's hard to remember your son when you have needles and meth to fill your time.

Mom has friends over. Loud friends that like to groan and moan. Forest doesn't know. He's too high. The cracks in our walls tell their secrets.

One of them is angry. Really, really angry.

I look out the window in my room and pray. Mom once told me God wasn't real. She said he was for people with money. So I pray in secret.

I beg for a way out.

Forest knows—I can hear him now.

The room is loud. So, so loud.

I fall asleep to the familiar lullaby of screams.

Chapter 1

My heels wobbled on the slippery tile in Nicole Knight's kitchen. Bodies were herded together, crashing into one another with flirty looks and lingering stares. I had a buzz in my bones, a tingling forgetfulness that tempted my good sense.

To some, it was a house party. To me, it was a rare escape.

"Have another drink, Roe," Nicole said while jabbing a dirty shot glass in my face. I'd seen at least a dozen of my classmates wrap their chapsticked tobacco lips around that very rim. I wasn't in the spirit to catch mono, but the clear liquid inside of it tantalized me.

I wasn't much of a partier. Wasn't much of an extrovert, either. But tonight—*just* for tonight—I needed to pretend to be someone else for a bit. Someone that didn't strategically know every danger in the room.

"I should stop," I replied. I had already devoured enough tequila to make my body chatter, and my cotton mouth pout was begging me to drink some water.

Nicole frowned. She was my friend of the month. Tragically beautiful, she had bright blond hair and sparkling jade eyes that seemed to spill with sad mischief. She moved here two months ago, which meant she hadn't been around long enough to know what I was about.

"Come on, you wanted to forget that asshole, drink up!" she encouraged, pressing the cool glass to my lips. I took it from her and swallowed, letting the scorching hot liquid land on my tongue before shooting it down my throat.

Some onlookers cheered. Bad decisions were more palatable when you had good company.

"How are you doing, girl?" Nicole asked while draping her slender arm around my shoulder. She smelled unmistakably of cheap beer and cotton candy body spray, but she was noticeably sober. I realized a couple of weeks ago that she liked to host the parties, not become them.

"I'm fine," I lied, the words like ash on my tongue. That expression was getting on my nerves. It was one of those lies everyone could see through, like a sheer blanket you wrapped around yourself before bracing for a blizzard. But it wasn't my recent breakup that had me out of sorts.

"Are you sure?" she asked. "You seem so sad tonight. It's a fucking party! Liven up!" Nicole fist-pumped the air just as a guy bumped into her, rocking us both as he staggered to the living room. She rolled her eyes at him when he didn't apologize, before turning her attention to me. "I didn't even think you liked Joel that much. I mean, you broke up with him, right?"

Joel was my ex. He was nice but vacant, and he worked perfectly for what I needed. He smoked pot on the weekends and liked to play video games. We lasted longer than most of my relationships, mostly because he seemed more concerned with getting high than asking questions. But of course, it didn't last.

Joel started to get *too* close. He started to want to know about my likes, dislikes, past, present, and if I could imagine a future with him.

So naturally, I ran.

"I know. I just wasn't expecting him to move on so quickly," I replied, the lie easily rolling off my lips. If I were being honest, I wasn't drinking myself into oblivion because of Joel, but Nicole didn't need to know that. I'd rather she think I was heartbroken than know what was really bothering me. The truth wasn't as easy to swallow.

Joel spent all week fucking through anything with a pussy, and any normal girl who could actually fall in love would feel devastated about that, but not me.

I wasn't healthy. I devoured affections and spun them into sophisticated insecurities, ending them without a care. I was a serial dater. A clingy friend that kept things surface level, then fled. There was a certain high I felt when getting to know someone. I was obsessed with hoarding personalities and hyper-focusing on the intricate tics of others to avoid my own. I liked making friends. I liked kissing random boys. It was sticking around that I struggled with. I was running out of people to fall for.

"You know what they say," Nicole began. "The best way to get over an ex is to get under someone else." She knocked my hip with hers and giggled. I doubted she had ever *gotten under* anyone. Nicole might've liked to host parties to piss off her parents, but she wasn't actually as rebellious as she claimed to be. It was another one of those quirks I'd picked up on.

"I'm tired of the dating pool at Mountain Prep," I argued. "It's a bunch of fumbling boys that use your vagina like a fleshlight before asking, '*Did you come?*'" My chuckles filled the room as Nicole gaped at me. Our school was nestled in suburban utopia just outside of Denver, where the middle class thrived and every day at school felt like a reality TV show. People liked to create drama so their small town boredom was more palatable.

Nicole laughed as she peered around the room, assessing the growing crowd in her house. "I don't know, I heard Chris is good in bed," she offered, nodding at the preppy quarterback currently hitting a Juul and blowing smoke in some poor girl's face. Oh yes, I knew Chris very well.

I shrugged, thinking back to our fumbling romp in the janitor's closet at school. In Chris's defense, it was standing room only, but our brief, messy moment was not worth remembering. "His dick is nice, but he's got no rhythm. It was like fucking someone possessed."

Nicole snorted, her eyes wide in shock. "You've slept with him?" she wheezed while looking at me. I saw the curiosity in her eyes. Our friendship was still fairly new. She didn't know just how reckless I was, but she'd soon realize that the rumors were true.

I'd developed quite a reputation over the years. Many called me a slut, and I guess they were right. I didn't think it was anything to be ashamed of. Those who were crueler liked to pick apart my alienation, blaming every indiscretion on my *daddy issues*. They just simplified deeper problems they knew nothing about. My body was a vessel for control. My heart was a rabid beast out to prove something. I cracked my soul wide open and watched as the world slipped on the oil that fell out.

"Yep," I replied, searching the counters for more booze. I'd need more liquid forgetfulness if this conversation dug deeper into my impulsive proclivities.

"Well then, maybe we should find you a college guy, someone that knows how to use his dick. My cousin attends Denver University. He could probably get us into a party."

I smiled at her determination but had zero desire to go. I had this odd contradiction warring within my soul. I hated being alone as much as I hated being around people. Parties weren't really my thing. Crowds made me anxious. But I was doing the whole teenage thing, drinking cheap tequila and laughing at all the right times. I'd even worn my tightest clothes and a shirt that showed off my toned stomach. There was a checklist of high school experiences, and I was ticking all the boxes tonight.

"Oh shit. What's he doing here?" Nicole asked, nodding toward the hallway. I turned my head and rolled my eyes at the sight before me. Joel, with his smirking face and punk rock style, was strolling our way. I wanted to skip the awkward *breakup* stage and go back to just hanging out without expectations. Was it really so hard to be friends after you've sucked someone's dick?

"You look good, Roe," he greeted over the loud music.

Joel hovered over me, and I could practically taste the smoke on his skin. Bouncing in his Converse sneakers, he looked down at me. He was lean and smelled like pot, his jet black hair curled at the ends, kissing the tips of his ears. He sunk his teeth into his bottom lip as those sweeping cobalt eyes looked me up and down.

"Well, you look like shit," I replied with a wink. I tried not to lean too much into the flattery of knowing he still thought of me. I didn't want to lead him on, but validation was a drug and I was an addict. I was a bunch of things, actually.

"You going to stop hiding from me?" he asked.

"Nope," I replied quickly. I never went back for seconds. Once I was done, I was *motherfucking done.* "I'm sure you can find someone here willing to suck your cock."

He braced his hand on the countertop beside me and leaned in, his minty breath feathering over me as I stared down at his chest. He was wearing a gamer T-shirt boasting one of his favorite characters. He used to get so excited when he explained his nerdy games to me. I liked that about him. There was a simplicity about Joel that I connected with. There wasn't much to learn about him because he wasn't particularly complex. We had chemistry. He was easy to please. But I didn't love the guy. I was a serial dater.

"Look at me, Rowboat," he said. That nickname made me quiver.

I let out a slow exhale and looked up at Joel, following his command out of boredom, not respect. Swarms of onlookers crowded closer, eyeing us with curiosity and pity. "We had fun, didn't we?" he asked.

"We did," I agreed. There was no denying that Joel was fun to pass the time with.

"What happened?" he asked, making me frown. How could I possibly explain to him that the idea of liking someone scared the shit out of me? I was drawn to validation like a moth to a flame. I thrived on lingering looks and flirty touches. I blossomed in blissful orgasms and heady moans. But I clung to surface level relationships because they were easy. Anything deeper was like opening a wound. I just wasn't capable of doing anything that wasn't...easy.

"I just wasn't feeling it anymore," I deadpanned while glancing over his shoulder at the growing crowd.

"I figured you needed space, but it's been a week. I really fucking cared about you," he said, as if he were annoyed with himself for having such trivial feelings about me. "We can work through this."

Letting out a huff, I braced both palms against his chest and pushed him away. This was exactly what I wanted to avoid. "While you were giving me space, you fucked the entire senior class," I argued, cocking my head to the side. He staggered back, his mouth dropped open in surprise. He had to have known this was coming. What did he expect? "I'm not interested. Go find someone else."

Instead of reacting how I'd expected him to, he smiled. "You're jealous."

"I'm done with this conversation."

His smile quickly fell, and his eyes turned cold. "So I guess it's true what they say," he replied, straightening his spine.

"Oh?" I feigned ignorance. "And what exactly do they say?"

"You're a tease. The worst fucking tease. You lead people on and drop them like it's nothing."

His words stung, but they weren't wrong.

"Last I checked, we fucked like rabbits," I offered. I was no fucking tease. I didn't lead guys on. If I wanted to fuck, I made my intentions known. I didn't like fluttering around the topic of sex.

He looked down at me with a sneer. "Yeah, Roe. We fucked. I fucked you hard. I ate that pussy like it was my last meal and claimed your ass while you screamed my name." His voice rang out through Nicole's house, echoing off the walls and forcing a ripple of attention to land on me. Joel was making a scene. Some stared and snickered. A few girls blushed. "You might not be a tease with your body, but you sure as hell tease with your heart."

With those parting words, he turned on his heels and left me standing in shock, feeling like the damaged goods he accused me of being.

"Fuck you, asshole!" Nicole screamed at his back like the devoted friend she wanted to be. "What a dick! I can't believe you dated that guy."

I smiled before turning to her, no longer feeling in the partying mood. "He was good in bed, though," I chuckled, though my humor felt empty.

Nicole shook her head and started reaching for more bottles of tequila. "We need to get you drunk. The *nerve* of that guy," she said as I glanced at my watch. It was almost midnight, which meant that Uncle Mack would end his shift at the shipping yard and haul his ass up here and drag me home. I'm pretty sure he had a tracker on my phone. As if on cue, my phone pinged, indicating a message from him.

Uncle Mack: I'm on my way. You better be outside waiting for me or I'll call the cops and shut down whatever party you're at.

I smiled to myself before pocketing my cell. I knew with complete certainty that he would absolutely drag me out of here if I didn't stumble onto the lawn in exactly sixty seconds. "I got to go," I said to Nicole.

She pouted beautifully, her round face falling at my words. "You're leaving? It's barely midnight!"

"Yeah, my uncle is on his way. He's threatening to break the party up if I don't go. Sorry." I couldn't have timed his overprotectiveness better. I had no desire to stay here much longer but was glad to make an appearance and play the part. Now everyone could go home and gossip about how Roe Palmer was the town slut. I welcomed it with open arms, burrowing the truth deep in my chest.

At least it was better than what they said back in New York:

Roe Palmer is the daughter of that crazy woman.

Nicole wrapped me in an Oscar-worthy drunk girl hug, swaying both of our bodies as she squealed her goodbyes. "Okay, text me tomorrow! We can plot your revenge on Joel," she called as I pulled away and started pushing through the crowd and outside.

Uncle Mack wasn't here yet. I didn't hear the familiar roar of his Camaro or feel his broody, pissed-off stare on my back. I walked over to the tree line, giggling to myself at the thought of his impending lecture. My heels sunk into the lawn with every step; the ground was soft from last night's rain, and cold mud splattered on my bare legs. I found a tall tree and braced my back against the trunk. Staring up at the night sky, I counted exhales until my uncle arrived.

"Tired of the party, too?" a warm voice asked to my left. I snapped my head in the direction of the voice and flinched when I saw a figure leaning against another tree and staring at me. He wore a hoodie and had his arms folded over his chest. I couldn't make out any of his features, but he carried himself like someone who had seen the world and didn't like what he found. He had proud shoulders and long legs that were rooted to the grass, similar to the tree he was leaning against. I could feel his eyes on me, though I couldn't see them. Even in my drunken haze, I sensed his energy. It was like drinking whiskey and letting it burn you from the inside out.

"I'm not much of a partier," I answered before staring up at the stars. "You?"

"I'm not really a fan of them. It's just a bunch of sloppy, stupid kids."

I snorted at his gruff declaration. "Are you a student at Mountain Prep?" I asked. Turning to face him, I watched his chest rise and fall in beat to his breath. A long, pregnant pause filled the space between us, and then he chuckled.

"Nope. I graduated a while ago."

"Ah. So you're a creeper waiting on vulnerable, drunk high school girls," I nervously teased as I reached for my phone. I might be reckless from time to time, but I was taught to read a situation, and something felt dangerous in his presence.

"Nah. I'm just looking out for a...friend. I wanted to be near in case something happened."

"That's what they all say," I joked, but there was a sense of honesty to his tone.

I could practically feel his eye roll, though I couldn't see it. It was pitch black outside. "So, if you're not much of a partier, why are you here?" he asked.

It was a pretty personal question, and my flight or fight response perked up, waiting to see what I'd do. If I had wings on my back, I'd be midair. "I felt like escaping for a bit tonight," I finally replied. Maybe it was the darkness of night, adding a sense of privacy to our conversation, or maybe it was the fact that I couldn't see his face, making our entire exchange feel anonymous. I'd never see this man again. I didn't even know his name. It felt like I was in a confessional all of my own. I didn't need a cathedral, I needed the night sky.

"Why?" His question was simple but felt weighed down with curiosity.

"It's a hard day for me," I whispered. "It's...it's my eighteenth birthday. I don't really like birthdays."

He went silent, as if debating my words. It was an overshare, but I had the crutch of alcohol boosting my confidence and making me bold.

"Why not?"

The words got stuck in my throat. My tongue shriveled up and died on the spot, leaving his question to linger unanswered between us. *Because I don't like to celebrate being alive when my entire family is dead.*

He pushed himself off the tree and took a step toward me. I felt myself leaning closer to him. "Sometimes the only way to stay sane is to ignore how you feel. I used to count the blades of grass in my backyard. I'd shove my headphones so deep in my ear and turn up the volume as high as it would go until my skull rattled with the heavy beat."

I nodded my head. Even though I hadn't told him what was bothering me, he got it.

The strange man took a step closer, and the spark of a very, very stupid idea settled in my stomach. "I do stupid shit to forget...like kissing strange men in the woods," I hinted as my lips stretched into a drunken smile. I also made friends. I broke up with boys that loved me. I talked to strangers until my throat was raw, picking apart the little nuances that made them tick so I could focus on something else for a while. He counted blades of grass; I collected and discarded people.

I didn't know if this man was beautiful or dangerous. I just knew he could pass the time between the painful beats of my heart, and right now that was enough.

He took another step closer. A rough palm cupped my cheek. He smelled like the woods. His presence felt steady. Time stretched, and his palm grew hot against my flushed skin. I breathed him in like I'd been holding my breath all night.

There were many types of kisses in the world, and I'd had my fair share. Something told me kissing this man would feel like pure anticipation. I loved the kisses that happened after hours of thinking of them. I might have only spent a few minutes with this man, but the building desire blooming within me felt like an eternity. "I'm not going to kiss you," he finally whispered before pulling away.

I found myself leaning closer, trying to minimize the distance between us. "Oh? Why not?" I asked.

His chuckle sounded like bells and mischief. "Because I'm not some creep preying on vulnerable, drunk high school girls."

"Roe!" my uncle yelled, snapping me out of our strange moment. I whipped my head toward the driveway and frowned when I saw my uncle standing by the hood of his Camaro, tapping his foot impatiently at me.

"Sorry," I began. "I gotta g—" I twisted to face him, but the stranger was gone. "Go," I whispered to myself before shaking my head. He was already gone? I guess I wasn't the only runner at the party tonight.

"Roe! Get your ass over here!" Uncle Mack yelled again. I took a deep breath, then released it with a sigh, silently thanking the stranger for the brief moment of forgetfulness.

Chapter 2

ROE

Uncle Mack was shifting his weight from one foot to the other on Nicole's crisp front lawn, all while staring daggers at me through the shadowed night. I forced a sense of sobriety through my body, praying he didn't see how the world seemed to tip sideways with each staggering step.

"You're drunk," he grunted the moment I was close enough for him to get a whiff of my breath. "You know I hate it when you don't update me on your whereabouts. And I especially hate when you pull shit like this." He was a predictable man that thrived on routine. Always up at four in the morning, he started his day with espresso as black as his wardrobe and then spent the rest of his day acting more like a personal bodyguard than my caregiver.

"I don't have to update you. You can just track my phone, Uncle Mack," I teased before reaching into my pocket and pulling out the smartphone beacon he'd relied on since I was ten.

Uncle Mack was brusque but affectionate. Kind but distant. We'd tested the sentimental bullshit when I first moved in with him eight years ago. He bought me frilly clothes and struggled to make up for the lost time, but it felt hollow. I didn't even know he existed until Mom died.

In the beginning, we both forced a relationship for the sake of survival. Uncle Mack was a gruff guy, not ready to take on a tween. I was a traumatized girl, not capable of handling any more upheaval in my life. Once he realized that I wasn't looking for a friend or father figure, he stopped tossing stuffed animals in my face and taught me how to curl a fist.

"I might have had a bit to drink," I admitted while cupping my forehead. Was I slurring? I wasn't so sure. I blinked twice and peered up at him as swaying bodies passed us by. They clutched red cups like trophies as my uncle pinched the bridge of his nose.

"Get your ass in the car. We're going home."

"You don't want to stay and take a couple of shots? You look like you could use it," I mocked as he gently grabbed my arm and steered me toward his Camaro. Uncle Mack was old, with a crooked nose and broad shoulders that seemed to carry the world. He had a beer gut but was handsome, in a weathered sort of way, and was about as cuddly as a cactus.

He was all I had, and that was enough. Permanence trumped affection.

"You don't even like parties. Crowds make you anxious, that house is pounding with bubblegum pop music, and you hate listening to anything that isn't classic rock. Why the hell are you doing this? I had a long ass day at the yard. The boss makes me work a double, and you decide to go all rebellious for the night," he cursed before wrenching open the passenger door of his sleek car and guiding me inside.

Once I was safely seated with my seatbelt on, he slammed the door shut, and I watched him circle the car through the windshield. Each stomp on the ground and muttered curse had me smiling to myself. We both knew why I was out tonight. He was just kind enough not to bring it up. My birthday was a sad reminder that his sister was dead.

He got in the driver's seat and turned on the car, the roar of his engine masking the grunts swirling in his throat. "Come on, I never party. Think of this as a rite of passage," I argued while leaning back and closing my eyes.

"Right. Usually, I have to drag you out of parked cars," he replied with a disgusted shiver.

Again—personal bodyguard. My uncle was the biggest cock block in the world. He liked to pretend I was a virginal, innocent little dove, spreading my wings in a secluded garden away from pollinating bees. His attempt at keeping me out of trouble was cute. Too bad I was addicted to the high of feeling wanted and spent my free time exploring meaningless flings.

He lectured me as we drove home, reminding me of the dangers of underage drinking and scolding me for not telling him where I was. "You've always been wild, Roe. I was just hoping you'd grow up a bit this year. Especially since you dumped that pothead. What was his name again? Hank? Jacob?"

I laughed. "Joel?"

"Yep. That's the dumbass," Uncle Mack replied with a nod.

He pulled up to our tiny house and put the car in park, twisting his bulky frame toward me with a furrowed brow. "I just worry about you, is all. You're impulsive and naïve. You don't make my job easy."

I frowned at his use of the word *job*. I'd always felt like a job to him.

I knew he cared about me, but there was a sense of responsibility in our dynamic that always made me feel uncomfortable. He didn't ask to raise his niece. He didn't ask to be burdened with my issues. But I literally had nowhere else to go.

I still remembered the first night I moved in.

I'd slashed my hand on broken glass while unpacking my nearly empty backpack. I remember crying to my uncle as crimson life poured from the cut. He washed it with a rag and wiped my tears with his course thumb. His care was tender yet foreign to me. I was so used to screams and overdramatic wails. The slightest injury would send my mother spiraling, and I'd be forced to kiss my own paper cuts as she rocked on the floor.

But Uncle Mack saw it and stayed calm. He was considerate and careful. It was jarring, and once he finished cleaning it, he patted my head and said, "I'm not putting a Band-Aid on it, kid."

"Why not?" I'd asked him through broken sobs. It wasn't a big cut; I think the idea of hurting was more painful than the actual laceration. I'd been conditioned to fear pain. I'd been conditioned to run like hell away from it.

"You gotta let your damage breathe, Roe," he'd responded with a sad, affectionate smile. He probably thought I'd sliced myself on purpose. The line was crisp and long, too straight to appear accidental. He didn't ask, though. I wasn't self-destructive, at least not in the physical sense. My issues were all emotional.

Let your damage breathe.

Let your damage breathe.

Let it fucking breathe.

I guess that's why I'd kept my heart wide open all these years. The broken thing pounding in my chest had become a symptom of my existence. Some said I was too much, but they didn't get it. I was just airing out my trauma for the world to see.

Shaking my head, I pulled myself out of those intrusive memories and cleared my tight throat. "I'll do better," I lied before unbuckling my seatbelt and shuffling outside. We walked in uneasy silence to the door, and once inside, he went to the kitchen and grabbed a beer, cracking his neck in exhaustion before sitting down at the table. I watched him with a grimace. He'd been working a lot lately. I cleared my throat. "Uncle Mack?"

"What?" he grumbled.

"Thank you. For, uh, everything," I began while shuffling on my feet. Thank you for taking me in. Thank you for being normal. Thank you for raising me. "Goodnight," I then whispered.

He hesitated, with his hand under his chin and words clogged in his emotionally stunted throat. "Hey, Roe?" he asked, making my blood pressure spike.

Don't say it.

Don't say it.

Please, don't say it.

The last words my mother ever said to me were *Happy Birthday, Roe.* I could still hear her raspy voice. It felt like a curse, and I refused to lose Uncle Mack, too. Superstitions might be dumb, but I was raised to cling to them.

"Yeah?" I answered back while squeezing my fist until my nails cut through my palm.

He paused, likely hearing the pain in my wavering voice. "Goodnight."

I wobbled down the hall to my room and shut the door. With a shaky exhale, I braced my back against the wall and slid down it, privately thanking him for not bringing up what day it was. Uncle Mack learned long ago that birthdays were a sore subject for me. My father died the day I was born, and my mom joined him precisely a decade later. It was better for all of us if we just pretended today didn't exist.

I reached into my pocket and pulled out a lighter, flicking it on just to stare at the dancing flame. "Happy birthday, Roe," I whispered out loud to myself before blowing it out. I didn't bother to make a wish. I watched the burning hope extinguish.

Maybe it was melodramatic and counterproductive to pretend that another year around the sun hadn't passed, but I guess I still felt like the ten-year-old shaking her lifeless mother's body. Maybe one day I'd eat cake and blow out my candles like an ordinary girl. Maybe one day I'd settle into love and find a sense of intimacy that didn't feel temporary or send me running for the hills.

But not today.

Chapter 3

ROE

"Morning," I said while settling onto the cozy couch and bracing my bare feet up on the coffee table. Unsurprisingly, I didn't sleep well last night. I kept seeing her. Lifeless and cold with foamy vomit pooling out of her mouth. I woke up clenching my teeth so hard I just knew they would crack.

"More like afternoon," Uncle Mack retorted, knocking me out of my memories. His voice was laced with hard sarcasm. It always irked him when I slept in late, probably because he couldn't sleep past five. His body was hardwired to be an early riser.

"Not all of us have to wake up at the asscrack of dawn, Uncle Mack," I joked roughly, refusing to admit that I'd gotten probably two hours of sleep. I spent most of the morning lying in bed and thinking about how fragile everything in life was. My mother's memory was a hard stain to shake.

Uncle Mack was flipping through channels on the television and leaning back in his recliner. Our home was a simple three bedroom with a nice deck and a spacious yard that had a generous view of the mountains. If I were being honest, it looked like no one even lived here. We didn't hang photos on the walls or decorate it in any particular style. We filled it up with functioning furniture, takeout, and a flat-screen TV.

"You hungover?" he asked. The eagerness in his tone hinted that he was looking forward to my pounding headache and dry mouth. If he hoped that I'd learned my lesson, it didn't work.

"Sorry to disappoint you, but no," I quipped with a smile while gathering my shoulder-length caramel hair and piling it on top of my head in a messy bun. "I'm still young, which means I don't get hangovers." I patted my stomach with a sly smile. "I've got that nice metabolism. You just look at a beer and you're grumpy for weeks."

"Watch it," Uncle Mack replied with a puff before crossing his arms over his chest. It wasn't my fault he was an old fart. "I guess we should discuss your punishment," he then said while giving me a pointed stare. Ah, the punishment.

"What's the damage, old man?"

Mack stroked his beard like he was trying to come up with something sinister. "No phone for a week?"

Good. I didn't have anyone I wanted to talk to anyway. "You can do better than that. I mean, I was underage drinking, Mack."

"You're right. Grounded for a month."

"What exactly is your definition of grounded? Because as it stands, I don't really go many places anyway."

"Good point," Uncle Mack replied, not even bothering to deny that he was strict as fuck. I had to be creative to get around his bullshit rules. It had become a fun game of cat and mouse over the years. "No pizza for a month."

My mouth dropped open in shock. "Pizza? You're taking away pizza? What kind of monster are you?"

I grinned at him for a moment, rolling my eyes at his ridiculous punishment. He'd be ordering a deep-dish within the week.

Most kids my age wouldn't appreciate Uncle Mack's overbearing nature, and even though it annoyed me sometimes, it was nice to have someone who actually gave a fuck.

He turned to look at me in that speculative way of his. Even though he was grumpy, he was still very intuitive and aware. Uncle Mack was always assessing me and observing the room. He probably already cataloged the bags under my eyes and the yawn threatening to escape my lips. "You sleep okay, kid?"

I swallowed, debating on pretending I didn't hear his question. If I ignored him, he'd press the issue, and we'd both then be forced to awkwardly attempt stumbling through a discussion about my issues. "Nah. You know how October fourth goes." I was proud of myself for expertly avoiding the word *birthday*.

Nodding, he didn't offer any words of comfort or empathy but still relaxed at my explanation. We had such a unique relationship. We were comfortable with one another, but Uncle Mack knew every fine detail of my habits, my fears, my self-destructive ways. He didn't prod, mostly because he had the emotional range of a coffee cup and was repelled by the vulnerability, but he cared.

Someone knocked on the door, a loud pounding that made me turn my head. "Can you get that?" my uncle asked while scratching his belly and rolling his neck. "It's probably the FedEx guy. I ordered a new part for the Camaro, and someone has to sign for it."

"You're always tinkering with that thing," I said. Getting up, I adjusted my tank top and sleep shorts while making my way to the door.

I could hear Uncle Mack's cell phone ringing from the living room, and he answered it with a gruff *what*.

I twisted the knob and smiled, prepared to greet someone, but... I leaned out of the threshold, squinting around with a frown on my face. "There's no one here," I called over my shoulder to Uncle Mack before looking down at the welcome mat. Maybe they just left the box.

But there was no box. There, I saw something that made my stomach clench. It was a flower—not just any flower—a lily. Bright and beautiful, it was deceptively cheerful. Some might find joy in nature's elegant display of petals, but I knew better.

Wisps of a faint memory stroked my mind. Mom used to tell me about all the flowers and what they symbolized. She was working at a flower shop in the city when she met my father. He'd come in to order an arrangement of lilies, and they'd hit it off immediately. They fell into a fast affair neither of them was capable of falling out of. Mom was like me, constantly diving into a shallow pool of passions without a life jacket. She lost herself in the excitement of it all. Maybe that was why I was so weary of staying in love. I craved it and despised it all the same.

During one of her...episodes...a few years after he'd died, she'd told me something. She said she should have known that the flowers he ordered the first day they met were a warning from God. He wanted an elegant bouquet, but she was too smitten to recognize the sinister symbolism hidden behind their pretty petals: *death.*

Goose bumps pebbled over my skin, and a foreboding sense of being watched washed over me.

"Get inside right now!" Uncle Mack yelled while wrapping his beefy arms around my stomach and dragging me out of the doorway. My feet skidded across the hardwood floors as my body flailed.

"What's going on?" I demanded as he set me down. Adjusting my tank top, I stared in bewilderment at my uncle. Why the fuck was he freaking out? Without answering me, he then twisted the deadbolt and locked the door.

"Fuck!" he yelled before running a hand through his thinning hair. "Did you see anyone?"

My eyes widened. "N-no. I didn't. No one was there, just that fl-flower."

Uncle Mack quickly worked to close the blinds on all the windows, muttering to himself all the while. "What's going on?" I urged him.

"Was it a lily?"

"Y-yes. How did you know?"

Uncle Mack picked up his cell phone and spoke into the receiver. "It's the Asphalt Devils. They left their signature." I stared expectantly at Uncle Mack for a moment as someone on the other end of the line spoke. "Okay. Meet you at the coordinates we discussed." He hung up his phone and slid it into his pocket before turning to address me.

"You have thirty seconds to get dressed. Leave your cell phone here," he replied before dropping to his knees and shoving aside the tattered red rug in our entryway. I watched on in shock, surprised to see that beneath the rug I'd obliviously padded across for the last eight years, there was a trapdoor with a padlock.

"What the fuck?" I asked while taking a step closer.

"You now have twenty seconds. Stop wasting time," Uncle Mack argued before pulling his keys out of his denim pocket and opening the nook. He worked like he'd been preparing for this day his entire life. I sensed the threat in the air but wasn't sure what he was so afraid of. Glued to the spot, I stared in dismay as he pulled a rifle and three handguns out of the compartment.

"Wh-what is that for?" I sputtered. None of this was making any sense. Guns? We didn't carry guns in the house. Instead of answering me, Uncle Mack checked his watch and huffed.

"We're out of time. We will go through the garage and get in the car. The second the door opens, keep your head ducked, got it?"

He rose up and holstered guns to his body before heading toward the garage, not waiting for me to respond. I remained rooted to the spot, staring at his back in confusion. We're leaving? Where? When? Why? What did that flower mean? And who the fuck was he on the phone with? Uncle Mack paused when he realized I wasn't following him. "Get your fucking ass over here, Roe. I don't have time to explain. Trust me, okay?"

I studied his expression for a fraction of a second. I noted the seriousness in his grave eyes and the frown on his wrinkled mouth. His cheeks were flushed, and his fingers shook with adrenaline. "Okay. Okay, let me put my shoes on."

I grabbed my sneakers from their spot by the door and jogged down the hallway after him. Once I was at his back, he opened the door and led me into the garage and to his Camaro. He inspected the tires, the engine, and underneath the car like he was looking for something. He must not have found anything, because he then spoke to me.

"Get in the car, Roe," he demanded while brushing his hands together. I hastily followed his orders and opened the passenger door, slipping inside while trying to control my breathing. He quickly joined me, and once we were both settled, he let out a slow exhale and shifted to face me. "Keep your head down. I'll protect you, okay?" I nodded, then curled my torso until my lips were touching the top of my shaking knees. He put the key in the ignition and turned on the car before pressing the button for the garage. I listened as the low rumble of the gate rose.

Time seemed to slow. I was functioning on confusion and shock, my body obeying Uncle Mack's orders while my mind tried to come up with reasons he was acting this way. Did he do drugs? Was he in some kind of trouble at work? He'd mentioned the Asphalt Devils. Wasn't that some kind of motorcycle gang?

Uncle Mack put the Camaro in reverse and pressed the pedal all the way down, shooting out of the garage with a vengeance as I squealed. We accelerated down the driveway, and he slammed the car in drive before spinning out and down our street.

I wanted to peek up and look around, see what he was running from, but I trusted him and kept curled down. Out of the corner of my eye, I saw Uncle Mack lift his phone up.

"We have two tails. Headed to you now."

"Headed where?!" I screamed. "Who are you even talking to?"

Before Uncle Mack could answer, the sound of shattering glass pierced my ears. Sharp slivers of the passenger window fell down like rain on my body. A shrill scream broke past my lips, and I felt the car swerve. "Shit!" Uncle Mack yelled while twisting the steering wheel to the left and hopping the curb. The engine whined, the wheels sputtered. I breathed in the scent of gun smoke, letting it coat my lungs as the Camaro lurched.

On instinct, I peered out my broken window and took in the sight of a blacked-out truck swerving in and out of traffic and trying to keep parallel with us. "Get down!" Uncle Mack screamed while shoving my head toward the floorboards with his palm.

I braced my arms over my head and tried to keep calm, but the jostling car made me sick to my stomach. I couldn't breathe. I couldn't think. "What's happening!" I shrieked when something crashed into us from behind. The sound of crumbling metal rattled my ears, and our car fishtailed out of control, sending us into a rolling pattern of suffering. The airbags deployed, smacking my skull and shooting my body backward. Glass grazed my lips. My mouth pooled with blood. My left arm snapped, and debilitating pain rocked through me.

Finally, we stopped. My vision was a blur of shapes and colors. I tasted rust and smoke. "Uncle Mack?" my garbled voice tried to choke out, but my throat felt blocked by emotion and the trauma from our wreck.

A groan answered my call.

The earth shook.

My body was shattered on the road. His old black Camaro, the same car in which he'd picked me up from the police station in New York, was nothing but crumbled metal and crunched memories. Footsteps on the pavement rattled against my brain, like a methodical warning.

My eyes were drowning in blood, a wound on my forehead felt like an offering.

Let your damage breathe.

Let your damage breathe.

Let it fucking breathe.

Tears mixed with blood filled my nose. The footsteps were close.

And then a shot rang out. Crisp and clear, it sliced through the air like a booming whip.

The footsteps stopped.

My eyes closed.

Chapter 4

ROE

Ripping to the surface of my consciousness took considerable effort. My mind felt entombed, alive in a pit of splintered glass and pain. Thundering, pulsing agony echoed around my skull. Everything hurt. Everything ached. Massive, coarse stones seemed to settle on my eyelids, making it challenging to pry open my eyelids and take in the room.

I knew almost immediately that something was very, very wrong. There was a peculiar unsettled feeling seeping into my bones, suggesting that something wasn't right with my body. When I first roused, I'd hoped to be greeted with the smell of antiseptic and the sound of beeping hospital equipment. After all, that's what people did when they were injured. They went to the doctor.

I was familiar with hospitals. When I was a little girl, back when I still had a mother, every cut, bump, scrape, and bruise had to be looked at by a doctor. Mom knew all the emergency room triage nurses by name. It was one of the perks of having a mother obsessed with her fear of death.

But I wasn't in a hospital. No, I was in hell.

Four midnight blue walls engulfed me. I sniffed the air and noted the distinct smell of fresh paint. After blinking the sleep away for a few moments, my vision cleared enough to notice that a single wooden door was in my direct line of vision. I wanted to get up and test the knob to see if it was locked, but my body wouldn't cooperate. The space was so cramped; I felt cornered. Trapped.

There couldn't have been more than two feet between me and the wall. Claustrophobia creeped up my awareness like a serpent, crawling along the ridges of my spine as I became more and more aware of the deadly reality I'd woken up to. I was on a full-sized bed, and the frame groaned every time I tried to move my body. The soft mattress had no support, so lying on it felt like drowning in quicksand. A thick white duvet comforter cloaked my naked body. Oh my God, where had my clothes gone? I peered beneath the blanket and winced at the dark bruises coating my skin. No panties. No... nothing. Just bruised skin and dried blood.

I struggled to lift my legs, but the uselessly numb limbs wouldn't respond to my earnest demands. My left arm was a tingly sort of paralyzed and lay heavy beside me, wrapped in a hard cast made of plaster.

What happened to me? I swallowed, my dry mouth painstakingly producing an insignificant amount of saliva. I eyed a clear, half-empty glass of water on the nightstand beside me but didn't dare reach for it. This was wrong, so wrong. I felt half-dead. What if the water was drugged? I was almost thirsty enough to test it, though.

Where the fuck was I?

A single lamp with a lazy, warm glow was perched on the nightstand to my left, but it was so dull that I could barely make out the room. The floor was rough concrete, blotched with various rust-colored stains that I couldn't make out. There was a slight chill to the air that made my teeth rattle and vibrate. I knew that if I somehow managed to get my feet to work, the icy floor would send a shock wave through me. I exhaled, wondering if it was cold enough to see my breath, but it wasn't. A cold sweat completely painted my body, making the freezing bite that much more intense.

My mind immediately started doing that timeless checklist, the one Mom used to burn into my brain. Look for all the things that could kill you. Observe your weaknesses. Fear everything. Trust nothing. I could feel the start of a panic attack coming on. Maybe I would survive the crash and this hell just to let my mind kill itself.

"Uncle Mack?" my strained voice choked out, too afraid to yell and uncertain if I actually could. My mind worked to make sense of what it could remember, cataloging all the brutal moments that led up to this.

The rolling car.

Bullets slicing through the air.

Blood.

Strong hands dragging me across the asphalt and pulling me out of the Camaro.

A soft, delicate touch to my tear-soaked cheek.

Then nothing.

"Uncle Mack?" I called again, this time stronger. My pleading cry echoed around the room. Vulnerability felt like barbed wire wrapped around my breasts. I was naked, bruised, battered, and weak.

I focused my eyes on the single door directly in front of me while willing myself to get up and investigate the lock. There was a complex disconnect between my brain and my body. My limbs felt so fucking heavy. It was like they'd been replaced with bags of cement. There were no windows in the room, no way of fleeing. There were no other sounds except for my harsh, erratic breathing. I was thankful for the heaviness, though. At least I couldn't feel the sharp pain in my arm. I knew it would come whenever the drugs wore off. But I couldn't escape if I was writhing in agony.

Just as I was about to scream out in stark terror, the single door slowly inched open, like a portal to hell slyly revealing itself. I held my breath and shot up in bed, gripping the bedding to my chest like modesty was something I cared about. I felt too defenseless, too weak.

Too confused.

"H-hello?"

I blinked twice, trying to see who was on the other side.

"You're awake," a voice answered me. Profound and brooding, the tone sounded authoritative yet somehow familiar. My chest expanded with air at his words, like he could command my lungs with a single syllable.

"Who are you?" I rasped, my weathered voice grinding against my raw throat. My veins felt hollow, like I hadn't had a drink of water in days. I debated taking a sip of water once more but refrained. I was too focused on the open door and the voice calling out to me.

The door opened further, and I gasped at the imposing shadow on the other side. The hooded figure was so towering that I felt tiny in comparison.

His shoulders were proud and muscular, veiled by the thick material of his sweatshirt. Gray sweatpants hung low on his hips as he calmly walked toward me. I squinted at his face, trying to find any recognizable features, but he kept it hidden completely from view. Something told me that was intentional. He didn't answer my question, the man simply hovered over the foot of my bed and stared at me in silence.

"What do you want from me?" I asked while inching backward until my back hit the headboard. Every movement made a dull ache pound through my sore muscles.

I was plotting my escape, trying to figure out if I was capable of running around him and outside. He was big, and my body was battered. I wasn't sure I could fight him off even if I tried. "Are you just going to glare at me?" I asked after a long moment had passed. I stared right back at him, speculating if he was even real. If it weren't for the persistent rise and fall of his chest, I'd think he was a phantom of my drowsy imagination. This felt more like a nightmare than life.

He took a step closer, and I gasped, forcing myself not to squeeze my eyes shut in terror. He took another stride, and my heart galloped like it was trying to pump a lifetime of blood through my veins in a matter of seconds. My body trembled. Anxiety and adrenaline swirled in my gut, floating along my nerves as I watched the shadowed figure stalk closer and closer and...

Once he was about a foot away, I smelled him. He was earthy, like patchouli and rosewood. The masculine scent was subtle but memorable. I felt suspended in time as he leaned even closer. I wanted to fight, to run. But my soul was trapped in his orbit, and I was too disoriented to make sense of what was happening or who he was.

"Are you going to hurt me?" I croaked. His shoulders lifted, and I wasn't sure if it was the tension that forced that movement or if his answer was a shrug. "Please don't hurt me."

"I already have, Roe." His clipped response confused me. How did he know my name? Unsettled certainty unfurled in my throat. This was who Uncle Mack was running from. This was the man that shot at me and caused our car wreck.

"Why? Please just explain what's happening," I urged while crossing my arms over my chest. Every single movement depleted my energy. I felt like a popped balloon, lazy and languid and utterly useless.

"No," he replied. I let out a shaky breath as he lifted his finger. Slowly, ever so slowly, he cut through the remaining space between us and pressed the pad of his index finger against the side of my neck. His touch landed directly on top of the centimeter-long discolored scar that I'd had since my childhood. The second our skin touched, I felt a zap of awareness and heat travel down my exposed collarbone and flow throughout my body. They say terror is chilling, but the response this stranger had evoked from my body felt like the burning fires of hell. It was uncomfortable, smoldering with intensity.

He paused, lingering on that spot on my neck for another long, penetrating moment. It was as if he were shocked to be touching me. Goose bumps pebbled over my skin, and I went rigid with fear, not wanting to provoke him with any sudden movements. He was touching me, fucking touching me. I assessed the dim situation I was in, the nakedness of my body, and the unfamiliar setting. This man had me in his fist and could squeeze me till I cracked if he wanted.

He let out a slow and steady exhale, like he'd been holding his breath, before speaking. "When you were nine, a little boy pushed you off the top of the slide at the park," he whispered. My mouth dropped open in shock. How did he know that?

"Y-yes," I replied with a flinch, trying to put more space between us.

"You cut your neck. There was a lot of blood. You're so easily broken, Roe." His bitter voice made me gasp.

I remembered that day, though it seemed so long ago. My pink dress had been soaked with blood. I remembered the little boy crying in shock. He hadn't expected to hurt me. We were a bunch of stupid kids testing the boundaries of our mortality. Mom rarely let me go to the park. She said it was a death trap, and falling that day had proved her point. She stopped taking me after that. Eventually, she stopped leaving the house.

"Who are you?" I asked again. "How do you know that?"

"I know lots of things." He trailed his fingers down my neck and over my shoulder, leaving a blazing trail across my arm until he landed on my outer wrist on my uninjured arm. "You burned this when you were thirteen. You wanted to cook Mack dinner, yes?" I stared at where our skin connected for a moment too long before turning my gaze to my other arm, and the cast currently covering it.

"Did I break my arm in the crash?" I asked. My voice slurred, and I wasn't sure if I was high on pain meds or poisoned from the venom in this strange man's presence.

Once again the man didn't answer me. Instead, he slipped his hand under the blanket with slow precision. I immediately shied away from the contact, my sluggish body responding the best it could. But he persisted, digging his fingers into my body until his gruff touch landed on my stomach. I sucked in another breath at the intrusive movement. His large hand nearly completely covered the expanse of my tight abdomen, his fingers stretching low enough to make my fears spike and the vulnerability I felt grow tenfold. I could feel the calluses on his palm and each groove of his rough skin. His forearm had brushed against my breasts, but all of his movement was hidden beneath the blanket covering me. I could only feel his perusal. It was a terrifying violation of my personal space, but I was still curious about what his intentions were.

He'd touched every injury I'd ever had. How could he possibly know about this one?

"Your mother kicked you in the stomach when you were six," he whispered to himself before lightly tracing the exact spot where she had pummeled me. "It was because you fell, remember? You were playing and nearly hit your head on the corner of your nightstand. She wanted to punish you for getting hurt. It was the only time she didn't take you to the hospital."

Tears filled my eyes at his words. He was right, and how he knew my painful past, I didn't know. She only did it once, but it was a memory that had stuck with me. It was like a cut that wouldn't scab. My eyes widened, and I peered up at his shadowed face. I couldn't see much of anything, just the slight frown, and his dark, scruffy facial hair. He had pillowy lips, which were currently stretched thin into a hard line of annoyance.

When he pulled away, relief flooded me as a wave of cool distance breezed along my pebbled skin. I could still feel the heat of his touch and the threat in his movements, though.

A million questions fluttered through my brain. I wanted to understand who he was, where I'd woken up, and what he planned to do with me.

"Where is Uncle Mack?" I insisted. Uncle Mack was the only family I had left. He was the only person I let stick around in my fleeting heart. What if he was dead? What if I was truly alone now? I needed to know if this man had killed him.

"He didn't do his job, Roe. We all have jobs to do."

My brow furrowed in confusion. His job? Was he mixed up in some shady gang activity? "I don't understand," I replied while shaking my head.

"He was supposed to protect you. He failed," the strange man whispered. Memories of my overprotective uncle flashed across my sluggish mind. Every time he pulled me from my dates. How he drove me to school because he couldn't trust me to drive myself. "He understood the consequences of failing. Once you're better, I'll let you see him again."

I brushed my hair behind my ear, shaking my head as I looked down at my lap. "Please don't hurt him." I started to cry, though my eyes were so dry the tears seemed to evaporate the moment they pooled in my tear ducts.

The strange man seemed to hold his breath, going impossibly still. Hovering on the edge of saying something, I watched him then sway on the spot. My lip trembled as shocking awareness flooded my system. I needed to get better and get the fuck out of here.

He pulled a syringe from the pocket of his hoodie, and I flinched away, willing my heavy body to move as he tapped at the needle. "You need to rest. The doctor will be back soon."

I stared at the threatening needle. "No, no, no. Please," I begged as his hand wrapped around my uninjured wrist, squeezing with a viselike grip.

My feeble attempts to get away were almost laughable. "Please," I cried out as he plunged the sharp instrument into my arm. I focused on the thick, warm liquid that filled my veins. He grunted in satisfaction as I whimpered.

"You always get hurt," he whispered in tense reverence as I slowly gave in to the darkness that clouded my vision. Those haunting words sounded too familiar.

I could have sworn I heard him say something else, but I wasn't sure if it was my nightmares talking or him. Maybe they were the same. "You always get hurt," he said again. "But not anymore."

Chapter 5

ROE

The next time I woke, I didn't let feeble confusion guide my movements. My eyes popped open like a bullet escaping a gun. I angled my head up and searched around the room, somewhat expecting that odd man to be observing me again, but there was no one there.

I could still feel him, though. My skin broke out in bumps like it could sense his stare. I might've been alone in that unfamiliar room, but his presence dominated the air. When I inhaled, the smell of rosewood slapped at my throat.

It took a few moments to stand. My body felt weakened but still better than before. With each step, my joints seemed to crunch with soreness. Once at the door, I rattled the knob and busted my bruised body against the wood. I screamed a lot. I urinated in a nearby bucket and guzzled down the glass of water on the nightstand. Rabid and scared, I freaked out for what felt like days, though it couldn't have been more than a few hours.

Every passing second had me feeling more and more on edge, and all the while, I felt his eyes on me.

Visions of the hooded man and his enigmatic words circulated throughout my mind. I scrutinized every sentence, every connotation of his tone and tried to come up with his motives for keeping me here. He said Uncle Mack didn't protect me. He knew about my injuries, some of them very private. He couldn't have known about them unless he was watching me.

How long had he been watching me?

Why?

I stank of salt, vomit, and body odor. My wavy, caramel hair was a snarled, tangled mess, knotted and drenched with my nervous sweat. How long would this psycho hold me here?

Thankfully, I was clothed now. Black sweats covered my scraped legs, and an oversized gray sweatshirt covered my torso, though my wounded arm wasn't threaded through the sleeve. Instead, I woke to it cradled to my chest. I was thankful for the comfort of clothes but didn't like the idea of someone putting them on me while I was vulnerable and passed out. The thought of the strange man touching me sent a shudder of fear throughout my body.

I examined the furniture in my room, trying to see if I could break it apart and use something as a weapon. Maybe if I found a blunt object, I could slam it against his skull. I wanted to see his face.

Just when I'd finally resolved to use the lamp on my nightstand as a bat, the door to my narrow room opened. I braced myself for the intense stare of my stranger.

My stranger?

My stranger?

What the fuck was wrong with me?

But instead of the hooded man with secrets and heat, I was greeted with the bruised face of my uncle. Relief and apprehension filled me. I would have shot up from my spot on the bed if my entire body wasn't a bundle of aches. Instead, I slowly shifted, gaping at his slumped form as he entered my small room. "Uncle Mack? What happened to you?"

He wore an identical cast to mine on his left arm and had a fresh cut along his neck. He moved with a limp like his right leg was bothering him. His face was peppered with bruises, and his strong jaw bloomed a dark purple.

"Get up, Roe. We're leaving," he gruffly replied before sitting on the bed, like walking into the room took too much effort for him.

My skin horripilated and shivers racked my spine. We're leaving? After days of confusion, and that's the first thing he wanted to say to me? "Leaving? Where are we? Why did we run? And who was that man that came in here to see me?" My questions escaped my lips in quick procession. I couldn't get my worries out fast enough. I sought understanding and answers. I didn't feel safe, and I knew the only thing that would give me control over the situation would be knowledge.

Uncle Mack blanched like he was nervous about my questions. "He's no one, Roe."

I frowned at that dull answer. The strange man didn't feel like no one. He knew me, knew intimate details about my childhood that I'd revealed to no one. His voice was familiar and his touch even more so. There was something about him that felt inevitable. I couldn't escape the unspoken idea that he knew me. Intimately. Dangerously. It was so odd, and yet the puzzle of his intimacy was addicting. In our brief but intense moment together, I felt like he held me gently in his palm, but I couldn't tell if he was stroking me like I was precious gemstones or an atom bomb.

Whoever he was, Uncle Mack obviously knew him; I could discern that by the way he planted a half-hearted excuse in the soil of my curiosity, then glowered when a flower didn't bloom.

"I'm not going anywhere until you explain to me what happened and why you look like someone took a sledgehammer to your body," I began, anger infusing my blood with newfound energy as I sat up straighter and used my index finger on my good hand to poke at his chest. "One second we were relaxing and watching a baseball game, and the next we're racing for our lives. Then, I wake up here, beat and bruised, to a strange man. He knew me, Uncle Mack. He knew..." My voice faltered. I hadn't even told him about the terrible things his sister had done to me, though I had a feeling I didn't have to. Uncle Mack might be a basic man, but he was intuitive. He could see the damage from my childhood written across my face. "He knew things...things I've never told anyone. None of this makes any sense, and if you think I'll just blindly follow you, then you don't know me at all."

Uncle Mack groaned and mumbled something under his breath that sounded like *I told him this would happen.*

"Told who?" I snapped while poking him again. This time, when my index finger connected with the soft muscle of his chest, he winced. I briefly wondered how many injuries were hidden under his clothes.

Uncle Mack rolled his eyes and gritted his teeth. He could be annoyed all he wanted, but I wasn't just going to let him be cryptic and settle for blissful ignorance. "The people chasing us have been taken care of, Roe. The man you met was a friend of mine. We can go home now."

I scoffed. As if I'd accept that bullshit explanation. Uncle Mack didn't have friends. He had coworkers and me. "A friend of yours?" I replied sarcastically with a roll of my eyes. "Why was he even chasing us to begin with?"

Uncle Mack pulled his bulky body back up to a standing position, his spine twisted to the side like he was compensating for a flare of pain in his abdomen. "Roe. He wasn't the one chasing us, okay? He saved us."

I blinked twice at that explanation. I'd hoped it would create a chasm of relief to flood me, but it didn't. I just felt more bogged down by confusion. "Listen," Uncle Mack began again. "You're going to get up and get in the car. We're going to go home and pretend none of this ever happened. Don't ask questions. Stop prying. I know you're shaken up, but I promise you it's better if you don't know. I'm trying to keep you safe, okay?"

Keep me safe? What was he even keeping me safe from?

"No." My single word response filled the small, quiet room. It landed like a heavy rock in the deep ocean of distrust growing between us. I crossed my arms over my chest in defiance while staring him down. I took in the dried blood on his thin lips and the rust-colored stains on his white shirt. I noted the tear in his jeans and the darkened blue-black color of a bruise on his eye. Uncle Mack was beaten to hell, and if I needed to, I could outrun him. Between the two of us, he looked the worse for wear.

I wanted to trust my uncle. I wanted to believe that he had my best intentions at heart. He was the only family I had. I knew this man—or at least I thought I did. But something in my gut was telling me to run. There was an innate wrongness about everything that had happened, everything he was saying. I wasn't about to lie down and accept his excuses.

"Yes," a deep voice said from the doorway. I snapped my attention there and stared at the phantom leering at me. He was still wearing his hooded jacket, concealing his face from my vision, but I recognized his commanding presence. It was like the room had dropped ten degrees from his chilling energy. I felt the gloom shadowing his soul.

He'd unzipped his hooded jacket but wore nothing beneath it. My eyes wandered along the hard hills of his body, noting each defined dip in his abdomen and the firm lines pointed in the shape of a V at his hips. I noticed deep gashes along his chest, old scars that had long ago healed but still seemed to define him. I thought the scars would make him look more dangerous, but instead, it just confirmed that he was actually human. On his hip, there was the distinct edge of a tattoo, but I couldn't fully make it out. "I got this," Uncle Mack retorted through gritted teeth while staring at the stranger.

My heart rate picked up, and I shuffled a little to create more space between us, though he hadn't moved past the threshold of the door. I wasn't sure there was even much room for the three of us, considering this room was a glorified closet.

"I thought you had it handled last time, but look where we are," the man growled in response, turning his attention away from me and to my battered uncle. I could feel the hostility rolling off of him, see the way his lips thinned in disapproval.

Uncle Mack froze before shaking his head. Tilting his head back to me, the man then spoke. "You're going to leave now, Roe. You're going to listen to your uncle. You're going to live a happy little life in your happy little house and forget everything that happened here. You're going to be safe and obey. You're going to not put yourself in harm's way."

I opened and closed my mouth, feeling indignant at the condescending way he spoke to me but also disturbed by his commands. I knew with complete certainty that I couldn't go against him. He was too strong, too fatal. I also bristled at the words *safe* and *obey*. My mother drilled those words into me for a full decade. I associated safety with her compulsive fears about death, and even though Uncle Mack was a bit overprotective, it was nothing compared to her obsession with safety. I didn't like feeling like I was being sucked back into a world where I was trained to fear everything.

My intuition was guided by self-preservation, and one look at this man had me shaking with the need to flee. "I just want answers," I finally whispered. It echoed like a pathetic plea.

The strange man seemed to study my words for a fleeting moment. He lifted his hand up and rubbed at his chest, like the pounding thing pumping blood there was paining him. We teetered on the edge of a decision. I prayed he'd open up and give me an ounce of honesty, but he didn't.

"I just want you to leave," he finally replied.

His answer felt oddly disorienting. Why was there a longing in his tone? Why did it sound like a lie?

He spun on his heels and walked away, carrying with him a truckload of confusion and suspicion. I observed his back until the darkness of the hallway consumed his tall, muscular frame. I squinted past the darkness for a single lingering peek, not sure why I was so invested in figuring out this dangerous man. I should want to leave, I should want to take this opportunity by the balls, escape and run with my tail between my legs. But there was something I was missing. I knew it.

But what?

The lights flickered overhead, jarring me out of my trance.

Uncle Mack exhaled before speaking again. "We have to go, Roe. Please don't fight me on this. I promise you it's better than staying here." He was right. I wanted out of this small room and back into the mirage of safe familiarity. Better the devil you sort of know than the devil you don't.

I flickered my gaze between the door and my uncle, considering my options. Nothing about this was right. Nothing about this made sense. "Please, Roe," he begged while running a meaty hand through his hair. I noted scars on his knuckles. What did I really know about my uncle? I knew he cared about me. He learned how to braid my hair when I was a tween. He would special order my favorite pumpkin pie on Thanksgiving. He listened. He cared. He painted my room pink when I first arrived at his house, then changed it to black when he realized I wasn't the sort of girl to revel in the frill of things. He worked hard for both of us and always made sure I was well taken care of.

Uncle Mack had a track record of caring for me, but it seemed convoluted now. Was I willing to throw all of that away for this?

Maybe.

My soul was begging me to flee. I'd always been so quick to let go of the people that had the power to hurt me. My mother let my father's death completely warp her reality. She loved him so much she let her grief ruin her, and I never wanted to give someone that sort of power over me—even

Uncle Mack, the man that had effectively raised me. I felt like he was about to reveal something painful, and not just the physical sort of bruising we already had endured. I felt like running because I knew that this was just the start of my world crumbling at my feet, and I didn't want to stick around to pick up the pieces.

"Okay," I whispered, though it felt like a lie. I wasn't completely on board with trusting him, but I realized I didn't have much of a choice. Staying here with the strange man wasn't an option, and if my aching muscles had anything to say about it, going off on my own wasn't really viable just yet either.

Uncle Mack's face lit up like I'd taken a massive burden off his shoulders. His happiness created a dark pit of sadness to boil over in my chest. It felt like my throat was constricting.

I'd go with him, for now. But the moment I had the chance to flee, I would.

After all, running from my feelings and from people was what I did best.

Chapter 6
HUNTER

I observed Mack and Roe as they drove across the long stretch of road leading away from my cabin in the woods until their tail lights disappeared into the distance. Every inch of space between us seemed like miles, and an odd mixture of relief and misery swelled in my chest. I planted my hand against the cool glass to ground myself, letting the chill seep into my blistered palms. I felt like a fucking pussy.

I spent the next three minutes reassuring myself that she was safe. I knew the immediate threat to her life was gone. I had six piles of ash in my backyard to prove it. All that was left of Rosemary's men was the stink of charred skin. Getting rid of the bodies was always the worst part. It was like a massive hangover after a raging night of drinking. It was messy and exhausting, a sloppy reminder of the sin I'd committed.

I didn't think that the Asphalt Devils would go after her. Roe was my dirty little secret. But secrets were tricky. No matter how hard you fought to keep them under wraps, they always came out.

I wanted to torment my enemies more. When I drove up to the scene and saw Mack's mangled car on the blacktop, I wanted to burn the world down. Luckily, Mack was on his way to my cabin, so it happened on a secluded road. No witnesses made my job easier. There was no one to hear the screams. No one to see the splattering of blood. The cleanup crew cost a pretty penny, something my boss bitched about after the fact, but I didn't care.

I'd killed them all. I'd lodged bullets through their skulls like the skilled marksman I was. Retribution was a drug, and addiction's in my blood. I wanted to torture them, but other things demanded my attention.

Things like a damaged girl passed out in Mack's trampled passenger seat. Things like her wild, light brown hair and chilled skin. Roe got hurt because of me, and I couldn't fucking see straight. I thought she was dead. An entire lifetime of regret came to a screeching halt when I saw her too-still form. It was the end of an era. The chains she had over my life seemed broken, but I craved the cold shackles digging into my skin.

And when I dragged her from the car, her faint pulse mocked me.

I'd imagined us meeting a thousand times, but I never wanted this. I never imagined I'd carry her home with her blood seeping through my shirt.

She was so close. I fucking touched her.

Her.

Roe.

My finger brushed against her skin, and it felt like caressing thorns.

I hated her.

I went to my kitchen and sat at my worn table. Picking up the pocket knife on my tabletop, I flicked it open and ran my thumb along the sharpened blade until my skin punctured and blood spilled from the cut.

It was surreal having Roe in my home. I'd been looking after her for the better part of a decade—hell, since the day she was born. It wasn't until around the time that her mother died that I was financially stable enough to take my obsession to a new level.

Fucking Mack. He had one job: keep her safe.

And he failed me.

I hired Mack eight years ago. I entrusted him with her. I'd known him for a while, and when he wanted to settle down, I figured he'd be perfect for the job. His daughter died of cancer fifteen years ago, and I sensed that he needed someone to care for. We both worked for the Bullets, but Mack was lonely. Despite his deadly expertise, he was a family man through and through. He took the job, convincing himself that it was just something to pay the bills, but kept it because he liked having a family again.

Back when I'd hired Mack, I told him that whatever happened to Roe, I'd do it to him. When she cut her palm on glass, I sliced his. When she fell and scraped her knee on the concrete, I took sandpaper to his skin. And when her arm snapped in the car accident, I cracked his bone with a hammer, relishing in his screams as I kept my promise. It was a moment of deadly weakness. I paid him enough for his trouble, and he knew he couldn't run from this—from me. I'd kill him. Besides, he cared too much about Roe to leave her to me. Smart man.

Mack blamed me for the attack, but I blamed myself more. I had a long list of enemies, but no one had ever connected me to her.

Until now.

I put the bloodied knife on the table and used my other hand to reach for my phone. Turning to my surveillance app, I frowned when I was greeted with Roe's distant expression as she sat in the passenger seat of the new car I'd bought them. Since the accident, I'd upped security, putting a camera in the air vent so I could watch while they drove. As if the GPS wasn't enough. Nothing was enough. Part of me regretted hurting Mack; it meant he was vulnerable against another attack. My anger had gotten the best of me, but I didn't mind picking up the slack for now.

A halo of sunlight kissed her hair, and an odd sense of pride filled my chest at the sight of her in my sweatshirt. A pout was planted on her thick lips, her gnashing teeth made her jaw flex. Peering at Mack with sideways glances, she seemed full of distrust. I couldn't blame her. The half-assed excuses we'd given her were insulting to her intelligence. Roe was smart, though she didn't give herself enough credit. It was only a matter of time before she figured it all out.

I dreaded that day.

I counted her breaths and gazed at the blurred screen, noting the dullness in her brown eyes and the cut on her lip. I saw everything. Heard everything. Watched everything.

Every time I saw Roe's face, I hated her more. So I watched her as often as I could.

My phone started ringing, disrupting the feed. I glanced at the caller ID and debated answering it when I saw the name: Gavriel Moretti.

My boss was a ruthless fucker, and I knew if I didn't answer, I'd have my ass handed to me on a silver platter.

I clicked the button and held it up to my ear. "Hello?"

"You failed," he replied. His gruff voice sounded like smoke and disappointment.

"I took care of the problem," I replied cryptically while glancing out my window at the spot where Rosemary's men were burned to the bone. Moretti and I had a code of sorts. Though our phones were encrypted, you could never be too cautious.

"You should have taken care of the problem before it got to this point. Someone found your weakness, and it's only a matter of time before the wrong people connect you to me. You know how important discretion is to me, old friend."

I shook my head and walked over to the sink to run cool water over the cut on my thumb. I was a hitman. An assassin. I'd always had a steady hand and a good eye. It felt odd to brag about being the best in the business, but I was. I never wanted to be glorified for killing; it took away from the sport of it all. The Bullets hired me on my eighteenth birthday when Roe was just eight years old. I saw an opportunity to better watch over her and took it. I'd been discreetly cleaning up their messes ever since.

Gavriel had settled down with his family a few summers back, but he still ran the business from a distance. He checked in on his associates to make sure they were doing their job and to cash the checks they'd earned for him. I only answered to Gavriel, though. Which meant he took a hands-on approach to my role in his business.

A motorcycle club had been crossing the line of the Bullet territory. Gavriel was territorial and trigger happy. I got the orders to take down their leader, Rocky Jones, two months ago. It was an easy job. He was drunk in his living room, stroking his cock to some shitty porn, and I caught him with his pants down—literally. He had a predictable schedule and was too egotistical to hire personal bodyguards. It was almost too easy to kill the fat fucker, but I wasn't expecting his daughter to walk through the door just as I was making my bloody exit. Rosemary Jones was wide-eyed and shocked when she saw me. I couldn't bring myself to kill her. I didn't kill women; it was just a rule I had. I didn't imagine she'd take over her father's job so quickly.

The thing about killing someone of power was that there was always someone quick to take their place. Rosemary claimed her throne as the queen of the Asphalt Devils. It wasn't a title worth bragging about; the gang was loud but lacked organization. Rosemary went looking for revenge but found a lot more than she bargained for.

"They won't be coming back," I promised. "I'm not even sure how they found out about Roe. They're nothing. No one. I've got it handled."

Gavriel let out a sigh. I imagined him sipping water at his desk, brushing his hand along his chin while debating how best to control the situation—control me. He was a decent man to work for despite his hardened personality. But I knew that when push came to shove, he would always choose his family's safety over mine. And if I became a threat to that, he'd have no problem taking me out.

I'd like to see him try.

"How is she?" he finally asked.

"Fine," I gritted. I didn't like when he talked about Roe.

He went silent again. Gavriel liked those long, pregnant pauses in conversations. He liked to have the world on the edge of their seat, waiting for his next play. "You know," he began. "I understand you, Hunter. I understand your need to protect her. I respect you more for it despite your reasons."

I hadn't told Gavriel about Roe. He'd discovered it all on his own. Gavriel collected knowledge like it was gold, holding onto the precious currency and using it to make deals. Though he hadn't threatened her, I knew that he wasn't above holding her safety over my head. "What's your point?" I snapped.

"Watch your tone, Hunter. Remember who you're speaking to."

I let out a sigh. Gavriel was the sort of man to demand respect. He didn't become the leader of the largest, most powerful gang in America by being passive. "Yeah, okay," I replied.

"As I was saying, if you need help, I'm only a phone call away. I take care of my people, Hunter. You might enjoy living alone out in the middle of nowhere, but you don't have to seclude yourself. I have the resources to take care of you and her."

I knew this. I knew that if I needed the Bullets' support, Gavriel would be here with his army by nightfall. But I didn't want to need anyone. Gavriel's help came with stipulations. He didn't do anything out of the kindness of his heart. Hell, I doubted he even had a heart. Being close to him just meant I was deeper in the trenches. I liked pretending I was in control of my own life. He was my boss, and I was a killer. I could handle this on my own.

"I'll keep that in mind," I replied curtly.

"Good," he replied, like the benevolent asshole he pretended to be. "I've sent you another assignment. It's local, so you won't need to travel too far. I know you are anxious about leaving right now. Once this is taken care of, I don't think we'll have any more problems. Rosemary has no idea what it takes to run a lucrative gang. She's angry and hurt, but the Asphalt Devils will be as dead as her father soon enough. We'll just keep killing until they get the idea. She won't want the blood on her hands."

At his words, adrenaline pounded through my veins. I always got like this. Killing was an elaborate chess game. How would I do it? Where would I be? Would I get caught?

"I'll take care of it."

"Good. I'll wire the reward to you once proof of completion has been submitted. Denver has been good for business, and I refuse to lose that territory to a shitty motorcycle gang."

It was all so transactional. The value of life got lost behind dollar signs and power plays. Humanity had no significance in our world, only power. "Sounds good."

I was about to hang up the phone when Gavriel stopped me. "Oh, and Hunter?"

I closed my eyes, then stared out the window again. "Yeah?"

"Don't fuck up this time."

The phone line went dead.

Fucking Gavriel Moretti. I tossed my smartphone on the counter and shut off the water. My thumb was still bleeding, so I grabbed a paper towel and pressed it against the wound.

Don't get me wrong, I was thankful for him. I'd probably be dead by now if he hadn't given me guidance and direction. Plus, he paid fucking well. He knew there was no one better than me, and paid accordingly. I couldn't pay Mack and take care of Roe without his generous compensation. Before working with the Bullets, I was a stupid teen trying to get by, floundering on the dark web and living on the streets. Gavriel offered a sense of stability in my life I hadn't had before. He molded me in his image and turned me into a cold-blooded killer. I wasn't disillusioned. I knew my role implicitly and didn't blame him for making me this way. I was always meant to be a murderer, regardless of who cut my checks.

I stared at my phone once more, debating whether to pick it up and watch Roe again. Fucking Roe. The bane of my existence. The devil on my shoulder.

My one weakness.

She knew me now. She might not have seen my face, but she knew the power I held over her life. My manic awe at seeing her in person had me by the balls. I gave in. I let too much slip. I let my life collide with hers instead of watching from the sidelines, and now I had a clusterfuck to clean up.

I knew there was a change in the air when I saw her on her birthday. It was reckless and stupid. I touched her cheek and flirted when I should have been running the fuck away. Now, she knew too much and it was all my fault. Keeping my distance had worked for the better part of a decade, but now I didn't know how to proceed.

I should have made her stay here. I might have taken care of my enemies, but more would come. I just couldn't handle having my weakness under my roof. Knowing how close she was gave me that high before a kill. I couldn't trust myself to keep her safe when every instinct in my body was screaming at me to end this torturous existence—end this torturous obsession.

Giving in, I reached for my phone and opened the camera feed again. They were home now. Part of me hoped she memorized the turns leading to my cabin. Part of me hoped that she'd come back here demanding answers.

But mostly, I hoped that she was too scared to return. She should be.

I switched to the feed in her bedroom and watched her sink onto her queen-sized bed. She stared at the wall for a moment while clenching her fist. She was angry. Good.

Minutes ticked by, and then she stood slowly. Grief-stricken, I watched her aching body struggle as she moved around her room, shoving clothes and other items into her backpack. Every shift of her body had both of us grimacing. She folded shirts and packed a toothbrush. A wide grin crossed my face as I realized what she was doing.

Roe wanted to run.

I'd seen her fighting spirit over the years. Her defiance. She barreled through life, living recklessly and without shame.

I'd let her run, sure.

But I would catch her.

I always caught her.

Chapter 7

ROE

My bag was packed, but I wasn't quite sure where I was going. I had no escape plan or place to go. I wasn't really suited for running away. I had maybe a hundred dollars to my name from Christmas and other days I refused to celebrate, and no real skills or experience to keep me going. I was leaving in the middle of the school year, so I didn't even have a high school diploma to get a decent job. Uncle Mack never let me work. He said I needed to focus on my studies, but now I wondered if he did that to keep me isolated.

I'd accepted that I'd probably end up sleeping on the streets until I could find a job. It would suck as my body healed, but I could do it. Mom and I had been kicked out of enough apartments for me to know that even if it wasn't ideal, I could survive. She was always too scared to work. She liked keeping me safe and under her thumb. The entire world was a death trap, and things like groceries, rent, and the electricity bill were inconsequential in comparison.

I stole my social security card and birth certificate from Uncle Mack's bedroom and stashed a full bottle of Tylenol, a sleeping bag from when Uncle Mack used to take me camping, and enough clothes to last a week in my bag. I wasn't a survivalist in the slightest, but I wasn't stupid either. My uncle was working with some deadly people. He was involved in something I wanted nothing to do with, and the fact that he wouldn't even explain what was happening made me want to flee. I wasn't equipped to leave, but I sure as fuck wasn't staying here, either. Maybe I could get on a bus and just ride until I found a place that felt right.

I was conditioned at a young age to trust my intuition. Mom said the night Dad died, it was like someone had taken a bat to her gut. I used to bite my tongue until it bled to stop myself from reminding her that it was the contractions hurting her. Dad died the night I was born, after all.

But my gut was telling me to run the fuck away. It was a stupid, hollow plan, but it was still a plan. At least I wouldn't be here.

I walked out to the living room, clutching the straps of my backpack with my good hand as I braced myself for Uncle Mack's questions. As expected, he twisted in his recliner to stare at me. His face looked even worse now than this morning. His eyes were so swollen that I doubted he could actually see me. "Where are you going?" he growled while struggling to stand up. His bulky body staggered with every move. I'd considered waiting a few days to go but realized now was my best option. Uncle Mack couldn't physically keep me here, he was too injured. Though I wasn't in much better shape, I could still get away if I needed to.

But I was clinging to hope. I'd give Uncle Mack an ultimatum. If he told me the truth, I'd stay. If he lied…

"I guess that's up to you," I replied.

"You can't leave, Roe," Uncle Mack said, his voice clouded with annoyance and skepticism. "You don't understand—"

"Because you won't tell me!" I interrupted. "We were in a car chase! Some guy locked me in a room in his cabin. He drugged me. And you just want me to pretend as if nothing happened?" I scoffed. "Fuck that. You raised me to be mindful of my surroundings and keep safe. If you were in my position, you'd be gone in an instant." I punctuated my words by snapping my fingers. "You're the one putting me in danger, Uncle Mack. Tell me everything, or I'm out of here."

He grimaced while stalking closer to me, and I wasn't sure if it was my words hurting him or moving his body. "I know you want answers, kid. I really do. There's just so much you don't know."

"Then tell me," I pleaded while taking a step backward. My backpack hit the front door. I felt trapped and, for the first time in my life, terrified of my uncle. I knew it was all in my head. He was too hurt to actually do anything. But the man that raised me and the man standing in front of me now seemed like two completely different people.

Uncle Mack chomped on his busted lip for a moment, making the dried blood crack open and fresh life pour from the laceration. "I'm not your uncle, Roe," he finally said after a long, contemplative pause. His worn voice was uncharacteristically small, and I'd barely heard him. It took me a few moments to consider what he'd said.

He wasn't my uncle?

"What?" I asked. Of course he was my uncle. The state contacted him after Mom died. He was my mother's estranged brother. He knew things about her, talked about their childhood together. Certainly, he'd not made all of that up.

"I was hired by someone to keep you safe. They were going to put you in foster care, and my employer figured a steady home would be better for you."

His employer? Who the fuck was his employer? I was wading through the thickness of this reality, trying to understand. "Why would someone want to keep me safe?"

"I can't answer that, Roe." His response was instantaneous and laced with guilt. His bruised face turned a blotchy red color as obvious shame filled his swollen and battered expression. "I've always loved you like you were my own daughter, kid. I promise. This doesn't mean anything has to change. Just because I was hired to be here doesn't mean I don't care." He was speaking rapidly like he was trying to get his truth out there for me to absorb as fast as possible.

But there was only one thing that stood out to me: Everything I knew was a lie. Who was it that hired him? Why? I was a nobody, the daughter of a crazy mother and a ghost of a father. My parents weren't important. Hell, *I* wasn't important. I was just a trivial, damaged girl.

"Of course this changes everything!" I yelled, my voice rough and full of rage. "I don't even know who you are anymore."

"You know me. I raised you, Roe. All of that is still true. I taught you how to ride a bike. I took you to school. I braided your hair. I cared about you." Those memories, which had once felt important to me, made me nauseous now. It all felt fake. "But you're right," he began again. "You need to know the truth. I can't tell you all of it, but I own up to my part. I was hired to raise you."

He was hired to raise me.

All this time, I thought Uncle Mack was the only person in my life that stayed. I pushed others away, but he seemed like an unmoving tree, an eternal force that proudly set up roots in my life. He saw past my toxic bullshit and really looked out for me. He broke my mother's toxic chains and slowly reintroduced me back into the real world. My mother didn't let me go to school. Hell, we barely left the house. The day she died, I thought I was leaving her hell, but I was leaving one form of control for another. All of it was a lie. He kept me around because he was paid to do it. And I couldn't cope with that reality.

"Who wants to keep me safe?" I asked again while shoving the rising betrayal down. I was determined to understand this. I definitely had no plans to stay now, though. My entire life felt orchestrated, and I didn't know what the end goal was.

Uncle Mack closed his swollen eyes and let out a sigh. Though he didn't say a name or a reason, the hooded man from the cabin stood out in my memory. "It's him, isn't it?" I asked.

Uncle Mack's busted lip twitched. His tell.

"Why would he want to keep me safe if he kicked us out of his cabin? If you thought revealing that you aren't really my uncle would suddenly explain everything and keep me here, you're an idiot."

Uncle Mack tugged at his wrinkled shirt as if debating about what to say. "Fine. Leave. He'll bring you back here within the hour. He *will* find you, Roe."

count on, though, and that was Joel's love of blow jobs. He didn't care who was attached to the mouth sucking his cock, as long as he got off.

"Oh you did, huh?" I asked, my throat still dry. Based on my chronic constipation and cotton mouth, I'd determined that my uncle and his friend had been pumping me with pain meds for the last three days. I guess it was a good thing because, now that the opioids were wearing off, there wasn't a single bone in my body that didn't hurt.

I was currently popping ibuprofen and Tylenol like it was candy, not caring if it fucked up my liver. My broken arm hurt like a bitch, but I was grateful to have control over my mind and body. It made me sick to my stomach to think that my body was an unconscious void. I didn't like not knowing what happened to me while at the cabin. Obviously, a doctor had put the cast on my arm, but there was still something violating about not remembering much of the last three days.

I still remembered him though. The handsome hooded stranger that knew my body intimately.

"You can't help it. You miss my dick," Joel responded gleefully. I imagined him beaming on the other end of the phone, sitting in his dark bedroom full of roaches simmering in makeshift ashtrays. My little fuck buddy was probably even stroking himself through his holey jeans. "I think about you in the shower," he added in a raspy voice.

Yep. He was definitely touching himself right now. Disgusting.

"I'm glad you take your hygiene seriously," I deadpanned. I had to literally bite my tongue to stop myself from telling him to fuck off. If I wanted Joel to come and get me, I had to play the part. I needed someone to drive me out of town or to a bus stop. I could try to steal Uncle Mack's new car, but I worried he had a tracker on it. I'd watched enough crime television to know that was possible. I had some cash saved up for a one-way bus ticket out of Denver but needed a ride there. Joel would be suspicious if I suddenly started acting like the lovesick fool he wanted me to be, but I had to at least pretend to want him. It was a precarious tightrope. One word too affectionate, and he'd know something was up. Even hinting I was disgusted by him would earn me a lecture and get my calls blocked.

"Look," I huffed. "Do you want to come and get me so we can fuck, or am I going to have to find someone else to get me off?" I asked while staring at the blood caked under my nails. He went silent for a moment, likely debating my offer. He probably struggled with his pride, but I knew his horny dick would win in the end.

"Fine, fine," he relented. I let out a sigh of relief. I needed out of here and fast. "I'll pick you up in thirty minutes. Just let me shower real quick and tug one out so I can last longer."

My mouth curled in disgust. "Lovely," I replied. Why did I ever date this guy in the first place?

Oh yeah, I was a desperate motherfucker.

He hung up the phone, and I tried not to imagine him stroking his cock in his bedroom.

"WHAT THE FUCK happened to you?" Joel asked the moment I slid into the passenger seat of his compact truck. His cobalt eyes raked over my cast and bruised skin, assessing me as I struggled to shove my oversized backpack into the small floor space at my feet. "You look like shit, Roe," he added, making me bristle. If I had to guess, he was seemingly speculating if I was up for sex. I might have called him here under false pretenses, but if I knew Joel, he'd still be down.

"I got into a car accident," I replied while squinting out the window.

"A car accident? What the fuck? When?"

I rolled my neck and twisted to face him. "Three days ago. I've been recovering since then."

Joel gnawed on the inside of his cheek. "Explains why you haven't been at school. Shit, Roe. Shouldn't you be asleep right now? I'm not one to turn down sex, but even I have my limits." He knocked at my cast and then looked back at me. "I mean, we could try some sexual healing, though."

I tried to stay cool but was too on edge to stretch my composure long enough to entertain Joel. I needed him to get the fuck out of here—the faster the better. "Yeah, about that. I didn't actually call you for sex." His face dropped, and I knew I had to hurry through my plea before he kicked me out of his truck. I could walk to the bus station if necessary, but I was still too sore to move. I didn't want to waste my limited funds on a cab, either. "Joel, I need you to drive me to the bus station in Denver, okay?"

I avoided eye contact with him, instead looking around his compact truck. It reeked of weed and cologne. I could sense his stare on me, though, and from the corner of my eye, I saw a peculiar expression that roughly mimicked pity on his face. "What's going on?" he asked.

I glared at the road while swallowing. "I'm not hooking up with you. I need you to be a decent guy for thirty minutes and drive me to the bus station, okay?"

He braced his hands on the steering wheel and gripped until his knuckles became peppered with red and white blotches. "Did someone hurt you, Rowboat?" he gritted. I blanched, shocked by his concern and warmed by the familiar nickname. I used to hate it when we were dating, but the familiarity and comfort grounded me now. It was nice to find footing in Joel's presence. "I'll kick his ass, Roe. Did your uncle hurt you?"

His question caught me off guard. My uncle did hurt me. Hell, he wasn't even my uncle. I was still processing that bombshell of a revelation. The hooded man at the cabin hired him and was the reason for this mess. I was sure of it. But something within me didn't want to blame Mack. I knew there was more to the story, and I wasn't willing to admit that this was his fault. "Not directly, no," I answered, the words tasting bitter in my mouth. "A lot of shit has gone down. I'm not safe, Joel. I didn't have anyone else to call. I really need you to take me to the bus station and pretend you never saw me, okay?"

His hand moved to hover over the gear shift, as if he were debating on listening to me. "Where are you going?" he asked before relenting and driving off. The carefree pothead turned serious in an instant, his face hardened in earnest determination. The switch surprised me. Maybe I'd underestimated him.

"I don't know. I'm just going to buy a bus ticket and get the fuck out of town."

"What happened to you, Roe? I know shit has to be serious if the ice queen is asking me for help."

His words stung, but I'd deserved them. Joel wasn't the love of my life, but we had fun. Until we'd broken up, he'd been a good enough guy. I could have stayed with him. I could have conquered my fear of abandonment and maybe fallen a bit for the asshole, but I didn't want to. I fell for souls, then ran when things got too real, leaving them behind in whatever mess I'd abandoned.

I'd seen what happened to people that loved, and wanted nothing to do with it.

"Mack isn't my uncle. I don't know the details, but he's involved in some shady shit, and there are people that want to hurt me. Someone wrecked our car on purpose."

"Fuck, Roe. That's a lot to digest. What do you mean he isn't your uncle?"

I quickly explained everything I could as he drove into the city toward the bus station. The more I spoke, the more he checked his rearview mirror and peered around the corner of every street. His spine was rigid, and he sat in rapt attention as he absorbed my words. The carefree expression he usually wore so well became worried.

"The guy that took us in was terrifying. He knew things about me, Joel. Things I've told no one," I whispered while thinking back on the hooded man with his tender touch.

"Roe, you need to go to the police," he finally said while pulling up to a stoplight. He reached for my hand but paused when he saw the cast.

Going to the police was a good idea. If I were being honest, it was smarter than buying a bus ticket and sleeping on the street. "I probably should, but…"

"But what? You were in an accident and some guy locked you in a fucking room and drugged you." He was shouting now. His anger on my behalf was endearing.

How could I possibly explain that I was scared to go to the police? Would they even believe me? Uncle Mack was able to convince the state that he was my biological uncle. The police would probably think I was just a stupid, pissed-off, and rebellious teen. I was a legal adult, too. Car accidents happened. They got me medical help, and I had no way of proving what kind of shady shit they were involved in when I didn't even know it myself. Sure, I could give them a tip to investigate, but would they? And then what would happen? Would he punish me for leading the police to their operations? I didn't know how to go up against something I didn't understand. I'd seen enough television to know that snitches get stitches. They already tried to kill us once.

"I can't go to the police," I replied steadily, hoping Joel didn't press the issue.

"You can. Or you can stay with me. I'll protect you, Rowboat."

I smiled but didn't immediately answer him. People were always about grand gestures, but I didn't want to be disappointed when Joel got scared and realized I wasn't worth the effort. "Joel..." I began, certain he could hear the distance in my tone. There was no way in hell I'd put that sort of responsibility on his shoulders. I just needed a ride.

Poising his lips in a firm line, Joel pulled up to the bus station and turned off his car. "Do you have money?" he asked.

I pulled cash out of my wallet and flashed it in his face. "Enough to get out of here and eat for a few days. I'll find a job when I get there."

"That sounds like a shitty plan, Roe. Are you thinking this through?"

He was right, but impulsivity was in my blood. I wasn't stupid. I knew this was a bad, terrible, ridiculous idea, but it felt right. Even if I wasn't thinking rationally, I wanted to see just how far Mack's employer was willing to go to keep me. I also wanted to give myself a chance to get away, and I definitely couldn't stomach the idea of staying in that house with a man that had been lying to me all these years.

When I didn't answer, Joel sighed and reached into his tight jeans to pull out his wallet. Flicking through a thick wad of cash, he pulled out a hundred-dollar bill and tossed it to me. "For the record, I think you should go to the police."

I clutched the cash in my palm and leaned over the center console to kiss his cheek. "For the record, you are kind of a good guy."

"Gee, thanks," he replied. "I was hoping for at least a blow job, but..."

I used my good hand to shove his shoulder. "I'm sure you can find someone that isn't bruised to hell to take care of that," I joked.

"But no one with a mouth like yours. That thing you do with your—"

"Nope. Not going there."

He frowned for a moment and leaned over to kiss me. I braced myself for the familiar soft touch of his lips and the smell of his cologne. It wasn't a devouring sort of kiss that left you drowning in passion. It was tender. Intimate. Kind and loving. I opened for him, but he pulled away, leaving me on the edge of a confusing battle within myself. "Call me if you need anything, okay? I've got an unlimited supply of orgasms," he teased before biting his lip. Cocky motherfucker.

"Thanks for the ride."

I got out of the car and watched as he pulled out of the parking lot and headed back toward town. It felt like just a moment—a blink in time.

I should have felt something in that moment other than self-preservation. I'd ripped Joel apart, and he still came through for me. But I couldn't force myself to feel gratitude or even love for the boy with cobalt eyes and scars on his wrist. I just felt relieved to be out of his hard stare.

They say that if you keep hurting the same part of you again and again and again and again, the nerve endings die, making you numb to the pain. The corner of my heart where Joel tried to find a home lost feeling long ago.

Chapter 9

ROE

I clumsily purchased a one-way ticket to Los Angeles. It felt like a cheesy cliche, but I was committed. The woman working the ticket counter eyed me suspiciously and asked to see my ID. Thank God I was eighteen, or she might have refused to sell it to me. I couldn't even fault her. I looked like I'd been tossed in a wood chipper and had that anxious energy that put off a suspicious vibe.

I'd always wanted to visit LA, and I figured it was far enough away that I could put some distance between me and the clusterfuck that was here in Denver. It was a big city, too, so I was sure I could find a job there and survive for a little. Plus, it wasn't as cold as Denver, so if I had to sleep on the streets, I wouldn't freeze to death. See? I could handle this. I was thinking it through.

How far would they go to bring me back, though?

The bus didn't leave for another thirty minutes, so I sat on a bench and bounced my foot on the hard tile while watching others lugging duffel bags and clutching tickets as they settled on the seats near me.

While I sat and waited, I felt the intrusion of an old habit hit me in the chest. I was conditioned to expect the worst in a situation. I knew this was reckless and foolish. There would only be two outcomes. Either the hooded man would drag me kicking and screaming back to Mack's house, or I'd end up homeless in LA. And even though neither option seemed good, I felt a thrill. Mom would have hated everything about this. I could almost hear her whispering in my ear.

"Never keep your back to the door, Roe. You'll never be able to see if a gunman enters the room that way.

"Eleven children die per year on school busses. I read it on the Internet. You don't need to go to school, baby. I can teach you everything here.

"I once read in the newspaper that, at any given moment, there are two million impaired drivers on the road in the United States. We should stay home. We can do Halloween next year."

"LA, huh?" a voice at my back that dripped with sinister honey said. It made the hair on my neck stand up. I recognized the tone, it had been haunting me ever since the car accident. He'd found me, just like Uncle Mack said he would—and in record time, too. Fuck. I hadn't even gotten on the bus.

Good. Maybe I'd get some answers out of him. A bulky body settled beside me on the bench, his arm brushing mine and sending a spiral of threatening heat through my body. I twisted my head to stare at the man sitting beside me, and to my surprise, he wasn't wearing a hood.

With dirty blond hair that was long and swept across his forehead, the man had bright blue eyes and a scar over his right eyebrow. His jawline was strong and defined, and his thick lips framed a bright, disarming smile. "Stop looking so terrified, Roe. I just want to chat."

His voice was cocky and lacked sincerity. It was like mountain climbing, one syllable could make my foot slip. "I'll scream," I promised while looking around. There was a security guard by the door currently engrossed with his lunch, barely watching the room.

"Please do. It's been a while since I've had to kill an entire room of people. You think that grandfather over there will put up a fight? He's got an Army hat; I bet he's a veteran."

I swallowed and followed his gaze to stare at the older gentleman with deep-set wrinkles. He was wearing an oversized, gray suit and clutched a veteran's hat in his veiny hand speckled with age spots. "You wouldn't kill everyone," I replied while shifting in my seat to put some distance between us. Every touch of his skin against mine sent me into a panic.

"I wouldn't?" he asked, genuinely curious about my opinion of him.

"N-no," I stuttered.

"You don't sound so sure. Maybe I went about this wrongly. Maybe I should have told you what I am. Do you want to know how I handled the people chasing you and Mack, Roe?"

At his question, I knew with complete certainty that whoever was after us was now dead. I didn't need verbal confirmation of his ruthless abilities. I could feel his danger.

I gnawed on my lip, drawing the attention of his icy eyes to my anxious tic. "What's your name?" I asked.

He paused, as if surprised by my question. "Why do you want to know?"

I ran my fingers along the hard cast covering my left arm and turned to face him. "I'm just curious if the devil has a name." I wanted to appear strong. Mom once told me that if I felt threatened, I should scream as loud as I could. I could practically feel the curdling yells bubbling up in my throat.

He smiled, flashing me a devious grin that was far too bright for the evil I could practically feel buzzing on his skin. "Hunter."

I rolled the two syllables and the meaning of that word around in my brain for a moment before responding. "How appropriate. Are you here to hunt me?"

He wrapped his hand around my waist and leaned in to whisper in my ear. His lips brushed against my sensitive skin, sending a spiral of confusing reactions zipping through my body. I felt flushed and attuned to every movement he made. "I caught you a long time ago, Roe."

That realization sent a flood of questions through my mind, and I found myself gaping at him as he pulled away. "Are you stalking me?" I asked.

A woman with her young child walked by at that exact moment, and he grinned at them, using his pretty face to charm anyone willing to look. He was pretty, as much as it pained me to admit it. When we first met, he hid his features from me, but out in public, I saw that he used his face like a shield, hiding his malicious intent behind a practiced smile. Once the woman, albeit a bit flushed, passed, he turned his attention back to me. "Stalking has quite the connotation. Are you flattered by the idea of someone being obsessed with you, Roe? You want someone that'll follow you. Watch you. Pine after you from a distance and long for something you have? You have quite the track record of clinging to affection. You strung poor Joel along for months."

How the fuck did he know all of that?

I must have spoken the question out loud, because he chuckled. "I know everything about you. But I'm no stalker. Stalkers are infatuated with their prey. They obsess and desire something they can't have. But that's not the case with me."

I swallowed and stood up, clutching my backpack as I walked as quickly as I could out of the bus station and onto the busy street outside. Crawling cars in the afternoon traffic passed by. Horns blared as I stared past the tall buildings and toward the mountains in the distance. "Running away?"

"Please leave me alone," I grunted while shuffling down the sidewalk.

"This is why you ran, isn't it? You wanted to see if I'd chase you. You wanted answers, Roe. I'm right here with them."

I spun around on the sidewalk, grimacing at the sharp pain in my side. My ribs were banged up, and all this walking was making me short of breath. "Why me? Why are you obsessed with me? Why did you hire Mack to be my fucking fake uncle?"

Hunter stopped in his tracks. "He told you that, huh? Guess one broken arm wasn't enough," he said while caressing his chin.

My mouth dropped open in shock. My throat closed up with apprehension as my eyes widened and the realization of his words dawned on me. "You broke his arm?"

"His negligence broke yours."

I looked down at the cast on my arm and took a step backward, but Hunter was too close. He wrapped his hand around my wrist and pulled me flush with his body. I could feel every hard, aggressive inch of him. His eyes were lifeless and wicked, peering back into mine as I shoved against his chest and tried to wriggle out of his grasp.

"Are you going to hurt me?" I hissed as pedestrians walked by. I could have screamed. I could have made a scene. Maybe someone would have helped me, but I wanted to know why.

"I see how excited you are, Roe," he said before looking over my head then back at me. "You like being wanted, but I'll tell you the truth. I want nothing to do with you. I hate you. You're nothing. No one. Just a debt I owe." None of this made sense. He was talking in riddles. "My prettiest debt," he then whispered before stroking my cheek. His hands were icy cold, matching his imposing stature hovering over me. I barely met the middle of his chest and had to lean all the way back to meet his hardened stare.

"I don't understand any of this," I whispered. The tall buildings surrounding us seemed to fall at the feet of his declaration. He was larger than life, and right then, I felt so small I could have stood on the quill of a forgotten feather and blown away with the simplest breeze.

"Why are you obsessed with someone you hate?"

His body shivered. "Why are you obsessed with the idea of being wanted?"

He knew me. Really knew me. This virtual stranger had been watching me my entire life, and that made me sick to my stomach. I exhaled and jerked my knee up, nailing him in the balls with a hard kick. He folded over with a groan, releasing my wrist and giving me the opportunity to run away. Well, shuffle away.

Hunter might have had an outsider's look at my life, peering through the windows of my existence. But he didn't know me. At my core, I wasn't obsessed with being wanted. I was obsessed with survival.

Men in business suits and joggers fluttered out of the way as I stumbled down the sidewalk, anxious to get away from Hunter. Seeing an alleyway, I slunk down it and breathed a sigh of relief when I saw it didn't lead to a dead end. Water dripped from drains, and people shouted on the street at my back. Each hard step away jostled my aching bones. I was out of breath, my lungs pressing against my bruised ribs. My blood felt too thick for my veins as it pumped throughout my body.

Rushing around another corner, I scraped my palm against the coarse brick of the building. Sweat poured down my face as I dodged a sleeping homeless man and made my way toward a park on the other side of the alley. I moved faster and faster, jogging lightly as my backpack bounced against my back. "You're going to hurt yourself," his tense voice called in a weary drawl that was almost insulting. I breathed in through my nose. I couldn't fight him off. I spotted a patrolling police officer in the distance, whistling and kicking at the sidewalk with his polished shoes. I opened my mouth to scream, the tip of my foot just out of the shadowed alleyway, with the light of day welcoming me to safety.

But a hand wrapped around my mouth. A bicep curled against my cheek. Soft lips pressed against my ear. "I wouldn't do that if I were you."

I groaned against his palm, trying to scream into the muffled barrier. My feet kicked as he dragged me across the pavement. My body thrashed, each jerking movement making scalding tears burn my eyes and trail fiercely down my flushed cheeks. "You're going to fucking hurt yourself," he grunted again while dragging me back into the dark alley, where the only witnesses to his danger were trash bins and a light scattering of apathetic men sleeping on the street.

The glimmer of an idea bloomed in my mind. It was a trick I learned at a young age, something I hadn't had to do since my mother's death. I swiftly connected the dots to his motivations and went limp, my body becoming dead weight until I crashed to the ground. I knew it would hurt, but my pain seemed to fragment his cruelty. If I had to hurt to get away, I'd bite off my own arm and shove it down his throat.

His fingers were outstretched, reaching for me as I fell onto my tailbone. I cried out the moment I landed, shocking pain surging through my already throbbing body. I fell sideways until my skull landed on the hard concrete, forcing my eyes to pepper with stars. "Fucking hell, Roe!" Hunter screamed before dropping to his knees and cradling me in his lap.

He tenderly stared at my face and brushed my hair out of my eyes. He rooted around my head, searching for a wound. His cold eyes melted, becoming soft yet intense. He shook with concern that felt so palpable I practically choked on his obsession.

This man might be dangerous and disturbed, but I was his weakness.

Chapter 10

HUNTER

Roe was stooped over and clutching her head as I drove us back to Mack's house. With her entire body forced up against the passenger door of my Jeep, she rocked with adrenaline and acted like she couldn't get far enough away from me. She kept stealing peeks at me, though, and I met each and every stare. I was greedy for her apprehension. It was intoxicating to have her so close yet feel so distant.

I'd debated on calling Mack and having him haul her crazy ass home, but he was resting. I was starting to almost regret breaking his arm. Almost.

Working as an assassin, I learned that there was a thin line between loyalty and fear. When it came to controlling people, you had to use everything in your arsenal. Loyalty made people forgiving. Mack was willing to overlook my brutal abuse because he felt a sense of loyalty to me. I'd found him at his lowest and gave him purpose. We had a unique understanding of one another, founded on years of established boundaries.

I had zero need to build that sort of relationship with Roe, though. I might have been shackled to her since I was a ten-year-old boy, but my burdens weren't bred from loyalty, they were rooted in guilt.

I needed her fear. I knew how to forge terror and use it to my advantage.

Fuck right and wrong. If Roe thinking I was capable of harming her would keep her tucked away in her pretty little house and safe from all the dangers of the world, then so be it. I didn't watch her for eighteen years just to lose her now. She was too negligent, too wild.

"Where are you taking me?" she finally asked. The white sweater she wore was coated in street grime from her fall. Her wavy hair was wild and windblown, and she was red in the cheeks. I'd carried her to my car once I realized she hadn't seriously hurt herself during the ridiculous stunt she pulled downtown. She didn't fight me or try to get away again, thankfully. She just peered at me with questions in her golden brown eyes. After needlessly hurting herself, I saw a spark there that she hadn't had before. She was smug, like she'd figured me out. I didn't like her thinking she had me under her thumb, but I could manipulate her curiosity. I was still in control.

"Home," I grunted.

"That narrows it down," she replied, her shaky tone dripping with sarcasm. "I don't really have a home. That place where I grew up with Mack is all a lie. Are you taking me to your home? I don't particularly want to sleep in that cage you call a bedroom again, but I'm thinking I don't have much of a choice. You just run my entire life, and I'm supposed to nod my head like an obedient little lamb and be okay with it." She punctuated her words with a scowl and rolled her eyes. Infuriating little lamb, indeed.

I forced myself to be patient. She was inexperienced. Though her life wasn't easy, she was still naïve about how the world worked. She didn't know she was sitting two feet from a seasoned killer. Instinctually, she sensed that I was dangerous. Her understanding of self-preservation was screaming, "Run away!"

But she didn't know how bad it was. I knew the specific amount of pressure required to snap her delicate neck. I could kill her quietly on a crowded street, and no one would know. I could hide her body where no one could find it. I had three guns hidden in my car within arm's reach. Commanding bullets was my calling, and if I wanted to, I could end her life in the blink of an eye. She might still have some fight in her, but she'd learn soon enough that she didn't control her fate, I did.

"You do have a home. I might have hired Mack to watch you, but that doesn't mean he doesn't think of you as family. Did you know that his daughter died? He took this job because he wanted a second chance at fatherhood. I'm not going to sit here and let you belittle how much that man cares for you." My words were heavy, but I didn't want her hating Mack. I might be vicious, but he was a good man. Just because I had fucked up expectations didn't mean I wanted her questioning his character. I wasn't planning on telling her any of this, but she needed to know that Mack wasn't some schmuck I got off the streets. He was a good guy. He took his job seriously, gave me updates, and watched her back. He was better than any foster family she would have ended up with.

Her eyes cracked open in wonder. I wasn't sure if she was more unsettled about Mack's past or my outburst. I needed to rein in the touchy feely shit. I didn't want her to have the wrong idea about me.

Maybe by some standards, I was the stalker she accused me of being.

I watched her. I...obsessed over her safety. But it wasn't because I found the way her heart-shaped mouth curved into a beautiful pout to be tempting. I didn't pine over her long legs or her delicate hands and defined collarbones. It wasn't those long as fuck lashes that left shadows on her cheeks or the way she dived head first into the world with an open heart and jaded past.

No. She was a debt I had to pay.

"I didn't know Mack had a daughter," she murmured before turning the vent in the car away from her. I noticed a bead of sweat dripping down her temple and immediately adjusted the heat in the car.

I was always doing this shit—always adjusting the climate to keep her comfortable. I spent my life keeping ten steps ahead of her. Fuckers at school gave her trouble? I spoke with them. She wanted to try ice skating? I got her classes with the best fucking coach in the area. But she didn't make it easy on me. She was the type to never be happy, always seeking the next thrill, the next passion. She rarely stayed with one thing for too long. Last month she wanted to be a photographer, this month a dancer. Next month she'd probably take up modeling, Lord knows she had the body for it.

She was the same way with hobbies, friends, and relationships, too. She fluttered from one intense obsession to the next, never feeling fulfilled long enough to stick around. Her sadness was her only constant, though. Her life was a whirlwind, but she grieved her dead parents like clockwork.

Exiting the highway, I watched from the corner of my eye as she opened and closed her mouth, as if deliberating over what to say. She looked like a fucking goldfish. Tired of watching her wrestle with her thoughts, I finally shouted, "Spit it out!" I wanted to know what was going on in her head. I could watch her all day, but that didn't mean I understood how her mind worked. It was infuriating. She wasn't just flighty, she was indecisive. It made predicting her needs fucking impossible.

Letting out a sigh, she finally answered. "I just want some answers. You don't have to tell me everything, but if you could just explain some of it, I'll d-do my best to keep safe."

Keep safe, huh? That sounded suspiciously like bargaining, and I'd be damned before she used her safety against me. She thought she could hold her wellbeing over my head and make me heel? Fuck that.

I reached over and gripped her knee, squeezing where I knew a severe bruise from the crash was. She winced but didn't cry out in protest. Strong, pretty little debt. I was hurting her, but she didn't want to even give me the satisfaction of her pain. I squeezed harder, watching as her gaze pinned my hand as I applied more and more pressure, letting her know just how much I didn't care. She whimpered, and my chest constricted. I watched as she squirmed in her seat, tears filled her eyes, and terror coursed through her expression. I leaned over her, trying to appear more threatening, but I couldn't stop watching the thudding vein in her neck or the way her face turned pale. Roe's fingers trembled as she reached for the door handle, but still I kept up. I felt my stomach drop, and somewhere between my desire to show how much she didn't matter and her pain, I realized that I couldn't do it. Eighteen years of paying a debt was a hard habit to break. I tried to send more pressure, but I couldn't fucking do it. Pussy.

Letting go, I shifted my attention to the steering wheel, gripping it until my hands went numb. "I work for some bad people," I began. I didn't see the use in sugarcoating it, but it was safer if she didn't know the details. "I've been watching you since the day you were born, and some of my enemies think you're a weakness of mine."

She gulped at the air and rubbed the ache in her knee before swiveling to face me. "Am I a weakness of yours, Hunter?" she asked, a bit of snark to her tone. I didn't like how smug she sounded.

"Depends on how you define a weakness," I rebutted. "I owe someone a debt. A life debt. I watch over you because I take my obligations seriously." The more I spoke, the deeper she sunk in her seat. I was more than happy to deliver disappointment on a silver platter. "Look, I don't give two shits about you. Don't romanticize what's happening here in that stupid little head of yours. I need you to keep safe because I owe it to someone to watch over you."

"Who could you possibly owe a debt to? Who could possibly care?" she asked. "My father died the day I was born, and my mother was a crazy recluse until the day she died. I can count on one hand the number of times she left her house. No one knows me. No one could possibly care."

I bound my mouth shut, swallowing my explanation like a bitter pill. "It doesn't matter."

"But it does matter," she urged. "What if I don't want your creepy protection? Do I have a say in the matter?"

No. She didn't. The only person that could relieve me of this duty was dead.

"I don't really care what you want. I gave you your stupid answers. You're going to listen to me. Go to school. Live your life. Give Mack a break. Nothing has to change here."

She shook her head. "Everything has changed, Hunter." The way she said my name made me shiver. It was tender and soft, but full of resentment.

I preferred anger.

I pulled down her street and parked the car. "Listen, I've always watched. Mack has always taken care of you. The only difference is now you know what's happening behind the scenes."

"How often do you watch me, exactly?" she asked. She ran her hand through her brown hair, a nervous tic I knew all too well. I looked down at her leg, watching as she bounced it.

I didn't know how to answer her without sounding like the creep I was trying not to be. "Often."

"Do you have cameras in my house?" she asked, her voice rising in pitch with every question.

"Yes."

"In my room?"

I didn't answer her squeak, but my silence weighed heavily between us.

"This is fucking insane. I should go to the police," she said before unlocking her seatbelt.

I rolled my neck and turned to stare at her. "I wouldn't do that. Like I said, I work for some powerful people. They have deep pockets and badges on the inside. You could try to go to the cops, but it would just put more attention on you—attention you probably wouldn't want."

She let my words sink in. I saw the indecision on her gentle, distressed face. "Fine. I'll play along for now. But no more watching me in my bedroom. A girl should be allowed to flick the bean in the safety of her bed without some old pervert watching."

I'd never actually seen her flick the bean, as she so eloquently put it, but now my fucked up brain couldn't stop imagining it. I could almost see her now. Her plush gray bedding ruffled from her writhing body. Her hand dipped between her thighs. Her back arched as she moaned into her pillow.

I didn't like the girl, but a show was a fucking show. She wasn't ugly, just too much of a pain in the ass for me to feel anything other than responsible for her. My traitorous dick hardened, though, making me clench my teeth.

"Sure. I'll stop watching you in your bedroom," I lied effortlessly.

"Liar."

She sat there for a moment longer, playing with a hole in her jeans until she found the courage to speak. "You say you've watched me since the day I was born. How old are you?"

"Twenty-eight," I replied.

"So you've been watching me since you were ten? That doesn't make any sense. Ten-year-olds don't have life debts," she quipped. She wasn't wrong.

Most ten-year-olds didn't have life debts. Most ten-year-olds had families and normalcy and a roof over their heads.

But not me.

I ignored her statement and nodded toward the house. "Go. Mack ordered you pizza."

"That's seriously all you're going to give me?"

"Yep. And if you don't get your ass out of my car, I'll give you another reason to be afraid, Pretty Debt.

She sputtered at the nonchalant way I threatened her before giving in to her good sense. With a huff, she pushed at the door and eased herself outside. I watched for any winces or staggering. Maybe I needed to have Gavriel's home doctor make another visit. "Oh and, Roe?" I called out as she grabbed her backpack.

"What?"

"If you try to run away again, I'll drag you back here. If you sneak out, I'll find you. If you go to the police, I have people that will rain hell on your naïve little head." I pulled my gun out of the glove box and flashed her the black metal with a menacing grin. "If you do something stupid, I won't be afraid to ruin your life. The only person allowed to hurt you is me, and I've been dying to end this debt for ages. Don't give me a reason to."

She stood there in disbelief for a moment, then slammed the door in my face. Stomping off toward her driveway, Roe looked furious. I watched her fume with anger until she was safely inside. I didn't leave, though. I grabbed my cell phone and opened the surveillance app like the creep I was. Sure enough, she was in her bedroom, looking around for the camera I had hidden there. It was almost cute how angry she was, but she'd never find the microscopic device I had stowed away in the vent. And if she somehow did find it. I'd just replace it. Again and again.

She started spinning around with her middle finger in the air, screaming *"FUCK YOU!"* as loud as she could.

I honked the horn in response, making her jump.

Stupid, pretty little debt.

Chapter 11

ROE

An entire week inched by, filled with empty moments. Most of my minutes were spent in a bedroom that didn't feel like mine anymore. I hid under my covers and read books, passing the time in my own little private space where Hunter's eyes couldn't see. Mack tried to pry me from the safety of my room, but I ignored him, leaving only to eat. I felt profoundly alone, yet I knew I wasn't. I could feel Hunter's watchful presence, though I hadn't heard from him since my half-assed runaway attempt. I hated how smug my uncle looked when I waltzed back through the door. He was absolutely right. Hunter brought me back, kicking and screaming.

I called Joel a couple times to update him on what was happening, but he didn't answer. His silence was strange, but I tried not to dwell too much on it. He was probably off somewhere getting high and ramming something with his whiskey dick.

Monday, my self-imposed imprisonment came to an end. Apparently, school was more important than an existential crisis, and I'd healed from the accident just enough for Mack to force me to go. I'd debated on putting up a fight, threatening to tell the world what he'd done so I could stay home, but when it came down to it, I was actually excited to get out of the house. At least at school Hunter couldn't watch me as much.

Or, at least, that's what I was hoping for.

Hunter. I'd whispered his name over my skin every day like a spell caster trying to ward off evil spirits. It was a haunting sort of name, one that induced nightmares and chronic paranoia that kept me awake most nights. The harmless collection of letters became my greatest fear. My questions became an anthem of doubt. I caught myself singing them out loud without reason. Why me? Why you? Why this fucked up existence of watching and waiting and protecting and hurting?

And in my darkest moments, I felt like my mother. She was obsessed with fear. She could spout death statistics better than any search engine. She focused on what could hurt her, and let it ruin her mind, and I was so focused on Hunter that I feared the same fate. He was a killer, the epitome of what my mother wanted me to avoid. Part of me felt drawn to him in some sort of rebellious outburst. The other part of me understood my mother. I'd always loved her in that special sort of way young children idolize their parents. She was my whole world, mostly because she intended it that way. But now that I shook hands with the deadliest man I'd ever met, I could understand how she let fear chew her up and spit her back out.

I was thinking of Hunter again when a concerned yet chipper voice called at my back. "Oh my gosh, Roe!" I struggled to put my books in my locker while bracing myself for the inevitable questions she'd have at the sight of my cast and bruises. I wore concealer to hide the ones not hidden by my clothes, but it was the healing beneath the skin I was worried about keeping secret. Mack made it clear on the drive to school this morning that I wasn't to say anything to a single person. Keep it simple, he'd said. Tell them you were in an accident and it was too scary to talk about.

It was good enough advice. Everyone I knew expected me to clam up when it came to difficult conversations. I turned around to face Nicole, who was eyeing my cast with trepidation. "Joel told me you were in a car accident. You poor thing!"

Joel told her, huh?

"Yeah, it was rough for a few days, but I'm better now. Not looking forward to all the makeup homework," I breezed, praying she didn't hear the anxiety in my tone or sense the lies hiding just below the surface of my smile. Lies had a sort of buzzing quality, like a persistent fly perched on the ridge of my ear. Hunter's threat was at the forefront of my mind: Tell no one. Continue as if nothing has changed.

"I was so worried. I would have called, but my parents took my phone. You wouldn't believe how they reacted when they found out about the party. My mom even canceled her business trip to Japan!" she squealed, a little too excitedly in my opinion. I figured out her motivations early on, but she could at least pretend to be disappointed about being punished.

Slamming my locker shut, I nodded and smiled at all the appropriate times while trying to ignore the tingling feeling traveling up my spine. She went on and on about herself, a habit I'd encouraged since the day we met. I was a pair of ears to this girl, nothing more. I preferred it that way.

"Mom is making us all have dinner together every night, too. She says she needs to keep an eye on me," she added while pausing at the door leading to her class.

I frowned like I was supposed to. "That sucks, bro," I responded. What I wanted to say was, *I guess you got what you wanted. You go, girl.* We couldn't actually say what we wanted, though. She'd continue to act out for the sake of feeling close to her parents, and I'd continue to push people away to keep hidden the fears I'm harboring deep inside.

"Let's catch up at lunch, okay? I want to hear all about your accident. An entire week off from school? Maybe I need to break my arm," she joked over her shoulder while waltzing into her classroom.

I wanted to tell her that I'd attend this shitty school for the rest of my life if it meant I didn't have to see Hunter again, but I kept my dry lips pinched shut and simply waved goodbye with my fingers. Even here, in a crowded hallway, I felt him. Hunter was a predator I couldn't escape.

I made my way to English class, and the moment I walked through the door, Mrs. Sellars glided toward me. "Miss Palmer, I heard you were in an accident. I'm so happy to see that you're okay!" Mrs. Sellars was probably the only teacher who actually gave a fuck around here. She was just a couple years away from retirement but treated each year like a brand new teacher, investing in the lives of her students and building us up. I liked the woman, with her kind brown eyes and sporadically speckled hair. She wore purple daily, like she didn't know any other color existed, and today was no exception. I looked her up and down, grinning at the sight of her periwinkle pantsuit.

English was always my favorite class. I wasn't an exemplary student by any means, but I found reading and writing to be a calming experience.

"I'm fine," I replied with a wave of my hand. I wasn't looking forward to a day of lies. I wasn't fine, not even in the slightest.

Mrs. Sellars went into a long discussion on the readings I missed and the homework she'd help me with. I was just about to ask for an extension on a paper due at the end of the week when a brusque body shoved past mine. "Excuse me," Joel gritted while pushing his way to his seat. I gaped at his harsh brush off before excusing myself and sitting down at the desk next to him.

I was just about to flip open my text book when Joel huffed and grabbed his bag. I twisted to ask him what crawled up his ass but gasped at the sight that greeted me. His right eye was black as night with an outer layer of shaded purple. There was a cut on his bottom lip and his eyes were bloodshot. "Shit, Joel. What happened to you?" I asked as he stumbled to put distance between us. More students filtered in and started to watch our exchange, probably hoping for another public lovers' spat.

Joel leaned over and hissed low and steady, anger coursing through his tone, "Stay the fuck away from me, Roe."

"What? You're acting like an ass," I replied, fixing my face up into a scowl.

Joel's nostrils flared as he watched me. "I want nothing to do with you, Roe. Don't sit by me. Don't talk to me. You're nothing but fucking trouble." At the end of his speech, he scurried over to the corner and plopped down with a wince in the vacant seat.

I knew Joel and I weren't exactly on the best of terms, but he'd never been this cruel before. My mouth dropped open in shock, and I tried to make sense of his hatred. The last time I'd seen him, he was helpful and kind, driving me to the bus station and offering me cash. Now he couldn't stand to breathe the same air as me. What changed?

I knew the answer to that question before I even had the chance to ask it.

Hunter happened.

He told me he didn't want his secret getting out, and I'd told Joel. If Hunter watched me as much as he said he did, then he knew I'd told Joel.

My gaze flared to the corner of the room, where Joel was now sulking in his seat.

I swallowed and tried to compose myself as Mrs. Sellars clapped her hands and ordered the class to settle. "Come on, everyone. Sit down and get out a sheet of paper."

I was stuck on Joel's words and couldn't force myself to move. Everything felt sluggish, and my reality was nothing but an echo of devastation. "Miss Palmer, are you alright? Do you need to see the nurse, dear?" Mrs. Sellars asked while peering at me. I felt the entire classroom's attention hot on my face, but I didn't look at any of them. I was too focused on the fact that Hunter had his fist wrapped around my life, and there was no shaking him off. School wasn't proving to be the distraction I'd hoped it would be.

"I'm fine," I gritted while picking up my pen and clutching it.

Mrs. Sellars smiled charmingly, ignoring my mood. "I know just the place to put that attitude, Miss Palmer. We're getting into the poetry unit, and I have a lot of amazing poets lined up to study." She started writing an assignment on the board as she continued to talk. "Maya Angelou. Sylvia Plath. Gwendolyn Brooks. I also have a few contemporary poets we will be studying, such as Rupi Kaur, Steve Roggenbuck, and Suli Breaks."

Each of those names went in one ear and out the other. I was too busy stabbing my desk with my ballpoint pen. "But before we can study the style, tone, and flow of a poem, I want you to try writing your own. It can be anything. It doesn't have to rhyme. It doesn't have to have structure. I just want you to write what you're feeling right this moment. I'll set the timer for thirty minutes, then each of you will read what you've written." She giggled at the various groans erupting throughout the room before continuing, "Begin!"

I glared at the blank page for a moment, taking in the perfectly perpendicular blue lines covering it. With careful script, I wrote my name in the top right corner, then tried to come up with something that made sense for the project. I was a mediocre student. Never really excelled at anything, not that I applied myself much.

I was too distracted by everything that had happened over the last week and a half to actually pinpoint what I was feeling, let alone write it down into something that could pass as fucking poetry.

My eyes slid over to Joel, who wasn't even bothering to write. He was staring back at me, his eyes like needles poking my skin. I could feel his hate, and even though I didn't know what exactly happened, I knew that it was warranted. I led him on, broke his heart, used him to escape, and probably brought Hunter into his life. Every blister and bruise on his face was my fault.

I started to write. I thought about all the relationships I'd fucked up. I thought about the distance I put between myself and others, my shitty fail-safe painted into a vibrant shade of self-preservation. I thought of how everything around me felt controlled. I pictured the illusion of safety I'd been wrapping myself up in. I wrote something that was probably total shit, but I drained all the things I wanted to say to all the people I'd run away from. There was no room for anger toward Hunter on the page. That would be for another day.

"Time's up. Pencils down!" Mrs. Sellars said while cracking her aged knuckles. The loud pop startled a sleeping student in the front, making some of my classmates giggle. "Who wants to go first?"

No one raised their hand, and I certainly didn't want to go. I watched as Mrs. Sellars scraped the bottom of the bowl as she walked between the rows of desks, daring anyone to avoid her request. The trick to not being called on was to not make eye contact. I made sure to stare at her glittery purple shoes instead of her determined face.

"How about you, Jeffrey?" she asked while nodding toward a kid to my right. I'd known Jeffrey for a while. Freshman year, he touched my boobs in the school parking lot and came in his jeans. I felt bad for the guy.

"M-me?" he asked.

"Yes. You."

Jeffrey smoothed out his paper and cleared his throat. "This, uh, is called 'Blow Jobs'."

The class howled with laughter, but Mrs. Sellars was a seasoned pro. "Oh really?" she began, a snappy twinkle in her eye. "You know, I always tell you to write what you know. Are you sure you're qualified on that subject matter, Mr. Moon?" The class laughed even louder as Jeffrey's pale face turned a bright shade of red. Mrs. Sellars was fucking savage, and even I cracked a grin.

"Calm down, class," Mrs. Sellars called out over the distracted class. It took a few threatening looks and a stomp of her foot, but everyone eventually quieted down.

"Fine, let's skip the blow job, shall we? How about you, Miss Palmer? Read what you got, sweetie."

A cold sweat broke out on my neck. What I'd written seemed too personal to read to the class. It didn't feel like a public announcement, it felt like an exorcism.

"I'm not so sure..." I began.

My teacher slammed her palm down on her desk. "I want to hear your poem, dear. There's no right or wrong way to do it. Unless you took the same route as Jeffrey over there."

A few more snickers broke through her stern demand, and she eyed the culprits with a ruthless warning.

"Fine," I replied. I'd been saying that word a lot today. I'm fine. I feel fine. I'll be fucking fine.

"My poem is called 'The Space Between Our Lips'."

My eyes scanned the words on the paper, and with a sigh, I read my scrawled, worthless words:

The Space Between Our Lips

I built a home for myself on the small plot of land between our lips.
With a foundation of sand and walls of straw, one exhale could make me fall.

I plant flowers in the garden of your affections with dry soil and seeds
out of season.

I don't unpack my boxes. My belongings stay tucked away, ready to move
at a moment's notice. I sleep on an air mattress and wear the hoodie I stole
from your dresser.

There's a cement fence surrounding the property, with a lock on the gate.

I guard my house of straw like it's diamonds mined from the cavernous hole in my chest. They say pressure breeds beauty, so I squeeze until the walls around my heart look like an engagement ring.

My yard keeps getting bigger and bigger. The space is now large enough to house a mansion with empty rooms and empty walls and empty promises to fill them all.

You stopped visiting me at the space between our lips.
You stopped whispering prayers over my offering.

But I have a home.
But I have a home.

A sense of wonder and finality filled the room at my last word. One asshole at the front tittered, but Mrs. Sellars cut his humor with her knife-like gaze before turning her attention to me. "That was hauntingly lovely, Miss Palmer. Well done."

She made her way around the classroom, and a few other students stumbled through their poems. One was about lunch, another was a terrifying serial killer poem that made me seriously question the sanity of the person writing it. I found myself interested in the thoughts of others. I'd always gobbled up souls like they were a genuine form of nourishment, and hearing their hearts bleed out on the page had my flighty passion project tendencies soaring into overdrive. Maybe I'd try my hand at poetry for a week or two.

The bell rang, and Joel hobbled out of the classroom like his ass was on fire, not even bothering to spare me a second glance. I wondered what he thought of my poem or if he was even smart enough to realize that he'd inspired it somewhat. "Miss Palmer, can I speak to you please?" Mrs. Sellars called out.

I slowly made my way to the front of the room as other students trickled out, gossiping and laughing as they made their way to their next class. "Yes?" I asked as she shuffled through papers on her desk.

"You've got some raw talent, girl. We need to work on your mechanics, and I would have changed some of your diction, but you evoke feelings, Roe. I really think this could be something."

I politely smiled, soaking up her compliments like a sponge. "It was fun," I replied noncommittally.

"There's this contest called the National Star Poetry Scholarship. I think you should enter. You have to submit ten pieces, and with a little guidance, I think we could have a great portfolio to submit. You could win ten thousand dollars!"

The money would be nice, maybe enough to give me a fighting chance at running away, but I couldn't do that. "I'm not so sure—"

"Roe. I love all of my students, but you are a giant pain in the ass, you know that?" Mrs. Sellars barked, startling me.

"Excuse me?"

"You don't take yourself seriously at all. You don't believe in yourself. You never apply yourself because you're afraid of failure. I mean, hell, I guess if you don't try, it doesn't hurt when you lose, right?" she asked while waving her wrinkled hands in the air. "I'm tired of watching you wade through life in the shallow end. I want you to try this. Dive in for once in your life, child. I'll help you swim."

I wasn't expecting to get a lecture today, but fuck, Mrs. Sellars could deliver. "Fine, I'll try," I replied like the lame troublesome teen she thought I was. I probably wouldn't stick with it long enough to have ten poems, but I'd amuse my favorite teacher if it made her happy.

"Good. I want your next poem at the end of the week. I'll provide some constructive feedback on the one you wrote today so you know how to craft it more strategically."

She was throwing a lot at me, and I dreaded adding yet another responsibility on top of my overflowing pile. "O-okay," I stuttered.

"Great. Go along now, dear."

While walking out of the room, my phone pinged in my pocket, and I used my good hand to wrench it out of my skinny jeans. I didn't recognize the number, but the moment I saw the message, I knew with complete certainty that Hunter sent it.

Unknown: Joel is a good listener. Nice poem, by the way.

My fingers shook, and I leaned against a locker as the bell rang, not caring that I'd be late to Biology with Mr. Vin.

Roe: What did you do to him?

Unknown: We just chatted.

Chatted? They just chatted? I felt incredulous and helpless. I saw the evidence of their little chat all over Joel's bruised fucking face. I quickly typed out my response.

Roe: Stay the fuck out of my business.

I watched the chat bubbles flash across the screen, as if he were debating on what to say. My heart was pounding in my chest. I knew he was the reason Joel looked beat to hell and angry as fuck. I could strangle Hunter for hurting him. And *nice poem*? What the fuck did that mean? Was he watching me through my phone?

I kept stalking down the hallway, my Converse squeaking across the tile with every step. I stopped at my locker just as another message came in.

Unknown: Your business is my business, pretty debt.

I stared at my phone in disbelief, trying to work out how he'd known everything. My eyes flickered to the small camera lens at the top of my phone. I moved my head closer and closer, like if I peered down it, Hunter's manic smile would meet me on the other side.

Fucking bastard.

I opened my locker quickly, then used my injured hand to hold the device where the door shut. In a fit of rage, I slammed my locker on my phone again and again and again, watching the technology and Hunter's presence crunch on impact. The hallway echoed with the loud bangs. My wounded arm ached from holding my phone there, but I didn't care. I slammed until the screen cracked, until the power was cut off, and until it was nothing but splintered control on the floor.

"Miss Palmer!" a voice rang out, shocking me out of my haze. "What on earth are you doing?" I spun around, feeling like fire and smoke as Mr. Allen, the vice principal, strutted up to me. He was a slender man with a toupee and green eyes. The man's personality was the equivalent of a mall cop but more annoying. "Is that your phone?" he asked in disbelief.

I looked down at the mess at my feet before replying to him. "Sorry," I began. "There was a bug."

He just gaped at me, but I felt a sense of relief.

I'd try my hand at this poetry thing and take my winnings if I could. I needed something to help me get away from Hunter and Mack, and this might be my ticket out of here.

Chapter 12

HUNTER

She was sharp as sin, twisting her delicate features up into a vehement expression as she smashed her locker shut and destroyed her cellphone. Luckily, I was already ten steps ahead of her.

By the time she realized I had hacked her iPhone to listen in on demand, I was already following the security feeds at her school so I wouldn't have a moment of interrupted viewing time. She looked so triumphant, so determined. She was irrational and yet somehow majestic.

I wanted to break her spirit.

That night, I left a new phone on her nightstand with a note:

Try not to destroy this one, Little Debt.

She left it in the box and shoved it in her dresser drawer, probably hoping that not touching it would preserve her idea of privacy. And because I was gracious, I let her think she had this little win and that I hadn't found other ways of watching, even though my obsession with her seemed to grow even more.

Before, I'd periodically check on her throughout the day whenever I had a free moment. Now, it was like I couldn't drag my gaze away from the window to her life. From the moment I woke until the moment I fell asleep, I glared at her, hating my addiction while compulsively needing to make sure she was safe. I counted smiles and watched the steady rise and fall of her chest. I listened as she worked on her homework. I watched as she spoke to her friend, as her mind wandered, and as her anger stirred. I told myself that the near-death experience had triggered my protective instincts. I was just watching because I had a debt to pay, nothing more.

But that wasn't altogether true, and I sure as fuck wasn't about to admit it now.

Frosty fall clung to the air and thrust dying leaves toward the ground. I woke up to the smell of rot and mold. My old cabin wasn't much to brag about, but I didn't need much. Most of my money went into savings or paying Mack and providing for Roe. I was conditioned at a young age not to require much, and I guess that simplicity overflowed into my adult life. I survived for ten years on a stained mattress with water and crackers. The more you had, the more you had to lose.

I breathed in. Death seemed to permeate the air and cling to the logs that made up my walls. The windows were foggy and clouded as a murky mist rolled through the woods outside my house. I'd been up for a couple of hours, staring at my phone and speculating over what Roe would spend her day doing. She was lying on her bed with a lollipop in her mouth, her feet swinging back and forth as her puckered lips wrapped around the bright red candy. I lazily watched as she scratched words onto a wrinkled sheet of lined paper. She was humming to herself as she worked, and occasionally, she'd look around, as if she could feel my tired, hungry eyes on her freckled cheeks.

My phone started ringing, and I quickly answered it, annoyed to have my one-sided staring contest interrupted. "What?"

Mack's gruff laugh answered me. "Nice to talk to you too, sweetheart."

I rolled my eyes at his sarcasm and let out an exhale. "What do you need?"

"Gavriel called me. He wants me to oversee a product delivery at the yard today. He let me off for the past two weeks since you went all caveman and broke my arm, but he doesn't trust the new blood to make sure this shipment gets to where it needs to be. Especially with the Asphalt Devils still sniffing around."

I let out a slow exhale. I was supposed to be finding a solution to the gang—and by solution, I meant killing their new leader, Rosemary Jones. I was not looking forward to killing a woman, but chivalry died within me a long time ago.

I'd seen a few of the Devils riding through town, but none of them had stayed for long, and none of them had messed with Roe. Apparently, killing six men with my bare hands sent a strong message. But that wasn't enough for Gavriel Moretti. He wanted Rosemary killed yesterday, and every second I wasted letting that bitch breathe was a second Gavriel was growing increasingly annoyed with me.

It wasn't that I didn't want to. I just felt distracted. Not to mention, she was hard to find. All my leads had dried up, and I needed a little more time to figure out where I could hit her where it hurts. Even her girlfriend was in hiding. The Bullets had a reputation for taking care of the competition, and they weren't fucking around. Especially when the competition was dealing in sex. Gavriel made it his personal mission to end traffickers, and the Asphalt Devils were dealing girls. I didn't understand how Rosemary could sign on for something like that, but I guess she was like her father.

These idiots might know when to lie low, but they wouldn't stay hidden forever. I just had to find and kill them before they got brave again.

"You sure you up for work, old man? I can go if you need to rest more," I replied while standing and making my way over to the coffee pot and pouring myself another cup. Mack worked for Gavriel's father and now Gavriel. He was in the family business, and the Bullets' empire was how we met. I had a feeling, once Roe graduated, he'd retire, though. If Gavriel let him. Mack was good with numbers. He liked the dull work at the yard because he was a man that flourished in stable parameters and mundane activities. It was a common misconception that gangs were all violence and chaos. If we wanted our lucrative business to keep running, we had to keep inventory and records just like anyone else in corporate America. The only difference was our records didn't get reported to the IRS. Gavriel was the fist, I was the gun, Mack was the paper pusher in the back, grinning at the idea of working with numbers. Don't get me wrong. Mack was brutal when necessary—you didn't grow up in a gang without getting your hands dirty. But he preferred to keep the peace.

"I'd be more up to it if I didn't feel like a fucking truck hit me, but you and I both know that I have little say in these things. Besides, Gavriel doesn't want his favorite pet overseeing product transfers and weighing bags of cocaine. I'm calling to let you know that Roe will be home alone tonight, so keep an eye on her. Though I'm guessing I didn't really need to tell you that."

I didn't answer him. It was futile to admit what we both already knew. I'd been projecting my new level of infatuation on Mack, calling him to check on Roe, making sure he gave me hourly updates and asking how she was feeling. Mack was enjoying having me by the metaphorical balls, and I needed to shut down whatever weirdness that was going on within me so he didn't get any crazy ideas. "I'll monitor her, but I've got plans tonight," I replied while gripping the countertops.

"Plans, huh? You finally getting laid?" Mack teased. He knew damn well I wasn't going out chasing pussy. If I wanted to get my dick wet, the opportunity usually presented itself, but that didn't mean I was actively looking for a woman eager to tame and maim me. I liked sex, I just didn't like the women that refused to leave the next morning.

In my line of work, you could never be too careful. Strange women staying over and wanting to know your life story over breakfast were an annoying problem. And not to sound like a pretentious dick, but I was talented in bed. Most women wanted a repeat performance once they realized I knew my way around a clit.

"You're one to talk. It's been, what, ten years since you've even seen a pussy?" I retorted with a snicker.

"I look at you every day, don't I?" he chuckled. Bastard was always fucking with me.

"Yeah, yeah. Whatever."

Our laughter died down for a moment, and we both stayed on the phone in awkward silence for a beat or two before Mack spoke again. "Roe has completely shut me out. It sucks, man. She's like my kid. I don't know how I will ever get her to trust me again."

I felt bad for Mack, but he knew when signing up that this was a risk. I encouraged his attachment to her because I knew that love was a good motivator for protecting someone, but he was a fool for thinking it would last forever.

"You knew it would eventually come out," I replied.

"Can you talk to her? Just make her see I'm not the bad guy here."

My teeth clenched at the notion, and I gripped my phone so tightly I could have cracked it. "You want me to talk to her? You want me to tell her I'm the bad guy so she can go back to playing house with you?"

"Yeah. I mean, why not?" Mack began. I sensed a lecture coming on. "She knows now. There's no point in hiding it anymore. You watch her all the time. Maybe it could save us both some headache if you actually attempted to, I don't know, be her friend?"

The words *absolutely* and *not* warred on my tongue. Mack spoke again, not giving me the chance to refuse him. "Just think about it, okay? Maybe we can migrate to a healthier level of obsession. One that doesn't invade her privacy. One founded on trust. Maybe we can get to a place where she just comes to us when she needs help instead of us anticipating her needs? I probably sound crazy here…"

His voice bled with sarcasm. But that was the entire point to my system. Mack was supposed to build up a foundation of care and act as a buffer between her and me. I didn't trust myself to be close. I hated her too much to mingle my responsibility with feelings. I was supposed to watch from afar and anticipate her flighty tendencies with Mack's guidance. Now, it was all just a clusterfuck of epic proportions. Maybe he was right. Maybe

I needed to switch things up.

"You still there?" Mack asked when I had been quiet for too long.

"Yeah. Stay safe at work tonight," I replied before ending the call, not bothering to hear his response. I didn't want to give Mack the satisfaction of admitting he was right. It was time to change things.

———————

IT WAS TOO easy to sneak into her bedroom. It pissed me off how oblivious she was. I silently watched outside her window until she disappeared into the kitchen for a snack, then let myself inside. I'd for certain be nailing that motherfucking window shut the first chance I got. It was too damn easy to break in. My anxiety spiked. Maybe I wasn't doing enough to make sure she was secure? She needed a watchdog. Maybe some more cameras.

I couldn't tell if my anxiousness was from me wanting to save her from everyone else or myself.

I walked around her room, feeling intrusive and odd while sweeping my fingers along the top of her dresser. Earrings, dust, and quarters had collected there in a disorganized array of life and clutter. Her mirror was smudged with fingerprints, and her desk had books stacked on it. I stared at the papers on her bed, inching closer while listening for footsteps. I didn't give a fuck if she caught me snooping, though I probably should.

I came here with a purpose. I wanted to patch things up between her and Mack and gain her trust. I was tired of worrying if she'd run away or do something stupid like go to the police. Maybe if we established a truce, it would make all of our lives easier.

Maybe.

I picked up one paper and scanned it, pausing when I realized it was a poem she planned to submit for the scholarship opportunity. She's never stuck with anything, but for some reason, she was determined to keep with this. Mrs. Sellars seemed to have Roe pinned down, and if shit with Mack didn't work out, I'd be hiring that sassy old woman next.

A Mother's Shame

She used to knock on death's door and rock on the floor.
Don't go outside, Baby. It's just another day.
Beautiful shell of a woman. I used to stroke her cheek
as she told me about cancer of the soul.
Car accidents are just God's choreography.
Funerals, a divine comedy.

I was drowning in her words, absorbing them like a sponge and trying not to blame myself for her arduous childhood. I was only a kid myself when I'd taken on the role of her secret protector. But it was one thing to know about what she'd been through and another thing entirely to have the portrait painted with dynamic, haunting words.

Roe's mother was obsessed with death. She feared it, studied it, and pushed those compulsions on her daughter.

And it was all my fault.

The slamming of the front door shocked me out of my reading. What the fuck? I quickly dropped the paper and ran after her, my chest constricted. As I traveled down the hallway, I tried to think of what she was up to. She didn't pack a bag or anything and was in her fucking pajamas. Where was she going?

The moment I opened the front door, a gust of icy wind slammed against my cheeks, and I twisted my body to search for her. Was she taking out the trash? Checking the mail? Running away? "I'm not going anywhere, Stalker," she said with a sigh to my right. I released some of the tension in my chest and turned to face her. Her pajamas were way too thin for the fall Denver chill. I couldn't help but stare at the threadbare top clinging to her chest and her pebbled, perky tits pointing at me.

No. No no no. I was not staring at her fucking tits.

She wore plaid pajama pants, and her hair was up in a messy bun with light brown wisps framing her face. Her rosy cheeks bloomed at the sight of me, and each exhale made a visible plume of her hot breath flow over my skin.

"You knew I was here?" I asked in a low voice as she crouched down on the patio and placed a plastic plate with tuna on the concrete. Her broken arm was useless by her side, and I fixated on it as she replied.

"Yep. Saw you parked outside. Figured you'd either sit there all night or try to murder me in my sleep."

I blinked twice, not sure if I was hearing her correctly. "I'm not here to fucking murder you," I bit back. "I'd have to care to kill." I was definitely losing my touch. I was a fucking assassin; part of the job was being able to find a person's routine. I hid in the shadows on the daily and could sneak up on the best of them. Was Roe as attuned to me as I was to her?

"And yet you care enough to keep me alive," she snarked back.

Rubbing the bridge of my nose, I trembled from the chill and spoke again. "Why are you even outside right now?"

A low meow answered me and drew my attention to a black cat slipping up the drive and running toward Roe. The thing was surprisingly fat for being a stray, and even though the weather was freezing, it didn't seem bothered. "I sometimes like to leave food out for our neighbor's cat. It's getting cold now, so she probably won't be stopping by as often." The plump cat moseyed over to Roe and wove between her legs with a purr before inspecting the plate of tuna.

Roe scratched behind its ear while shivering, her bare arm pebbled with goose bumps from the icy wind. "You'll get sick out here in the cold. Let's go inside," I offered.

"Fine."

After scratching the cat behind the ears one more time, she finally stood and headed back inside with me following her. Once the door was shut and locked, she spoke. "Why are you here, Hunter? Are you going to make me use that cellphone you got me? Threaten me? Beat up my boyfriend again?" she gritted while letting down her hair and brushing her nimble fingers through it.

"Ex-boyfriend," I corrected, not sure why of all the defiant, ridiculous things she'd just said, that was the first thing that stood out in my mind.

"Right." Her face twisted into a poised scowl that somehow looked both beautiful and fierce. "I thought you wanted to pretend things were normal. This," she began while gesturing between us, "is not normal, Hunter."

No, it fucking wasn't. But what the fuck even was normal? I'd been watching this girl in secret for eighteen years. I controlled her entire life, hired her guardian. Normal wasn't in our dynamic, it never has been. "Mack said you're giving him trouble. I just wanted to chat about it."

She scoffed, her honey eyes widening with disbelief as she shook her head. "Trouble? I've done nothing wrong. I go to school, come home, and stay in my room. We don't talk. I keep out of his way, he stays out of mine. I stopped sleeping around. I even skipped out on a party tonight. I'm doing what you've asked. How can I be giving him trouble when we don't even talk?"

She strutted over to the kitchen and opened the freezer, pulling out a pint of ice cream. "That's the problem. He...he misses you." My words seemed clumsy and shallow, but I didn't really know what the hell I was supposed to say. I was definitely out of my depth, chatting about feelings and shit.

"Well then, he can talk to me about it himself. He's a big boy and doesn't need his stalker boss mending fences for him."

I watched as she shuffled through the utensil drawer. Settling on the biggest spoon she could find, she then started stabbing at the frozen treat while mumbling to herself. I just stared like I always did, cataloging her willowy body as it swayed. I bit my lip as her hand gripped the handle to her spoon. "You can leave now. I'm not going anywhere," she finally sputtered with a full mouth. Some creamy chocolate gathered at the corner of her lips, and I was tempted to lick it right off of her.

My next words were fucking ridiculous. "I read your poem." She froze up at my admission. Her pout dipped and her eyes turned glassy. There was a split second of pure, raw feelings. It was like lifting the veil of her consciousness and getting a front-row seat to all the things that worried her. My fingers itched to reach out and stroke her cheek.

And as quickly as her vulnerability appeared, she locked it down behind her stone-like eyes and continued to eat her ice cream. "I should probably bring up the gross invasion of privacy, but that would be redundant, hmm?" she said with a humorless laugh before slamming the pint of ice cream on the granite countertop.

"I didn't realize..." my voice trailed off. This was not how I thought this evening would go. "I knew your mother was a recluse and a bit obsessed but..."

"Didn't realize?" She scoffed while shaking her head incredulously. "You're so pious. You thought just because you've been watching me all this time that you somehow know me? Fuck that. You know nothing."

She was wrong, though I didn't vocalize that. I knew her better than I probably knew myself. I'd seen how she processed trauma. I'd watched her find happiness in the hearts of unworthy, fumbling boys. I'd seen how it took years for her to open up to Mack, and one mess up on my part built those walls back up. I knew how she searched for death in every room, how she was trained to read danger like an open book. I knew how her laugh sounded when it was real. I knew that she didn't give herself enough credit.

"I have no desire to know you," I lied. "Don't flatter yourself."

"You're a fucking liar," she said before wiping her hands off on a towel and taking a step to move past me. I wasn't ready for our conversation to be over, though. Reaching out, I grabbed her wrist, yanking her toward me. Our chests collided like a car crash. My bones curled and groaned at her closeness. She let out a breathy little gasp that didn't sound like shock or surprise. No, it sounded like lust.

"Let go of me," she whispered, though she did not try to put distance between us. She breathed in slow and deep, pressing her breasts against my chest with each methodical inhale. Her cheeks were flushed, and her breath smelled like chocolate.

"My foster home was three blocks from your mother's apartment in New York. Well, one of your apartments," I admitted. "I'd climb the stoop and check on the two of you when I could. You moved, and I lost you for a year. But I found you again. I always found you." I didn't mention how that year felt like a prison. Or how I barely slept and worried something had happened to the girl destiny had saddled me with.

She squinted at me, like I was a crossword she couldn't figure out. What's a six letter word for obsession?

"So you really have been watching me since you were ten?" Her question was drowning with confusion and fear. "Normal ten-year-old boys aren't creeping on newborns. You said you were in foster care? Didn't you have anything else? Anyone else?"

She was hovering right over the truth, and it made me want to squirm. I had nothing and no one. I was born alone and would die alone, too. Sure I had my job, and Mack was a good enough friend, but I was destined to only share my life with a one-sided obsession.

She was leaning so close that one bad impulse could close the distance between our lips. I let go of her wrist just to see if she'd pull away. She didn't.

"I had nothing. I just had you, Pretty Debt." My admission made bile crawl up my throat and burn me from the inside out. Silence. Total silence. We stood staring at one another, too close to be appropriate and yet too far, as well. She pressed her tongue against her cheek while assessing me. Had I said too much? Too far?

"You staying the night, Stalker?" she finally asked.

"Yes."

"There're sheets and blankets in the linen closet, and the couch folds out into a bed. Goodnight."

And like the skilled runner she was, she disappeared down the hallway and away from me.

\

Chapter 13

ROE

"Let's skip class," Nicole said while twisting a lock of blond hair around her index finger. We hadn't been talking a lot lately, though I'd seen her on Joel's heels in the hallway. She'd invited me out to a party, but I spent the weekend hiding in my room, with the devil sleeping on my couch.

I wasn't expecting Hunter to stay as long as he did. Something came up at work for Mack, and he didn't come home until late Sunday night. I was fine with being alone, but Hunter took it upon himself to be my babysitter. It pissed me off, but part of me liked having the opportunity to get to know him better. The only problem was we refused to speak to one another. We even stayed on complete opposite sides of the house.

Honestly, I didn't trust the level of empathy I felt for the lonely boy with nothing but an obsession with me to keep him company. Empathy was one of those slippery slope emotions that burned up your better judgement. Not to mention, the man was too damn sexy. It was easy to forget how fucked up he was when he looked like a walking Calvin Klein ad. It was thirty degrees outside, and he spent all of Sunday shirtless and lounging on the couch. It felt like he was testing my reaction to him, and every time my cheeks bloomed with a harsh blush, I felt like a failure.

"Why do you want to skip class?" I asked Nicole before slamming my locker shut. Usually her reckless ideas stemmed from a deeper issue, and I was curious just how far she was willing to go. She looked good today. She wore a short, little skirt with black tights and high heels. Her sweater was more like a crop top, and her cropped hair was curled perfectly.

In stark contrast, I was wearing long jeans and tennis shoes. My hair was a wavy mess, and I couldn't be fucked to use concealer to hide the dark bags under my eyes. It was hard to sleep last night, knowing Hunter was near. My imagination kept conjuring him at the foot of my bed. I almost preferred him watching me from a distance than sleeping just down the hall.

"Well, if you'd check your phone, you'd see that my parents are going out of town again to some bullshit conference in New York they just have to attend. They're missing my piano recital."

I nodded like this was something I understood. I never really put expectations on my mother. She was far too lost in her own grief and mental illness to focus on me. She taught me how to fear. She taught me that relationships were weaknesses, and the only person I could trust was myself.

"I'm sorry, girl," I replied. I had empathy for her. The last eight years, I'd been given a father figure that cared. Even though I didn't really give Mack that many options to attend extracurricular activities, I bet he would attend whatever bullshit I tried. He'd probably show up wearing a fedora to my poetry reading and would snap louder than all the other parents combined. This strange distance between us was getting harder and harder to navigate. Maybe Hunter was right, we needed a truce.

"Let's just go for a drive or maybe out to eat? I just don't feel like going to class," Nicole pouted. "Or we could drive up to Denver University? See what kind of trouble we could get into. Joel could get us some edibles, probably. I have a friend that could buy us beer." Every statement got progressively more self-destructive, and I started to worry. I bet she wanted to go somewhere she'd get caught so her parents would have a reason to stay. Nicole was nice enough and yet also painfully transparent. She'd never admit that she acted up for that reason but didn't deny it either.

"I don't know if I should," I began, my voice trailing off as I felt that familiar sensation of being watched travel down my spine. Hunter was pretty clear on the rules, but rebellion was in my soul. My sense of self-preservation pushed me to listen, but I also wanted to show him that I wouldn't roll over and heel just because he threatened me. And aside from my broken arm, my body had healed some, which meant I was more capable of putting up a fight.

There was a deeply buried part of me that wanted to rebel, if just for the chance to be chased. It was electrifying to be on the receiving end of his obsession, in a petrifying sort of way. He'd given me breadcrumbs to his past over the weekend, but it wasn't enough. I wanted to learn where he came from and why...me? The hate he felt was palpable and toxic. It was such an odd contradiction to loathe the person you wanted to save. I wanted to figure him out, and the only way to do that was to force him out of hiding. He reacted when I pushed him.

"Yeah. Let's cut class and go shopping in the city? I'm itching to buy some new boots," I said loud enough, as if Hunter were listening to us now. I wasn't sure what he was fully capable of, but refused to put anything past him. I didn't have my phone on me, but he still seemed aware of every fucking thing going on in my life. A trip to the mall wouldn't be too crazy, which meant I didn't have to worry about Nicole doing something stupid to get her parents' concern.

"Ooh! I like your style, Roe!" Nicole shouted while clapping her hands together. "Let's go!"

It was ridiculously easy to sneak out after the bell rang. No lingering teachers in the hallway stopped us, and we walked out the front door without a hitch, the sunshine hitting our cheeks and the chilly wind caressing our skin. I eyed the parking lot with apprehension as we walked to her Prius. I half expected Hunter to jump out from behind a car and tackle me to the ground.

But no. He didn't. I got in her car, and we headed to the city. I told myself that I wasn't disappointed for the lack of fanfare. Surprisingly, she brought up Joel quite a few times. "He sure was beat up. I can't believe he got jumped! I brought him some dinner the other night…" she trailed off while eyeing me out of the corner of her eye. She was obviously trying to gauge if I was going to be mad that she was spending more time with him. "Joel is so sweet. He told me that he'd come over and keep me company while my parents were gone. Did you know he wants to go to California after graduation?"

Her rambling was annoying me. "Nicole?"

"Yeah?"

"Ask what you want to ask already; you don't have to tiptoe around it."

She swerved on the road, and I clutched the door handle, flashbacks barreling through me like a tidal wave. "Sorry," she squeaked. "I just wasn't expecting you to be so blunt."

"You like Joel, yeah?" I asked.

"I mean, he's nice. Totally not what my parents would want me dating but—"

"I didn't ask if they approved or not. He's not some guy you can use to make your parents angry so they'll pay attention to you," I spit out while eyeing the window. Sure enough, Hunter's car was following behind us. Predictable little stalker. I didn't want him lashing out at Nicole, but I was invigorated at the sight of him.

"Excuse me?" she stuttered.

"You heard me. Look, your parents are absent most of the time, and your rebellious shit works to bring them home. It sucks you have to go to such drastic measures, but I won't let you use Joel for your Mommy and Daddy issues. He's a tatted pothead that's good in bed, but he's actually a decent human, too."

Behind us, Hunter's electric blue Jeep was riding our ass, but Nicole was reeling too much from my statement to really pay attention.

"I don't even know how to respond to this," she murmured while exiting the highway. Hunter exited right behind us.

"Just answer my question," I replied with a shrug as she pulled into the mall parking lot. "Do you like Joel? Not for any other bullshit reasons. Just him."

The car came to a stop, and she unbuckled so she could turn and face me. Her jade eyes assessed, and she gnawed on her nails while thinking over my question. "I like him," she whispered. "I think. But...I don't want to upset you. Girl code trumps everything, and I won't go for it if it makes you uncomfortable."

I tried to assess how I was feeling but came up empty. There was a sense of fondness for Joel but no jealous lingering need for affection. He was just someone that made me feel desired. Someone to pass the time. I cared, but there wasn't love. Love was just some abstract condition I couldn't relate to. "I don't care if you like Joel. I'm not the type of girl to get worked up about shit like that."

She gave me a look like she didn't believe me. "Riiiiight," she said with an eye roll.

"I'm serious! I'm not interested in Joel anymore, and I want you to be happy."

"You can't be over him; it's only been a couple of weeks. Not unless you took my advice and got under someone else," she replied with a nudge of her elbow. I let out a huff of air, trying to come up with a way I could convince her I didn't care when a stark knock on the window made me pause.

Motherfucker.

"Who the hell is that?" Nicole said while stretching her lips into a broad smile. "Oh my God, forget Joel..." I turned to look at our intruder, already knowing who it was before I'd even seen his face. There was only one man that was crass enough to knock on our window and hot enough to make any woman melt.

I smiled at Hunter, who was scowling and wearing tight jeans and a hoodie, his staple attire. Opening the door, I greeted him with a saucy grin.

"Babe! I didn't think you could make it." My voice was loud enough for Nicole to hear, which was exactly my intention.

He looked quizzically at me, like he wasn't sure what game I was playing with the ridiculous pet name. Wrapping my arms around his waist, I leaned in and inhaled his woodsy scent while Nicole gaped from inside the car. I then whispered my threat. "This is the only friend I have. You will not threaten her. You will play along, or I will jump in front of moving traffic."

He went rigid. "I'm not doing anything. Why are you cutting class? You're a fucking pain in my a—"

His hissed words were cut off with a shrill squeal. "Oh my goodness, hello!" Nicole shrieked while getting out of the car. She patted her hair and smoothed her sweater while all but drooling at Hunter. "I'm Nicole!" she circled her Prius then stretched out her hand to shake his. Naturally, the antisocial psychopath just stared at her French manicure for a moment. I could have throttled him for being so stunted. Finally, he turned on the charm and slipped on the mask he wore when out in public, the mask that disarmed the masses.

"Hey, I'm Hunter," he replied in his honey voice.

"I didn't realize Roe had invited anyone...how do you know one another?" Nicole asked.

I swooped in to take control of the conversation. I didn't really want Hunter meeting Nicole, but since he followed us here, I'd do everything I could to keep her off his stalkerish trail. "Hunter and I have been seeing each other for a couple weeks. Apparently, he has a kink for girls in casts," I joked while placing my uninjured palm against his chest. I felt his breathing stall for a moment beneath my touch.

"Oh my! How nice! Will you be shopping with us today? I wanted to skip class, and Roe was kind enough not to let me go alone," Nicole practically purred.

He dug his fingers into my hips, pulling me flush with his body. "I don't think so. I just had a break at work and wanted to check in. Would you mind giving us a moment?"

Hunter didn't wait for Nicole to respond. He seized me by the neck with mock tenderness and lugged me toward his Jeep, his boots stomping the pavement with every step. To an oblivious onlooker, it probably looked like he couldn't wait to get his dick in my mouth and just wanted me alone, but I knew the truth. I was about to get a scary lecture, and for some reason, I was excited for it.

"Take your time," Nicole's sultry voice called at my back, teasing us like she was in on some sort of dirty secret.

The moment we were at his Jeep, he banged my body against the driver's side door and bound me there with his pelvis. I hadn't completely healed from the accident, so the hard collision made me wince.

"Why are you skipping class?" he asked while gripping my hips. His fingers dug into me, like he could hurt the truth out of me.

I studied his question for a moment. I had lots of reasons for skipping class. I didn't want to see Joel again. I had a math test I wasn't prepared for. I wanted to see how far Hunter would go to track me down.

But of all the reasons, there was one that really stood out.

"Nicole is probably my only friend," I replied timidly.

"And?" Hunter's question was filled with annoyance.

"And sometimes she does reckless things to get her parents' attention. I didn't want her cutting class alone and ending up on the evening news. I feel a bit protective of her, and you more than anyone should understand that."

Hunter froze but kept his body pressed firmly to mine. I watched as he dragged his index finger along my hard cast, staring at the damage done to my body with a sense of regret. "I don't like you skipping class and going where I can't see you. I also don't like you going to crowded places without Mack or me present."

His rules triggered old memories within me, and I felt the urge to rebel. I tried to be patient with this infuriating man, but I didn't owe him my cooperation. I was a grown ass woman who was more than capable of taking care of myself. But he'd already made it clear that my boundaries were simply silent suggestions, so there would have to be a sense of cooperation with my puppet master if I wanted the pretense of a normal life, at least until I had a detailed plan and money to escape. "I'll start using the phone you gave me so you can keep an eye on me," I promised in a rush, though the words made me squirm. Agreeing to his terms felt a bit like giving up, and I didn't want to be some helpless woman giving in to a dark, handsome man's demands. I wanted to stand up for myself, but being strong meant knowing when to pick my battles.

He seemed to think over my words for a moment. It was short-lived, though, because he immediately started spitting out more demands. "I also want you to tell me if and when you're going somewhere. I won't have to invade your privacy as often if I don't have to monitor."

That was somewhat of a compromise. I liked the idea of not feeling observed all the time. Part of me wanted to tell him to fuck off, but the other part wanted to meekly obey his request. I was trying not to seem completely fucked in the head. "My…" I began. For some reason, I wanted to explain why my independence was so important to me. "My mom never let me leave the house. She homeschooled me. I didn't go to parks. I spent more time in the emergency room than anywhere else. When she died, Mack eased me into freedom."

Hunter's eyes softened, and he nodded, encouraging me to continue. "I really value my independence. It's been kind of a mind fuck to know you've been pulling the strings behind the scenes. I just…I can't go back to that sort of control, Hunter."

He chewed on his lip before responding. "Okay."

"Okay," I replied, and it looked like all the tension in the world drained from his broad shoulders. His crystal eyes softened to deep pools of relief, and his hard body leaned into mine without threat. I did not understand the burden he carried. I recognized that it disturbed him, but this pressure to protect me didn't seem to come from a sick place. The pressure of my happiness and survival weighed him down, and I wanted to know why.

I glanced over his shoulder and saw Nicole watching us with a broad smirk on her face. She would definitely have questions about Hunter, and I wasn't looking forward to answering them. I wrapped my good arm around Hunter's neck, pulling him close. "What are you doing?" he asked.

"I'm pretty glad you're here. I was trying to convince Nicole I'm cool with her dating Joel. She doesn't think I've moved on."

He faltered for a moment, then a flash of determination crossed his features. He leaned impossibly close, resting his forehead against mine. I wasn't expecting this response from the broody man, and I felt trapped against him yet somehow comforted too. My pulse had picked up at his nearness, and part of me hated the way my body responded to his hard body and sexy smirk. It seemed wrong to be drawn to someone that was obviously not good for me, but he had this captivating presence about him I couldn't ignore. There was something between us that was potent and needy and protective. My fucked up brain didn't worry about love or running. Raw chemistry and an unavoidable attraction simmered between us. It was impossible to fake.

"You want me to kiss you, Pretty Debt? You want to put on a show for your friend and let me feel you up against my Jeep?"

His sultry words made my lips part, but I couldn't meet his gaze. The truth was, I did want that. I'd always been impulsive with my body. I'd always craved affection from people. The first ten years of my life were spent alone, and it warped my sense of self. I needed to touch, to feel others.

But it wasn't right. In fact, it felt unbelievably wrong. I didn't want to kiss my stalker, nor did I want to feed the roaring monster within me. Hunter was wrong and twisted up about a lot of things, but he was right about me feeling flattered by his obsession. But the more I got to know him, the more I realized he resented me. I couldn't let my needs turn this into some complicated sexual conquest, no matter what the heat between my legs suggested.

"No," I replied without meeting his gaze. "I don't. This should be enough to convince her."

My words were calm and steady. I didn't sound desperate for affection or shaky from the feel of his body pressed against mine. I was proud of myself for not doing the self-destructive thing. His eyebrows shot up in surprise.

"You don't want me to devour your mouth right now?" he prodded.

"You don't want to get off on feeling wanted?"

I shivered at his cruel words. I did want to feel wanted—just not from him. I didn't want to encourage his obsession.

"I don't want to be on the receiving end of your regret," I admitted. My response was threaded with truth but barely skimmed the surface of my base needs in that moment.

Hunter placed his palm against my chest, stretching his fingers around my neck with threatening pressure that made me whimper. His lips brushed against mine slowly, yet so briefly it made me lean even closer to prolong the contact. "Don't worry, Pretty Debt," he began before lowering his mouth to the sensitive spot behind my ear. I looked up at the clouds above us, praying for relief as his hot breath caressed my skin. His teeth dragged sharply across my skin, then he pulled away and cupped my cheeks. "I don't regret the things that mean nothing to me."

And with those savage words, he pressed his lush lips to mine. I didn't see fireworks, and there was no explosion of relief. It was like planting a seed and watering the beginning of a towering tree with deep, unmoving roots. I sighed into his mouth and hated myself for it. He moved like this kiss was my punishment. He nipped at my bottom lip. He sucked on my tongue and threaded his hands through my hair. The bite in the cold air struck at my heated skin, adding another sense of harshness to his kiss. I moved my hand to the waistband of his jeans and curled my fingers until they teased at his growing length.

He groaned out curses and forgiveness and hate. His guttural tone caressed my body in time to every stroke of his tongue. My body seemed to react on pure instinct. I widened my stance as we kissed, as if hoping he'd take his hand and cup my sex. He didn't.

His hands were everywhere. His tongue like a snake. We moved like waves, his hard muscles flexing as his hand explored my hips, my stomach, and the spot right under my breasts. We were in a public parking lot with Nicole's watchful eyes following everything we did, but the world seemed to waste away. I fed on his coffee taste.

We kissed.

And kissed.

And devoured.

And flicked.

And tasted.

And the hate died a bit. And the fascination grew. And my panties became coated with forbidden lust for a man that I should run from.

And every nerve ending in my body seemed to startle with want. I was getting off on his experienced desire. He knew how rough to explore. He knew where to stimulate. He knew exactly where would drive me fucking crazy without giving me what I wanted.

I cursed the cast on my arm, keeping me from using both hands to search the feel of his humming body. I ached to lift my leg and wrap it around his waist. I wanted to open the door to his car and lie down in the backseat. I wanted to feel the friction of our bad decision on my cunt.

But he pulled away.

And away.

And he got into his car.

And he turned it on.

And he left me standing there.

And the regret I didn't want him to feel suddenly became my lust-filled anthem. My body felt cold and shocked senseless. One second I was debating the benefits of public sex, and the next he was peeling out of the parking lot. My heart seemed to sink as I pressed the tips of my fingers to my pulsing lips and gawked at the sight of his retreating tail lights.

"Fuck you, Hunter," I whispered.

Chapter 14

Bee Sting Kisses

Needle tongue. Whiskey breath.
Cinder hands and agonizing death.
You frown with your eyes and kiss with your fist.
Leaving me wishing. Lust dismissed.

Hammer heart. Bee sting pout.
Lovely lies and delicate doubt.
You walk with corruption and argue with venom.
Leaving me...momentum? Phantom? Random?

Fucking A. Fucking stupid poem. I was trying to take the creative route of working through my anger, but it was just making me more frustrated. It had been six hours since Hunter left me in the mall parking lot with my lips parted in desire. He left without a word, trying to convince me that he wasn't affected by the confusing make out session we shared. But I felt it. I felt his erection pressing against my stomach. I felt his nearly inaudible moan caressing my tongue. He was just as turned on as I was, so why stop?

There were a million and one things stacked against us. I knew it. He knew it. Hell, anyone with a basic understanding of right and wrong understood that kissing my stalker was probably the first sign of Stockholm syndrome. He was ten years older than me, and I didn't really know where he stood on the creeper scale, but he was attractive. There was this undeniable connection between us buried in his mind and blossoming in my soul. I couldn't quite put my finger on it, but that kiss felt like the most tragic, inevitable thing in my life, and I wanted to explore it more. I wasn't bothered about a little PDA. I'm all for sexual freedom and empowerment, but I didn't like the dismissive way he just dropped me like a hotcake on the asphalt.

I deserved better than that. I deserved better than everything this stupid man was doing to me. I deserved answers and freedom and a bit of trust. I hadn't gone to the police, and I hadn't tried running again. I was being cordial with Mack—for the most part. I was the best damn behaved captive this world had ever seen. Would it kill him to at least pretend some part of him cared about me? I'd seen the evidence of his affections in his deeply protective nature. A simple scratch sent him reeling. You didn't protect what you didn't care about, and I wanted to understand why he was so hell-bent on convincing me this was nothing—this meant nothing.

Was he ashamed of being a stalker? I couldn't necessarily blame him. Peeping through the windows at unsuspecting toddlers had my pedophile warning bells shrieking. But I didn't get that sort of disgusting vibe from him. In fact, nothing about our situation felt sexual up until yesterday. I think what started as a responsibility turned into lust, and he wasn't sure how to handle that.

I was going to handle his dismissal with gritted teeth and a fist.

My phone pinged, and I turned to look at it, frowning at the notification.

Hunter: You're using your phone. Good girl.

Good girl? I was *nobody's* good girl. I rolled my eyes. The patronizing tone transcended the simple text and washed over me. That asshole had no problem letting me know how pathetic I was. For a stalker, he sure did juggle the contradiction of not giving a fuck about me with ease. I debated on how to respond to him and finally settled on something snarky.

Roe: If it means what happened today never happens again, I'll happily keep this cell phone on.

I smiled at my text for a moment, feeling proud of myself. It took him all of thirty seconds to respond.

Hunter: Yeah. Today can't happen ever again.

Gritting my teeth, I quickly typed out an immature response just to fuck with him.

Roe: It was awful. I felt like I was drowning in your saliva. And what the fuck did you eat for lunch? Sauerkraut?

Beneath the anger and sexual frustration, I felt insecure—which was fucking ridiculous. I shouldn't *want* Hunter to want me. But for fuck's sake, most stalkers were obsessed with their victims. Would it hurt him to be at least a little bit nostalgic about our kiss? Maybe he knew that I got high off validation and he didn't want to fuel my already hard-to-handle ego. Maybe he just didn't want to admit his attraction to me. Maybe the kiss meant nothing. Either way, I wanted a reaction out of him, and I think I knew just how to get it. My phone pinged again, and the message there made me want to throw my phone through the window or find another locker to slam it in.

Hunter: Liar. You enjoyed it.

Tossing my phone onto the bed, I rolled over onto my back, letting my sleep shirt rise a bit as I digested his words. I stared at the sliver of skin exposed on my abdomen and wondered what it would feel like to have his lips press there. Would he suck on my skin? Would he leave a mark everywhere he went?

I wasn't wearing shorts. I made the choice to be half-naked on the off chance he was watching. I dropped my knees open, and my body went wild with awareness. An electric feeling made me buzz as I slowly slipped my good hand lower and lower, teasing the boundary of my nude lace panties with my middle finger.

I just wanted some fucking relief, and I wanted to make him frustrated in the process. He left me wanting, and here I was touching myself, hoping he was watching; maybe a little torture would help him admit that he *liked* kissing me. I was so frustrated with myself. So frustrated with the unaffected asshole that just left without a word. So confused with why I craved his touch.

I curled my finger and touched my clit, closing my eyes and imagining rough lips wrapped around my sensitive nub, sucking and teasing. I knew he was watching. I could feel his presence. Hell, I could practically smell him. Had he been in my bedroom recently?

I was just about to finger fuck myself into oblivion when my phone rang. I smiled broadly with my eyes closed, knowing he could see the sense of satisfaction on my manic, lusty face. Hunter was getting predictable at this point.

I didn't bother to answer my phone, though. I was in the middle of getting off, and Hunter didn't deserve my full attention right now. He deserved my *vengeance*.

I ran my fingers along my slit and arched my back, moaning to try to get myself in the mood. It wasn't good enough. I needed release, but I didn't want to do it myself. I was about to call some of my previous hookups when my phone rang again.

Sexually frustrated, I reached for the phone and answered. "Hello?"

"Stop touching yourself." Hunter's voice was gritty and harsh. With one demand, he had my body thudding.

"Are you watching me, Stalker?" I asked coyly.

"Are you trying to get off, Pretty Debt?" he replied. Instead of answering him, I propped the phone between my shoulder and ear, then slowly trailed my fingers down my body and back inside my panties. "*Fuck*," he growled.

His whispered curse made my lips part and my back arch. "Stop watching, Stalker," I moaned.

His breathing grew ragged as my finger circled my clit. I'd been getting myself off for years. I never understood being ashamed or scared of masturbation. It was normal. And with Hunter watching and listening, it felt *fucking good*. Knowing I was pissing him off was half the pleasure. "Are you trying to get back at me, Pretty Debt?" he finally asked. "You think that touching yourself while I watch will make you feel better?"

"You don't have to watch," I replied simply. "You don't have to kiss me." With each word, I teased more and more. "You don't have to hate me."

I pinched my clit between my fingers and writhed in bed. Hunter gasped through the phone. The effect I was having on him made me preen. "Tell me something," I demanded. It was nice to feel in control for once. Our dynamic had always felt one-sided.

"What?"

"When did you start to be attracted to me?"

He cursed. "I'm not fucking attracted to you," he replied. It sounded like he was clenching his jaw.

"Could have fooled me," I rasped. "When, Hunter?"

"Shut the fuck up and hurry. I'm tired of watching you," he growled. Oh, he was mad. So, so mad. It made me bite my lip.

"Was it after the car accident? Did you like seeing me bruised and broken, Hunter?" I asked. "Was it when I ran away? Was it just today?"

"Stop talking and come, Pretty Debt," he begged.

"I'll come when you admit it," I promised, forcing my fingers to a full stop.

Silence stretched across the phone. We battled the tension with nothing between us but pants and wanting. I had the worst case of blue balls, but I wasn't about to give him the show he craved until he admitted it to me. I didn't expect anything more than hate, but I wanted the truth of his attraction.

"When?"

"I met you the night of your birthday," he replied lamely.

Shock plummeted in the base of my stomach as I processed his words. Hunter was the man in the woods. I'd been too drunk to remember or really care much about that interaction, but it all made sense. "It was you," I replied in astonishment.

"You got your fucking answer, so finish what you were doing now," he gruffly replied. He hadn't officially admitted that he was attracted, but we had a starting point for lust, and that was enough.

"What did you like about me?" I asked, a teasing hint to my voice.

"What the fuck does it matter?"

It mattered to me. I didn't understand why or how we'd gotten to this point, but it *did* matter. I wasn't about to get off for an audience without some payoff. And the only currency Hunter had to offer right now was knowledge and validation. I wanted to get drunk off his desire. The silence stretched, and I looked at my legs, raising the left one up slowly so I could brush my fingers down it. "You're ridiculous," I replied.

"Don't make me come over there," he said.

"Please do," I dared him.

Lowering my leg, I started rubbing on my clit again with quick fingers, giving him the show he wanted. I let the conversation fade into harsh breaths and moans. I let him listen to how my needy body responded to touch. I imagined him stroking himself on the other end of the line. I imagined him feeling as frustrated as I felt earlier. It was wrong to want one another, but our mutual need to suffer bonded us.

The line went dead just before I came. It was like he could feel the blooming pleasure sparking within me. I smiled to myself at the silence that answered me, knowing that his absence spoke louder than his presence. He felt wrong for wanting me.

I got off quickly. It was good enough to ease the friction of my soul, but it wasn't the explosion of pleasure my body craved. Regardless, I moved my body like it was the best damn orgasm this world had ever seen, putting on a show for my stalker because I wanted him to suffer.

And when it was all done, I felt disgusted with myself. I lay there for a moment, wondering if I was crazy but also feeling proud that I'd gotten him to express something other than hate or dismissal toward me. I just couldn't figure out if my fucked up brain was finding attraction where it didn't exist, just for the chance to feel something.

I grabbed my pen and a scrap of paper, writing a line that crossed my mind.

Bee Sting Kisses

What a tragic thing, to crave what kills you.

Chapter 15

HUNTER

I thought we were taking things too far when we kissed, but of course Roe couldn't stop there. Last night left me feeling disgusted with myself. I wasn't oblivious to how messed up this entire situation was. My commitment to keeping her safe bordered that line of appropriateness on the daily.

My only consolation was that I didn't watch her come. I didn't deserve the pleasure of seeing her perfect, tight body blissed out and writhing. I didn't deserve to see her arched back and parted lips. I turned off my laptop and hung up the phone just seconds before I knew she was coming all over her nimble little fingers. I wanted to punch myself. It was wrong.

I wasn't expecting to get up early and drive to their house. I had spent more time at their house in the last three weeks than I'd ever been there. It was so strange, yet with each passing day, it took on a sense of familiarity I was clinging to. Being an assassin cut me off from the world, and what was once a thin thread tethering me to humanity was now weaving its way into a thick rope.

With my hand hovering by the door, I once again asked myself what the fuck I was doing. I convinced myself that I was simply here to tell her that what happened last night couldn't happen again, but that was a fucking lie. Maybe I was messed up in the head. Maybe I wasn't the chivalrous protector I built myself up to be.

I didn't even get a chance to knock before Mack was opening the door, a wide grin on his face. "Roe and I were just sitting down for breakfast; want me to make your plate?" he asked in greeting, like he already knew my sick ass was headed over. He loved Roe like a daughter, and if he knew what kind of sick things I'd done, he would kick me off his porch.

"Is she actually speaking to you now?" I asked. I was happy to hear that they were having breakfast together instead of avoiding one another.

"Yes!" Mack replied with a clap of his hands. "She even asked how my weekend was. Whatever you said definitely worked!"

I was happy for the guy. Having them on the same page would be better for me in the long run, but having a family breakfast wasn't necessarily on my agenda for today. I was here to draw a clear boundary between right and wrong, a boundary I wasn't very familiar with but knew needed to be established nevertheless.

"I'm not really hungry," I said.

"Sure you are. Don't come here looking all broody. Roe hasn't had breakfast with me in three weeks, and I'm not letting you ruin this for me." I felt sheepish while looking up at him. I might be the boss, but there was a lot of give-and-take where Mack and I were concerned. He let me be the ruthless bastard I was, and I let him be the father hen from time to time. "You're gonna come inside, sit down, and we're all going to have a nice breakfast."

"Sure," I replied before following him inside.

At the kitchen table, Roe was sitting in her pajamas and struggling to cut her pancakes with one hand. She was wearing pajama pants, and her wild hair was thrown up into a bun on top of her head. She didn't turn to face me; I bet she was too embarrassed to look me in the eye.

The tips of her ears were red as I sat down in the chair directly next to her, making sure to brush my leg against hers in the process. I felt like a bastard, but I wanted to see those rosy cheeks bloom a bright shade of red, like the flush coating her skin last night.

"And why are you here?" she asked while stabbing her pancakes with her fork. I eyed Mack and noted how the temple in his forehead was throbbing furiously, as if daring me to fuck up his happy little breakfast.

"Just making sure the two of you don't burn down the house with your one-handed cooking," I joked. My attempt at humor wasn't amusing enough for Roe, though, because she simply scowled at me.

"You're the one that broke his arm. And whatever gang activity you're involved in is what broke mine," she argued with an unamused roll of her eyes. She had a point.

Mack spoke up. "I knew the deal when he hired me. I'm not afraid of a little pain, and I'm more than compensated for it."

I knew that was the absolute worst thing to say, and judging by the look on Roe's hurt face, Mack had just completely fucked up his pleasant breakfast.

"Oh. I almost forgot for a second that you were my hired fake uncle. Now I can add that you're bat shit crazy and let some psycho hurt you to the list of things I'm absofuckinglutely not okay with."

Oh, she was utterly pissed now. Vibrant and beautiful. It was a sticky situation, but my cock wasn't getting the inappropriate memo. He grew hard in my pants, and it was taking everything I had not to groan in discomfort. I couldn't help it. The fight in Roe's personality was not only the most annoying thing about her, but also the hottest. I loved when she stood up for herself and got pissed off at the world. I loved that she wasn't some helpless little lamb. It made feeling obligated to keep her safe an easier pill to swallow if I knew she wouldn't go down without a fight.

"You wanna talk about this?" Mack asked with a huff while dropping his fork. I felt like I was assigned the job as their therapist, mediating this fight from a distance. What the fuck?

"Yes. I think I do," Roe replied while crossing her arms over her chest. "Why do you work for this psychopath?" she asked before nodding at me.

Psychopath? I wasn't a fucking psychopath. Delusional, maybe. But not a psychopath.

"We're friends," Mack answered with a shrug.

"Friends don't break each other's arms, Mack. Not good enough."

Mack let out an exhale and looked at me for help. Nope. I wasn't touching this conversation. If he wanted to mend the fence in his own home, he'd have to man up and do it himself.

"My daughter is dead," he blurted out. It was like dropping a bomb on the conversation. No warning, no bracing for impact. Four words that hurt and rocked Mack. "She died of cancer, Roe," he added. His shoulders slumped. His eyes turned to the door. His mouth quivered with emotion. No tears graced his eyes. I'd only seen Mack cry once, and it wasn't when I was breaking his arm. "I was a single dad. Worked for the same...family...my entire life. Guess you could say I was born into it. I wasn't the best father, but I loved my little girl something fierce and provided for her the best I could." I glanced at Roe and noticed the moisture swimming in her light brown eyes, the empathy sliding down her face. "I'm so sorry, Mack," she whispered.

"After M-May died," Mack stuttered on her name, making even my cold, dead heart pang, "I went a little crazy. I did...aggressive things. I hurt people. I wanted to take on my daughter's hurt, but you can't steal away someone's cancer. I had so much fucking guilt. Hunter understood me. He offered me redemption. He offered me a chance at a family again. You could never replace my daughter, Roe. But I'm so happy that I got another chance to save someone, ya know? I needed to feel capable of that."

I watched as Roe took in his words, staring at the table as she gnawed on her lip in contemplation. I've known Mack since I was ten years old. He's part of the reason I got hooked up with the Bullets when I became older. I'd seen him work through his pain. In many ways, he was another one of my obsessions. But I didn't feel the need to protect Mack. I just wanted to help him feel like a man capable of saving someone.

"How did you meet Hunter?" she asked. Mack averted his gaze to me, asking with his eyes just how much he was allowed to share. I gave him a look that said *fucking tell her nothing*, and the corner of his mouth tilted up in amusement.

"We met at the hospital once. May was there for treatment. He was just a boy, separated from his family, looking for labor and delivery." I gritted my jaw. He better not go much further into detail. "I ended up walking him. I'd just gotten bad news that May would need to go on hospice, so the distraction was nice. We started chatting, and here we are. He kind of followed me around after that. I'd run into him occasionally around New York, and when he was old enough, I got him out of foster care and set up with my employer. Things just progressed from there."

That was definitely more information than I wanted to share, but it was good enough for now. "And here I was, thinking I was special," Roe said with a sigh. "You just stalk everyone."

Mack let out a relieved laugh, like he was thankful for the heavy conversation to be over. But I wasn't as willing to let this conversation drop. "I don't like hurting Mack. But sometimes he...needs it," I interrupted, slicing through the attempt at lightheartedness with a knife. "Whatever happens to you, I do to Mack."

Roe snarled at me. She didn't seem to like my explanation. I wasn't a therapist, but I understood Mack's needs. I never pretended to be anything but myself, and the ruthless solution might be unconventional, but it worked for us.

"Don't use Mack's grief as an excuse to be a terrible human being. You like hurting people. You like feeling powerful and in control. It's why you control my life. It's why you're always watching." Roe's words were focused and razor sharp. She put me under her thumb and pressed. She was right, in some ways. I did like being in control. I did like handing out pain. I'd been on the receiving end of it for the majority of my childhood, and I liked dishing it out more than taking it.

"You're a control freak with anger issues. Don't pretend you're doing

Mack or me any favors. I didn't ask for you to hurt him. I didn't ask for your protection, either."

Mack looked like he wanted to stab my eye with his fork. I'd definitely ruined his idea of a pleasant family breakfast.

Getting up from her seat with a frown, Roe didn't even bother excusing herself. She simply marched to her bedroom, her tight little ass swaying with every step.

"Well, that went just perfectly," I muttered under my breath while turning to look at Mack. The man was staring at his fist. Clenching. Unclenching.

"What? She'll come around," I offered when he didn't say anything.

The silence seemed to go on forever. I waited for him to provide some sort of commentary about her assumptions of me, but Mack just sat there in his own world. Lost in his grief. He'd given in to the memories he'd been running from since May died, and I knew the only way he'd come back out of it was either from a slap to the face or with a lot of time.

I decided not to be the villain today and give him time.

Roe walked back out of her bedroom, ready for class and still angry. "Mack, I'm ready for school."

Mack didn't even acknowledge her. He was too busy staring at his good fist.

"Mack?" she called again with a huff while taking a step closer. "I'm ready to go now."

She cocked her head to the side while observing him.

"I'll take you to school," I spoke up while standing. Roe wasn't going to get anything out of Mack right now, and we needed to discuss what happened last night anyway.

147

"Fine," she replied. I was really starting to hate that answer. She used it practically every time we talked.

"Fine. Fine. Fine," I mimicked as she slung her backpack over her shoulder and headed toward the front door. "Don't you know any other single-syllabled teenage words of rebellion?"

She walked toward my Jeep and got in the passenger side. The chill in the air made goose bumps pebble over my skin, and I could see my exhales.

Once we were both in the Jeep, I locked the doors with a sense of glee. There was no escaping this conversation, and I wanted to watch Roe squirm.

"That was quite a show you put on last night," I said while putting the car in reverse and pulling down the drive.

"Can we please pretend like last night didn't happen?" she asked.

If I were being honest, I'd like nothing more than to pretend like nothing had happened last night, but that just wasn't possible. I couldn't forget her creamy skin. I couldn't forget the way her body moved or the raspy way she spoke to me. It was like this continuous loop in my mind.

"No, we can't."

"Well, if you're hoping for a repeat performance, you're shit out of luck."

Part of me was a little disappointed, but I pushed that emotion down while stopping at a red light. "Why'd you do it?" I asked. I had a good grasp on the human condition. I'd seen the worst and best of it over the years. Motivations were easy to figure out if you paid enough attention. I just needed to figure out what was motivating Roe right now. Hate, I could work with. Interest would be a problem.

"I wanted to prove that you aren't as indifferent as you pretend to be," she snapped back with a satisfied grin before twisting in her seat to stare at me.

She looked so beautiful with her shoulder-length caramel hair and those warm brown eyes staring back at me. Her lips looked blushed and tender, like she'd been gnawing on them all night. Her outfit of plain jeans and a simple black long-sleeved shirt wasn't anything to obsess over, but she looked good. When did I stop seeing her as a girl I needed to protect? When did she become this...woman?

"You kissed me, then acted like it meant nothing. I just wanted to prove that you're a lying sack of shit with a hard-on for me."

I nearly choked on the spit gathering in my mouth at her words. Well alright then. Those motivations were pretty damn clear. So she wanted to get me back? Fine. Two could play that game.

"You shouldn't want me to be affected, Pretty Debt."

"We shouldn't want a lot of things, Stalker."

Against my better judgement, I reached out and lightly grazed her knee. I doubted she could actually feel it through the thickness of her jeans. My fingers were a feather light, teasing touch. "Is this what you wanted? You want a reaction out of me? You want me to admit that you're hot? That shit doesn't mean anything."

"I just want the truth," she breathed out before shoving my hand away. The light turned green, and I started driving toward her school again, taking each turn slowly to prolong our time together.

"I've given you as much of the truth as you're entitled to," I replied with a frown.

"Bullshit. You won't explain why you feel so protective of me. You won't explain why you seem hell bent on keeping me safe but hate me all the same. I'm getting tired of the contradictions. I just want you to admit that you give a fuck about me. You wouldn't have kept me safe all these years if you didn't."

I pulled into the school's parking lot and turned the car off. "Caring is relative, Roe," I replied. "Stop trying to push me for answers."

She stared at me for a moment, smiling like she had me figured out. There was a halo of light surrounding the crown of her head from where the sunshine hit through the window. "If you won't give me answers, I'll find them somewhere else. You can pretend all you want, Stalker. There's something here, and I'm going to get to the bottom of it."

With those ominous words, she got out of my Jeep and left me to wonder what she had up her sleeve.

I watched her on my phone the entire drive home.

Chapter 16

ROE

The club downtown was thudding with rebellious music. Hard beats and loud guitar riffs rattled my ears. They crammed bodies into every nook and cranny of the club, and I felt like I was walking through the personification of Nicole's cry for help.

I wore a black tank top and skinny jeans. My hair was curled and my makeup smoky. I didn't even have to show the bouncer my fake ID. I got in with a flirty smirk and a wink, and I hated myself for it.

Nicole was easy to spot. She was like a flare of naivety in the club's corner, sipping on what was probably a virgin cocktail and waving her arms above her head. It wasn't until I squeezed through the dancing bodies and got closer that I realized she was sitting on Joel's lap. He looked better than the last time I saw him. The club lights camouflaged the bruises on his shadowed face. A couple more weeks, and he'd be back to his beautiful self.

My cast stood out like a bright neon sign, glowing an electric blue under the lights. I made my way over to them, not thinking about the beacon in my pocket or how I had to climb out of my bedroom window to get here. Mack and Hunter would be at the club soon enough, but until then, I planned on being rebellious and free.

"Hello," I greeted before sitting next to them on the small couch. It looked like Nicole used her parents' credit card to book a private alcove somewhat away from the booming speakers and screaming crowd. A cocktail waitress sauntered over with a bottle of Patron and set it down with a wink. Guess she paid for bottle service, too.

Nicole squealed and shifted from Joel's lap to mine, wrapping her thin arms around my neck while squirming her bony ass against my thighs. "You made it! I figured you'd be busy with your new boyfriend," she practically yelled. I didn't miss the way she side-eyed Joel as she spoke, as if making sure he knew I was fucking someone else.

"I needed out of the house," I replied with a shrug before leaning over her lap to grab a shot. I downed it with a hiss, letting Nicole's screams of approval drown out my better judgment. I didn't like clubs, though I'd heard enough of my classmates brag about this place. It was one of the few clubs in Denver that turned a blind eye to underage girls. If you had money, you could shake your ass with the rest of them.

But crowds made my sense of self-preservation spike. There were too many variables, too many statistics about death, rape, and alcohol poisoning in my mind to really enjoy myself.

Once the burning liquid was down my throat, I turned my attention to Joel, fixing my expression into an indifferent facade. "Hello."

"Surprised they allowed you out, Rowboat," he said before leaning back on the velvet loveseat, reaching an arm back to rest it behind my head. I didn't like the insinuation in his tone.

"Yep. Escaped the warden for a bit," I replied with a frown.

"Let's take a picture!" Nicole interrupted before wiggling between us. Pulling Joel close, she pecked his cheek while holding her cellphone up, capturing an Instagram-worthy shot of the three of us living it up illegally in a downtown club. I guess it didn't happen unless you posted about it.

Within three seconds, she had it captioned and shared, the likes popping up like jealous little reminders that we had a life. She stared greedily at her phone, stroking the screen with her thumb while Joel and I sat there in silence. It was awkward for a moment until the real reason we were all gathered here lit up her phone. I glanced at the caller ID with bored interest.

Mom.

"I have to answer this..." Nicole got up, her pearly white teeth digging into her bottom lip to keep the grin from breaking out across her face.

I stared at her back as she retreated to a side hallway. "Does Nicole know what kind of shit you're involved in?" Joel asked before leaning forward to get his drink from the coffee table.

"What exactly am I involved in, Joel?" I asked while cocking my head to the side.

He glanced at me over the rim of his glass. A flash of terror crossed his features before he put his glass down. "All I know," he began while leaning closer, "is that one second I was taking you to the bus station, and then a few hours later some guy was breaking into my house and kicking my ass. He held me at gunpoint. He told me not to say a word and to stay away from you."

I swallowed. That sounded about right. "And then you ran away like a little bitch," I replied. I was still angry about the way he brushed me off in class, but I understood that he was scared.

"What does it matter to you? We break up, you call me for help, then rope me into some fucking gang activity bullshit, and then get mad when I cut ties. I don't get you, Roe."

He wasn't wrong. "And then you date my friend," I snapped, though of all the things leading up to this moment, I didn't care about that.

Joel tossed his head back and chuckled. "You don't do friends, Roe. You do temporary projects to help pass the time. To have a friend, you'd have to actually stick around."

I leaned forward and glared at Joel. "That may be true, but if you're fucking around with her because you're hoping to get back at me, you're wasting your time."

"Am I?" Joel asked while placing his hand on my upper thigh. "The way I see it, Nicole wants someone to make her parents pay attention. I think the town slut and local bad boy fit the bill nicely. We're all just using each other. It's up to you if there's a payoff," Joel said. He swayed in his seat while snaking his hand higher and higher, pressing the tip of his middle finger against my cunt as his whiskey breath feathered over me.

His words pissed me off and made me doubt myself. I thought I had Nicole figured out. Was she just hanging out with me to make her parents mad? I thought she did that with Joel, but I never imagined she was playing me, too.

I felt the impulse to run. It was a recognizable feeling. Breathing in the smoky club air, I prepared to stand up and leave this clusterfuck alone. I wanted a taste of freedom, not a slap in the face of reality.

"Keep touching her, and I'll break your fingers off and fuck her with them," a cruel voice said to my left. Joel turned ghastly pale and dropped his mouth open. He snapped his fingers back, and I enjoyed the drunken, stark terror crossing his face as he scrambled off the couch and away from me.

I grabbed another shot and downed it before slowly turning around to face my devil knight, and fuck if I didn't swoon at the sight I saw.

He was wearing a leather jacket, cut and tailored perfectly to his broad shoulders. His hair was disheveled in an effortlessly sexy way, and the dark denim jeans he was wearing fit his thick thighs perfectly. He leaned forward and yanked the shot glass out of my hand.

Neon lights danced across his skin as he stared me down. I could feel the intensity sizzling between us. Blood boiled in my veins, heating me up from the inside out. "What are you doing here?"

"Just wanted to have a little fun," I replied with a noncommittal shrug I just knew would piss him off even more.

Hunter looked over my head at Joel, and I watched as his chest expanded with air. Anger bled through the thin line of his lips and his dark glare.

"I'm going to go find Nicole," Joel stuttered before running out of there.

I gnawed on the inside of my cheek to keep from laughing at his quick departure. Hunter watched Joel's retreating form until he was completely out of sight, then turned his attention back to me.

"Where's Mack? He's usually the one to drag me out of these things," I said before glancing at my watch.

"I'm thinking you *want* to be pulled from these things. You don't like parties, you don't like crowds."

I averted my eyes, choosing to stare at the scuffs in the wood floors at my feet. Hunter grabbed my chin and forced me to stare at him. "You want to have some fun, Pretty Debt? Let's have some fun."

Hunter led me out of the private corner of the room, dragging me through the parting crowd to the dance floor. Bodies crowded me, sweat and swaying limbs stuck to my skin as he dug his fingers into my hips. I focused on the feel of his fingers to stop my intrusive thoughts.

Stay away from crowds, Roe. They could trample you.

I forced my mother's trembling voice out of my mind.

"You going to dance with me, Hunter?" I asked, my lip quirked in amusement.

The song switched to something dark and heady, the beat electric. Hunter leaned over to shout in my ear. "No, Pretty Debt. I'm going to get you off."

I gasped as he shoved his thigh between my legs. His hard grip on my hips guided my grinding movements against his thigh in time to the music. My lips parted on an exhale. I looked up at him through my lashes, taking in the deliciously devious man playing my body like an instrument.

The room was dark aside from the neon flashes of lights flickering around us. Lasers danced along the ceiling. It didn't take long for the grinding to awaken that harsh need within me. I wrapped my good arm around his neck and pressed my body against his.

His lips found my ear again. "How's that feel, Pretty Debt?" he asked. His thumbs pushed up my shirt, teasing my hot skin with his rough touch.

I couldn't even form my answer; I was too busy humping his leg like some sick, needy animal. From the corner of my eye, I saw Nicole and Joel dancing. Her mascara was smeared like she'd been crying. Joel looked oblivious, staring at me with his haunting gaze as he swayed.

"Don't fucking look at him," Hunter said while removing his leg from between mine. I whimpered at the loss of friction.

Pushing me away, Hunter spun around, like a predator looking for someone else to demolish. A blonde with a tight little body and a shirt so thin I could see the dark color of her nipples approached. He wrapped his arms around her and buried his face in her neck as they started grinding on one another. The song changed, and I stood there like a statue, rooted to the spot with my mouth hanging open in disbelief.

I was two seconds from coming on the dance floor, and he left me for someone else. He was trying to prove something here, something I didn't understand. But I wasn't about to give him the satisfaction of winning the who-cares-less game.

I looked around the room and settled on a guy dancing near me. He was lanky and high, his delayed movements and vacant face made him the perfect partner.

But I didn't even get the chance to walk over to him. I simply looked away from Hunter, and he drew away from the woman dancing on him and stole my attention back for himself. Wrapping his arms around my waist, he whispered in my ear, "Pretty Debt, you didn't think I'd let someone else get you off, did you?"

I almost melted at his touch, but I wasn't so easily controlled. Instead of answering him, I walked off the dance floor with an angry clit and wobbly legs.

I walked past Nicole and Joel, not bothering to tell them goodbye. I hated that Joel's words had affected me so much, but I needed room to think. I walked past the bar and out the front door, welcoming the icy city air with gritted teeth. In my epic storm out, I forgot to grab my jacket.

Nope. I definitely would not be going back in. I just had to make it until my Uber arrived. I pulled up my phone and started ordering a car when I felt him at my back.

"You're cold," he observed.

"I'd make fun of your observation skills, but you're a stalker," I replied while typing in Mack's address. Hunter plucked my phone out of my hand and put it in his back pocket.

"My Jeep is just around the corner."

Of course it was. Hunter wrenched out of his jacket and placed it over my shoulders. The friendly gesture almost made me forget his torturous idea of fun on the dance floor. I was getting genuinely fucking tired of being led on and then getting left to take care of matters myself. I just wanted to get home and get rid of the tension. I couldn't help but wonder. Would he watch me again? Would he call? Would he stay on the phone this time and listen to me come?

"You hear me?" Hunter asked while holding his arm out, pointing in the car's direction. "I'm parked over there, let's go."

I nodded. "All right," I replied before walking along the sidewalk.

The Denver night air smelled like pot, booze, and burgers. Drunk girls walked past in their short skirts, oblivious to the nasty chill. Hunter kept close to me, eyeing everyone that passed.

Once in the car, I pressed my forehead to the glass and tried not to let him see how frustrated I was. He drove us home, and I thought about Joel's words. I thought about my friendship with Nicole. I thought about Hunter showing up and threatening Joel. I thought about our dance—boy, did I think about our dance.

It took us thirty minutes to get back to Uncle Mack's house. I didn't even bother to question Hunter when he pulled up the drive and turned off his Jeep. He got out of his car and stalked up the driveway with angry steps, not explaining himself.

I noticed that Uncle Mack's new car wasn't in the drive and briefly wondered where he was.

"Mack is working late," Hunter said while walking down the hall and toward my bedroom.

I followed him in confusion. Hunter reached behind his head and took off his shirt with slow precision. I watched the tense ripple of muscle on his back in morbid fascination. I knew he was stronger than me, but why was that so alluring? I didn't want to crave him, but we'd been doing this dance for a while now.

"You going to finish what you started?" I asked while shrugging his leather jacket off my shoulders.

"No," he replied while looking over his shoulder at me. "We're going to sleep."

I balked at him. "You're sleeping in here?"

Hunter spun around to face me, showing off each dip and groove of his abs in the process. "Yep. I am."

"Why?" I asked incredulously as he sauntered over. Lifting his hand up, he then fingered the strap of my tank top and shoved it gracefully over my shoulder.

"I have a few reasons. I'd like to sleep without worry that you're going to run off. I don't particularly like the couch. I want to feel you squirming with need against my body all night. I want to smell your arousal on these sheets."

I couldn't fucking stand it. His words made me press my thighs together for some semblance of relief.

He grabbed the band of my jeans and tugged me closer until our bodies were flush. "Yeah, just like that," he whispered before unbuttoning them and easing the zipper down, his knuckles grazing my cunt in a slow, torturous move that had me whimpering.

"I thought I had to control you with fear, but this works much better," he whispered before bending to ease the thick fabric over my hips and down my legs. "You're a physical person, Roe. And I will ruin your life with a single touch."

I stepped out of the jeans while panting, observing Hunter as he tossed them to the other side of the room. He shrugged his own pants off and popped the band of his boxer briefs. "Let's go to bed."

I was stunned. Short of breath. Achy. He smirked at me before walking over to the bathroom and shutting the door. It wasn't until I heard the sink running that I closed my mouth and took control of the situation again.

Taking off my tank, I shimmied out of my panties and let the cool air kiss my naked body. I then waited at the door for my turn in the bathroom.

Hunter took his sweet time, and every tick of the second hand, I felt more and more ridiculous, standing naked outside the bathroom door. What the fuck was I thinking? I had convinced myself that this was the worst idea ever when the bathroom door opened, and I was greeted with his smug face.

"Are you trying to entice me?" he asked with a small laugh. "Because don't get me wrong, Pretty Debt, you have a nice body. But I think wanting you is hotter than the real deal, and I'll happily keep my distance if it means watching you squirm."

After a split second of wanting this infuriating man, I shoved past him to get in the bathroom. Grabbing my toothbrush, I put toothpaste on it to brush my teeth, but once again Hunter stole it from my fingers.

"Open your mouth, Pretty Debt," he challenged.

My traitorous body did exactly as he asked. My mouth slipped open, and he beamed in triumph. Grabbing my chin with his free hand, he started brushing my teeth with gentle precision. It was such an odd, compassionate gesture, but it felt like a power play too. I was putty in his hand, but I also felt cared for. This man had me exactly where he wanted me, though, and I was wondering how I went from fighting my stalker to wanting to fuck him. What was I trying to do?

"Spit," he demanded while pulling my hair back. I bent over the sink and did as he asked, keeping my eyes on him in the mirror's reflection.

His eyes never went to my ass. He didn't look at the curve of my spine or my dangling breasts as I bent. His eyes bore into mine.

Once done, I stared at the ground and brushed past him, making my way back into my bedroom and feeling more confused and conflicted. I stumbled to my dresser, but his words stopped me in my tracks.

"What are you doing?" he asked.

"G-getting dressed," my stupid, weak voice replied, though the lift at the end made it sound more like a question.

"No. Get in bed, Roe," he ordered while motioning toward my mattress. Slumping my shoulders, I followed his command and made my way to the left side of the bed before slipping under the comforter and sheets.

The lights turned off, and I squeezed my eyes shut. It wasn't until the mattress dipped beside me, I realized I'd have to spend an entire night vulnerable and naked with my stalker. It felt like some weird conditioning exercise. He was grooming me to want him, but I didn't feel manipulated. I felt in control, despite it all. He wanted me. He wanted me so badly he drove to Denver in the middle of the night to pluck me from a club. He cared about my safety. He may be stronger, but I motivated his actions.

"Your thoughts are too loud for sleep, Pretty Debt," he whispered into my ear while wrapping his arms around me. His forearm settled between my breasts, making them sensitive to the taunting idea of being played with.

Slowly, ever so slowly, he slipped his palm down, down, down my stomach. He eased his fingers between my thighs until he was cupping my pussy. My breath hitched, and I tried desperately not to squirm. The friction was just there.

"If you keep still all night, I'll reward you in the morning," Hunter whispered. I felt his hard cock drilling into my back. There was no way I'd be able to keep still all night. His hand was hot and already slick with my desire.

But maybe that's what he wanted. He wanted me to fail. He wanted me to want him with no relief. Fuck that. I was in control. Using my good hand, I reached down and pressed against his. He went rigid. "What are you doing?"

"I don't want your reward, Hunter," I whispered before pressing once more. His fingers slipped, and I could feel it just at the edge of my entrance. "I want to get off."

I ground against his palm, holding him in place with my other hand while whimpering into the pillow. He could have easily moved if he wanted to, but we allowed ourselves to believe the lie that I was making him do this. That he didn't want to feel me come against his skin. That I was just a toy to fill with desire and abandon.

I was already so close, every interaction of the evening building up to this crashing, flooding orgasm. "Fuck," I cursed while riding his palm. I moved fast and hard, whimpering and moaning with every movement as he rocked behind me.

I came hard. My entire body tensing and releasing with a force as I trembled and moaned in Hunter's arms. Hunter froze like he couldn't believe he lost the upper hand.

Once the roaring blood in my veins slowed to a quiet whisper and my body relaxed, I whispered to him, "Goodnight, Stalker."

And I fell asleep, with his palm on my cunt and my cum on his fingers.

Chapter 17

ROE

I expected the cold vacancy of my mattress to greet me the next morning. I ran my hand along the sheets, seeking his warmth and finding pleasure in his absence.

Hunter left because I scared him. I knew it deep in my gut. You didn't run from things that comforted you. You didn't escape things that felt easy. My mother taught me that you ran when you were scared, and Hunter was fucking horrified by the idea of being comfortable with me.

I rolled over and sat up in bed, reaching my arms out with a loud yawn. My cast felt heavy, and the skin beneath it was hot and sweaty. I was so damn ready to get this thing off.

It was Friday, and I wasn't looking forward to school. I didn't want to see Nicole or Joel. As much as I hated to admit it, what he said last night at the club had stuck with me. I felt used.

"You smiled when you saw I wasn't here. Why?" a voice called out against the dim morning light. I spun around and frowned at the towering, imposing figure sitting with his legs spread out in my plush gray reading chair.

"I thought you'd left," I replied, trying to keep my cool. Why was he still here?

"And that made you happy?" Hunter asked while leaning forward. He rested his forearms on his knees, and fuck if the sleepy look didn't make him even more devastatingly handsome.

I got out of bed, feeling the chill of the morning air brush against my naked skin. Hunter's eyes raked over the swells of my breast. It was like I could feel his stare. "Not necessarily," I replied. "It was more the reason that had me smiling."

Hunter stood up and wrapped me in his arms. The move swift yet jumbled all the same, like he was at war with his desires. "And what reason do you think I have for leaving?"

I leaned up to murmur my response over the thin line of his mouth. "You're afraid of me."

He closed the hairline of distance between our kiss, scalding my lips with his for the briefest of seconds, not long enough for me to worry about morning breath or if we should be doing this. It was a faint blink, so quick you'd miss it if you weren't paying attention.

"If the idea of fearing you put a smile on your face, I'd hate to see how you'd react if you knew how I was actually feeling," he whispered before pulling away. I felt rooted to the spot, overanalyzing his words. "Get dressed. I'm taking you to school today."

He didn't even give me a chance to respond with snark, and he simply disappeared out of my bedroom door.

I got ready quickly, but for some reason, I took care to pick out one of my favorite tops. It curved my body graciously and was a deep shade of blue. I paired some ankle boots with my skinny gray jeans and added a couple of loose curls to my brown hair. After swiping on some mascara and chapstick, I grabbed a granola bar to eat before class and made my way outside to Hunter's electric blue Jeep, where he was already sitting in the driver's seat.

I wouldn't say he was sulking, but there was a distinct contemplative expression on his face that made me pause. I didn't want to talk about this dangerous line we were dancing along, so I kept my mouth closed as he pulled out of the drive and made his way toward my school.

I caught him looking at me from the corner of his eye numerous times. His hands gripped the steering wheel as he drove. He must have showered at our house because his hair was still wet and his face was freshly shaved. He wore dark denim and a black shirt with a skull on it. I was getting used to the dark aesthetic of his wardrobe. He dressed like his energy—doomy and broody.

I wanted to ask him what all of this meant. There wasn't a label that felt right for us. Enemies. Friends. Lovers. I felt like I didn't know him enough to feel the way I did. But the little bits of information I did have weighed heavily on my shoulders.

Hunter was devoted.

He was alone.

Hunter had a bad childhood.

He was obsessive. Jealous. Territorial.

He was skilled with his tongue and touch.

He didn't just skim the surface of a person. He seemed to understand my motivations and needs—even the things I was ashamed to admit.

We were driving along, me with my head resting against the passenger window when I saw Mrs. Sellars huffing on the sidewalk, headed toward the school. She wore a large purple coat wrapped tightly around her frail body, and her cheeks were rosy from exertion. "Stop the Jeep!" I shouted.

Hunter took three seconds to peer outside, and the moment his gaze landed on my favorite English teacher, he stopped. I found myself feeling briefly thankful for my stalker because I didn't have to explain who she was or why I was concerned that she was walking in the cold, three miles to school.

"Check on her. See if she needs a ride," Hunter said with a sigh before putting the car in park.

I peered at him. "Promise you won't go all crazy on my English teacher? I like her."

Hunter rolled his eyes. "I'm not going to murder Mrs. Sellars. She cracks me up. Last week, she told a boy off because he was snoring in class."

"It's so weird that you watch me in class."

"Why don't you worry about Mrs. Sellars, and we can discuss how crazy you think I am another time, hmm?" Hunter replied sarcastically. I was about to tell him that it would take an entire team of experts to understand his fucked up personality but stopped myself.

Rolling down the window, I called out to my teacher. "Mrs. Sellars, are you alright?"

She stopped her brisk walk and greeted me with that spunky smile I loved. "Hello, Miss Palmer. How are you today?"

"Are you walking to school? Is everything okay?" I asked her.

Mrs. Sellars marched up to the car and rested on the passenger door while catching her breath. Her gray eyes flickered to Hunter, then back to me. "Would you believe my old Buick died? I would have called an Uber—is that what they're calling taxis these days? I couldn't find a telephone number for it in the phonebook. I figured a good walk would do my old body good, but..." She looked in the backseat of the Jeep and smiled wickedly. "I see you have two perfectly good vacant seats, and we're both headed to the same place. Why don't you give me a ride, and I'll tell you what I thought of your last poetry submission, yes?" she asked. I cracked a smile at the unabashed way she invited herself without even greeting Hunter. She simply opened the door and lifted herself inside the Jeep, which was not an easy task considering how lifted this off-roading monstrosity was.

"Hello," she finally said to Hunter once she was settled inside. "I'm Mrs. Sellars, Roe's favorite teacher. And you are?"

Hunter bit the inside of his cheek, then put on his public approval face, flashing her a smile in the rearview mirror before putting the car back in drive and merging onto the street. "I'm Hunter, a friend of Roe's uncle. I'm taking her to school since he had to go to work early this morning."

"I really should call Mack," Mrs. Sellars said while rifling through her briefcase. "Roe needs to get her license. Especially if she's going off to college next year."

Hunter gave me a look out of the corner of his eye that suggested he hadn't even thought of college. I guess in some ways, he felt like I'd always be this girl he felt responsible for. But we both knew that wasn't the case anymore, and the reality of my future was at our feet. I just didn't know if he'd let me go. And with our developing...thing...I wasn't sure how easily I'd leave.

"If you need someone to teach you, I'll have some time once the Buick is fixed, dear. Just let me know."

"I'll teach her," Hunter said in a low voice before switching lanes and hitting his accelerator just a bit too aggressively. I was twisted in my seat, alternating my gaze between Mrs. Sellars and Hunter. My wry teacher was currently squinting at our chauffeur as if trying to figure him out.

"Look at that, Miss Palmer. You've got an entire team of people willing to show you how to drive. Who are you again?" she asked Hunter.

"Just a friend, Mrs. Sellars," he replied smoothly, her name too familiar on his tongue. Was this how he was with me? Did he assume familiarity because he watched me my entire life? The label "friend" felt hollow for what we were but seemed to appease my teacher. Shaking her head, Mrs. Sellars continued digging through her briefcase until she pulled out a few brochures.

"I found a few colleges I'd like you to apply to. They have wonderful creative writing programs and are well-rounded with their offerings if you decide to go another route. But with your skill level, I really hope you take a creative writing plan. Your last poem was powerful, Roe. Deeply powerful."

My mouth dropped open in shock. Maybe picking up Mrs. Sellars was a bad idea. "I wasn't planning on attending college—"

"Nonsense," she interrupted. "You have decent grades. What were you planning on doing? Staying here for the rest of your life?" she asked with a scoff, like settling down in the suburbs of Denver was the worst thing that could happen to a person. I found her reaction ironic, considering she'd lived here her whole life.

"You're going places, dear. I want you to see the world. I want you to grab life by the balls and find something to be passionate about."

I cautiously looked at Hunter. His eyes were void of all emotion, and his lips were pursed.

"Can we go over your poem now?"

"Uh…"

She pulled out a sheet of printer paper and cleared her throat. When she started speaking my words, a chill traveled down my spine. My poems were always little whispers in the back of my mind. It almost felt intrusive to hear someone else read it out loud:

Trapped by Roe Palmer

I see you there, strung up with silk.
Struggling against cloud restraints.
Drowning in that open air.

I see you there, choking on your words.
Like rocks lodged in your throat.
Saying NO feels a lot like dying,
I suppose.

I see you there, held down by your fears.
Chained to death. Crying with glass in your palm.
Girl in the mirror. She looks like me. She cries like me.
She's trapped like me.

Hunter pulled into the school parking lot as Mrs. Sellars let out a low whistle. "The concept of this is excellent, Roe. I like your imagery here and the play on words. She's not trapped. I think stylistically the same line for each stanza works, but I want to work on the flow of the second and third lines, they feel a little disjointed. Come see me at lunch, and we'll fix it, okay?"

Mrs. Sellars unbuckled and turned to Hunter, tapping him on the shoulder until he rotated in his seat to stare at her. "It was nice to meet you, Friend of Roe's Uncle. It was nice of you to drive her to school. Please tell Mack to call me. We want to set Roe up for the best life possible, and we can't do that if she's stuck here."

Hunter clenched his jaw before responding. "I'll be sure to pass along the message."

Mrs. Sellars gave him a half-smile before exiting the car with one last farewell. "See you in class, Roe. Please do be careful. Last time you made out with a boy in the school parking lot, you got detention for a week."

I jumped when she slammed the door and then sat there silently, waiting for Hunter's response to my eccentric teacher—waiting, waiting, waiting. I was starting to learn that Hunter rarely spoke without dissecting his thoughts first. I added it to my list of things I knew about him.

"Do you want to go to college, Roe?"

I wasn't expecting that question but welcomed it all the same. "I'd like to get out of Colorado. I'd like a chance to figure out my passion. I like writing a lot. The more I learn, the more fun it is for me. But I don't know, I never really thought about the future until now. I kind of just figured I had time. And my mom..."

Hunter reached out and grabbed my good hand, squeezing it lightly. "What?" he asked. "Your mom what?"

"I don't know. She kind of conditioned me not to want things like that. I keep thinking I've let go of her influence over my life, and then shit like this comes up. I haven't once considered going to college. It just makes me wonder what else I'm giving up on without even realizing it. It scares me. I loved my mother deeply, but I don't want to end up like her."

Hunter nodded, absorbing my words. "People sometimes confuse pity with love, Roe."

"No," I snapped, a little too harshly. As much as I hated to admit it, I did pity my mother. I pitied her so much that it felt wrong to be angry at her for leaving me. I pitied her so much that I used her anxiety as a wall around me.

Hunter leaned back in his seat, scratching behind his neck. "If it's any consolation, I think you're less like her than you think."

"Oh?" I asked.

"You were in bed with a killer, after all. I'm the deadliest thing in this town, and I don't say that pretentiously."

I swallowed his words. He was right. "You sound so full of yourself right now," I joked, trying to lighten the mood.

We stared at one another; my gaze zeroed in on his lips. I licked mine. "You better get going. Wouldn't want you to get detention," Hunter said with a grin.

I leaned over the center console of the car and kissed him on the cheek just to see if he'd let me. His eyes closed in poetic reverence the moment my chapstick lips touched his stubbled cheek. "Mack will pick you up tonight.

I've got work."

"Work? What kind of work?"

"The kind you don't want to know about," Hunter said in a low growl.

"Okay," I whispered before pulling back and getting out of his Jeep.

I watched him slowly pull away while thinking about all the things I didn't know about him. I didn't know what *work* meant to him or where he came from. I didn't know his last name or why I felt so close to someone I should fear. This thing between us was a dangerous game. There was a shift in the air, so subtle you'd have to be paying attention to notice it, but it was there all the same.

My stalker stopped hating me.

I stopped wanting to run away and started wanting to understand.

Chapter 18

HUNTER

I didn't want to be sitting outside a shitty motel that looked like it was coated in a layer of cum and smelled like every STD in the books. I wanted to be with Roe. I wanted to figure out what the fuck was wrong with me where she was concerned. I'd watched her for the better part of almost two decades. Shit had changed, and I wasn't sure if it was for the better or not.

But no, here I was, watching a seedy motel the Asphalt Devils frequent. And watching out for my target—Rodger Stump. It took a few days for me to find the asshole. Gavriel gave me a local hit while I dealt with Roe, but that didn't mean he made it easy on me. If Gavriel had his way, he'd have every single member of the Asphalt Devils six feet under.

The problem with gangs was there was always someone waiting to rise up in the ranks. Rosemary Jones was losing her grip. It was only a matter of time before she was killed by someone in her own organization.

Gavriel said she wasn't worth worrying about anymore, but he wanted to prepare for the next asshole who would rise up in the ranks. Her vendetta with the Bullets had gotten too many of her members killed, which meant Rodger Stump would quickly take her place as leader. This was more of a preemptive strike. No one else was good enough or organized enough or ruthless enough to do a good job.

You had to attack the competition from two angles. First, kill the smartest leader in the bunch. Then, cut the gang off at the root, starve them of money so they have nowhere to grow.

Gavriel was taking care of the money issue. He could navigate deals better than anyone I knew. My job was to clip the excess stems growing. You could never let one grow too wild; it could throw the entire operation off and save the plant.

Rodger Stump was one of those pesky, ambitious stems. He was eager and trigger-happy. Gavriel heard whispers that he was working to revive some deals with a supplier, and that wasn't going to work for our long-term goals. In other companies, you could monopolize the market, negotiate competitive prices, or buy them out. In our line of work, you had to kill or be killed. There were no laws here.

I could have stormed into their motel room. I could have easily shot Rodger and his fuck buddy point-blank and been done with it. But that didn't sit right with me. For starters, I didn't like to kill hookers. They were just doing their job, just like I was doing mine. And if I were being honest, looking at Rodger made me think I had the better one. I doubt the bastard had showered in the last week. Nasty fucker.

But two, I wouldn't be storming in, because rumor had it my second target for this bullshit gang also liked to stick his dick inside this same hooker—directly after Rodger. Willie Goffet wasn't as smart or dedicated as Rodger, but I had a feeling he'd be third in line for the Asphalt Devils' throne based purely on the fact that he was a scary looking motherfucker. Gavriel didn't put him on the list, but I figured a nice *buy one get them free* deal would put me in his good graces again. I was a good businessman, after all.

I spent four days watching this motel. Learning their habits, researching their routines. I knew which room they'd get, based on what was available. I talked to housekeeping and learned how often they frequented here. I checked the weather for visibility and packed weapons with silencers on them so I'd have time to escape. The motel was busy most nights, and I didn't want any heroes stopping me or interfering.

My blank car with fake plates smelled like cigarettes. I was pissed the fuck off that I had to be here. This gang was really starting to be a pain in the ass. When we first moved to Colorado, it was because Gavriel wanted to expand his business. Soon, other gangs flocked to it like flies on shit. You can tell a lot about the integrity and success of a person by the way they make business plans. If they copy someone else, then they have no grit or determination of their own. They like to go where the opportunity is. People like that rarely survived in this business.

My phone pinged, a notification from Gavriel.

Boss: Is it done yet?

So fucking impatient. I quickly typed out my response and put my phone in the glove box.

Hunter: Almost.

The roar of a motorcycle filled my car, and I watched the road as a large man whose gut was pouring over his Harley Davidson pulled up to the motel. I observed him as he got off his bike, slicked back his greasy gray hair and removed his wedding ring.

Bastard. I was probably doing his wife a favor. Willie was a sorry fucker of a human being and wanted Asphalt Devils to start dealing women. I watched him walk up to the motel room and knock with a sinister grin. My time to shine.

Getting out of the car, I follow after him, keeping to the shadows, with my ears peeled for any sounds of approaching footsteps. Willie went inside and was greeted with a man's laughter and a woman's squeals of mock delight. I cringed as his belly shook and the door slammed behind him. Disgusting.

Easing my body against the brick, I pulled my suppressed Glock from my holster and made sure there was a bullet in the chamber. I didn't think I'd need more than one magazine, but I kept a few holstered to my chest in case anyone else showed up.

I pulled the mask over my head and checked my gloves. I'd leave no trace. Make no sound. Do nothing. I was a ghost.

Making my way over to the door, I listened to the sounds of giggles and groans, preparing myself for the sight I was about to see.

One. Exhale. Two. Inhale. Three. Exhale. I kicked open the motel door and let loose a rain of bullets. Two went directly in Rodger's skull. My precision was almost boring. The ugly bastard was sitting in the corner on a chair, stroking his limp dick with his eyes rolled back in his head. I stared for a second as blood and brain poured from the head wound.

Willie was faster, but not by much. His head was buried between the legs of his hooker, licking up the cum Rodger left behind like a fucking sicko. He scurried off the mattress like his pimpled ass was on fire. "Don't shoot!" he screamed. I never understood why they always said that, like it would make a fucking difference.

"This is for the Bullets," I said ceremoniously before pulling the trigger. One shot. One single bullet was all it took. Right between the eyes.

Willie fell forward, landing on his face with a thud. That was easy.

I turned, brow raised at the hooker whose name I'd already forgotten. Of all my research and preparation, she was both the most and least important variable. She was the bait.

Lying spread eagle on the ruffled bed, she stared at me in boredom with her slick pussy on display. She hadn't moved or made a sound. She didn't beg for her life or scurry to cover her nakedness. She just rolled her neck and watched. "Are you high or just indifferent?" I asked. I was certain she'd be screaming her head off by now, alerting everyone and the cops.

"A little of both," she replied with a cough. Makeup was poured into the deep crevices of her wrinkles. Her gray teeth looked rotted.

"You should probably get dressed and get the fuck out of here," I said with a sigh before putting my gun in the holster of my jeans.

"You're not going to kill me?" she asked while snapping her legs closed and sitting up lazily in bed. Her eyes had that empty look about them. The kind of look that made you pity them and wonder if the edge of the universe was lost in their brain. I knew that look too well. That look made me sick to my stomach.

"You're already dead inside if you were fucking these two idiots," I replied with a dark chuckle. "Besides, I don't kill women."

She stretched her arms out, then reached under the sheets, probably feeling for a needle to shoot up with.

"Well, I probably should thank you." She kept reaching for something. Suddenly, it felt off. "But you might want to rethink your killing women policy. We're all dead inside." As quickly as her high body could, she pulled out a revolver and aimed it at me. In the time it took me to reach for my Glock again, she had pulled the trigger. Her shaky aim sent the bullet toward my arm, grazing the muscle there with burning pain. I didn't have time to crouch over and curse the blooming agony there. I aimed my own gun at her skull and sent a bullet straight through her nose. Blood splattered, and I watched it artfully scatter across the stained motel sheets like a Jackson Pollock painting.

I hissed out in silent agony while bailing from the motel room. Fucking bitch. Hot blood spilled down my arm as I walked to the rental car and got inside. My vision blurred as I picked up my phone to send Gavriel a message.

Hunter: It's done. Willie, too.

Gavriel: Good work.

Chapter 19

ROE

"Fuck, Mack. You're killing me here, man."

I shot out of bed, listening to the angry sounds coming from the kitchen. I was sleeping in a tank top and cotton panties, and after slipping on my black robe, I padded out to the kitchen where I was surprised to find Hunter sitting on the countertop. Mack was blotting at the steady flow of blood trailing down his arm with a paper towel.

"You try doing this with one arm," Mack growled while tossing the bloody paper towel in the sink. "I can't stitch it up, but I think you'll be fine. It's just a graze. I'll clean it, wrap it tightly, then go find the antibiotics I took last time I got shot."

"And some pain killers," Hunter gruffed.

Hunter was shirtless, his body tanned and rippling with muscles. I should have been concerned about the shower of blood pulsing out of his arm. But I was fascinated by his calmness. Despite the wound, you couldn't tell he was hurting. The only sign that anything was wrong showed in the way his bulky muscles were coiled with tension. I couldn't help it. I stared for a long while, drinking in the sight of him without shame or worry. I was convinced that neither of them were aware that I'd joined in on their little party, but of course, nothing escaped Hunter's notice. "Come here and make yourself useful, Pretty Debt." I snapped my eyes away from his corded abs and back to his face.

"Hard day at work, Stalker?"

"Nah, it was easy," he replied with a pained smile. Hunter was pale, his lips nearly white.

"Watch him," Mack said to me before running off to his bedroom for more supplies.

I stared at the rubbing alcohol on the counter and picked it up. "Want me to flush it out?" I asked.

Hunter stared at me for a long, steady moment. His blue eyes bore into my skin, and I watched as he sucked on his lower lip. "Sure," he finally said. "Get it over with."

I poured it on his upper arm while staring at the long gash there. As the blood cleared, I noticed that his skin almost looked burned, like charcoal with curled edges. He didn't hiss when the stinging pain punched him in the arm. He didn't flinch. Hunter remained rooted on the countertop and stared at my lips as I poured all of it on the wound. "You don't have to pretend like it doesn't hurt," I said while pulling away, the bottle now nearly empty. The alcohol dripped over the counter and floor, seeping into his jeans and making the room smell sterile.

His answer was steady and haunting. "I'm not pretending. I taught myself a long time ago to be indifferent to pain."

I nodded as if I understood—but I didn't. My mother had hurt me, sure. But I was so sheltered my entire life. I hadn't conditioned myself to accept pain—physical or otherwise— because I ran before it could hit me. My mother taught me well.

Uncle Mack reappeared with a bottle of pills and a wrap for Hunter's arm. "I'm going to check out the scene and see what we're dealing with. It would be just our fucking luck that you left blood on the carpet. We've been using a lot of favors lately, and I don't want your fucking DNA on the scene," Mack said. My ears perked up with interest. I was dying to ask my questions as visions of dead bodies and sin assaulted my mind's eye.

"I was careful. I wore gloves and a mask."

"I'm still going to check. If the police are already there, then I'm going to have to call our contacts. Get some sleep."

Hunter chuckled while shaking his head. "I thought I was the boss," he replied.

"And I thought you were smarter than this. Leave no one. Trust no one. Kill all witnesses."

Dread pooled in my gut at Mack's words. He was crass and careless; life was nothing more than baby teeth—an inevitable loss.

"I got it. Now get your grumpy ass out of here," Hunter growled in response.

Mack swiftly left, making me jump when the door slammed. I stared at Hunter, then at the gauze on the countertop. "I'm not sure if I like knowing all the fucked up things you're involved in," I whispered before reaching for the gauze.

"It sure makes my job easier. It was nice just showing up and not having to worry if we woke you. One year I had a concussion, and Mack hid me in his bathtub."

Of course he did. I opened and closed my mouth, not sure how to process that information. Instead of commenting on it, I picked at the gauze with my good hand and fumbled with it. Hunter placed his hand over mine while staring at my cast with a hard look. "I've got it."

I made myself useful and started a pot of coffee as he wrapped his arm. Once again, he didn't flinch or wince. He simply tightly tied the gauze around the wound in methodical fashion, keeping his expression cool and free of pain. It was like staring at stone.

I reached up to grab a coffee cup from the cupboard and set it on the counter, then lifted the coffee pot to pour him a cup, but my trembling hands slipped, sending a steaming hot splash of the coffee to land on my upper thigh. "Fuck!" I cursed while taking a step back and rubbing at the raw and red skin blooming there.

"What did you do?" Hunter asked while jumping off the countertop and sinking to his knees to look. I looked down at him in shock, the intense expression on his face stealing all thoughts of pain. He reached up and slowly, slowly, slowly pulled at the tie keeping my robe closed, revealing me to him. I let out a barely audible gasp. He lifted his hand, rubbing his thumb around the area I'd burned. "It's nothing," I said breathlessly.

"You burned yourself," Hunter replied softly.

"*You* have a gunshot wound." I rolled my eyes as he continued to move his hot hands along my thigh, leaving little swipes of his blood along my creamy skin.

Hunter looked up at me through his thick lashes and leaned forward to kiss the pained spot. I closed my eyes when his rough lips touched my scorched skin. His hot breath feathered over my inner thigh, traveling up to my thudding sex.

"I...I'm fine, Hunter. Let's finish getting you cleaned up so you can rest," I stuttered while placing my good hand on his shoulder to steady my shaky legs.

He leaned forward and kissed my sensitive inner leg again. And again, leading his lips up to the apex of my thighs before briefly kissing my thin panties right over my clit. It took me two seconds of intense lust before I shook my head and shoved his face away from my sobbing pussy. If I let my vagina make the decisions, she'd be sucking his face.

"Are you trying to make me come so I won't ask questions?"

"Maybe."

Hunter stood up and ran a bloody hand through his blond hair, licking his lips like he was trying to taste me on them. "Why don't you take a shower?" I asked.

"You going to help me?"

I lifted up my cast-covered arm and raised my eyebrow. "Yeah, that's not happening."

"Fair enough. I'll be right back."

I got cozy on the couch as he showered, trying not to let my imagination run away with me. I went to that safe space in my mind where I didn't think about trauma or death or empty, glassy eyes staring back at me. Hunter seemed so comfortable with death. He was fearless and devoted to destruction. It made me wonder what made him the way that he was. While my mother was consumed with her fears, Hunter became them.

But why?

When the shower shut off, I sat up a little straighter on the couch. I pulled the soft gray blanket over my legs and forced my eyes not to stare at the hallway, waiting for Hunter's return. His bare feet padded down the hallway, and I gasped when he rounded the corner.

Wearing nothing but a fluffy white towel and a tired grin, Hunter strutted toward me. The only thing hiding his cock from me was the loose grip he had on the towel.

"You're naked," I said, sounding stupid.

"My clothes were bloody."

"I'm sure you can borrow something of Mack's," I said.

"Come to bed with me, Roe."

Hunter grabbed my hand and pulled me up, dragging me down the hall toward my bedroom.

He pushed me on the bed with a gentle shove, then dropped his towel. I stared at his glorious body, watching his proud cock jerk to attention. Like everything else about Hunter, his dick was impressive and thick, long enough to make me nervous and round enough to make my mouth drop open in shock.

"I'm not fucking you," I said, feeling like a liar while staring at the little delicious bead of precum collecting on the head of his cock. I licked my lips.

"I was thinking I would give you some answers tonight, actually," Hunter replied before climbing onto the mattress. He crawled up my body in a predatory way that made me hum.

"Do you know the different bases?"

I snorted, a completely unattractive sound. "Bases? As in baseball? Like kissing is first base, second base is some boob action, third is oral and home..." my voice trailed off.

"You don't seem like the type of girl afraid to say *sex*, Roe," Hunter joked.

"I'm not," I replied defiantly.

"Right..." Hunter continued to crawl up my body until he was hovering over my lips. I glanced at the bandages covering his arm and frowned at the blood pooling beneath the bandage and seeping through. "Ignore it. I'm fine," he ordered. "I'm going to let you ask a question. Each answer, and I get to steal a base."

I looked him up and down, my eyes peering at the bandage on his arm and the way his muscles were flexed. "Seems like a fair game. I can ask anything?"

A flash of uncertainty crossed his face. "If I don't want to answer, then the game stops. I know you want me as bad as I want you right now. So I guess you should ask smart questions if you want to get off, Pretty Debt."

Fucker. I guess that means any questions about the past or how he knew me were off-limits. I leaned forward to whisper in his ear, noting how he smelled like my citrus body wash. "Deal."

Hunter smiled, then bit his lip, moving his body to lie beside mine as I settled on the mattress. "What's your first question, then?" he asked, almost impatiently.

"Did..." I began slowly. "Did you kill someone tonight?"

Hunter broke out in a deep belly laugh before rolling over to face me. Our eyes collided, mine mirroring fear, his filled with amusement. "Why are you asking questions you already know the answer to, Pretty Debt?"

Shit. He did. I knew Hunter was dangerous, deadly, and dark. But the reality of it was now staring me in the face. Hunter didn't bother answering directly. I wasn't sure if it was his way of keeping his crimes under wraps or if he didn't see the point in admitting what we both already knew. He simply leaned forward and pressed his lips to mine with unbridled passion. His sweeping tongue and certain mouth poured passion like sweet honey into me. Our teeth clashed. We nipped at one another, and I felt every prod and groan.

We kissed forever. Long, slow, hard, fast. We groaned, and I ached for our bodies to move. I wanted his palm on my breasts. But he didn't cross the barrier of passion, no matter how much I urged him with my body. I craved his touch and knew the only way to get it. "Next question," I rasped while pulling away. He grinned wickedly at me.

"So needy, Pretty Debt," he teased.

I was desperate for him and worried that this question would stop everything. I debated for a moment about asking but decided that I couldn't continue if I didn't know. "Does killing get you...off? Are you turned on because you murdered someone? I just need to know if..."

"If I'm hard as a rock because I split three skulls?" he spat with a cruel look.

"Th-three?" I sputtered.

"Three," he confirmed. "You know I work for bad people, Roe."

I swallowed. "I'm scared to waste a question asking what you do for those *bad people*," I admitted.

Hunter wrapped his large hand around my neck and leaned in to growl his response. "I wouldn't answer if you did." His lips trailed the edge of my ear as he continued to speak. "I'm not turned on because I killed, Roe. I'm not a serial killer that fetishes death. I'm hot because I was in pain and you walked downstairs in your skimpy little robe and you didn't get scared. You cared for me. You took care of me and tried dressing my wound. Compassion is what got me hot, Roe."

"Are you not used to compassion, Hunter?"

"Is that another question?"

"Sure."

"No. No, I'm not. I'm used to the worst of humanity. I grew up thinking I was born in hell. I've spent my life meeting devils and ending their lives."

"I...Hunter..." I was speechless.

"No more questions. Come here and let me taste you."

In one swift move, my robe was gone and my tank top was torn down the center. The sounds of fabric being ripped filled my small bedroom, and then his hot mouth wrapped around my nipple. My back arched off the bed, and my body thrashed. I felt so fucking hot and sensitive.

He grabbed at my breasts, kneading and squeezing, whispering prayers over my skin as he worshipped me. "You're so fucking beautiful, Pretty Debt. I feel like you're too precious to touch."

"Please don't stop," I begged.

"I couldn't even if I wanted to," Hunter assured me before moving to hover over my body once more. The blood on the bandage continued to pool as he licked swirling designs on my stomach and sunk lower and lower *and lower*.

His teeth pulled at the waistband of my panties, and he tugged them down, over my rounded ass, over my thick thighs, down my shins and completely off.

I wasn't a shy person. I'd had sex before. I was liberal with my body. But being completely bared to Hunter while knowing he was about to taste my cunt was a vulnerable experience I treasured. He made it all feel like new. He dove in and breathed in my scent, moaning as he wrapped his arms around my thighs, effectively pinning me down.

The anticipation was brutal. I wanted his tongue on my clit. I wanted to squirm with pleasure and feel him pull bliss by his teeth, but he made me wait. He exhaled and waited for me, waited for me to be so over the edge of desire that a single touch could send me soaring.

"Are you going to make me come or what, Hunter?" I asked.

He hummed and tenderly kissed my inner thigh. There was delicate affection in his touch. I preened at the look of adoration in his eyes. I was terrified by how easily his touch comforted me.

"With pleasure, Pretty Debt," he replied before licking me long and slow up my entire slit. He savored and moaned until stopping at my sensitive nub. He wrapped his lips around it and hummed.

"Oh fuck!" I cried out as his tongue flicked over my bundle of nerves. I was practically purring as his skilled tongue circled and teased and vibrated against me. Slick heat coated his chin as I rode his face. He was determined, licking me in that punishing sort of way that felt like too much and not enough at the same time.

His hard body pinned me down, though I ached to writhe. He groaned and cursed and prayed into my pussy as he tasted every drop of my pleasure. "Fuck, you taste so good," he said with a gasp before diving back into my heat. I wasn't sure how long we'd battled for bliss. He was a determined little soldier. His obsession became a tangible sensation that built and built and built within me.

I came unexpectedly, the passion so sudden and intense that it shot out of me like a bullet from a gun. I cried out and gripped the sheets, my mouth dropped open in ecstasy. Pure life and pleasure exploded on his tongue, and he lapped it up like the greedy fucking stalker he was.

When I was done, he got up and wiped my cum from his mouth with the back of his hand. The look was erotic, his eyes burning hot with intensity and desire. I looked down and noticed his hard cock staring back at me. I wanted my fucking home run. I wanted to feel him pulsing inside of me.

But I wanted answers more.

"Last question?" he asked while easing his way back up and positioning himself at my entrance. He was greedy and ready. "Ask it," he begged in a raspy voice.

I swallowed, bleeding with hope and acceptance. I was hoping he wanted me enough to give me the answers I craved. But I knew without a shadow of a doubt that this sensual moment between us would end the second my question left my lips. I was giving up a chance to feel this god of a man inside of me for the idea of truth.

"What debt are you repaying, Hunter?"

Hunter stilled.

His face slipped back into that familiar expression of pain. He pulled away from me and sat on the bed.

"Game over, Roe."

Yeah. Game over.

Chapter 20

Lies

Paint designs in the shape of intimacy on my skin. Laugh like it's a sin.

You hold your breath. The air I breathe is a secret you keep.

Filthy, nasty, dirty man.

Knowledge hoarder. Pleasure destroyer.

Hooded eyes and shadowed face.

Disgrace.

I try not to think about my mother. I rarely invited her into my everyday thoughts. I didn't linger on her death or make decisions based on the trauma she smeared across my soul. I didn't want to be a cliche of parental issues.

My loss was more like a living, breathing intrusion. Mom's memory came to me at odd moments. She snuck up on me, like a knife in the back.

I'd be doing normal things—like showering—when I'd remember that it's possible to drown in two inches of water.

Or when I crossed the street, I'd think about how easily one could get hit by a car.

My favorite meals were ruined by thoughts of poison and food contamination.

My favorite places were ruined by crime statistics.

My favorite people were ruined with the idea that nothing ever lasted.

Her manic face flashed across my mind as I was trying to get to the bottom of Nicole's reasons for befriending me. She was talking to my cheek as I put my books away. I wondered what would happen if I put my head inside of the locker and someone slammed it shut. My dead mother whispered over my skin that my impulse to escape this conversation with Nicole would certainly snap my neck.

"You haven't returned any of my calls and are avoiding me in the hallway. I don't understand the problem," Nicole said, drawing me out of my morbid thoughts. I let out a sigh before turning to face her as she whined. "You said I could date Joel, but now you're ghosting me."

I tapped my foot on the tile floor, wishing I could drown in a pool of coffee. I was so fucking tired. So fucking plagued with thoughts about everything. Hunter had been distant since our almost fuck. I wasn't sure if he was dealing with the aftermath of his murder or if he was avoiding me, but I spent a ridiculous amount of time focusing on Nicole to keep myself from overanalyzing it too much.

"I'm not avoiding you because you're dating Joel, though you might want to talk to him about his motivations," I finally replied.

"What? What is that supposed to mean?" Her tone was snappy and quick. Too defensive for a productive conversation.

I debated on telling her that Joel was just with her to get back at me, but that sounded petty and self-centered. Even if it was the truth, Nicole wasn't in the headspace to hear it. Joel was this odd mix of compassionate, protective, assholish, and selfish. I never knew which emotion I was going to get from him. Just because he showed me his asshole side at the club didn't mean he wasn't showing Nicole that he knew how to give a fuck from time to time.

"Why are you friends with me?" I asked Nicole. "I mean really. Why are we friends?"

Her face turned pale. "What do you mean? We hang out and get along well enough."

"But you don't really know me," I replied. "I'm sure by now you know my reputation. We hang out when we're bored. But there is zero substance to our friendship whatsoever."

"Don't be ridiculous. We spend time together," Nicole said.

"But we don't really know anything about one another."

She crossed her arms over her chest. "It's not like you've given me much of an opportunity. I've asked about your life—your parents—and you shut me out. I learned fairly quickly that you wouldn't open up to me." She wasn't wrong, but that didn't make this any easier. "I mean, does your uncle even know you have friends? My parents know about you," she added.

"Of course your parents know about me," I said in a low voice. "That's the part that worries me. Everyone in this town has their ideas about me. Most of those notions aren't very good. Are you friends with me to get back at your parents?" I asked.

Nicole averted her gaze, and I knew then what her answer was. I was nothing but a tool to get her parents to listen. I knew they were absent. Hell, they were gone so often that even I hadn't met them, not that I wanted to. Mr. and Mrs. Knight were like abstract shadows over her life, and I didn't understand it.

Nicole looked around the crowded school hallway before responding to me. "At first I didn't really care who you were. I'll be honest, you wouldn't have been my first pick of a friend around here. I'm more pep, and you're like the broody alternative girl that gives herself bangs during a mental breakdown."

My eyebrows shot up at her assessment of me. "I see. Well, I guess Joel was right then..."

I spun on my heel, prepared to run. I didn't know where I was going, but I had to leave before I was left. A flash of my mother's vacant face crossed my mind, and I squeezed my eyes shut.

"Will you let me fucking finish?" Nicole asked before grabbing my shoulder and forcing me to turn around.

"I don't really want to talk—"

"That was *before* I got to know you. And I'm not talking about the stupid surface level shit you tell me, either."

I let out a huff of air and looked down at my cast, avoiding her gaze. "Everyone talks like you're this party-girl slut. You act like you'll spread your legs for everyone, but I doubt you've even slept with your boyfriend yet, right? I have to beg you to come to my parties or go out with me. And when you do manage to leave the house, you stick yourself in a corner and talk yourself out of having fun."

I looked up at Nicole. "You know what I think?" she continued. "I think you kissed—or fucked—a couple of dumbass dudes. I think you didn't get attached, so they labeled you something you aren't so that they could put ice on their bruised ego. And worst of all. I think you let them. It's easier to let people think you're wild and reckless. Because when you leave, at least it's expected. Hell, you were just going to leave me and never look back, right?" She peered at me.

"I had no intention of being your friend after this, no," I agreed.

"I don't know about your parents. I don't know why you're so fucking scared to stay. But I'm not going anywhere. Yeah, I fucked up with my reasons for getting to know you, but I'm staying because I got to know the real you, and she's fucking cool. I mean, who else would defend their ex-boyfriend and encourage their friend to date them?"

I cracked a small smile and rolled my eyes. "Okay, okay."

"I've been chasing my parents since the day I was born. I'm not afraid to work for a relationship, Roe. You can be skittish all you want, but that doesn't mean I won't track you down, own up to my shit, and demand we work through it, okay? Don't make me start doing reckless stuff for your attention, too."

Shame filled me from the bottom of my toes all the way up. She had a point. She was determined as fuck. "I'll do better," I replied just as the bell rang.

"Good. See you at lunch," Nicole replied before disappearing down the hallway. I stared at her back, wondering how the crazy girl I was passing the time with turned out to be a real friend.

———

"I SENT YOUR submissions into the prelims," Mrs. Sellars announced proudly after the rest of the class had filtered out.

"What?" I asked while gripping my skirt.

\

"I didn't want to tell you when the deadline was because I was worried you'd cancel or freak out. I just submitted them myself and hoped for the best."

I shook my head and glanced around her desk. "I didn't even know this thing had prelims."

Mrs. Sellars rolled her eyes before clapping her hands. "Which is exactly why I've been collecting your poems and compiling them into a nice little portfolio without your knowing. You'll have to take over for the rest of it, but I'll help you."

I sat down on the top of her desk as she started stacking papers. "So… When do we get the results?" I asked. What if they hated my work? What if it wasn't good enough?

"Oh, I already have them," Mrs. Sellars replied, a bit too nonchalantly for my tastes.

"I was just looking for something before I told you…" She grunted while pulling her briefcase out from under her desk and flipping open the clasp. "Ah! here it is." She then handed me a sheet of paper, and I glanced at it. A permission slip?

"What is this?"

"Finals are in Dallas. Two other students made it to the next round in other writing categories. I think you'd enjoy Joanna Lovelace's short story submission. It's very poetic. I need your uncle to sign this permission slip and bring it back tomorrow so the school can order a charter bus to take us there."

"Wait, so I made it to the next round?" I asked incredulously.

"Yes, Roe. Believe it or not, you are capable of wonderful things. You've made it to the next round and have glowing comments from the judges. I look forward to hearing you read your poems at finals."

I was still processing all of this information. I couldn't believe that this was happening. "Wait, I have to read it? In front of people?"

"Yes. And with feeling, too. I've already emailed you a list of videos I want you to watch to help prepare."

"So I'm in?" I asked once again, in disbelief.

Mrs. Sellars spun to face me in her little kitten heels, her weathered face fixed into stern compassion. "Yes, Roe. You're in. I'm so proud of you."

I wrapped my arms around her frail frame and squeezed her tightly in a hug. I couldn't believe it. I'd made it. I'd actually done something and stuck to it.

"Thank you, Mrs. Sellars. I couldn't have done this without you," I squealed.

"Yes, you could have," she replied while pulling away from me. "Sometimes we just need a little shove is all. And right now I'm going to shove you to your next class because I have papers to grade."

I laughed at her bluntness and nodded. "Okay. I'll watch those videos you sent," I promised while backing out of the classroom.

I felt myself walking on cloud nine.

While heading down the hallway, I glanced at my phone, noticing that

Hunter had sent me a text. Maybe he was done working and would actually talk to me. I was ecstatic to tell him about the competition and Dallas. I couldn't believe this was actually happening.

But all the excitement and hope within me deflated the moment I saw his text.

Hunter: It's not safe to go to Dallas right now.

I stared at his words, digesting each disappointing part of them. No congratulations. No understanding or encouragement. Just a resounding refusal to let me go. I typed out a million responses, each of them filled with anger and hurt until I realized the best response of all would be silence. I turned off my phone, revoking his access to me with one simple move.

Now I just had to figure out how to get rid of his control over my life.

Chapter 21

HUNTER

I 'd stared at the photo for two hours, running my rough hand over the image with reverence. I found it on the windshield of my Jeep with a white lily delicately placed beside it. I didn't understand the significance of the flower, but it was the second time she'd used it to let her intentions be known.

She will die.

Those three words were scrawled on the back in dainty handwriting. There was no signature, just a heart drawn around the word die. The ink was a hot pink, which seemed odd for such an ominous threat. But I was learning that nothing Rosemary did was normal. She and I had never officially met, but she was becoming quite the threatening presence in my life.

The photo was nice, though. It was Roe and I together in her bedroom. She was smiling at me mischievously as I sat in her chair. Whoever took the picture had a telephoto lens and found an opening in the drapes in Roe's bedroom window. It was a rookie mistake on my part. I should have been more aware, more observant. I was the best of the best. I practically wrote the book on stalking, but I was so preoccupied with Roe that I hadn't noticed the enemy slipping past our defenses.

I was hoping the Asphalt Devils were a problem of the past. Rosemary's need for revenge lost her the faith of her members. And now that Willie and Rodger were dead, the pulse of their gang had hit a dead stop. So many people had died in the Bullets war that no one was willing to fight anymore. It was exactly what Gavriel wanted, but he created a monster in the process. And where Rosemary was terrible at running a gang, she was good at hiding. I hadn't seen her anywhere. The only intel I had was from an informant that told me about Willie and Rodger. Rosemary was an uncharted variable, and I wasn't letting Roe out of my sight until Rosemary was taken care of. I was even debating on pulling her from school. Rosemary had nothing to lose. She was desperate, and desperate people did desperate things.

Mack had left to pick up Roe from school, and I was waiting in his kitchen for them both to arrive. I would have gone to get her myself, but I was worried there were eyes on me. My...infatuation...with Roe was already out there. Rosemary knew that I was connected to Roe. But that didn't mean I wanted to show her that the threat affected me. Mack picked her up every day from school, and he'd continue to do that. We had to be smart—protect ourselves without appearing weak.

I needed to learn more about Rosemary. She'd already proven to be bloody, impulsive, and vengeful. I needed to find her weak spot. As of right now, she didn't appear to have one. She didn't care who died as long as she got to me, and that was a problem. I needed to find what she cared about and crush it in my fist.

The front door slammed, and I prepared myself for Roe's fiery frustration. She'd gone against our deal and turned her phone off when I texted her. It pissed me off to not be able to listen in on her, but I understood her anger. Hell, I was kicking myself for how I handled it. I should have waited. I should have worded things better. I should have congratulated her. Roe was timid when it came to putting herself out there. She never committed herself to anything because her hermit of a mother taught her to fear failure. Failure was the equivalent of death.

I didn't mean to make her upset, but I'd gotten Rosemary's threat and immediately checked her phone to see if she was safe. When I heard Mrs. Sellars say that she was invited to Dallas, my blood turned cold. That would be too dangerous. There was no way I could keep Roe safe. I quickly texted her without thought, but the way she was stomping her feet toward me made me regret how I handled the situation.

Roe's caramel hair was wild around her flushed face. She was wearing a brown miniskirt and boots with tights. Her tight, button-up shirt was tied at her bellybutton. Her fist was clenched at her side, and the overall effect of her rage and the outfit she wore was too damn irresistible. I had to focus to keep myself from closing the distance between us and swallowing her anger with a kiss. "I'm going to the contest, Hunter," she snarled. I licked my lips.

I bit my cheek to keep from smirking at her. I knew I was in trouble, and this wasn't a laughing matter, but hell she was hot when she was pissed. Mack disappeared down the hallway, shaking his head. I knew he was probably annoyed that he had to pick up an angry Roe from school.

"You're not going," I replied simply, my voice like a concrete wall.

Roe moved closer to me. "I'm fucking eighteen, Hunter. You can't just keep me here."

"I can. And I will." That was definitely the wrong thing to say, because her scowl deepened.

"Why?" she asked, her voice choked with emotion. I could practically feel her disappointment. "I don't get it. Why do I have to suffer because you're involved in some shady shit? No one has bothered me since the car accident. I thought you took care of it."

I crumbled the photograph with Rosemary's threat in my fist, then shoved it in my pocket, with Roe's mother's mental illness heavy on my heart. I wanted her to know how dangerous it was without triggering childhood fears that had been ingrained in her. Her mother was right, this world was a scary fucking place.

"I'm still working on the situation. You feel safe because I want you to feel that way. You don't know what's going on behind the scenes for a reason, Roe. Hell, I came home with a gunshot wound a couple days ago."

Tears filled her golden brown eyes, and I could have kicked myself for making her cry. "You sound like her," Roe cursed while averting her eyes. The long-dead thing in my heart panged. "You tell me how dangerous it is. You act like you have a right to lock me up, tell me it's for my well-being."

Roe started pacing the floors, and I reached out to grab her shoulder. She shrugged my hand off and continued to stomp her feet along the wood floors, spouting off past hurts as she moved. "You know we once went eight months without leaving the house?" she whispered while wrapping her thin arms around herself. "She heard about a car bomb in the city, and she said it wasn't safe to leave..."

"Roe," I began.

"She unplugged the oven because she was scared I'd crawl in it."

I squeezed my eyes shut. I knew that I was just a kid with my own problems. It wasn't until I was older that I could do anything to help Roe, but I still felt like a failure. I was supposed to protect her. There were many times I envied how much her mother cared. Aside from the one time she lost her mind and kicked Roe in the stomach, she was obsessive about watching out for her daughter. I'd never had that, so I thought her protectiveness was normal. Hell, how did I even know what was normal and what wasn't?

"Roe. I wouldn't do this if I didn't genuinely think it wasn't safe," I reasoned, keeping my tone soft and compassionate.

"She'd say that too," Roe said with tears running down her eyes. "She said she was keeping me inside, away from friends, away from people, because she loved me. Because it was safer. She lost my father and didn't want to lose me."

Those words made my chest constrict. The mention of Roe's father had me clenching my teeth.

I reached out for her again, and this time she didn't push me away. A steady stream of tears were falling down her cheeks now, making her creamy skin slick with pain. I wiped at it with my thumb and pulled her body flush with mine. "Roe. I'm not like your mother," I promised.

She scoffed. "Aren't you, though? You're obsessed with protecting me. You won't tell me why or what debt you owe. Once again, I have no say in my life." Her voice was raw with emotion. She was choking on every syllable.

I placed my forehead against hers. I felt like shit for doing this to her, but Rosemary's threats were vivid in my mind. Until I could eliminate all of my enemies, I wouldn't be risking Roe. I'd come too far to lose her now, and the dynamic of my obsession had changed. Roe was no longer an obligation I was saddled with. She'd become more. She was like the fucking air in my lungs. "I was sad when she died," Roe whispered against me. I let her go, and she took a step back. "I cried. I mourned her. She was my mom, you know? I was so mad that she spent her life convincing me how terrifying death was, then went and willingly died. Such a hypocrite," she said while rubbing her eyes.

I nodded my head in encouragement, pretending to know what it was like to have parents worthy of grief. "But when Mack took me in, I vowed to never hide from life like she did. It's taken years to break through the toxic walls she built around me. I still can't handle crowds without thinking of all the ways I could die. I can't imagine too far in the future because I've been trained to think that I won't survive the year. I'm...naïve," she choked out. "I'm all or nothing when it comes to people. I run away because life is one big decision between flight or fight."

As she spoke, all I could think of was how badly I'd failed. Roe was supposed to have a good life. She was supposed to be loved and healthy and successful. My entire purpose since the day she was born was to pay my debt. Roe was my purpose. She reminded me that I was capable of good things. She taught me that I wasn't like my parents, that I was able to care for another living being.

But I'd failed.

"Roe," I whispered while reaching for her hand. She pulled out of reach and shook her head. Snot dripped from her red nose, and she wiped at it with the back of her hand as more tears fell down her face.

"I don't want to live my life this way, Hunter. And I'm not going to let you turn me back into the little girl scared of the world again. I've been working way too fucking hard to escape her."

She spun around and headed toward her bedroom. I was helpless to say something comforting or useful. I just stared at her back and wondered how she'd ever be free with me in her life.

Chapter 22

ROE

I spent most of the next day in an angsty haze. I felt stuck in this never-ending cycle of confusion and discontent with Hunter. Every time a breadcrumb about our past was shared, he took a step further away, creating distance between us with his cruel words and dismissive actions.

I refused to feel trapped. I knew what it was like to spend my life afraid of the world and controlled by a person convinced they were doing right by me. It would never happen again. I wouldn't be manipulated by empathy anymore.

I hated how vulnerable I sounded while spilling my past at his feet, but every word I said was true. My mother loved me very much, but she let that love turn her into a recluse. She let love give her a sense that her actions and decisions were validated. She did the things she did because she honestly felt it was in my best interest, and I refused to let another person's *obsession* with keeping me safe and alive ruin all the progress I'd made.

Sometimes I wondered if my mother loved me or if her illness just made her obsessed with the idea of keeping me alive. Maybe Hunter had the same problems. He was twisted by his ideas of protection. He was dangerous. Though we'd been exploring each other's souls and bodies, I didn't feel like a girl capable of claiming Hunter's heart. I was his redemption, not the love of his life. I just didn't understand what sins he was working through—or in his words, what debt.

I felt so angry but also intrigued. There was something about Hunter I couldn't escape, but I couldn't let my infatuation trap me here. I wasn't my mother. I wanted to try new things. I wanted to look toward the future with a smile and hope. I wanted to *live*.

And in all of this, I was angry with myself. I was angry that I got wrapped up in the idea of Hunter. I kissed him. I gave my body to him willingly, and I didn't know if I did it because I craved human contact or if I was falling for my stalker. There was a lot about myself I just didn't understand, and I wasn't sure that I'd figure it out unless I put some distance between us or got some answers about our past. I needed to know just how far he'd go to keep me—and why.

I was sitting on my bed, scrolling through emails from Mrs. Sellars, when a chat notification popped up on my screen.

Unknown: Do you want to know more about Hunter?

I stared at the words for a moment, disbelief and dread filling me up. It was like the universe had gifted me with some information, but I couldn't quite trust it. Just because something was wrapped in a pretty bow didn't mean it was safe to open it. I licked my lips and hovered my hands over my keyboard, debating on how to respond. I was almost scared to even acknowledge it.

Roe: Who is this?

I watched the chat bubble appear and disappear a few times as if the person talking to me was trying to decide how to answer. I noted their uncertainty while biting my lip. At least they hadn't planned what to say. Maybe it was a prank. Or Joel.

Unknown: Not Safe.

Unknown: He could be watching.

Unknown: If you want to know about the man stalking you, meet us at 7898 Lawry Street in fifteen minutes.

I laughed to myself. Though the temptation for more information had me salivating, I wasn't willing to just go meet up with a complete stranger to get it. For all I knew, this was another one of Hunter's tricks. He could be looking for an excuse to test my loyalty, and although I felt no sense of camaraderie toward him at the moment, I wasn't in the mood to push him tonight. I needed to focus on how the hell I was going to get to Dallas.

Roe: No.

The chat bubbles became a flurry of activity, disappearing and appearing in an instant. I watched in amusement while using a pencil to lazily scratch at my skin beneath the cast on my left arm.

Unknown: Perhaps this will change your mind?

The sinister undertones in the message had me holding my breath as an image downloaded on the screen. I stared at it in rapt attention, my mouth dropping open in shock the moment I realized what the photo was and who was in it.

It was my mother. Her stomach was round, plump with a baby in it. She had glossy, pink lips stretched into an inauthentic smile that I recognized immediately. Her hair was auburn, wild and curly. She was sitting on a faded couch, her head tipped back in amusement with beer bottles and needles at her feet. She was glowing but seemed out of place. The rigid set of her spine gave off the impression that she was uncomfortable. In some ways, I didn't quite recognize her. This photograph seemed to be taken before my father died. Before fear corrupted her mind. Before the idea of death turned her into a hermit.

But in all of this, the sight of my mother wasn't what made me bristle. It was the little boy with blond hair, sunken in cheeks, and bright blue eyes sitting next to her that had me reeling.

I knew with the utmost certainty that this was Hunter. Where my mother was light and hope, Hunter looked dark and broken. Even in the blurred photos, I could make out bruises on his arm. His bones stuck out of his shirt, and he looked malnourished.

This was a photo of my mother and Hunter. But what the fuck did it mean? Another message came through.

Unknown: I know you want answers. I can give them to you. See you in fifteen minutes, Roe.

This person definitely had my attention now, but I still wasn't so easily convinced.

Roe: How did you get this photograph?

And then there was nothing. No response. The unknown account went completely offline, and I stared at the screen for six minutes. The time passed with every exhale, and I waited for them to get back on and give me more. I had leaned in so close to the screen that my nose had brushed across it. My chest felt tight. Had the time started? Should I be leaving to meet them now? They said I had fifteen minutes, but I wanted to see just how desperate they were.

Another minute passed.

Another.

I hovered my hands over my keyboard and waited for the person to go online again. I wanted to see how desperate these people were to see me. I debated on calling Hunter, but we weren't on good terms. I also felt like he hoarded our past, burying it deep in his chest and hiding it from the world. If he thought I had even an inkling of information, he'd be pissed.

Fifteen minutes passed, and I crossed my arms over my chest. Pulling my bottom lip between my teeth, I gnawed on it until the unknown person's chat appeared online again. I then smiled. Gotcha, motherfucker.

Unknown: I found the photo.

Roe: How do you know Hunter?

The chat bubbles danced again.

Unknown: He stalked me too. He's delusional. If you want to know more and how to escape, you better meet me.

I averted my eyes while rubbing at my chest. For some reason, the words this strange person typed sent a searing pain right to my heart. Who else was Hunter obsessed with? He wasn't kidding when he said I wasn't special. How many girls was he grooming and protecting?

These words hurt, but I still didn't trust the person talking to me.

Roe: I don't believe you.

Unknown: Fine. Years from now when he has you trapped, you'll think back on this.

I swallowed, not sure how to take that. Feeling trapped was my worst nightmare. I was raised to fear death, but it really just made me fear the idea of never really living. I chewed on my nails for a moment while debating on what to say. I knew for a fact I wouldn't be meeting this stranger at some strange address in a part of town I rarely went to. I wanted answers, and they obviously wanted to see me. I just had to do it in a place that didn't put me in harm's way.

Roe: I'll meet you. On my terms. Spin and Margie's Diner off Highway 20. See you there in thirty minutes. If you want to chat, it's going to be in a public place.

The response was instant.

Unknown: See you soon.

Letting out a breath I didn't even know I was holding, I stared at those three little words until they didn't feel so threatening. See you soon.

Fear enveloped me in a cocoon of anxiety as I got ready and climbed out my bedroom window. Walking down the street, I took steadying breaths while thinking about the photo they'd sent. I knew our pasts were intertwined, but I didn't realize he knew my mother. It made sense, though. His protective tendencies felt like her. He was obsessive. Dark. Determined. All I knew was that I would finally get the answers I sought. I'd find the ties that bound us together and cut them.

Chapter 23

ROE

As I walked, a cloud of air framed my face with each exhale. The chill was unbearable, and I wrapped my coat tighter around my body. I couldn't put my cast through the sleeve, so I simply cradled my arm against my chest.

The diner I'd told them to meet me at had been many things over the years. A craft store. An antique place. A restaurant. Right now, it looked like an ominous haunted house holding all the secrets to my future. Spin and Margie's was a busy place, but it was eclectic and falling apart. Staring up at the grime-filled brick and the flickering lamp illuminating the walkway, I wished that I'd picked a brighter place in a better part of town. But this was one of the few crowded spots within walking distance.

My cell phone was turned off and in my pocket. I patted it reassuringly but frowned when I remembered I had no one to call. I suppose in a pinch I could call Mack, but he was so closely tied to Hunter that I wasn't sure

I could trust him. I briefly considered calling Nicole but decided not to. I didn't want to drag anyone else into this fucked up situation. Joel was the last person I told, and he got beat to hell.

I fixed my gaze on a cracked window while steadying my breath. There was a cute couple sitting inside, staring at one another from across a cluttered table. Their hands were clasped together, and the sly smiles on their faces looked intimate, like they were sharing a joke for only the two of them. I wondered if Hunter and I would ever date or if the kisses we shared were just inevitable side effects of our fucked up situation.

"They look cute, huh, Roe?" a soft, feminine voice said at my back. I froze, digging my shoes in the concrete while taking a steadying breath. It wasn't a threatening tone, but the familiarity in her voice clued me in that this was my mysterious messenger.

Slowly, I turned around and found myself facing a young-looking woman. She had dark blue hair and grooves in her face like she'd been doing meth for the last five years. She was skinny—too skinny. The woman looked deceptively weak, and I felt a bit better, though I wondered if this was her intent.

"Are you the person that's been messaging me?" I asked, keeping my feet firmly planted on the ground. "How did you have that photo of my mom? How do you know Hunter?" Each question ran out of me in rapid procession. My mouth couldn't keep up with my brain, and I watched her smile in satisfaction with every syllable. I knew that look. It was the look of someone that thought they had you right where they wanted you.

"Why don't we go somewhere private? Hunter Hammond is a nosy fucker. He'll probably be here any second," she replied softly while holding her hand out for me to take. I eyed the offering with suspicion. The glow of the streetlamp above her cast shadows on her face, giving this woman a demonic look that made my nerves go haywire.

Hammond. His last name was Hammond. If this strange woman wasn't staring, I would have rolled the name along my tongue like a decadent treat. It had a certain ring to it, and I liked knowing it. It was almost shocking how satisfying it was to have Hunter's full name. I hadn't realized how desperate I was for information, and this girl was already proving to be useful. I took a step closer to her while tilting my head to the side. I didn't trust her at all, but she was bribing me with what I wanted most. "Who are you?" I asked.

"My name is Rosemary." There was something off about this woman, something other than the holes in her face or her gray teeth. She was wearing a leather jacket too thin to truly protect her from the cold. "I've seen what Hunter is capable of. He's a bad man, Roe."

"Is that why you reached out?" I asked while tapping my foot and glancing around. The shadows of the chilly night were messing with my eyes, making me think I was seeing people hidden around the corner and in the alley across the street.

"I wanted to warn you, Roe. Do you know what Hunter is capable of?" she asked.

I mulled over her question for a moment as the truth slapped me in the face. In fact, I *was* sure what Hunter Hammond was capable of, I'd just been pushing it to the back of my mind for the sake of my sanity and survival. I knew he'd killed the men in the car chasing after us. I knew that he was ruthless. I knew that he worked for a dangerous gang and broke

Mack's arm. I knew that he'd been watching me my entire life. I knew that he wanted to control me out of some convoluted need to protect me.

"He's dangerous," I admitted.

"He's insane," Rosemary replied while running a hand through her blue hair. I watched her while taking a step back. For some reason, I wanted more distance between us. "He was obsessed with me. It started with simple control. He'd watch me and convince me there was no other way," she began, and my heart sank.

He'd done that to me. He manipulated me with threats and his version of sound reasoning to keep me from going to the cops. Rosemary must have seen the wheels turning in my mind.

"He did that to you too, huh?" she asked. "I bet he told you he was teamed up with powerful people. Did he tell you he knew cops? That he could end you if you talked?"

I looked down and studied the cracks in the concrete as tears filled my eyes. "Yeah," I replied.

"Then he started showing physical affection, right? He started to kiss you. *Taste* you. He made you feel good so you'd stop asking questions. So you'd stop fighting."

I nodded, my mouth too dry to speak. My blood had run as cold as the air between us. I couldn't believe what she was saying. "How did he know my mom?" I finally choked out.

Rosemary gave me a sad smile. "I don't know. I found the photo when I was going through his things," she replied. My hope plummeted right then and there as she continued. "I'm sorry. I needed to find a way to get you here. Hunter took something from me, Roe. I ran away for a little bit, but when I came back, I saw that he'd moved on and was lying and obsessing over someone else. I couldn't in good conscience leave you here with him. I have a van around the corner. If you come with me, I'll get you out of Colorado. I'll help you start a new life, away from him. I won't let you be trapped by Hunter like I was."

Her promises sounded so good. I'd been looking for a way out since the moment I woke up in his cabin in the woods. I didn't really know Rosemary, but she seemed so accurate. Could this be my way out?

"I don't know..."

"It's Stockholm syndrome, Roe. It took me a long time to clear my head of Hunter's lies, too."

I nodded and patted the phone in my pocket again. Something still didn't feel right. I took another step back, and she took a step forward. "Roe, we don't have much time," she said, this time her voice was less soft and compassionate.

"I just can't leave Mack," I whispered while looking around. "My life is here. Maybe I can convince Hunter to give me some space. Maybe he'll leave me alone..."

She took another step closer and reached out to grab my wrist. Squeezing hard, she pulled me closer with a strength that surprised me. "He'll never leave you alone. Your only way out is with me. Come on. He'll be here soon."

"I-I don't think so," I stammered. My intuition was screaming *danger*, no matter how appealing her explanation and escape may have seemed. I was trained to read a situation, and this woman reeked of desperation and evil. I needed to get out of here.

Just as I'd bolstered enough courage to run, a hand wrapped around my waist, and my body became flush with a soft stomach and hard chest. The smell of whiskey and tobacco invaded my senses as I lifted my hard cast to try and slam it against my attacker's face.

"You took too fucking long, Rosemary," the man holding me said as I screamed and jerked my body away. His meaty, greasy hand clung to me. "Let's get her to the van and be done with this shit," he grunted while dragging me.

Rosemary rolled her eyes. "I was *trying* to avoid a scene. This place is fucking crowded. Try not to make any noise. I almost had her convinced, too. Good call on bugging her place, by the way."

She'd been listening to me? Watching me? It felt wrong when Hunter did, but knowing this woman was invading my privacy too made me sick. I did the complete opposite of what Rosemary wanted and opened my mouth to scream, but a gloved hand covered my mouth, muting my sounds of distress. I braced my feet against the concrete as the strange man tugged my body along, keeping my arms pinned at my sides with his stronghold. I glanced at Rosemary and pleaded with my eyes for her to help me, but it was useless. She had a cold, cruel gaze that seemed smug. She practically strutted like a proud peacock as the strange man dragged me down the alley.

"Hunter is going to lose his shit. I'm finally getting revenge for Dad, Willie, and Rodger," she said while rubbing her hands together. The strange man yanked me around the corner and down a dark alley. "The Asphalt Devils will never question me again."

I jerked my body and stared at the man dragging me, trying everything I could to get out of his grasp. I couldn't see much, thanks to the dark night and the way he was pinning me. But he had a round, scruffy face and beady little eyes. My movements felt futile, and though he didn't have the muscle mass of Hunter, he was still impossibly strong, moving me like it was nothing. The only weakness he had was displayed in the subtle grunts.

An hour seemed to pass in mere seconds. I struggled and screamed against his hand, begging someone—anyone—to come to my rescue. And then flesh scattered, a shot sliced through the air. Rich, deep red blood splattered across my cheek, and the beefy body holding onto me went completely limp.

Strong arms pulled me to a hard body, and I melted at the familiar woodsy smell. Hunter. "Stay still," he grunted. Wearing his typical uniform of dark jeans and a hoodie, I stared slack-jawed at my knight in shining denim.

"What took you so long, Hunter?" Rosemary said while pulling a gun from inside her jacket. Her teeth chattered as she stared maniacally at us both.

"Figured I'd give you a head start," Hunter replied with ease. I glanced sideways at the gun in his hand. From his posture to his tone, Hunter sounded and felt completely confident. He wasn't fussed at all about the crazy woman pointing a pistol at us in the creepy alley.

"You can't just kill my father, end the Asphalt Devils, and get away with it," Rosemary gritted. "There are consequences for what you've done!" Her voice was shrill and shaky as her posture staggered. Her entire existence seemed unsettled.

"And there are consequences for trying to take the Bullets' turf. Your father knew the dangers of going up against the Bullets, and now you do, too. Put the gun down, or I'll make your death painful and slow," Hunter replied.

Rosemary laughed like his threat was inconsequential. My vision seemed to blur as I hyperventilated. All the fears my mother had buried in my soul bloomed to life with vibrant devastation. This was it. I was going to die.

"An eye for an eye, Hunter Hammond," Rosemary said with a giggle before aiming her gun at me.

She didn't even have time to pull the trigger. In a split second, Hunter was shooting at Rosemary with calm precision. Another silent bullet traveled gracefully through the night sky and landed between her eyes. I gasped when chunks of brain and bone splinters scattered around her. One second she was alive, the next her brain was nothing but cells and blood on the concrete. Her body went limp, and she fell to the ground with a thud. I watched with rapt attention as her legs twitched and her blood watered the ground. It was so fucking fast. Efficient. Tragic.

Hunter sighed and holstered his gun. Strong arms that should have terrified me wrapped around my middle, and I sunk into the familiarity of it. Hunter. He was here. He'd saved me. He...shot them.

I breathed in and out, the feeling of panic coursing through my veins. Death was holding me in his arms, and my mother's warnings seemed more tangible now. "Roe?" he said. "Are you okay?"

I panicked some more, breathing until the spots in my vision had disappeared. "Roe?" he called, this time louder. "We have to get out of here. Do I need to carry you?"

The tender way he spoke seemed uncharacteristic. I was expecting him to yell.

I stared at Rosemary as her broken body bled. It was gruesome and gritty. Hunter kept asking me questions, but I couldn't get past the sight of her body on the street. Her blue lips were parted like there was still a scream on the tip of her tongue. For some reason, Mack's words played in my mind on repeat.

You've got to let your damage breathe.
You've got to let your damage breathe.
Let it fucking breathe.

Chapter 24

ROE

"Who were those people?" I rasped while bracing my good hand against the dash. My heart was racing. My skin felt alive with adrenaline as I stared at my deadly savior. Hunter looked murderous. His ice-blue gaze could kill.

"Why did you go to them, Roe?" he asked stoically, not bothering to look at me as he entered the highway and pushed the gas pedal down.

"They had a photo of you, Hunter," I replied, like the reason was excuse enough. It sounded lame and ridiculous now. I willingly walked into a trap and nearly died for it. Adrenaline was still coursing through my veins, and my fingers felt numb. Was I in shock? Every word felt laborious to spit out.

"A photo? You fucking risked your life because of a photo? I have half a mind to spank your ass," Hunter growled in response. My eyes unwillingly snapped to where his hand was gripping the steering wheel. His white-knuckled hold lacked the calmness he exhibited when he shot Rosemary and her man. Little tremors traveled up and down his arm, making him shake as he drove.

"It was a photo of you with my mom. You were just a little boy..." My voice trailed off as I spoke. After I said it out loud, it seemed foolish for some reason. "How do you know my mother, Hunter?" I wanted to focus on that. I wanted to tunnel vision my mind on the information I was given today instead of letting my thoughts wander to the brutal murders I'd witnessed. Oh shit, I was an accomplice to murder. "H-how do you know her?" I asked again when he didn't immediately respond. I craved a distraction like it was air and I'd been tied to a cement block and thrown into the ocean.

"I'm not going to reward you with answers when you deliberately put yourself in harm's way," Hunter said before cursing and exiting the highway. I was so busy watching the glow of the moon casting hazy light onto his angry face, that I wasn't paying attention to where we were going. The woods looked ominous, and the trees lining the street towered overhead, causing a wave of dancing shadows to caress the road and block the night sky from view. I shivered when he turned onto a dirt road.

"Where are you taking me?" I asked in a soft voice.

"To my cabin. Rosemary was the last of the people wanting to kill me, but I want to make sure she doesn't have any lingering loyalists knocking on your door."

"Why do you need to keep me safe, though? Why do they want to hurt you—hurt me?"

Hunter continued down the drive, his face downcast as he gripped the steering wheel. I could see the thoughts circulating in his mind. How I'd started to understand his mannerisms in such a short amount of time, I didn't know. But he was mulling over his answer with a vengeance. He was weighing the pros and cons of revealing his truth. I hadn't necessarily earned his trust, but I craved it all the same. I didn't want to be his best friend, I just wanted to understand him.

He drove down the long drive, where extended, barren branches scratched the exterior of his Jeep. I bounced my leg on the floorboards, anxious about what had just happened and terrified to be back at his cabin. Would he force me to stay in that closet again? Would he lock me away as punishment for what I'd done?

I didn't want to be alone. I felt disconnected from my mind, focusing on the problems that were easier to swallow so I didn't get swept away in the trauma of what had happened. I swayed in my seat, biting the inside of my cheek to force my fears at bay.

Hunter pulled the car up to his drive and turned it off. The cabin looked different in the dark. The sight of Hunter's secluded home in the woods made me shiver. It felt like death and secrets. It felt like Hunter.

The wraparound porch was covered in dead leaves. Gravel covered the walkway, and when I got out of the car, a brisk chill coated my bones. It was colder up here in the mountains. The air felt icy, and the wind blew with a brutal intensity I couldn't shake.

I wordlessly followed him to the front door in defeat, knowing that there would be consequences for what I'd done. He opened it with ease like he hadn't even bothered to lock it when he left. Once he turned the kitchen light on, I took a moment to observe his appearance. The shirt he wore looked wrinkled like he'd grabbed it off the floor and threw it on in a hurry. His hair was a wild mess, and his eyes looked whiskey bloodshot.

"Were you asleep when..." my question trailed off. I couldn't vocalize the second half of it. *When I was almost kidnapped and killed.*

"No. I was watching you. Good thing, too," he growled before going to the cupboard and grabbing a bottle of bourbon. I watched as he methodically took a swig directly from the bottle. "Didn't take long to find you, but I wish I would have shown up earlier."

"Why did they try to take me?" I asked.

He let out a huff. "I'm an assassin, Roe."

Hunter dropped that bombshell of a revelation in my lap. He'd said it the same way you'd say normal things such as:

We're out of milk, so I'll pick some up from the grocery store.

I need to get my oil changed.

I paid my taxes last year.

I'm an assassin.

Three simple words with destructive meaning. In some ways, I knew that Hunter wasn't normal. There was a danger about him that had always felt like clenching your teeth; I just didn't know how deadly he truly was.

"So you kill people for a living," I murmured.

"I do. Are you scared of me now, Pretty Debt?"

I swallowed his question and let it fester in my gut. Was I scared of him? I should be. My mother would have told me to run the fuck away. Maybe my answer stemmed from wanting to rebel against the fear my mother taught me to embrace, but I said it anyway.

"No."

Hunter ran a hand through his blond hair and cursed under his breath. *Fuck.* He then turned around and slipped outside, leaving me standing alone in his kitchen with more questions threatening to burst at the seam of my lips. I wanted to know more about Rosemary, mainly if the things she said were true. I walked up to the window leading outside and placed my hand on the glass, watching outside as Hunter *Hammond* paced and punched the sky. He looked feral underneath the twinkling stars. He'd turn his face towards the cabin, and I'd be gifted with flashes of his murderous expression. He was furious, and I wished I could crawl into his soul and understand every nuance of it.

After two hours of watching from his kitchen and feeling too scared to touch anything, I wandered through his house until I came across the bedroom I'd woken up just weeks ago. It looked the same. The midnight walls were still dark. The floor still had that rust-colored stain that made me now wonder if it was the blood of his enemies.

Trembling and willing the terrifying thoughts away, I lay down on the mattress and curled my knees to my chest.

I was almost kidnapped. I watched a woman die. A man, who knew my mother, is the reason these people want me.

Shock was a fickle thing. It hit you like a bucket of ice water, lighting up your senses with a cold, harsh sort of reality. Round and round my mind went, circling through all the events that led to this moment. It all started with Hunter. It all ended with Hunter.

I trembled on the bed as hours casually slipped by. I waited for him to return. I knew he would return. He had to return. I let my mind bubble with all the questions. I let my heart pound.

I wasn't the type of woman to be easily impressed by gore. I numbed my soul so it wouldn't destroy me like it did my mother. Hell, I'd pressed my own index finger to the too-still vein in her neck on my tenth birthday. I learned long ago to bury my trauma deep within my chest and let a rose bloom from the seeds of pain. But this was too much.

The bedroom door opened, and I squeezed my eyes shut. I felt the small mattress dip and a hard body settle next to mine. Warm, muscular arms wrapped around my body, and I went completely still when hot lips pressed against my ear. "Little Debt, you're in so much trouble."

His words didn't feel playful or teasing. It felt like one wrong move and he'd wrap his massive hands around my throat and close, close, close—squeeze until the air in my chest turned to cement. "You scared me, Hunter," I whispered before gnawing on my lip. "Where did you go?"

Hunter squeezed me tighter before responding. "I went outside to sit for a bit and calm down so I didn't kill you," he offered nonchalantly, like it was another one of those simple little sentences that didn't mean anything.

"Do you want to kill me?" I asked. Maybe not facing his cold expression was making me bold, or maybe I just wanted to know how this ended.

"It would make things a lot easier."

His answer made me sick to my stomach. I rolled over to face my stalker, cupping his stubble-covered cheek with my good palm while staring into his eyes. It was like I could see the entire world in its fucked up entirety at the edge of his nose. I stared until my eyes burned.

"How did you know my mother?" I asked quietly.

"What does it matter?" he replied.

"I just want to know why I matter to you, Hunter. I want to make sense of this crazy connection. I want to know why you hate me so fiercely yet are protective. Just give me something, Hunter. Anything."

"It's so wrong to want you, Roe," he whispered. I'd expected a denial or maybe even more regret. I was holding my breath for the truth. But Hunter kissed me, instead.

His lips were soft and insistent. He threaded his hand through my wild, caramel hair and groaned against my sealed lips. My leg wrapped around his hip, and I whimpered. We let go. We collided.

We gave in.

His sharp teeth tugged on my lip, pulling, pulling, pulling. I knew my bruised lips would forever feel his presence. His mouth worked to convince me that the truth was just a minor detail. His touch massaged me past the reserved rigidity of disbelief. He kissed and savored me. "You're my prettiest debt, Roe," he whispered like a prayer over my altar lips. "When I saw you'd gone, it scared the shit out of me."

To emphasize his fear, he squeezed my neck, making my mouth pop open in lust. "They could have hurt you, Roe," he whispered before kissing me again. His tongue explored my open mouth, and our teeth clashed. It was messy and hot. We didn't look like two practiced lovers aching to kiss away the pain, we were exploratory sadists wanting to hurt with intent. "You've always been mine, you know. Since before you were born."

My mind went back to the photograph of my mother's pregnant belly and Hunter's pale, childish face.

I didn't know how that made me feel. I was willing to explore this between us, but I needed more to work with. He didn't seem willing to tell me about our shared past, but maybe I could work more out of him in other ways.

We stopped kissing, and I placed my ear to his chest, listening to the consistent beat of his rebel heart. "When did you become an assassin?" I asked.

"So many questions," Hunter breathed out while snaking his hand up my shirt. Resting his fingers on the clasp of my bra, he replied while working it free. "My first kill was when I was eighteen. My employer said I was a natural at it and let me do it again. And again."

His hand drifted to the front, and I gasped the moment he pinched my nipple between his index finger and thumb. "Do you want to be a killer?" I asked, my voice shaky. I wasn't sure if it was fear or lust making my words tremble, but I wasn't ready for the reality of that answer either.

"When I first started, it felt like redemption. I had so much anger in me with no place to go. Now it just feels like a means to an end. It pays the bills. It keeps a roof over my head. It allows me to watch over you..." His words trailed off as his fingers traced lazy lines up and down my abdomen, each swipe leading lower and lower.

"I guess you could say killing is in my blood. You were born nothing but a debt; I was born a murderer."

His words were dark and complex, everything stirring between us felt too complicated, too confusing. "So what does that make us together?" I asked.

Hunter leaned forward and pressed his lips to my forehead, murmuring his response over me. His tone was full of haunting regret. "I'm still trying to figure that out. I'm going to kiss you until I do."

Hunter eased me out of my clothes, stumbling a bit to get my cast out of my T-shirt. He kissed the awkwardness of our movements away, lapping up my mouth with his tongue as he unbuttoned my jeans and helped me ease them over my thighs. I ran my hand under his hoodie and traced the lines of his stomach, begging him with my touch to undress, too.

He undressed with taunting moves. Slowly, he shrugged out of his shirt. He unbuttoned his pants and made me watch as he shoved them off. His body was hot and slick with sweat. He smelled like the outdoors.

Moving his lips to my neck, he then sunk his sharp teeth into my collarbone. I whimpered as he sucked on my creamy skin. He hovered over me, and I wrapped my legs around his body and lined up our sexes as he focused on the sensitive skin on my neck. His hard cock teased at my entrance. Hunter was so close to sliding all the way inside, but I wanted one last answer before I'd let him find a home in my cunt.

"Tell me why you hate me, Hunter," I pleaded between kisses. I knew that once our bodies were joined, there would be no going back. I'd need to cling to his hatred if I was going to survive this.

"I hate you for many reasons, Roe," he replied before thrusting inside of me with one harsh move. My eyes widened. My mouth dropped open in lusty shock. He felt so fucking thick. I was so full. "I hate you because we were destined to be together," he began before sliding all the way out and slamming back into me.

"Oh fuck," I whimpered.

"I hate you," he began before sliding out again and pounding me with another punishing thrust. "Because you represent every bad thing that has ever happened to me, and you don't even know why."

I wrapped my good arm around his neck and pulled myself up to a sitting position. Hunter stayed on his knees as I rode him. We gazed into each other's eyes as I moved. "I hate you," he rasped before searing his lips to mine. We fought with our mouths. We shared unspoken remorse and a history I didn't understand before he continued, "Because I wasn't taught anything but hate. I know obsessions and pain. I wouldn't know affection or care if it slapped me in the face, Roe."

I drank in the look of his hooded gaze. I bobbed up and down again, watching his eyes roll back, his lips part, his head tilt up in bliss as I waited for him to explain. "It's wrong to want you, Roe. I was just supposed to protect you."

"It's not wrong," I moaned. He placed his palm against my chest and shoved me, sending me flying towards the mattress. In an instant, his mouth was on my left breast. His tongue was dancing around my nipple. He shoved apart my legs with his hand and started playing with my clit, running his rough thumb around it in circular motions timed perfectly to my pleasure.

My back arched off the bed, and I moaned. "*Fuck*, Hunter."

"I don't hate you, Pretty Debt. My obsession turned into something more."

He moved to suck on my neck, finding that sweet, sensitive spot and biting it. "More?" I asked, but I wasn't sure if I wanted clarification on what he meant or if I wanted him to fuck me into oblivion. His touch wasn't enough. I wanted to feel full again. I wanted to come on his cock.

Hunter circled my clit faster and harder, coaxing a harsh orgasm out of me with ease. I cried out and bit his shoulder, riding the waves of ecstasy as he sucked on my skin. "More, Pretty Debt," he replied before aligning us once more and sliding into me.

He fucked relentlessly. He didn't hold back. I felt how hard he wanted to deny this thing between us. I felt his determination to keep me safe. I felt his fear. I felt just how dangerous he was with each and every deliberate pound. Sweet heat made our movements slick, and the sounds of our slapping skin echoed around the small room. I cried out as loud as I could. There was so much energy and pleasure building between us with nowhere to go. Again and again and again he pounded. Another orgasm flooded me.

I was so fucking sensitive to his touch, but he didn't stop. He moved his hand to the apex of my thighs to circle my clit with his thumb. He wanted me to feel it all.

Another thrust. Harder. Our slapping bodies fought for dominance. I writhed on the bed. Another orgasm, this one smaller, wrecked me. My body was exhausted, but Hunter didn't seem close to stopping at all. I reached down to shove his hand away from me, but it just pissed him off.

"You want me to stop?" he asked while grabbing my hand and moving it over my head. Pinning me to the mattress, he stopped fucking me to hear my answer.

"I'm too sensitive," I cried out. Hunter threaded his fingers through mine, then slowly slid in and out of me. I was so slick.

"You feel too much," he said, and I wasn't sure if it was a question or not.

"I do," I replied as he moved faster and faster.

Hunter smiled, that wicked smile that felt mischievous and dangerous all the same. "Feel my obsession, Roe. Feel it all," he replied before finally letting go of all restraint and fucking me raw.

He was fast, every muscle in his body tense as he drove into me. I cried out, the pleasure too much. In and out. Harder. Harder. Harder.

Let your damage breathe.

He fucked me until we both came. We were an explosion of bad decisions and compatibility. He grunted and gasped but never closed his heavy eyes. He watched me with every spurt of his cum. I felt filled to the brim with his release, and never wanted it to stop. He collapsed on top of me, and I wrapped my limbs around him, begging him to stay. I wanted to feel this connection forever.

"Pretty Debt," he whispered into my ear, his hot breath trailing across my skin.

"Yes?" I asked.

"I don't hate you."

"I know."

Chapter 25

HUNTER

I watched her sleep this morning while counting all the ways I'd fucked up last night. I killed someone and left the mess for the police. Gavriel was pretty pissed but pulled some strings. Surprisingly, murder was one of the easier mistakes to cover up.

I woke up knowing exactly what needed to be done. This would probably be the last time I woke up holding Roe.

I'd told Roe what I was. I spilled out my job title like it was nothing and watched as her faith in me slipped. The terror in her eyes taunted me. I liked finally getting through to her—finally showing her just what I was capable of. But it hurt, too. For the first time in my life, I didn't like feeling like a monster. I didn't like feeling ashamed. She claimed to not be afraid of me, but I saw the tremor in her lips. I saw the way her eyes widened and her skin turned pale. I was the type of man to insight fear, and there was no escaping the terror Roe felt.

And then I held her. And then I kissed her and admitted that this fucked up dynamic between us had somehow shifted over the last couple of weeks, and I stopped seeing her as an obligation and more as this constant entity in my life.

I fucked Roe. I slid inside of her and felt the way our bodies pulsed with intent. It was the most erotic sex I'd ever had, but I felt regret the next morning. We experienced a shift in our dynamic. She started to mean something to me in ways I hadn't expected, and now I felt sick to my stomach.

"Good morning," she whispered the moment her sleepy eyes opened. She stared at me like I was deserving of being the first thing she graced those pretty deep pools of depth on.

"How did you sleep?" I asked, though I knew damn well that she slept much better than I did. This bed was too soft, too small. I could feel all of Roe's inhales. Her breasts spent all night pressed against my chest, and I spent all night reminding myself to keep my hands still. Sex once could be written off as a mistake. Twice was intentional.

"Okay," she replied. "I'm surprised the police aren't knocking on your door, though. It feels like last night never happened..."

Her voice trailed off, and I had to force myself not to smirk at the naivety of her words. Something definitely happened last night—a shift in my reality happened. One second I was watching from afar, obsessing about each tic in her jaw, and the next I was worried that I was too late, that I wasn't enough, that my enemies had killed her. Last night made me realize that I wasn't just obligated to keep Roe safe. I was terrified to lose her.

"The people I work for pay a lot of money to make sure things like last night get swept under the rug," I replied, not bothering to sugarcoat it.

"You're not going to school today."

She sat up in bed, forcing the soft sheets to pool at her hips. The large swells of her breasts strained against her tight shirt, and I had to practically swallow my tongue to keep from licking her neck. There was still a mountain of things fundamentally wrong with how fucking much I wanted her. But I guess I shouldn't grow a conscience now.

"Why not?"

"Because we need to talk," I said slowly. The words turned to ash on my tongue. I knew this day would come. I needed to explain everything. I needed her to know what I'd done, why I was infatuated with her.

"Talk?" she asked, her adorable button nose wrinkling in the process. "You're actually going to tell me everything?"

"I am," I replied. Bile rose up my throat.

"Why?"

Because I need to scare you off. Because I need you to live a full life without me. Because if we keep doing this thing, my obsession will trap you far worse than your mother ever did. You'll never leave. I'll own you, Roe.

I didn't say any of these things. "Because it's time you knew the truth."

She stared at me for a long moment, distrust making her eyes squint. She then stretched her arms above her head. I watched as her shirt rose up, gifting me with a sliver of creamy skin as she moaned in satisfaction. Her willowy body welcomed the day despite the destruction that happened last night. "Okay," she began. "Let's talk then."

"Shower first. I'll meet you in the kitchen."

Rolling her eyes, she said, "Sure thing, Stalker."

She showered and got ready for the day while I made us a pot of coffee. Roe liked her coffee so saturated with cream that it resembled snow. I'd always gagged from afar when watching her make it. It was brutal to know that these little facts were all I'd have of her after she was done.

When she strolled through the kitchen, an overwhelming sense of awkwardness settled between us. She was wearing my clothes, an oversized shirt and sweatpants that swallowed her thin body up. I had to swallow back lust. I just stared for a moment, stuck in limbo.

The truth was just on the other side of me prolonging the inevitable. I was stalling, we both knew it. I just wanted to enjoy the morning a bit longer. "Are you going to stare at me all morning, or are you going to pour me a cup of coffee?" she asked with a raised brow.

"You are more than capable of pouring your own, even with that bulky cast. Have any trouble showering?" I asked.

"Nope. But if you feel the need to help me, I wouldn't mind your assistance next time," she teased before pinning her mouth shut. It was almost as if she'd realized that she was flirting with me. The rose color kissing her cheeks was addictive, and I wanted to see it again.

An idea came to me. If I was going to tell her the truth, I might as well tell her all of it. I wanted to show her the parts of me even Mack didn't know about.

Grabbing two to-go cups and filling them with coffee, I then told her to grab one of my jackets. "We're going out," I declared cryptically.

"I thought we were going to talk," Roe argued while cocking her head to the side. I had a sudden urge to kiss her lips.

"We will. I just…"

"Want to prolong the inevitable?" she offered.

"No," I began while shifting from one leg to the other. Each tick of the clock seemed to pass too quickly. No, this had to be done. "I just need to show you something."

Roe didn't fuss or fight anymore, and I watched her slip her slender arms through the sleeves of one of my old flannel jackets hanging by the door and then slip her feet into her Ugg boots.

It didn't take us long to get in the Jeep. She didn't ask many questions. I suppose I had conditioned her not to expect any answers. Just another mistake. Just another way I was breaking her. I steered my Jeep off the road and bit my tongue, wondering how someone like me could even have a normal conversation with Roe. The two of us didn't get normal introductions, we got fear and declarations and ultimatums. I threatened her into compliance, and now I wanted to learn more. But how did I transition from observing her life to living it with her?

No. I didn't get to live life with her. I got to scare her away and save us both. I wasn't capable of continuing this thing between us. I just wanted this morning. I wanted one moment.

"What kind of music do you like?" I asked while fumbling with the radio.

She clutched her chest before answering. "You mean you don't already know?"

Her mocking made me want to clench my teeth and stop trying. I synced my phone to the radio and turned on one of her favorite artists, Halsey. "You listened to this song forty-seven times one day after breaking up with some asshole with a snaggle tooth," I said with a frown before clutching the wheel.

She stared incredulously at me for a moment before clasping her hands together in her lap. "What's my favorite meal?" she asked quietly.

"Sushi, specifically the Philadelphia roll. Mack hates the stuff, so you usually go by yourself," I answered easily.

She turned her attention outside. "What's my favorite season?" she asked.

"Summer. You used to spend every day at the community pool. I almost had one put in at Mack's house so he could watch you better."

Roe nodded. If I was creeping her out with my extensive knowledge of her, she wasn't admitting it. If we wanted to get ahead of this, we needed to openly rip apart our dynamic. "What's my least favorite day of the year?" she asked.

"Your birthday."

The silence stretched between us. "You're wrong, you know," she finally whispered, just as the song ended and another one began.

"Halsey is good, but my favorite band is Nirvana. Mom used to listen to them all the time. I like sushi, but it's not my favorite. My favorite meal is the deep dish meat lover's pizza from this little pizzeria in New York. Mom and I used to go there all the time."

I stored each nugget of information in my brain and clutched the steering wheel like it was a lifeline. "You can look through a window and watch me eat pizza, but you'll never know how it tastes," she said. Her metaphor lacked depth, but the point still came across.

"Point taken. So tell me about yourself," I offered lamely. Roe had me feeling all out of sorts, and I wasn't sure what to do about it.

"You can't just demand facts about me and expect to know who I am," Roe replied with an exasperated sigh. "You learn about someone through experience, and you can't just demand information without sharing some of your own."

I continued to drive. I'd been on this path so many times that my tires had killed the grass. Some leaves had fallen since I'd been here last, covering the road with their dead decay. But I could explore these trails with my eyes closed and still end up where I needed to go.

"You could start by telling me where we're going," she prodded while lifting her chin at the window.

"We're going to my safe house," I replied, though *safe house* didn't feel like the right term. *Killer's headquarters* was probably more accurate, but I wasn't about to terrify her with that.

"So the creepy, secluded cabin in the woods where I woke up locked in the basement *isn't* your safehouse?" she asked, sarcasm dripping like syrup from her plump lips.

"No. That's just where I hide some of the bodies," I replied jokingly.

Her doe eyes popped open in shock, and I realized we weren't at the point where I could joke about my profession yet. "Kidding," I quickly added.

"No, you aren't," she mumbled dejectedly under her breath before gnawing on that poor lip of hers. I didn't like the idea of her splitting it open with her teeth.

"You're right. I'm not." There was no use lying about it. She already knew too much.

We continued our drive. It only took about fifteen more minutes before we were pulling up to the secluded hut. On the outside, my headquarters looked like an abandoned garbage pile. I strategically built rotted wood around the steel exterior to hide the fortress inside. Large trees surrounded it, and I kept trip wires hidden along the property, alerting me if anyone went snooping.

"And just when I think you can't get any creepier, Hunter. You go and bring me to a place like this," Roe mumbled while shaking her head. I couldn't even blame her. It did look like I'd brought her here to die.

"Get out of the Jeep, drama queen. If I wanted to kill you, I wouldn't have bothered bringing you here."

We walked up to the hanging door, and I quickly flipped the hidden keypad and typed in the entry code. Three beeps greeted me, and the door slid open, revealing the steel cage under all the rotted wood. At my back, Roe gasped, and I had to hide the pleased, prideful smile I wanted to show. I'd worked hard on this place, and her reaction to it for some reason was very important to me.

"Whoa," she murmured while following me inside. It wasn't a large cabin. It had plumbing and a kitchenette for when my research forced me to stay long nights. It was just four walls, but each inch of space was strategically planned with technology, gear, and weapons.

Naturally, Roe gravitated toward my wall of guns, knives, bombs, and other weapons. She looked up at the rows of black metal poised on the wall, with her mouth hanging open. "Do you know how to shoot all of these?" she asked.

"Yep," I replied, popping the _p_ for emphasis. I wasn't one to brag about my abilities. I had an unusually steady hand, great vision, and an aim that couldn't be matched. I was a natural when it came to lodging bullets in skulls. I was probably the best damn shot in the world. I never missed.

But of all the things in my little safe haven, the weapons were the least impressive. Although each gun here had a unique purpose, they all were used for the same thing. Killing.

I liked my computer deck. I wasn't nearly as skilled of a hacker as some of the other guys on Gavriel's payroll, but I had the best equipment money could buy. It was untraceable and got the job done. The programs I ran could help me find anyone, hear anything, trace anywhere and hack into most accounts. This self-automated machine was the next level in criminal activity. You didn't need a man living in his grandmother's basement to access the FBI anymore. Now you just needed an Internet connection and enough money to buy code.

"I wanted to show you something," I said while motioning towards my wall of monitors. Roe tore her eyes from the large shotgun I got three years ago as a gift for my fifteenth kill, and moved to sit by me. This was it. This was where I'd tell her everything.

I sat down in my seat and booted up the computers while staring at Roe out of the corner of my eye. She seemed uncertain and distant. I reached out and wrapped my arms around her waist before tugging her closer to me. She stumbled a bit then settled on my lap. Her entire body seemed stiff, but I ignored it. Wrapping around her, I logged in and pulled up the file called *Roe*.

Thumbnails of photos covered the screen. "Is that?" she asked while leaning closer.

"You?" I offered. "Yes, it is."

"You really have been watching me my whole life," she whispered as I clicked on a photo of her at the hospital the day she was born. The day I met Mack. The day her father died.

"I don't have a lot of photos of you when you were younger. I didn't really start taking photos until you moved in with Mack, but this is the first."

"You were there the day I was born?" she asked while twisting on my lap to look at me.

"Yes," I replied solemnly.

"Rosemary said you stalked her, too. Is that true?"

I was surprised by this line of questioning. I'd just showed her a server with a lifetime of photos I'd taken saved on it, and yet she wanted to know if this thing was exclusive? "No. She was lying. She's been watching us and played you. You're my only debt," I whispered.

She got off my lap and ran her hand through her hair, looking around the cabin with wide eyes and a newfound sense of understanding that she didn't have before. I watched her take it all in, wondering if the beautiful, strong girl I'd been taking for granted would finally crack. I was hoping she'd do what she does best: run the fuck away.

"Is this you?" she asked while pausing at a space of wall with a shelf of personal effects on it. Of course she would single out the one photo I had of myself.

I stood up and made my way over to her. Once at her back, I breathed in her cinnamon scent as she reached up to pick up the dusty frame off the shelf.

She blew on it and wiped at the glass, cocking her head to the side as she stared at it. "That's my mother," I said in a soft voice while staring at the photograph. It was one of the only photos we had together. It was one of those things that hurt to look at, but you felt obligated to keep it, all the same.

"She looks..." Roe's voice trailed off like she was trying to place her

243

face somewhere.

"She looks sick. Fragile. Like she's dying," I finished for her. In the photo, my mother's blond hair was frail and scraggly. Her bones were poking through her scarred, blemished skin. Her cheeks were sunken in, and her teeth had that grayish glow only a drug addict would have.

Oh but there was love in her eyes. Despite her weakness, I knew she did care for me—when she was sober enough to remember that I existed. There was love there, definitely. But she was an addict, and addicts always loved themselves and their addiction more than the people depending on them. I wanted her to keep me safe, and in the end, she didn't.

"I was going to say familiar..." Roe's voice trailed off again. She was so close to the truth, so close to the tragic secret that bonded us together the day she was born. "It's like I've seen a photo of her before... The photo of you with my mother. Were our mothers friends?" Roe asked before turning around to face me. She bit her lip as if nervous I'd punish her for figuring out another puzzle piece to our life.

"Yes, they were friends," I whispered.

Roe's eyes brightened at my honesty. "And where is she now?"

"With your mother. Probably rotting in hell," I bit back before plucking the picture frame from her hands and putting it back on the shelf. Roe's eyebrows shot up in disbelief.

Roe took a steadying breath. Inhale. Exhale. I could see the *run* on her face. I'd watched her get it many times before. She was quick to leave and hard-pressed to stay. If she was mildly uncomfortable, she got out of there as quickly as possible.

And yet, I kept tossing her all these impossible scenarios. I kept secrets.

I told her lies, fed her fear on a silver spoon. So why was she still here?

Lifting up on her tiptoes, Roe leaned in to kiss me. Her lips were incredibly soft. Her coffee breath didn't bother me in the slightest. Her chilled hand cupped my neck as she closed her eyes and drank me in with a tantric kiss. "Tell me," she pleaded. I kept the words lodged in my chest.

Slowly responding to her touch with my sweeping tongue, we kissed for a moment as our past unfolded at our feet. She pulled away, and I didn't like how in charge of our kiss she seemed or the smug look on her face or the way her eyes seemed to burn with a newfound understanding.

"Tell me."

"Our mothers were friends. Both of them were in love with the same man," I explained. Her eyes went wide, and she shivered in disgust.

"Are you my brother?" she choked out.

"No, no," I quickly replied. "Come here. Let me explain." I grabbed her hand and brought her over to the small leather couch. Once we were both settled, I continued.

"Our mothers were in love with the same man. He chose your mom," I replied, the oversimplification of my mother's heartbreak making a sharp pain rock through me. "They ended up taking very different paths. Your mother found love. My mother found drugs and Forest."

Roe frowned but nodded for me to continue. "Forest wasn't a good guy. Your mom tried to keep the friendship alive for my sake, but it got harder and harder. My mom just got destructive…"

Misty tears filled her eyes, and she reached out to grasp my hand. I reveled in the contact for a moment, knowing that the moment she learned the truth, she'd let me go. "Did he hurt you, Hunter?" Roe asked in a timid voice.

I coughed back the anger burning in my chest. I was a man now. Forest was dead. No one would ever hurt me, ever again. But whenever I talked about this, I couldn't help but feel like the hopeless child that was forced to endure his hits. I didn't even answer her question, and Roe sensed the truth. She closed her eyes and scooted closer to me, wrapping her arm around my waist.

"Your mom tried to be a good friend to mine. But my mom didn't make it easy. There was addiction and toxic jealousy between them. Your mom loved me, though. She wasn't always so scared of the world. She was brave, once. Brave enough to call my mom out on her shit. Brave enough to show up in the middle of the night to bring me food. And then she got pregnant with you."

Roe tilted her head up to look at me. "Mom asked for some money. She said she was going to finally get away from Forest. Move out of the city. Get clean. Start over. It sure sounded good. Mrs. Palmer gave her two thousand dollars in cash. Of course, my mom blew it. Mom was afraid of change; I guess that's why things always stayed the same."

"What happened?" Roe asked, her voice raw with emotion.

"Your father, Lake, got fed up. You were due any day, and he was sick of my mom pulling this shit. It was a Thursday. The air was hot. I was hungry. I was *always* hungry."

Talking it out reduced me to shortened sentences. I felt like a caveman. "Lake arrived and asked for the money back. My mom cried. She cried a lot. I came out of my bedroom. Lake was always nice to me, though he kept away out of respect for your mom."

I closed my eyes and opened them. "My mom kissed your dad. She was high as hell and started taking off her clothes, offering him sex in exchange for the two thousand dollars. He tried to push her away. Lake was ready to get out of there."

When I opened my eyes, Roe was staring at me. Grounding me. Showering me with wordless support as she clutched me tightly. "Forest showed up. He was so fucking mad. He started hitting Mom. Lake tried to stop it. There was...a gun. I later learned that it was a single-action revolver. They fought over it. Mom was shot in the neck. Then Forest in the stomach. Then...Lake. In the head."

It all happened so fast. My childhood brain turned my memories into a flash of sequences, like blurred lights. I couldn't see it all, but I remembered the outcome. I remembered standing over the three dead bodies. I remembered Lake's lifeless eyes staring at me as blood flowed from his skull. I kicked Forest's dead body and cried at Mom's naked, still form.

"Oh, Hunter," Roe cried while nuzzling my neck. I was too shocked to hold her. I didn't understand. "It wasn't your fault."

"Lake's phone was ringing," I continued. "Your mom had called. She was in labor. I listened to the voicemail. I think I was in shock. It's funny how death means nothing to me now."

"Don't say that, Hunter. Of course death means something."

"Not to me," I promised. "I walked to the hospital where you were born. It's how I met Mack, actually. He helped me find you. I remember staring at you in the nursery. Your mother had no idea Lake was dead. She had no idea what her best friend had done. I vowed to take care of you, Roe. I promised to repay the debt."

Emotion clogged my throat. I hadn't spoken of this in so long, yet the wound still felt fresh. My vision blurred from unshed tears. "Hunter, it's not your fault," Roe whispered. "You don't have to pay for the sins of your parents."

I knew she was right. I was reasonable. But trauma didn't pick and choose obsessions. It just felt right to take care of Roe. Even when I was in foster care. Even when her mother wanted nothing to do with me because I reminded her of my mother. Even when Roe grew up to be a beautiful woman. I couldn't let go of that debt. I couldn't let go of what I'd seen. I couldn't let go of my anger.

"Your mother feared death because of my parents. Your father died the day you were born because of them, too."

"I'm releasing you of your debt, Hunter. It wasn't your fault. I'm so sorry you've convinced yourself that you have to watch me because of something your mother did," she said.

Her response wasn't what I was expecting, but I felt off. *Run*, I silently urged her. Run because I wasn't not good enough. Because our past was too tangled. Because my family was the source of all her troubles.

"I'm here, Hunter," she whimpered as more tears traveled down her cheeks. "I'm not going anywhere." She might have forgiven my debt, but there were still sins to atone for. Her compassion and grace left me at a standstill, but I knew what needed to be done. It was only fair that I released her of my obsession.

Chapter 26

ROE

He held me for a while. I traced lines along his strong forearms while simmering in silence. I reveled in the truth he offered while mourning our shared history. Mom told me that Dad died in a car accident while rushing to the hospital. I'd grown up thinking it was just a cruel twist of fate. I didn't realize her best friend had a hand in killing him. No wonder she secluded herself from the world. She couldn't trust anyone. I felt a new layer of pity for my mother.

Hunter's obsession made sense. He had a toxic childhood. Although he didn't explain much, I filled in the blanks. In the photo sent to me by Rosemary, he'd looked starved to death. He'd been abused, neglected, and forgotten. I hated my mother for not checking on him after Dad's death. I knew my mother didn't have the headspace to obsessively care about anyone else but the two of us, but it still made me sad to think that Hunter ended up in foster care. He was all alone. My heart desperately hurt for him.

Hunter wanted to right the wrongs of his parents and feel some control over his life. Maybe that's why he was an assassin. It was kill or be killed in his world, and he'd seen firsthand how quickly he needed to pull the trigger to save himself.

My heart hurt for my father. I wished he'd never gone to their house. I wished he'd let the money be. There was no debt worth the cost of a life, in my opinion. It was just money. It was just a mistake. I was furious with his selfish mother.

"You know," I began while sitting up. I'd been lying in his lap, the two of us sitting in silence on his leather couch as we absorbed everything. "You've already paid back the two grand, Hunter. I mean, I'm sure Mack isn't cheap."

Hunter breathed in. "It's not just the money I owe," he explained while running a hand through his hair. "In many ways, Lake was both the reason my mom was so fucked up and the reason I was finally free," he explained. "He was the first guy she really loved. I was just the product of a one-night stand; she didn't even know his name. But Lake? She would watch him. Follow him home. Mom worked at a flower shop with Mrs. Palmer. They both met Lake at the same time. Both flirted. Both asked for his number. They were all friends for a while, but he always loved your mom." He cracked his knuckles before spitting out the last of his admission. "Mom got off the wagon when they started dating."

I clenched my teeth. It wasn't my dad's fault he didn't like her. No one should blame him in this scenario. I'd never say it out loud, but it sounded like Hunter's mother was just a weak soul looking for an excuse for substance abuse.

"I know what you're thinking, and you're right. But he was a trigger. She dated Forest to make him jealous. Everything started with Lake, but it ended with him, too."

"That's why you hated me," I whispered.

"You look a little like him," Hunter admitted. "Same honey eyes. Same brown hair and freckles. I guess I was scared to like you because I saw what that sort of infatuation did to my mother. She was obsessed, and I…"

He was my stalker. He followed in the same footsteps as his mother.

I stared at Hunter. At the scar over his right eyebrow, at the dirty blond hair curling at the ends. I stared at the veins in his hands. I stared at the tight shirt stretched across his chest. "I've always been scared to love, because I saw what the fear of loss did to my mother," I admitted with a shrug. "But we aren't our parents, Hunter. We can start over. We can live our lives…" I was nervous to finish that sentence. The word *together* hovered behind my teeth. "We don't have to tie ourselves to the past."

Hunter's eyes grew wide with fear as if my suggestion were the last thing on earth he could possibly want.

"No. This is over, Roe," Hunter said while standing up. He looked around the room, and I watched him take in every single detail, like he was committing his safe space to memory. What did he mean this was over?

"What?" Hunter grabbed a duffel bag from the corner and started putting guns and various supplies in it. "Where are you going?" I asked, my voice turning shrill.

"I'm leaving," he replied. His voice was short and curt. I didn't understand. I was getting emotional whiplash and hated the feel of the sting in my soul. "I don't want this for you, Roe."

"What? Don't I get a say in this?"

Hunter stared at the photo of his mother and picked up the frame. I watched him drag his thumb across the glass for a slow, steady moment. His face twisted up in pain as he stared at the woman responsible for all of this, and then in one defining moment, he tossed it in the trash. "Last night, you almost died because of what I'm involved in. If I'm in your life, I'm going to hold you back," he explained.

"No," I stammered. "It doesn't have to be this way. We're just starting to understand one another." Now that I knew of our shared past, I wasn't willing to let him go.

Hunter stopped and turned around to face me. "You said you never wanted to be chained again. I'm not healthy for you, Roe. This thing between us can't go on. It's wrong. I want you to live your life. Experience things. Go to Dallas."

"It doesn't feel wrong," I sobbed. "It feels like it could be very right. We just started, Hunter." My chest constricted with pain. So this was what it felt like. This was the sort of loss my mother was trying to avoid. This was the all-encompassing pain she refused to let dampen her soul. But I wasn't losing Hunter to death, I was losing him by choice. His choice.

Hunter put his duffel down and stalked over to me. As he cupped my cheek, I peered up at his hardened expression, and a steady trail of tears streamed down my cheeks. "You can't do this," I croaked.

"You're releasing me of my debt. I'm releasing you of *me*."

I stood up while protesting. "But I don't want—"

He slammed his lips to mine. I sobbed against him, my skin wet from tears. Our kiss tasted like salt and sadness. I savored the taste of him as he wrapped his arms around me. Neither of us wanted it to end. I curled my body against him. I clawed at his back. I groaned and bit, doing everything I could to keep him with me.

"Don't do this," I pleaded as he ripped off his shirt.

He refused to answer my pleas. I was sure I lacked sex appeal. My skin was probably blotchy with emotions. My lips were dry. My hair a mess of tangles as he ran his hand through them. Within seconds, we were both naked, and I allowed myself to hope. Maybe I could convince him to stay. Maybe we could figure this out. His personality made sense. Hurt people *hurt* people, and Hunter was a boy that never let his damage breathe. My empathy had bloomed into full-blown love, and now that I had Hunter, I wasn't willing to let him go.

"Stay," I whispered when he shoved my panties off.

"Don't leave," I begged when his cock sprung free from his boxers.

"Please don't go," I whimpered when he slid slowly inside of me, stretching me, filling me up with his thick cock as I mourned into his neck.

I breathed in the smell of his woodsy skin as he thrust. I committed the scent to memory. I wasn't disillusioned. I knew what kind of sex this was. I knew that he wasn't promising me forever, he was saying goodbye.

"Come for me, Roe," he grunted. I refused to give in to the sensations flooding me. Because I knew, the moment I did, he would leave. I wanted this to last.

"Look me in the eye," I demanded while reaching up to grab his chin and turn his attention toward my face. Hunter closed his eyes to avoid the pain and sadness leaking from my eyes. "Look at me, Hunter," I pleaded. "It's the least you could do."

Hunter slid out of me and grabbed my hips. In one swift move, he flipped me over until my cheek was on the cool concrete floor. He yanked my ass toward him and slammed into me. I twisted to look back at him, and he pulled my hair. The stinging yank made me moan.

"Please look at me," I begged. "Don't do it like this. Don't break me," I begged. I wanted slow and sensual. I wanted his tenderness. I wanted to feel the invasion of his cock fill me up so I could remember him when he was gone.

"This is why I have to leave, Roe," he rasped. His hands dug into my hips as my body thrashed against the concrete. Each thrust had my cheek grinding into the floor. I could already feel bruises forming from his demanding touches. "I'll only hurt you."

Hunter fucked me relentlessly. Everything was so devastatingly painful. His arduous movements were both a punishment and a lesson. I took every last bit of his relentless, challenging pushes. My heart shriveled up and died on the floor. I broke before him. He came hard and fast, then pulled out, leaving me nothing but a puddle at his feet.

"You'll come back," I croaked as his cum spilled out of my throbbing, unsatisfied cunt. I refused to come for him. I needed this moment.

"I won't," he promised.

"I'll find you," I whispered.

"You won't."

I closed my eyes and focused on my breathing. In and out. In and out. I was naked on the floor, dripping in sweat, cum, and tears. I was completely broken. Damaged. Breathe, breathe, breathe.

A prick pierced my arm, and I shot open my eyes. Thick liquid pushed through a syringe and filled my veins. "No," I cried out as Hunter pulled the needle out. He stared at me with soft, sad eyes full of determination.

I felt the exhaustion hit me. I didn't cry or scream or beg. That was what he wanted, after all. I didn't whisper goodbye. I didn't reach out to hold him as my body grew too heavy. I simply exhaled a promise to myself.

I will find you, Hunter Hammond.

I will find you.

A Lovely Obsession

A lovely obsession.
I'm caught between mourning you and thanking you.
Death tastes like sour milk from my mother's breast.

I taught you how to speak,
how to form truths with the curve of your mouth.
Honesty sounds like footsteps walking away.

I became the hunter *and* the prey.
I'll watch you. I'll find you.
Hope smells like rosewood and rain.

You traded your sanity for a petty debt.
I traded my damage for a full set of lungs.
Redemption feels like trading words for your heart.

I'll still spill poetry at your feet.
And you'll exclaim,
What a lovely confession.

My voice trembled as I read my poem to the crowded auditorium. Mrs. Sellars sat in the front row, beaming up at me with pride. I looked out over the crowd, my eyes grazing over Mack, who was sitting in the back row. There, in the corner, a shadow flickered in and out of view. I held my breath.

No, it wasn't him. It was never him. I had waited and waited and waited. I cried. I screamed at Mack. I didn't understand how he could just leave me like that.

Mack, Joel, and Nicole clapped loudly for me as I exited the stage and made my way to the lobby. I didn't want to sit and listen to the others read their poems. I was too nervous.

It felt good to make it here, but there was one person missing. The success of making it this far in the competition felt hollow. I hadn't felt Hunter's eyes on me in weeks.

"Excuse me, miss?" a voice called from behind. I spun around and faced a flushed man with a rounded stomach as he stumbled toward me. "Are you Roe? Roe Palmer?"

I nodded. "That's me."

"I have a delivery for you. Please sign here." Holding up his clipboard, the man waited eagerly as I took the pen from his grasp and signed my name. "Thank you!" he said before handing me a box and disappearing.

I lifted the lid and gasped at the single rose resting on a pile of tissue paper. There was a gold card perched beside it. I picked it up to read the printed words typed there.

Good Job, Pretty Debt.

A LOVELY
CONFESSION

CORALEE JUNE

Editing by Helayna Trask with Polished Perfection
Cover design by Olivia Pro Design
Book design by Inkstain Design Studio

A LOVELY
CONFESSION

For the broken heart I ripped from my chest and planted in the ground.

Thank you for growing into the oak tree I shade my family with.

Thank you for teaching me that life blooms from broken things.

Chapter 1

ROE

I fucking loved throwing punches. A cool bead of sweat dripped down my chest and onto my bare abs. My muscles ached with each swing of my fist. I had been jabbing at this bag for hours. Throbbing pain shot down my spine and warmed my shoulders. Every tendon was burning from use. I didn't even know what time it was, but I knew it was late enough for club-goers to drunkenly saunter by on the sidewalk outside. Downtown Denver was alive and thriving.

I wasn't just working out, I was feeding my demons.

The twenty-four-hour gym I frequented smelled like sweat and body odor. Vintage motivational posters lined the walls in bright orange frames, and the various workout equipment was worn down from use. The gym was old and small and probably a health hazard, but it was all I could afford on my salary. Working at a local bookstore was fun and allowed me the freedom to write on the job, but it didn't pay very well.

A couple of off-duty night-shift cops I regularly saw here were lifting weights in the corner. They occasionally glanced my way when I grunted, but I didn't care. I had frustrations to work through.

I bounced on my feet. My shins burned. My forearms ached. My jaw throbbed from how hard I was clenching my teeth. I welcomed the pain. Pain made people change.

I started boxing lessons six months after Hunter left. It seemed like the only way to get the anger out. And I had *a lot* of anger. Tonight, I had more anger than usual. I woke up this morning with fury flowing through my veins. I knew what day it was the moment my eyes opened. I had been dreading it all year. I had a lot of reasons to hate October fourth.

It was the day my father died while trying to collect a debt.

It was the day I found my mother's dead body.

It was the day I first spoke to Hunter Hammond.

Five years had passed since he fucked me on the floor of his cabin, drugged me, and disappeared. In many ways, I moved on. I got stronger. Smarter. Independent. I went to community college, then finished my English degree online with University of Phoenix while working at a bookshop—without taking a single dime of Hunter Hammond's money. He'd left me quite a bit of cash laced with his guilt when he vanished, but I wanted nothing to do with it. It still sat in the bank, untouched.

Despite the personal and physical growth I'd managed over the years, I still couldn't shake him. I still looked around corners, hoping to find him watching me. I still stared at the camera on my phone, wondering if he was watching. Every time Mack called me, I still asked if he'd heard from Hunter, and every time I was answered with vacancy. He really was gone.

I licked at the sweat on my upper lip and threw my body into a final punch. The impact boomed and made my entire body vibrate. *It felt fucking good.* Almost better than sex.

Almost.

I gasped for air. My heart was racing, endorphins and pleasure rolling through me. I breathed heavily as I walked over to the bench and unwrapped my hands. The moment my fists were free of the tape, I stretched out my knuckles, uncurling my fingers and watching them shake.

One of the other regulars at the gym passed by me, and we exchanged an exhausted nod of solidarity. I never thought I would be the type of girl to spend all her free time at the gym, but it became a regular part of my routine. I liked to work until I was drenched in sweat and trembling from exhaustion. I liked to run until my lungs felt like they were on fire. This safe haven was a controlled space for working out my demons. The last few years had turned me into quite the masochist.

And when I wasn't purging sweat from my pores, I was looking for *him.*

I could hear my phone ringing in my duffel bag. I already knew who it was. Nicole Knight was determined as hell. I guess that's why we got along so well. You had to be committed to be in any sort of friendship with me. Maybe Hunter's commitment issues were why he left.

I let it ring, not ready to deal with her insistence, but when she started calling again, I reached in my bag and pulled it out with a sigh.

"Hello?" I answered breathlessly.

"Where are you?" she asked in a whine. Her voice was like congested bells. "I thought you'd be home by now. I have a surprise for you." I listened as she let out a squeal. Despite my broody mood, I cracked a smile at her excitement.

"Nicole," I began in exasperation. She knew how I felt about my birthday. "I really hope you aren't planning anything. We've talked about this."

Nicole Knight was my best friend and, aside from Joel, my *only* friend. Getting to know me was like digging with your bare hands through cement, but that woman had claws of steel. She knew about Hunter. About my mother. About my fears. My likes. My dislikes. She probably knew what color my underwear was today simply because she had no personal boundaries and liked to storm into my bedroom while I got ready for the day.

With my free hand, I grabbed a towel and started wiping my face. My hair was drenched. My sports bra clung to my skin like a suction cup. "It's not a birthday party," she explained. "It's a *housewarming* party. I thought we should celebrate the new apartment."

"The apartment we moved into a year and a half ago?" I deadpanned. That sounded like an awfully big loophole, but I wasn't about to argue. Nicole and I had been roommates ever since our high school graduation. We went to Denver Community College together, but she dropped out her sophomore year to become a stripper—and *damn* did she finally catch her parents' attention. They completely cut her off, and she finally accepted that they cared more about their careers than her. She still stripped, and she was pretty good at it, too. Last month Nicole mentioned going back to school for her business degree so she could open a club of her own. She was no longer pretending to be the wild child for her parents' sake. She'd owned up to her sexuality and really found herself.

When I switched to online classes at University of Phoenix, we decided to move closer to the club where she worked. I loved the location.

Rent was pretty much my entire salary at the bookstore where I worked, but we got a very good deal. Nicole promised me that if I was ever short on rent, I could easily make the money up at the club where she worked. I have yet to take her up on that offer, though sometimes when I saw her fat stacks of cash, I considered it.

We didn't live a grand life. We didn't go off to our dream college or leave Colorado. But we made it work. We found adventures in the survival of it all.

"I really hope you didn't invite a lot of people," I said with a sigh. I wasn't in the mood to talk to people. My head had been a very dark place all day. Hunter had been on my mind. I was almost ashamed of myself for still fantasizing about a man I hadn't seen in five years. What was wrong with me? I couldn't help but compulsively think back on our first conversation in the woods. When I closed my eyes, I could still smell his rosewood scent and hear his honey voice.

I'm not going to kiss you. . .

Why not?

Because I'm not some creep preying on high school girls.

I scoffed at the memory. You would think, after all this time, I would've let him go, but I couldn't for some reason.

"Just come home already. It'll be fun," Nicole whined once more. I pictured her stomping her stilettos in our kitchen with her petite arms crossed over her chest. "I have a really awesome surprise that took a lot of planning."

A surprise? That sounded awful. I couldn't stay at the gym forever, though. "Okay. I'll see you in about thirty minutes," I replied before hanging up. I wanted to punch the bags until I passed out, but Nicole would've probably dragged me out of here, kicking and screaming, if I didn't show up soon. That woman had superhuman stripper strength.

Maybe this would be a good thing. Maybe it would be the first step to celebrating my birthday. I could handle a *housewarming* party.

The walk home was short, and like a bad habit, I found myself looking over my shoulder for shadows lurking there. It was wishful thinking to hope that Hunter was following me, *watching me*. And when I took the elevator up to the seventh floor of my building, I stared at the security camera in the corner, daring Hunter to watch me get home.

I was pathetic.

The apartment was surprisingly quiet when I slid my key into the lock and turned the knob. Inside, all the lights were on, and the blinds were open, revealing the Denver city lights. I really did love our apartment. The open floor plan and chic decor was all Nicole's idea. It wasn't cluttered, and the furniture was minimalistic and comfortable. During the day, every inch of space was illuminated with natural light, thanks to the large, sweeping windows.

"Hello?" I said while setting my duffel bag on the kitchen island and rolling my neck. If this was Nicole's idea of a housewarming party, then I was all for it. No one was here.

"Hey there, kid," a gruff voice said from the hallway. I recognized it instantly. *No way.* I spun around and grinned.

"Mack?" My voice shook with disbelief. I was shocked to see him. Mack moved back to New York two years ago, and I hadn't really seen him since. Our relationship was strained at best. I struggled to trust him when I found out he was hired, then hated him when he wouldn't tell me where

Hunter went.

But at the end of the day, he was the only family I had. I still loved him—but at a distance. We spent holidays together when we could, and he called like clockwork every Friday afternoon. Our relationship had evolved to a comfortable dynamic, though sometimes I missed the simplicity from when it was just the two of us in our tiny house. Back before I knew about Hunter. Back before I knew my entire life was an orchestrated attempt at forgetting a debt.

I ran up to him and wrapped him in a big hug. "You smell awful," he choked before pulling away. Nicole's desperate threats to get me home didn't give me much time to shower, so I took a Febreze bath and hoped for the best.

"I was at the gym," I explained sheepishly. Mack wrapped his beefy hand around my wrist and lifted my arm up. With this free hand, he squeezed my bicep and made a low whistle of amazement.

"I wouldn't want to get into a fight with you. You've been toning up," he admired, and I smiled. That was kind of the idea. Over the last five years, I'd somehow found a way to bridge my mother's fear of death with my need to feel free. Instead of conquering those fears by going into hiding, I made myself strong enough to handle whatever came my way. I wouldn't say I felt invincible. But I did feel more capable than before.

"You think I could take you, old man?" I asked teasingly.

"Probably. I'm no spring chicken anymore."

I playfully flexed at him and made a face. He chuckled for a long while, then locked his eyes on the script tattooed on my arm. "When did you get this?"

7

I looked at my forearm and smiled at the script there.

Let your damage breathe.

"Few months ago," I replied with a shrug.

"I remember when I told you that," Mack said in awe. His eyes started to fill with moisture. It was probably the most emotion I've seen from the man in my entire life.

"Guess it stuck with me," I replied.

Mack and I chuckled and caught up for a little bit, though he evaded my questions about what he was up to in New York. I had assumed that he still worked for the Bullets with Hunter, but didn't know for sure. Part of me wanted answers, but I also had experienced firsthand the consequences of getting involved with gang activity. I'd almost died because of it.

Mack complimented our apartment and asked me about work and my writing. The last couple of weeks, I'd been unable to write. My birthday liked to muzzle my muse, turning her into nothing but a whisper, but she would find me again.

"Where's Nicole?" I asked finally.

As if summoned by my question, Nicole came barreling through the front door, carrying a white pastry box. Behind her was Joel. "It's time to party, bitches!" Nicole shouted in greeting. Mack squeezed the bridge of his nose, and I just shook my head while grinning at Joel. Nicole was wearing a mini skirt and black tights with a pink crop top tied at her bellybutton. Her pixie hair was perfectly styled, and her long fake eyelashes cast shadows on her cheeks.

Joel was staring at her ass but quickly remembered that he was living in the friendzone and accordingly dragged his gaze to me. He smiled, his teeth bright and warm. Joel still had those piercing blue eyes but had grown paler since getting a job bartending at a nightclub. We jokingly called him a vampire on occasion.

"Happy birth—*housewarming*," Joel said, correcting himself mid-sentence. Nicole put the box on the kitchen island, then elbowed him in the ribs. Joel and Nicole didn't last very long on the relationship front, but all of us ended up making our weird friendship work. Once the angsty teenage love triangle had worn off, Joel was actually a decent friend to have. He sometimes caught himself flirting, but we were determined to not go down that path. Joel even lived in the same building as us. We would've gotten a three-bedroom, but we decided we didn't want to meet all the girls that Joel liked to bring home every night. He had terrible taste in women—not including us.

He was one of the few people who knew Hunter existed—who witnessed the full story. Sometimes, I'd wondered if those few short weeks were even real. It was nice knowing I wasn't crazy. I had a habit of getting lost in my own head. Joel and Nicole were always the people to pull me back out.

"I got a housewarming cheesecake to celebrate," Nicole said while clapping her hands.

"And I swiped some top-shelf whiskey from the club," Joel added, shrugging.

"I don't even like whiskey," I replied with an eye roll and curled lip of disgust. "I'm more of a boxed wine gal now."

"But *I* like whiskey," Joel teased. "I mean, if it were your *birthday*, I might have gotten you some chardonnay, but since we're only celebrating a *housewarming*, it's BYOB, bitches," Joel replied with a cackle. "Shit," Joel began. "I'm going to go grab some edibles from upstairs. Anyone want some?"

"No, thank you," I replied with a giggle, and at the same time Nicole said, "Hell yes!"

Mack offered to accompany Joel so he could see his video game collection, and they both disappeared out of the front door.

Once they were gone, I hugged Nicole. "How'd you get Mack here?" I asked.

"I called," she replied simplistically. "It wasn't that hard to convince him. I think he'd visit a lot more; he's just waiting for you to invite him."

She was right. Things were just weird between us. I wanted to go back to how we were before, but I didn't know how. I guess Mack didn't know how either.

"I want you to think of a housewarming wish," Nicole said while clapping her hands together. "I won't make you blow out any candles, but you have to tell me what you wish for."

She looked thoroughly proud of herself. "Do *you* get a housewarming wish?" I asked with one eyebrow raised.

"I already got mine. Joel is bringing edibles, remember?"

"Riiiiight," I replied. "Mack being here is my wish."

"Nope. Not good enough. Think of a wish, any wish."

I bit my lip to keep my mouth from forming a name that was banned in our house. Nicole was really adamant that I move on from my obsession. She didn't understand why I was still holding on. How could I possibly explain to her that he was rooted in my past, a shadow that had always been there and always would be? She didn't like how I was always looking up mysterious deaths online, trying to trace them back to a hoodie-wearing assassin. She didn't like that I obsessed over his name. I typed it into Google more times than I could count.

She wasn't outwardly cruel about it. She understood that I had fixated on him for reasons neither of us could explain. She entertained me but didn't encourage me, and I didn't want to ruin our night with the sight of her disappointment.

"I'll have to think about my wish," I lied before wrapping my arms around her. "Thanks again for bringing Mack here."

"Of course. You have a lot of people that love you, Roe. Don't ever forget it," she said into my neck before pulling away.

When Joel and Mack returned, we all settled in the living room to eat *housewarming cheesecake*. Nicole suggested we celebrate the housewarming every year on the same day, and I gave her the side-eye. Even though I still struggled with October fourth, this wasn't so bad. Maybe I could do this in the future.

The night continued in a blur. Within an hour, Joel was laughing at stupid shit and was blazed as hell. Nicole, too. Mack mostly spoke to me, but I noticed him checking his phone numerous times. Every few minutes, I'd catch him with his head dipped and his face twisted in concentration as he typed on the keyboard. He *never* texted. His thumbs were too big to form words, so he avoided doing it completely. I briefly wondered if he was conducting Bullets business, and an idea sparked in my mind.

I knew what my wish was. I never allowed myself to wish before, but this year I just wanted one thing. I just had to convince my very high and super reluctant roommate to help me. Just this one more time.

I wrapped my arm around Nicole and murmured in her ear. "I'm going to go take a shower. Would you mind getting Mack drunk?"

Nicole tipped her head back and laughed loudly, drawing the attention of both Joel and Mack. "So it's that kind of party, huh?" she asked. "I'm so down. I bet Mack is a flirty drunk."

I curled my lip in disgust. "Ew. That's not what I meant." I leaned in closer to whisper in her ear. "I want his phone."

I knew that Mack and Hunter were still in communication with one another. No matter how hard I tried or how much I snooped, Mack would not tell me where he was. I almost ended our relationship over it. Mack was devoted wholly to Hunter, and after a couple of years, I finally accepted that he wouldn't reveal Hunter's location. But my…birthday…had me feeling bold and sentimental. I'd been searching for Hunter the last five years, and maybe tonight I'd finally get a lead.

I pulled away from Nicole, and she gave me a sympathetic look. "Let's get more cheesecake, hmm?" she asked before grabbing my wrist and pulling me toward the kitchen. Joel started talking to Mack about drunk girls at the club. "Are you sure you want to do that? You're finally doing better," she whispered. I knew this was how she would respond. But I had to try anyway.

Nicole had seen the worst of my depression when Hunter left. I explained everything to her, and she held my hand when I cried. She watched me work out until I was puking on the sidewalk. She read all my angsty poems and would come over in the middle of the night with a gallon of ice cream and wine. Ironically, Hunter leaving solidified my friendship with Nicole.

"I just want to try one more time."

"You've searched his cabin," she hissed. "You've checked Mack's computer and his cell phone already. There's nothing left. It's like he didn't exist."

I winced at her words. That was my greatest fear, that I'd imagined it all. My mother had delusions and mental health problems, so it terrified me to think that none of this really happened. He was like a ghost, leaving nothing but a scar from where my arm was broken.

"And don't forget the road trip to Vegas because you thought you overheard Mack on the phone with him," she added. "Or the time I gave that post office worker a blow job so we could check the forwarding address."

I cringed. Hearing it out loud made me sound deranged. "I know."

"I'm sorry," Nicole said. "I just feel bad enabling your heartbreak. You know I'm all for chasing after the people you love. It's how you got stuck with my crazy ass." I cracked a smile, and she continued, "But it's like chasing after someone not there."

"I'll stop after this," I lied. I didn't think I'd ever stop chasing after him.

"You said that last time," she countered.

"I promise. It's my...*our* housewarming. It's time for a new beginning. You wanted my wish, and this is it. I want his cell phone."

Nicole squinted her eyes and gnawed on her lip anxiously. We both turned to look at Mack, who was joking about car parts with Joel. "Okay," she agreed in a whisper. "But next year, I get to sing you happy birthday."

I swallowed. That song gave me panic attacks, but I needed her help if I wanted to get my hands on Mack's phone. If I tried getting him drunk, he'd be suspicious. He guarded his phone and secret involvement with the Bullets like it was a precious diamond.

"Deal," I replied hesitantly. "I'm going to shower," I then called over to the group.

"Thank God," Joel teased.

Nicole gave me a halfhearted smile, despite her reservations about the pipe dream obsession of mine. She wanted me to let Hunter go.

A moment of indecision crossed her features before she fist-pumped the air. "Let's do shots!" she screamed, and Joel cheered with her.

I slipped down the hallway and disappeared into the bathroom with the sound of Mack reluctantly agreeing to have a shot ringing in my ears.

———

WITHIN TWO HOURS, Nicole was handing me Mack's cell phone. She even managed to figure out his passcode from watching him unlock it throughout the night. I was impressed. My girl was a damn hustler. "With great power comes great responsibility," she slurred while sashaying over to the couch and sitting on Joel's lap. She had matched Mack drink for drink and was about two seconds from passing out. Edibles and whiskey were a bad combination, and she was cross faded as fuck.

It seemed almost *too* easy. My mother's age-old warnings about things being too good to be true made my stomach twist. If I thought too long, I'd convince myself that Mack *wanted* me to find Hunter. That this was some predestined link to draw us back together. My brain liked to imagine perfect scenarios where this was all just a giant misunderstanding. I liked to pretend that he wanted me just as much as I wanted him.

I stared at the phone as I padded down the hallway and made my way over to my bedroom. Even though Nicole was concerned with my obsession, it didn't even scratch the surface of all I wanted to do. I should have tried harder over the years. Hunter disappeared without a trace, but Mack still tethered us in a way.

Then again, part of me wanted to see if I could move on. Part of me wanted to get over him. But it'd been five years and still I woke up thinking about what he was doing. Where he was.

Who he was with.

I clicked on the message icon and started scrolling, noticing that most of his messages were weird collections of words from contacts named Cousin Joe, Mom, and Dad. It seemed like some weird code for gang activity, and I wanted nothing to do with it. I kept scrolling until I found a message from earlier today. The contact was listed under the letter H, and my gut told me that it was Hunter.

I wanted to be greedy and scroll through previous messages, but this was the only one. I wasn't sure if Mack deleted them as he got them or if Hunter only checked in once.

H: How is Roe doing?

Mack: Fine.

I wasn't sure if Mack kept things short out of loyalty to me or because he didn't want any details on his phone. Either way, I felt proud of Mack for not divulging any updates about my life in the text. If Hunter wanted to know how I was doing, he was more than capable of reaching out to me.

I debated on texting him. My fingers hovered over the keyboard for a moment. I was so fucking close. I'd built him up so much in my mind that I didn't know if the reality of talking to Hunter again would meet my drawn-out expectations. I once read that when we deny our emotions, they owned us. Maybe that's why I felt completely and totally owned by Hunter Hammond. The world wanted me to move on and forget he ever existed. I tried pushing down my obsession and ignoring the ache in my chest, but I only felt better when I gave in to the compulsion to chase him.

I started typing.

Hello.

How are you?

Why the fuck did you leave?

When are you coming back?

None of my questions or texts felt right. There was an emptiness about them that wasn't enough.

And then, as a last-minute impulse, I decided to call him instead.

As the phone rang, my breathing became labored. The sense of panic ricocheted behind my rib cage. What if he answered? What would I say? Why did I do this? I should hang up. As the shrill tone of the phone rang against my skull, I felt all the shadows of our past creep up my spine and burrow deep inside of my skin.

"Hello?" his honey voice answered casually as if this were just another call. As if my happiness weren't hanging by his greeting. I felt starved and full at the same time. My legs became weak, and I sat down on my bed while clutching the phone like it was a lifeline. His voice. I'd heard his actual voice.

"Mack? How was the deal at The Velvet Lounge? Gavriel give you a hard time?" he asked with a chuckle over a crowd. Wherever Hunter was, it was loud. I could hear a woman's voice in the background. My heart shattered at her sweet tone. I couldn't make out what she was saying, but he told her to hold on just a second, and my breath stalled. "Sorry, it's loud here."

I forced my lips to move, but no sound came out. I felt so ridiculous, listening to him on the other end of the line. I had him, but I couldn't even say all the things I wanted to.

"Mack? Are you there?" he said again. This time, his tone had turned serious. Pretty soon he'd know who he was speaking to. Hunter had a sixth sense about me—or at least he used to.

Nothing. I said nothing. I just wanted to hear him talk.

Eventually, the background noise faded, and I listened to him take steps somewhere. Neither of us spoke as another minute ticked by.

"Roe?" he whispered.

I sucked in a deep breath and exhaled before responding. "Hey, Stalker," I replied. I wanted my voice to sound cool and confident, but I choked on practically every syllable.

"Roe," he sighed. God, I wanted to hear him say my name again. I wanted him to whisper it over my heated skin. I wanted him to scream it until his throat was raw.

"Where are you?" I blurted out, not sure what else to say. "Actually, forget I asked that. I know you're not going to answer. I don't even know why I called you. I guess I like to suffer on my birthday."

"You shouldn't have called," he replied. I couldn't tell if he was angry or not. I tried not to imagine the longing in his tone, but there was a soft

17

and tender quality to it that made me wonder.

"Mack is here," I offered conversationally. "I stole his phone."

"Of course you did. Roe, why are you calling?"

I swallowed and debated on my answer. The truth felt too crazy. I'd become the stalker in our dynamic. It was a hard pill to swallow. "I miss you. Do you miss me?" I asked, praying I didn't sound as insane as I felt.

He didn't answer. We both let the clock tick by. I wasn't sure how much time had passed. Minutes stretched, and we just breathed together. We opened our lungs and let the damage of our past bleed out. "I hope you're okay, wherever you are," I finally whispered. "I'm going to find you, Hunter," I promised. Hearing his voice had ignited a fierce need within me. I felt so fucking close and so far all at once. I craved more. "I'm going to find you," I said again, this time my voice was sterner. I clenched my fist and punched the top of my thigh, smiling at the spike of pain produced there by my hit.

"For both our sakes, I hope you don't," Hunter replied. "Don't call me again."

Hunter hung up the phone, and I stared at the screen in disbelief.

I dialed his number again.

And again.

And again.

Each time, it went directly to voicemail.

I dropped Mack's phone on the floor and stood up. I walked over to my mirror and stared at my reflection, willing the tears building in my eyes to stay away. I wouldn't cry over Hunter Hammond. Not anymore. I was a woman of action now.

I hope you don't. . .

It sounded like a challenge and regret all rolled into one punch of a statement.

Or maybe he said, *I hope you do. . .*

I replayed the conversation in my head, feeling giddy and on edge. He'd said my name. He thought I was Mack.

What had he said? The Velvet Lounge.

I quickly looked up The Velvet Lounge in New York on my phone, my fingers flying across the keyboard as my eyes scanned the search results. Nothing came up. I gritted my teeth and tried not to get discouraged. I refused to lose a lead. A forum on Redditt caught my eye, and I found a thread discussing a voyeur club called The Velvet Lounge recently purchased by someone called Blaise Bennett. It took some digging, but after three subthreads and a quick chat with a sex addict, I had an address.

I had an address.

It took me fourteen minutes to find a flight. Though I vowed never to use the money Hunter left me, I figured a red-eye to New York was reasonable. I scribbled a note to Nicole, Mack, and Joel. They'd be worried about me, and I'd have hell to pay when I got back, but I was acting purely on impulse. Speaking to Hunter had turned me into the reckless teen he'd abandoned.

I didn't know how to explain what I was doing. I knew it was crazy, but nothing about Hunter and me was ever normal. So I kept it simple.

I'll be back in a few days. Thanks for the housewarming,

Roe.

Chapter 2

The gun in my backpack felt heavy and unfamiliar. I couldn't stop thinking about it. My mind was focused on the deadly weapon I was carrying. I was wholly consumed with the danger of it. I also ached to know how Hunter felt about holding the difference between life and death by the threat of a trigger. I wasn't prepared to hold the cool metal in my palm and aim it at someone. I'd been conditioned to have a sense of reverence for life, and you didn't buy a revolver from a pawnshop if you didn't intend to use it.

My impulsive recklessness probably should have terrified me, but I just didn't care anymore. With this gun, I was one step closer to becoming what I feared most about Hunter.

The street was almost empty. I walked along the damp concrete, dragging my high-heeled boots as dread and anticipation fought for dominance in my gut. What I was doing went against every cell in my body. Self-preservation was a thing of the past, I'd completely given myself over to reckless hope.

Obsessions had a funny way of twisting your thoughts and making you feel sane. You gave yourself little allowances.

I'll only search his name *once*.

I'll only go to the cabin *one more time*.

I'll cross the country to track down the gang he worked for *once*.

Once. Once. Once.

I'd been lying to myself since he left. I was stuck in a repetitive cycle of seeking him out.

All those little moments of weakness added up fast, and before you knew it, you were walking down the streets of New York with a gun in your backpack.

The streetlamps above me were flickering. It didn't take a lifetime of being aware of my surroundings for me to surmise that I wasn't in a safe neighborhood. Everything looked run down. Bars covered the windows. Rats scurried by, and trash littered the sidewalk. Sex workers pushing needles into their arms eyed me with resentment as if daring me to judge them. I didn't. Life had a habit of testing how far you'd go to survive, and my addiction was far less accessible.

They wanted drugs; I craved a man. A ghost.

I was willing to compromise my sanity and morals to get him, too.

I turned a corner and grimaced when I saw shadows dancing along the grimy red brick towering on either side of me. My heart raced, my mind was reminding me how ridiculous this was, but I felt like there was no other way.

All this freedom Hunter Hammond was determined to give me with his distance felt a lot like suffocation. I'd vowed to find the man that stole a part of me, then disappeared. Maybe the loss made me crazy.

I left my phone at the motel. Nicole, Mack, and Joel had been calling me nonstop since I landed. I knew it wouldn't take them long to find me. Mack probably saw who I called and guessed that I was spiraling. Mack would easily track down my credit cards and be at my doorstep within twenty-four hours at the most, which was why I needed to work fast and keep moving.

I traveled down the walkway, clutching the straps of my backpack as I traveled. My eyes slid side to side as I watched my surroundings. I knew there were eyes on my back; I could feel them burning into my skull. To someone that didn't know where they were, it looked like any normal creepy alleyway. But I saw the shadowed cameras perched overhead and the large man staring at me from a window on my left.

Beneath my trench coat, I'd dressed the part. I wore a lingerie corset and fishnet stockings. My hair was curled down my back, and my thigh high boots clicked on the pavement. Every forum I could find said that The Velvet Lounge was a sex club, specifically for voyeurs. I wasn't sure what I would find on the inside, but I hoped for answers.

At the end of the street, there was a large door with chipped, forest green paint. Based on what my research had told me, I'd have to knock and give a passcode. I'd been rolling the odd phrase over my tongue since learning it, wondering if my contact was fucking with me.

Sunshine Fever.

I lifted my fist to knock but froze. Staring at my trembling hand, I willed my body to move.

"You looking for someone?" a playful voice said at my back. My shoulders tensed, and I dropped my hand before whirling around. I curled both my hands into fists and raised them up to block my face. I then dipped into a ready stance, flexing my muscles and tossing my intruder a stern look. I moved purely on instinct. I guess I didn't need the gun. The last five years had transformed me into my own weapon.

The man standing there surprised me. Despite the dark sky, he was wearing aviators and a smile. His reddish-brown hair glowed under a flickering street light. He wore jeans and boots paired with a tight band shirt. Although he was blatantly smirking at me, there was an obvious mischievousness I couldn't quite place. He didn't look threatening, but he didn't look nice, either.

"I'm here to speak with the Bullet boss, Gavriel Moretti," I said, surprising myself when my voice remained steady. My heart was pounding so hard that I had to force myself not to grab my chest. "I heard he frequented this club."

The strange man laughed. "You won't find him here." He nodded up at the building for emphasis. "Gavriel doesn't really like a show. He prefers to control."

I didn't know much about Gavriel, but the strange man snorted at his own joke before taking his sunglasses off and looking me up and down. It was a curious perusal that lacked any heat, so I allowed myself to drop by fists—but not my guard.

"So he's not here?" I asked.

"Nope. He just funds the place as a gift to my wife and me," he explained. "I'm Blaise Bennett." My mouth dropped open in shock. This guy with his ripped jeans and cotton shirt owned this club? My guard instantly went up even higher. What kind of man owned a sex club? Was he dangerous? Should I be worried?

I slumped in defeat. This was my only lead. When I found out Gavriel ran the Bullets, I knew in my gut that he could lead me to Hunter. But if I couldn't speak to him, I had no hope. It wasn't like crime bosses had secretaries to leave a message with.

"Why do you want to speak with Gavriel?" he asked. I noted the familiarity in his tone. Gavriel Moretti was the sort of man worthy of announcing his first and last name. He was the kind of entity people feared. "And don't tell me some bullshit like you're pregnant and he's the father. I know for a fact that's not true, so you won't be getting no damn check."

Was that something that happened often with these people? I shook my head. "I'm not pregnant. I don't even know him. I need his help," I replied.

The man furrowed his brow. "What's your name?"

"Roe Palmer."

"What do you need Gavriel's help for, Roe Palmer?" he asked while taking another step closer. I gripped my backpack, and his eyes flickered to my stronghold on the black straps. I noted how his posture turned stiff. This was the sort of man trained to read a room. He was probably already thinking of ways to disarm me.

"I need his help in finding someone. An old...friend," I explained. Friend wasn't an accurate term for what Hunter and I were, but I didn't know how else to explain us. Fuck buddy? Enemies? "Hunter Hammond, do you know him?"

Blaise's eyebrows lifted in surprise. "You're friends with Hunter? The Assassin? I didn't think he did *friendships*. He just kind of kills, then disappears for a while. The man is creepy as fuck," Blaise replied.

"I guess who doesn't kill you makes you stronger," I replied with a tight smile. It also gave you a lot of unhealthy coping mechanisms and an extremely dark sense of humor. "Do you know where he is?

"That's classified. Only Gavriel knows his location."

"Of course," I replied with an eye roll. This Gavriel person seemed to control everything. He kept his cards close to his chest, likely for good reason.

Blaise pressed his tongue against the inside of his cheek, making it bow out as he thought about my words. "I happen to know Gavriel Moretti. Hell, I've known him my whole life practically. If you want to chat with him, I can take you there. But I have to know something first," he said.

Though his words and demeanor felt casual, there was an underlying sense of loyalty in his tone. I wasn't sure if I could trust this man, but I was desperate. Every year that passed put more and more distance between Hunter and me. I just needed to see him one more time. I needed closure. Our conversation had changed me. I craved more.

"Go on and ask," I barked.

"Why do you need to find Hunter? Don't spit some bullshit that you're just friends, 'cause I can see the lovesick in your eyes. Admit you love him, and I'll take you there."

"I love him," I snapped. I blurted those words quickly and easily. "I'll do anything to find him." I probably shouldn't have told him that, but my words didn't really matter. This man could probably feel the desperation rolling off of me. I reeked of it.

Blaise nodded, mulling over my declaration for a long moment as I stood there in the alleyway. I wrapped my jacket tighter around my small body. I couldn't remember the last time I ate. The moment my flight landed, I found a motel and made my manic plans. I bought a gun and my costume, and lost myself in the determination of it all.

"Well, you're in luck, Roe," Blaise said with a grin. "Not only am I a hopeless romantic, but I'm damn good at finding people."

"Is that so?" I asked. His cockiness made me want to laugh. I felt relieved, too. Maybe he could help me. Maybe I'd finally track down Hunter and be able to let him go.

"It is. I'm about to go to a family dinner. Do you want to join me? I can have the missus set out an extra plate for you."

"That's nice, but I really need to speak to Gavriel—" I began, but Blaise cut off my words with a laugh.

"He'll be there. Sunshine would kick his ass if he bailed," Blaise replied. Sunshine? Who was that? "Besides, you look hungry. I bet you haven't had a good meal in ages. Let's get this sorted out."

He turned around, not bothering to give me a chance to decline or run. He just started walking toward the street and whistling. He knew I wouldn't pass on the opportunity to meet Gavriel. I looked around for a moment and debated running off in the opposite direction.

But Blaise just continued whistling, and I took one step toward him. And then another. And then another. Hope moved me forward, and I clutched my backpack as I went.

Chapter 3

ROE

"**W**ere you hoping to defend yourself with this piece of shit?" a gruff voice at my back asked with a chuckle. I squeezed my eyes shut and gnawed on my lip. The moment I walked through the door with Blaise, a team of security stopped me and patted me down. They were efficiently intrusive, making sure to strip me of my jacket and sweep their beefy hands over my corset to check for a wire or weapons. When they found the gun, a group of them laughed.

"Is something wrong with my gun?" I asked as he tossed it back in my backpack.

"Nothing's wrong. You just forgot the bullets," the tall, muscular man replied with another laugh. I tilted my chin, looking up at him defiantly as he thrust my backpack into my chest.

I had bullets; I just didn't load them into my revolver. I was worried the gun would go off accidentally. I wasn't pretending to be the best at this.

I was more of a boxer, not a shooter.

I curled my hand into a fist and gave him a scathing look. "I don't really need a gun to get the job done," I threatened. The man who patted me down raised his hands in mock surrender and smiled at me.

"You really were dressed for The Velvet Lounge," Blaise said with a teasing laugh. I blushed, even though he kept his eyes respectfully up and away from my chest and long legs. Surprisingly, the club owner didn't give me any creeper vibes. If anything, he talked about his wife the entire ride here. Wrapping my jacket tight around my body, I wished I would have had the foresight to pack clothes with more coverage.

"I was determined to find answers," I replied with a simple shrug. It was completely out of character for me, but I haven't been myself for years.

"You're about Sunshine's size. I'll go steal some clothes of hers while you chat with Gav." I hoped Sunshine was the type to prioritize comfort over style.

I told Blaise thank you, and the guards led me down a long hallway and into a large sitting area where the original Bullet was waiting for me. I knew who Gavriel Moretti was the moment I saw him. He was perched in a leather wingback chair by the fireplace. He sat tall and proud, but there was an easy and cocky air about him that gave off a leisurely vibe. For someone that quite literally ran the world, he was completely at ease. He was quiet— too quiet. He seemed like the type to sit and observe for hours on end.

My eyes swept over him, lingering at the scars on his hands, neck, and cheek. "Roe Palmer," his smoky voice greeted. "I was wondering how long it would take you to find me."

My eyes widened in surprise. I wasn't expecting Gavriel to know who I was. His face turned smug like he was pleased to catch me off guard. Even though I wanted to ask him how he knew my name or why I was here, I didn't give him the satisfaction. "I want to know where Hunter is," I said. My voice trembled over Hunter's name. I hadn't really been able to say it out loud since he left. As a poet, I understood the power of words. They could transform a person's entire identity and sense of self. But before he left, I didn't realize the power of a name. It could punch you in the gut with a single murmur. The harmless collection of letters and sounds could bring tears to your eyes and make flashes of memories transcend your mind.

Gavriel nodded in approval. "I like it when my associates are direct. No sense in exchanging small talk when we're both here for a reason." I didn't like that he loosely called me an associate.

"I don't work for you," I said. I wanted to make my intentions very clear. Gavriel smiled. His white teeth glistened, and I stared at the sharp points of his incisors. This man was all predator. I thought Hunter was dangerous, but if this room were a pack of wolves, he would be the alpha.

Gavriel slowly stood up. I watched every movement and noted how his face flashed with a wince. "On the contrary," he began while walking over to the fireplace. He stared at the dancing flames for a moment before continuing. "Technically speaking, I've practically funded your entire life. Mack is on my payroll, and Hunter *was*," he explained before looking at me.

What did he mean by *was*?

"Doesn't Hunter still work for you?" I asked.

"We'll get to that in a moment. But first, I want to be very clear with you. You *are* an associate of mine. An employee. There's no interview. No choice. You proved to be brave enough to come to my house, so these are the consequences. And if you go down this road—if you reach out to Hunter—your entire life will be tied to the Bullets. I suggest you think that over before I give you an answer."

I swallowed and nervously grabbed at the strap of my backpack once more. It was starting to become a tic of mine. I guess I thrived on the idea of protection. "I really just want to know where he is," I said. My voice wavered once more, and I felt ashamed for showing so much weakness in front of this powerful man. Gavriel spun around from the fireplace and took slow, steady steps toward me. Once he was about a foot away, he crossed his arms over his chest and glared at me.

"Why do you want to see him?"

"Many reasons," I began with a shrug. "At first, I convinced myself it was for closure, but...I just feel like I can't believe he's done with me until I get answers."

Gavriel nodded, his eyes soft and the snarl on his lips relaxed. It was like he could relate. "Let's have dinner, Roe. My wife is trying a new recipe, so please keep your face neutral if it tastes like shit."

His wife? I thought Blaise's wife was cooking. I let the hint of the smile escape. "I lived with Mack for ten years. I can handle some bad cooking."

After changing into some yoga pants and an oversized shirt, the guards led me to a dining room that hosted a long mahogany table with sixteen chairs. I was thankful to be out of my lingerie and in something comfortable, especially since I was about to meet Gavriel's wife.

Naturally, the broody mob boss sat at the head of the table. He motioned for me to sit in the chair to his right, so I settled there, trying to ignore the beady stares of the guards surrounding us. They were lined along each wall, looking on with dull, protective interest. I wondered what it was like to have my entire life watched by security, then remembered that I *had* been watched. Hunter was always there; he was just less visible than these guards.

Blaise reappeared with a new hickey on his neck. His rusty hair was mussed and wild, like he'd just had a quickie. He tossed me a wink before sitting down two seats from my right. Another man with blond hair entered the room. He whispered something in Gavriel's ear that I couldn't hear, then straightened to address me.

"Hello, I'm Callum. It's a pleasure to meet you," he said politely while thrusting his hand out for me to shake. I took it and smiled amicably. He looked clean and polished and refined. Like the boy next door who somehow got wrapped up in the crime industry.

Lastly, a man with his head shaved and muscles that looked like he could snap my neck with a simple flick of his wrist strolled into the dining room. "Ryker, we have a guest," Gavriel said to the new man.

He nodded at me without saying a word, then sat down. He seemed like the silent, intimidating type, and I was perfectly fine with not speaking to him.

I felt anxious, surrounded by all of these men. They gave me polite nods of acknowledgment, but none of them seemed to care that I was there. It wasn't until a woman with raven black hair and tattoos up and down her arm entered the room carrying a platter, that their entire demeanors shifted. It was like sunlight decided to glow in the room. Callum shot up from his seat and went to grab the platter from her, kissing her on the cheek. Gavriel bit his lip. Ryker slowly got up and sauntered over to her before wrapping her up in a big hug. Blaise just rubbed at the hickey on his neck while licking his lips.

"Hi, I'm Sunshine," the woman said. I got out of my seat to shake her hand, but she wrapped me up in a hug, instead.

I was surprised by her strength. Her hug nearly cracked my back. "Blaise told me all about you. I hope we can find who you're looking for. I know what it's like to be separated from people you care about." I gave her a polite nod, then sat down. I wasn't really good at making connections with people, and I felt completely out of my element. If you had told me three hours ago that I would have dinner at a crime boss's house, surrounded by large men and a surprisingly kind woman, I would've laughed.

"So who are you looking for?" the muscular one asked. I think his name was Ryker.

I let out a sigh as Sunshine grabbed scoops of her casserole and plopped it on the fine china in front of me. It looked like noodles and melted cheese that was somehow both uncooked and curdled. "Hunter Hammond. He's an assassin for the Bullets. He left me five years ago, and I've been searching for him ever since. This is admittedly the closest I've gotten," I whispered.

At Hunter's name, the men at the table exchanged dark looks. I knew immediately that they knew something about Hunter. Callum spoke to Sunshine. "Sunshine? Would you mind—"

"Yeah, I'm not gonna run off while you guys have a serious conversation," she interrupted. "Go on. Tell us all the ominous things about Hunter Hammond."

I smiled. I liked her.

Blaise was too busy stuffing his face to contribute to the conversation, but Ryker dove right in after exchanging a meaningful look with Gavriel. "Hunter is somewhat of a lone Bullet. He's been on our payroll since he was eighteen but has his own thing going on."

"I know what he does. He's an assassin," I said. I'd had five years to come to terms with his career. It didn't make sense to me, and it completely contradicted my respect for life. But it's who he was.

Gavriel's brow furrowed. "He told you?"

"The night before he left," I explained.

I took a bite of the food and fixed my face into a neutral expression like Gavriel instructed. It wasn't terrible, but it wasn't quite edible, either. I turned to look at Sunshine and smiled encouragingly.

"Five years ago, Hunter Hammond stopped accepting my calls. We assumed he had died, but he wasn't good enough at clearing his tracks. He currently lives in the middle of nowhere by himself. I could give you the coordinates to his house, but I want something in return. I've let him mope for long enough; it's time to get back to work."

Hunter quit? That didn't make sense. From what I heard, he knew what Mack was up to. "He still talks to Mack," I said while squinting my eyes. "And you're saying he doesn't work for you anymore?" That didn't make sense. What if he didn't want to be an assassin? What if he realized it's not what his life was anymore? Even though we were having a pleasant dinner, I wasn't convinced that this job was easy. It was dangerous. Part of me wanted to think that Hunter left because of me, but maybe there was more.

"Mack and he have always had a unique relationship. I'm not surprised they've kept in touch. Speaking of, Mack will probably be here by tomorrow.

You'll want to leave tonight if you don't want to deal with him. I've always thought he was overprotective," Gavriel replied.

"I like Mack. He's a big ol' teddy bear," Sunshine said with a smile. It was weird knowing that Mack had this entire separate life from me. In some ways, I was happy to have a glimpse at who he spent his time with while in New York.

"Are you going to tell Mack what I'm up to?" I asked. I felt like a scolded child.

"If you're here, he already knows," Blaise teased. I didn't want Mack to interfere. I was ready to find Hunter once and for all, and no one was going to stop me.

"So you want me to bring Hunter back? What does that even mean?" I asked.

"It means I'll tell you where he is if you promise to bring him back to the Bullets where he belongs. He's the best in the business. No one compares. It's serendipitous that you showed up. I've had quite the problem that requires his expertise."

I opened and closed my mouth, debating on what to say. I needed to know where Hunter was. I craved those coordinates like it was my last breath. But how could I convince Hunter to come back? I couldn't even convince him to stay with me. "I don't think he'll listen to me. And if you know where he is, why not drag him back yourself?"

"Family is a choice," Callum said. My eyes snapped to the blond man in a sharp suit, but he wasn't looking at me. He was exchanging a meaningful stare with Sunshine.

Gavriel nodded. "I want Hunter back in the fold on his terms. Family is a choice, and I think you can convince him to come back. I could threaten him, but his loyalty would be skewed."

"And what if I can't bring him back?" I asked. "He left me in the first place. I'm not convinced he'll even want to see me. He could slam the door in my face."

At this, Gavriel tipped his head back and let out a smoky laugh. His dark chuckles made everyone in the room pause. "Hunter and I are very much alike," Gavriel said before looking at Sunshine. "If you show up on his doorstep, he'll come back."

"And if he doesn't?"

"Then I'll find other methods of persuasion. I'm not a fan of buying loyalty with threats, but I'm motivated enough to do whatever is necessary to get him back on the job," Gavriel snapped irritably before picking up his glass of water and taking a steady gulp.

Sunshine rolled her eyes. "Can we please stop talking business at the table?"

"Sure, Baby," Callum said with a wink. Based on how she interacted with each of the guys here, I couldn't quite pinpoint the dynamic of all of their relationships. Both Gavriel and Blaise said their wife was cooking dinner, but the only woman I saw was Sunshine.

"Thank you," she sang.

The rest of the dinner went by without dramatics. Ryker, who I found out was a professional-fighter-turned-coach, discussed his latest training with me. He even said, if I was ever back in New York, to stop by his gym. Blaise, a bounty hunter, talked about going camping next weekend and invited Sunshine with him. Occasionally, guards would whisper something in Gavriel's ear, but for the most part, he stayed silent and watched on. Callum ate every bite of the disgusting pasta and even asked for seconds. Sunshine bloomed at his request. My food felt like bricks in my stomach. I just wanted to get the information and get out of there.

Once everything was cleaned up and it was time to go, Gavriel asked me to go to his office with him. Sunshine told me goodbye and said I was welcome over anytime. Even though I really liked her, I seriously hoped I wouldn't be back here for a long while. She seemed nice enough, but this was a life I wasn't sure I wanted for myself.

On the surface, it wasn't the deadly encounter I envisioned when thinking about the mob. But there were dark undertones in everything they did. There was a heaviness about all of them. It was like they each were weighed down by responsibility and history I couldn't even begin to understand.

But I would do anything to find Hunter again. Even if it meant a deal with the devil.

Gavriel's office was masculine and dark. His large desk was organized, with neatly stacked papers everywhere. He looked like the CEO of a Fortune 500 company and not the head of the snake. He grabbed a sticky note and started writing something down on it. I held my breath in anticipation. Whatever he wrote down would lead me to the man that left me all those years ago.

"It's a fairly remote town. He won't make this easy on you, you know," he said before handing me the paper. I snatched it out of his grip greedily, then apologized with my eyes. Gavriel continued to speak as I looked down at the scribbles he wrote down. "Good luck."

"Why do you want me to bring him back? What if he doesn't want to be a killer? What if he realized that that's not who he was?" I hoped that I didn't offend Gavriel, but I wanted to make sure that I was doing this for the right reasons.

"Once a killer, always a killer, Roe. People change, I won't deny that. But some things are undeniable. I have this theory, would you like to hear it?" he asked before circling his desk and sitting down in the plush leather chair.

"Yes," I said.

"If you want to win him back, embrace who he is. Something tells me Hunter left because he didn't feel good enough for you. That man has guilt buried so deep inside that it's become part of his marrow. Show him how you feel."

I nodded. "I'll do my best," I said. I wasn't expecting relationship advice from a mob boss.

"Good. Bring him home, Roe," Gavriel replied with a wave of his hand, effectively dismissing me.

Chapter 4

ROE

Joshua Tree, California, was a hippie's paradise in the middle of the mountainous desert. A single strip of shops and restaurants greeted me as I drove down the winding highway. Vintage resale boutiques, with their doors painted turquoise and fur coats in their shop windows, passed by. The eclectic town both blended into the desert landscape and stood out. I smiled at the lavender Volkswagen bus parked on the side of the road.

The sky was a hazy shade of pink as the sun dipped behind the mountains, casting a glow on the sand on both sides of the highway. I clutched the steering wheel of my rental car as I followed my GPS onto a sandy road lined with cacti and Joshua trees. The moment I left Gavriel Moretti's home, I took a taxi to the airport and got on the first flight to LA. I landed four hours ago and drove here.

I was exhausted and burnt out. I was afraid that if I didn't chase this opportunity now, it would slip from my fingers. I had this ridiculous, chronic fear of Hunter escaping me again.

As I drove through town, I couldn't help but wonder what drew Hunter here. Was it the seclusion? The pink sky as the sun set behind the mountains? The air was dry and a bit chilled, but nothing like Denver. I barely had any cell service out here. It seemed like the type of place you'd escape to if you wanted to forget your responsibilities and sense of time.

Or if you wanted your responsibilities to forget you.

I accelerated, traveling down more winding roads as the night sky shrouded me in darkness. The sunset was swift and beautiful, and once the sun had completely disappeared, my headlights could barely make out what was in front of me.

I felt a crazy sort of courage. A terrifying sort of tenderness. The further I drove, the more my heart panged. It's like I could *feel* his nearness. My GPS pinged that I was at my destination, then off in the distance, I noticed a small silver airstream parked alone in the desert.

Fuck. This was it.

The RV was so quintessentially Hunter. Lonely. Picturesque. Mysterious. It *felt* like him. Not to mention, we were so far out from civilization that no one could hear you scream. Gavriel said he'd quit, but I couldn't help but wonder how many bodies were burned and buried out here.

I got out of the car and slammed the door. My sneakers kicked up sand as I walked. I probably looked like a mess. After sleeping at the airport and traveling all day, my long hair was a tangled clusterfuck, and my wrinkled clothes smelled like airplane food. I quickly thought about the last time he saw me. My hips were wider now. My hair longer. My mind clearer.

I was obsessed now, too.

Using my phone as a flashlight, I walked up to the airstream with my heart pounding in my chest. I could have poked a hole through my lip with how intently I was gnawing on it. A million questions circled my mind:

Why did you leave?

Where have you been?

Do you remember me?

Do you still care?

Now that I was close, I didn't know what I would even say. The entire trip here, I was so busy thinking about finally finding him that I didn't practice the words I'd use once seeing him.

I tried to come up with something to say as my steps slowed.

Hello, Hunter. Miss me?

Hey, fucker. Why'd you leave?

Hunter Hammond, you are *going* to fucking talk to me.

At the door, I didn't hesitate. I knocked the moment my knuckles were close enough, pounding my fist against the metal with all the anger I could muster.

I waited for an answer while listening for movement in the camper.

Nothing.

I knocked again.

Nothing.

I circled the camper while looking for a car, still using my cell phone flashlight so I could inspect the area. Fresh tracks in the sand showed that someone drove here often, but my confidence was slipping. What if Hunter didn't live here? What if Gavriel had it wrong? What if I drove all the way out here just to find out that Hunter Hammond was one step ahead of me. What if he left?

It made sense. I had a feeling it was the sort of thing he would do.

I stared at my rental car, debating on driving back to the first major city I could find and booking a hotel room for the night. But I didn't want to wait there.

A coyote howled, and a shiver traveled up my spine. Spotting a lawn chair by the airstream, I walked over to it in defeat. Hunter wasn't here. I wasn't even sure if he ever was. *Maybe it was time to give up?* I thought while plopping down in the chair.

Cold tears streamed down my cheeks, and I wiped at them in anger. Why was I being like this? Why was I so desperate to find him? I should have just let him go. I just didn't understand why I'd developed such an obsession with someone that didn't want me back.

I closed my eyes and let the night air wrap me up in a hug. It was dark and creepy, my loneliness amplified by the still desert. But above me, the stars were the brightest I'd ever seen. They sparkled with hope and infinite possibilities.

As I stared, I whispered into the wind, hoping the mountains would carry my plea to wherever Hunter was.

"Where are you?"

A TRUCK DRIVING up the road woke me. I didn't know what time it was, but the moon was high in the sky and there was a hint of light kissing the outline of the mountains in the distance. I licked my dry lips and sat up straighter in my seat, not sure what to do or who this was. I still didn't know if this was Hunter's place. It was probably really dangerous to stay here. Luckily, I was hidden completely in darkness when the truck pulled to a stop and turned off.

A sense of awareness flooded me. I'd always known Hunter to drive a Jeep, but the truck felt like him. It was hard to see in the dark, but the headlights illuminated it just enough to see the electric blue paint, the same as his Jeep. It was rustic and lifted. I bit the inside of my cheek to hold back a smile. It was him. I knew it was him. I uncrossed my legs, nervously prepared to stand and say hello, but my elation plummeted when I heard a feminine giggle as two bodies got out of the truck.

I could barely see them, but I heard her voice clear as a bell.

"Fuck me against your truck, Hunter," she slurred.

I knew what I'd heard, but it took a long, staggering moment for it to sink in. I had to clutch my chest to stop the pain from making me cry out. I was a foolish girl. Of course he was seeing someone now. I probably looked like a crazy ex, sitting outside his house in the middle of the night. What the fuck was I thinking?

"I just had the truck washed. I don't want your ass prints all over it," Hunter replied in a low tone.

Tears fell from my eyes, and I nearly bit off my tongue to keep from whimpering from the pain. I was foolish, and Gavriel was an asshole. Maybe I was sent here to see firsthand that Hunter was over me. Maybe he wanted to teach the stupid girl knocking on his door a painful lesson.

"Then let's go inside," she purred.

I kept still as a statue, forcing myself not to move and draw attention to myself. "Or you could put that mouth to use and drop to your knees out here?" Hunter offered, his voice smug. I prayed to every god in existence that she didn't take him up on that offer. I couldn't imagine suffering through the slurping sounds of her mouth and his moans.

"Are you a voyeur, Hunter?" she asked.

"Ain't nobody around here for miles," he replied. His voice was littered with a playfulness I'd never had the pleasure of enjoying before. With me, he was always so serious. There was no room for flirtatious banter. Our fucks were hard and harsh, an explosion of bad decisions and regret. We cut each other with emotions and words. We didn't play.

"Oh really?" she asked. "Then whose car is that?"

Fuck. I'd completely forgotten about my car.

There was a split second of silence, probably him inspecting what she'd pointed out. Then, all hell broke loose. "Get in the truck," he growled. He was protective of her; I could hear it in his tone. I clenched my teeth as she squealed. I heard the door slam, and I knew there was no way I'd escape without him seeing me. I debated on hiding in the dark or running to my car, and then I heard a familiar click of a gun. I knew if I didn't speak up soon, the skilled assassin would shoot me between the eyes without question.

I swallowed. "It's me, Hunter. It's Roe. If you just give me a second, I'll leave, okay?" My throat was as dry as the desert we stood in, and embarrassment made bile rise up my throat.

I watched the dark outline of his tall, bulky body. Hunter went completely still at my greeting. I didn't hear his footsteps move. The only sound I could hear was my thudding heartbeat. It was like he was in shock.

"Roe?" he asked. My name sounded like heartbreak on his lips.

"I'm so sorry," I choked out. "I shouldn't have come."

In a flash, I stood up from my seat and started sprinting toward my rental car. I wanted to get away from him as quickly as possible. Why did I come here? What could I possibly want to gain from tracking him down? If it was closure I wanted, I sure as fuck got it. He was with someone else now. He was happy.

For the last five years, I'd been obsessing over a man that had moved on.

I was no better than his mother. Affection and love made people crazy.

I unlocked my car and threw myself in the front seat. I pressed the push start and threw it in drive, my headlights illuminating his truck. The masochist in me hoped for just a glimpse of Hunter. I wanted to just see him once. But he wasn't there. With tears streaming down my cheeks and a pain so palpable in my chest that I had to force my lungs to expand, I put the car in drive and pressed on the accelerator.

And then he appeared. Standing in the middle of the road leading back to the highway, Hunter glared at me. My headlights illuminated his face. Hunter had a beard now. His hair was wilder. His shoulders were broader. It was like he spent the last five years working out nonstop. He stood strong and tall, and his face showed no emotion; but I was used to the stoic way he locked up his feelings.

He wore jeans and a button-up plaid shirt, and the only slip in his blank expression could be seen in his gaze. His eyes were furious and stormy.

I slammed on my brakes at his feet and whimpered when his hand beat the hood of my car. Fuck fuck fuck. I couldn't talk to him. I couldn't see him after what I'd heard. I shouldn't have come.

He circled my car, heading toward the driver's side with his fist clenched. I was hyperventilating, stuck between wanting to see him and wanting to flee.

His harsh knocks on the window made me flinch. "Open the door, Roe," he said. My heart fell when he didn't call me Pretty Debt. The nickname I once loathed was a thing of the past. There was no familiarity between us now. Instead of opening the door, I locked it.

He closed his eyes in impatience, then opened them again. I cracked the window a smidge, just enough to speak to him.

"Get the fuck out of this car right now," he growled. He looked at me like I was the enemy—like I was the villain in his story.

"I-I can't—" I stuttered while keeping my gaze fixed forward on the road. I knew if I turned to look at him, I'd lose my strength. I'd pray for his anger, because at least it was something.

"Open the fucking door," he demanded again.

"Hunter, who is that?" the woman's voice called.

"No one. Get in the fucking truck, Roxanne."

No one.

No one.

No one.

I really was no one to Hunter Hammond. He'd become my obsession, and I became nothing.

I braced myself for another round of searing pain slicing through my chest, then turned to face him. His eyes were sharp and cruel, boring into mine. He looked older. Harsher. Tan from the desert sun and bulky from working out. I could smell the pot on his clothes through the crack in the window.

"Goodbye, Hunter," I said with a half-smile, though tears were streaming down my cheeks.

I pressed on the accelerator and fled the scene. Every mile between us made my heart die. I willed my feelings into hibernation. I swallowed my pride and accepted the closure. Even if this wasn't how I wanted things to end, I was happy it did. Hunter was in love with someone else, and it was time I let him go.

I let the words "she's no one" become my anthem. Maybe if I said it enough, I'd really disappear. Words were the greatest magic, after all.

Chapter 5

ROE

I couldn't stomach the food in front of me, though I was getting weak from the hunger pangs. Every time I lifted my spoon to my mouth, I heard that woman's voice with Hunter.

Who is it?

I felt insane. I shouldn't be bothered by a man that had moved on. Five years had passed, and it was ridiculous to expect him to spend all that time mourning the loss of me. Hell, I slept with a few guys over the years. Nothing crazy, but I didn't stay celibate. I suppose it was the climax of it all that bothered me. For five years, I dreamed of seeing him again, of feeling those butterflies again. For five years, I craved closure and understanding. For five years, I craved *him*.

So when I finally saw the person who had been occupying my mind with someone else, it stung.

Well, it more than stung.

I took another sip of coffee and debated ordering another cup. I'd need the caffeine if I was going to survive the trip home. I wasn't looking forward to going back. Everywhere I went reminded me of Hunter and what happened between us. Nicole, Joel, and Mack would want to discuss my little disappearing act. They were concerned, and I didn't know how to explain to them that I felt out of control. I didn't have a choice. I had to do this, or I would lose it. I had six missed calls from her and Mack. I really needed to call them back.

I didn't know where I belonged anymore or what my purpose was. I didn't know what the fuck I was doing with my life. What kind of person tracked down their ex-stalker?

"Is this seat taken?" a low voice asked. I closed my eyes and breathed in before opening again.

He didn't bother waiting for my answer. Hunter pulled out the seat across from me and sat down. A part of me was hoping he would find me. I ended up sleeping in a motel forty-five minutes away so I could cry and rest in peace. Thankfully, I'd showered and brushed my hair. At least I didn't look as crazed as I felt last night.

I slowly lifted my eyes to meet his heavy gaze. Blue pools of heat greeted me, and I felt my entire body clench. He was real. He was here... *here*. In the stark reality of daylight, Hunter looked dashing. He wore a tight black shirt, his usual, and jeans. His scruffy beard was a change. I liked the messiness of it all. It was like he'd grown a little bit wilder out here in the desert air.

"Hello," I croaked.

"Hello, Roe," he replied. No nickname. No playfulness to his tone. I felt like an acquaintance. There was something raw in the lack of familiarity.

"You live in a cute place," I began while scraping my spoon across my bowl. "The weather is lovely this time of year—"

"You show up at my camper after five years and want to talk about the weather?" he asked, eyebrows raised in beautiful challenge.

"You never were good at small talk, Hunter," I replied with a dark chuckle before reaching for my coffee and taking a sip. He stared at my neck as I gulped the hot liquid down.

"Why are you here?"

"I was in the area," I lied. "I thought I'd say hello."

"Bullshit. You live in an apartment with Nicole in Denver."

It was both exciting and painful to hear that he knew where I was. Was he still keeping tabs? Was he watching me? "How do you know where I live?"

He clenched his teeth like he was pissed at himself for revealing that bit of info. "Don't be stupid, Roe. I'm still friends with Mack. He bitches about how much he misses you from time to time," Hunter explained with a wave of his hand.

I should have been surprised, but I guess it's nothing new. All this time, I was dying to know what he was up to, and he didn't have to suffer the same way.

"How'd you even find me?" he asked. I knew my answer would probably piss him off, but I didn't care.

"I had a nice chat with Gavriel Moretti. His wife made us dinner," I breezed triumphantly. At the mention of Gavriel, Hunter's face turned red with anger.

"You did *what?*" he asked incredulously. "Why the fuck would you talk to one of the most dangerous men in the country, Roe. Why are you here?"

"I mean, I fucked an assassin, Hunter. Dinner with a gang banger isn't that big of a deal." Hunter blanched, and I reveled in catching him off guard.

"I'm not going to ask you again, Roe. Why are you here?" He punctuated every syllable with gritty animosity. I stared at his white-knuckled grip on the edge of the table. I'd forgotten how quick to anger he was. I'd forgotten how much I loved it.

"I wanted to see you," I replied with a shrug. It was the simplest explanation but wasn't the full truth, either. Telling Hunter I'd been obsessed with seeing his face again felt hollow. I'd been thinking of him ever since that night—the night he left my naked body on the ground with cum seeping out of me. It was such a brutal goodbye, and I still hadn't come to terms with it. Maybe obsessing over him was my way of coping with the trauma.

"Why?"

I scoffed. "You can't demand answers from me. I owe you nothing. I was here. I wanted to see you. I've seen you. So now I can leave."

I wiped my hands on the napkin and waved the waitress back over. If I stayed much longer, my cool facade would fade, and all that would be left is a crying girl in the middle of a restaurant, asking why everyone always left.

"Are you going back to Denver?" he asked.

"Probably," I murmured while staring over his head. I wasn't strong enough to look him in the eye and see nothing in his gaze. "I might just drive around for a bit. My boss probably fired me for just leaving, and I'm not looking forward to Nicole and Joel hosting an intervention." At the mention of Joel, Hunter's lip twitched.

"Typical," Hunter growled. "Running away when you can't accept reality."

"That's rich coming from you," I gritted in response. "You drugged me and ran with your tail between your legs when shit got real. Does your girlfriend know you've killed people, Hunter?" I hated how jealous I sounded but figured I already sounded like a crazy bitch, I might as well commit to it.

"She's not my girlfriend, and we don't do much talking," he replied with a pointed stare. "We're too busy doing other things to get a word out that isn't my name or *oh God's*."

That stung. It stung a lot. "Well, I'm glad you're happy and living your best life," I replied as the waitress put the bill on the table. I reached for it, but Hunter was quicker. I didn't bother fighting him on it. He quickly slipped some cash on the table to cover my meal. "Well," I began with a forced smile. "I'm sorry to intrude on your happy little life. I honestly don't know why I came, but it's obvious I've...romanticized the time we shared together."

I stood up while trying to keep calm. This hurt so damn much. "Roe." Hunter said my name. Some fucked up part of me wanted him to call me his Pretty Debt again. Tears streamed down my face as I spun on my heel and bolted from the cafe. I heard the sound of his chair scraping against the floor and his steps stomping after me.

"Roe," he called after me as I ran across the parking lot. I stopped when I reached my car and turned to face him.

"I just have to know," I choked out. "Did you miss me at all? Did you think about me? Did you...c-care at all?"

His answer would be the nail in the coffin. "I didn't."

"Then why go through all that trouble?" I asked. "Why make me fall for you if you were just going to leave?"

"I didn't plan on it. I was just projecting my own bullshit on you. By the time I realized that we couldn't keep doing what we were doing, we took it too far."

I shook my head and stepped closer to him. "It wasn't just that," I insisted. "There was something between us."

Hunter balled his fists at his side. "There's nothing between us. There will be nothing between us. Go home, Roe. Live your life. I've moved on, and so should you."

No, no, no. This wasn't how any of this was supposed to go. I took a bold step forward, cupped his cheeks in my hands. If he wanted me to leave, then I was going out with a bang.

I stared at his lips. It felt like the night I first met him, with me feeling desperate for his kiss and him refusing to give in. I didn't care about all the reasons I shouldn't want him or that this would make it even harder to leave. But I craved a sense of closure.

Or maybe I wanted to open Pandora's box.

His eyes swept me up and down before lingering on my mouth. He still knew me well. He knew what I was thinking. The indecision was clear across his face. He looked away for a brief moment, then tore his eyes back to me.

"Take what you want from me, Pretty Debt. Then get the fuck out of here."

How could permission feel so painful and beautiful all at once? He called me Pretty Debt.

I refused to be a cliche. Though every bone in my body absolutely ached to slam my lips to his, I wanted to make him wait. I wanted to see the evidence in his longing expression that he wanted this, too. Even if I meant nothing to him, even if this was a one-off. I'd leave here knowing I affected him.

"Take what I want, huh?" I asked while removing my hands from his cheeks. "What exactly is it that I want, Hunter? It's been a while, maybe you don't know me anymore."

He looked up. My eyes locked onto the scruff covering his jaw, and I wondered how it would feel against my skin. I wanted my lips to be red and swollen from it. "Don't play games with me, Roe. You and I both know I'll win."

Pride was lifting me up by my bootstraps and dragging me out of my pity party. "On the contrary, Hunter. Coming here kind of helped dispel the illusion. I'd built you up in my mind all those years ago."

Hunter did a quick sweep of the parking lot with his eyes before pulling my body to his. I gasped at the quick, hard contact of his muscles against my softness. A tremor traveled down my spine, and I had to force my eyes open so I didn't melt into his touch. "You're here because no one fucked you like I did. You're here," he rasped while leaning closer to hover his lips over the shell of my ear, "because you miss my mouth on your cunt. Because no matter how hard you try to fuck me out of your system with those fumbling college boys that wouldn't know a clit if it slapped them in the face, you want to taste me again. You want my hand on your pussy. You want me to make you come so you can have the pleasure of screaming my name again."

I turned to brush my nose against his neck and let out a shaky exhale. "No," I replied.

"If you're going to lie to me, Roe, at least make it worth it."

I wrapped my arms around him and kissed his lips. And the moment my tongue swept across the seam of his mouth, he shuddered. *Yeah, fucker. You want this just as much as I do.*

He ran his hands through my hair and tugged at the scalp, making me gasp and moan into his mouth. He sucked on my tongue and clipped my bottom lip with his teeth.

"Fuck you, Hunter," I cried out while running my hands over his chest.

"Fuck you too, Pretty Debt. Why'd you have to come back, huh?"

I pressed my palms to his abs, choking on lust as I felt each hill of his muscles. Someone in the parking lot whistled, but I didn't let embarrassment or shame ruin this moment. His hands roamed lower until he was cupping my ass and drawing me closer to his hard body. I felt his cock against my stomach.

And then he ripped me away from him. The force of his shove made me fall on the ground. Sharp pain spiked up my tailbone, and I let out a little scream.

Looking up at Hunter, I watched as he ran his hand through his hair and spat on the ground like he was trying to get rid of the taste of me on his tongue. "I was happy, Roe. Really fucking happy. I had my life. And then you show up here, reminding me of everything I was running from."

Tears filled my eyes, and shame coalesced over my soul. I scoffed. "Happy men don't kiss the girls they're running from."

He stared at me on the ground, clenching his fist. "Get up," he growled. "Get up and leave. Go home, go somewhere else, go on an adventure or go to hell. I don't care. Please just go anywhere but here. I don't want you."

I scrambled to get to my feet while staring at him. "Bullshit. You want me, and it pisses you off. Why all this guilt? Why care?"

"I don't care. Get in your car and never come back, okay?"

I was crying now, hot tears gathered on my lip, washing away the remnants of him on my skin. "Hunter," I choked.

"Go. Go or I'll make you disappear."

"You're threatening me?" I asked, shock making my skin chill.

"I'm telling you to leave, or the consequences will be irreversible. Go home, Roe. I don't like who I am when you're around."

I swallowed and wiped my eyes. "Fuck you, Hunter. Fuck your guilt. This thing between us is real. It's why I haven't stopped thinking about you since the night you left. It's why when we kiss, you forget that you're supposed to be pushing me away. It's why you know where I live. Why you sigh when you say my name. I'll leave, but it's not because you scare me, Hunter. It's because I don't deserve this."

I walked to my car and got in the driver's seat, refusing to look at the hate in his eyes as I put the car in drive and left. His words were cruel, but they did their job. I wasn't going to sit there and let him threaten me.

When I got on the highway, my phone rang. Seeing that it was Nicole, I answered it. I needed my best friend. She would probably be pissed, but she'd put the scolding on hold to comfort me.

"I saw him. I really saw him. It went terribly, Nicole. He hates me. He threatened to kill me if I didn't leave," I cried out. "I think I built it all up in my head. I romanticized it all. I should have stayed away."

"Roe, stop talking," Nicole said. I could hear the terror in her tone. I furrowed my brow.

"Nicole? Are you okay?"

"Not really. There's someone here that wants to talk to you," she croaked out.

I listened to the phone as she handed it over. What the fuck was happening?

"Hello, Roe Palmer. This is Gavriel Moretti."

Chapter 6

ROE

"H-hello," I said while pulling over. My hands were shaking so badly that I wasn't sure I could see from the waves of dizziness assaulting me.

"How was your reunion, Roe? I hope it was everything you wanted."

Cars zoomed by as I sat on the shoulder on the desert highway. The sun was high up in the sky, casting rays of bright light through my windshield. I took off my sunglasses and rubbed my eyes, pausing for a brief moment of confusion to think before speaking. Why was Gavriel on Nicole's phone? What was going on? "It was awful," I began truthfully. Something told me Gavriel didn't like wasting time with lies. "I was at his house, and he showed up with some woman wanting to suck him off in his yard."

"That's unfortunate," Gavriel agreed plainly. Unfortunate didn't even start to cover how fucked up our reunion was. "How did that make you feel?"

What was he, a fucking therapist? "Jealous," I admitted. "Then he told me he hated me and that life was better without me."

Gavriel went quiet for a moment, dissecting my words. "Jealousy is a weak emotion, Roe. If you can conquer that, you can conquer anything."

I let out a dark laugh. "I can't be jealous of something I don't have."

This time, it was Gavriel's turn to laugh. His booming chuckles made my spine go taut. "You definitely have him, Roe. What happened after he said he hated you?"

I stared out the window in defeat. My mind wanted to find hope at the bottom of Gavriel's statement, but I refused to let him manipulate me. I knew how Hunter felt deep in my heart, despite the pity party I was throwing. Hunter loved me.

But love was a choice.

Chemistry and our binding past weren't enough to sustain me. I needed him to choose me, too. "Then I got in my car and drove off. I'm headed home. I think you overestimated my abilities to bring him back. Hunter Hammond wants nothing to do with me," I explained before punching my steering wheel.

"That's not going to work for me, Roe. We had a deal."

My stomach dropped. "Excuse me?"

"You didn't think I had Nicole brought to New York for afternoon tea, did you? I needed to make sure you didn't give up easily."

I sputtered. "Hunter hates me. He threatened to kill me if I didn't leave," I rambled. "You're going to have to bring Hunter back yourself. He's not going to listen to me."

"You have more creative methods of persuasion than I do," Gavriel began. My mind immediately flashed to the intense kiss Hunter and I shared in the cafe's parking lot. And then his cruel words rang clearly in my ear.

Take what you want from me, then get the fuck out of here.

"I can't," I choked out.

"You can. And you will. Figure your shit out and bring Hunter back. I have a job only he can do, and I have a feeling you're the only one that can lure him into cooperation. Bring. Him. Back."

The phone line ended, and I sat for a moment, staring out my window as rage simmered beneath my skin. A text message came through, and I clenched my teeth.

Unknown: You have two days.

How the fuck was I going to convince Hunter to go back with me? He didn't give a fuck about Nicole, so the truth would just make him dig his heels in. I could seduce him, but there was no telling if that would work. Especially after the things he said. And even if it did work, Hunter would be devastated once he found out it was all a ploy to get him to work for Gavriel again.

I didn't really have a choice, though. Either way, I lost him. I just couldn't stand the idea of losing Nicole to this mess, too.

I'd have to go back to see him. I'd have to seduce him. Maybe drug him like he did me, then throw him in my car and drive all the way to New York.

No matter what, I'd have to see Hunter again. And it was going to piss him off.

So why the fuck was I giddy about that?

Lipstick

She keeps warpaint in her purse, at the ready.

She colors her lips with a shade called Boy's Tears.

Then, she dances naked in her bedroom, like Cosmo told her to do.

A broken heart feels a lot like a battle.

You have to wear armor of lace and smile with grace.

You can't let them see your weakness.

A Queen guards her kingdom with a short skirt.

She sips vodka on the dance floor and finds comfort

at the thrust of a thick, sharp sword.

And then she cries the next morning on the city bus headed home.

And then she paints poems with war.

After getting checked back into the motel, I showered and got dressed with purpose. I put on some high-waisted cut off shorts with a deep red crocheted bralette and a black lace kimono. My ankle boots made my toned, tanned legs seem even longer.

I applied makeup slowly while letting my wavy hair air dry. As I lined my lips with rouge, I thought of how the color would look smeared along Hunter's chest. It was the same shade as blood and was named Lust. I worried that the moment Hunter saw me, he'd end this little reunion between us once and for all. Would he kill me?

No. He wouldn't.

Seeing as it was a Saturday night, I asked some of the locals where the hottest place to hang out was. Nearly all of them said Jobe's Place, a dive bar illuminating the sand-covered road with its neon lights.

I wasn't sure if Hunter would show up there, but based on the drunk woman he'd brought home last night, I figured he regularly attended a local bar to chase pussy. The thought of that made me sick, but I tried to focus on the task at hand. This was no longer a mission to win him over, I just needed to get him home.

Honestly, I was too much of a chicken shit to show up at his house again. I refused to believe that Hunter would hurt me, but I wasn't stupid, either. Besides, I was stronger now. I could put up a fight. But being strong meant being smart, too. Things had changed so much that I wasn't about to test his code of ethics or sense of right and wrong on his *very* secluded property. No one could hear me scream.

This was a small town. People talked. I hoped to walk in the bar, flirt with a few guys, and get the locals to notice. I had every intention of standing out in a public place that would safely garner Hunter's attention. He wouldn't hurt me if we had an audience. I just needed another chance to chat with him. Maybe if I asked him to be just friends, he would go for it.

I sighed at the smoky eye shadow smeared across my lids and wished

Nicole were here. I never partied without her, and knowing she was with Gavriel made me sick. Maybe she could answer her phone?

I dialed the number and listened to the phone ring. Nicole answered just before I was sure it would go to voicemail. She didn't even give me time to greet her. "Girl, you better go get your man. The Bullets are not fucking around," she said.

"Shit, Nicole, I'm so sorry I dragged you into this. Are you okay?"

"I'm fine. Pissed as fuck at you, but fine. Before I bitch you out for writing the most basic ass note, leaving town, not answering your cell, and working with gangsters—are you okay?"

I cringed. Yeah, I really had lost my fucking mind. "Yes and no?" I offered. I went into a long explanation over what had happened from the time Hunter answered his phone until now. "I can't do this. He wanted nothing to do with me, Nicole," I argued while staring at my reflection in the mirror.

"You better take your panties off and handle this like a woman because these fuckers mean business. What's your game plan?"

I quickly explained how I was going to a local bar to get intel and hopefully run into him. "You should just show up at his house naked," she insisted.

"Absolutely not. I have to play this smart, Nicole."

"Yeah, you do. I don't particularly want to die. Although the team of guys they have making sure I don't run away are kind of cute. I mean, what a way to go, am I right?"

I rolled my eyes while setting my phone down and turning it to the speaker. "Only you would joke about dying from a hot guy," I teased.

"You're one to talk. We're in this mess because you're obsessed with your assassin stalker that now wants nothing to do with you." I pushed up my boobs and smacked my lips. The sun had long ago disappeared over the mountains, which meant it was almost time to leave. "You'll handle this, right, Roe?" Nicole asked after a long, lingering moment of silence.

I didn't know if I had this handled or not, but I wasn't about to worry her any more than she already was. "I'll figure this out. Even if I have to drug Hunter and bring him back in the trunk of my car."

"Atta girl," Nicole said with a sigh of relief. "And I was serious when I said no panties tonight. Give the bastard easy access, then trap him with your pussy."

"Good night, Nicole," I interrupted.

She was rambling about well-timed hip thrusts when I managed to hang up the phone.

The clock read ten o'clock, and my mind fumbled over every detail from our kiss earlier. Now that I had a clear head and had purged all thoughts of his cruel words, it didn't feel like the sort of kiss from someone that hates me. If felt reluctant, like he didn't want to admit that he missed me as much as I missed him.

I would have to push him, I decided. Biting my inner cheek, I shimmied my red lace panties off and kicked them to the side.

Let's do this.

Chapter 7

ROE

The entrance to the bar had swinging doors like an old west movie. There wasn't anyone waiting to check IDs, but I had a feeling that everyone in this town knew everyone. I also got the sense that underage drinking wasn't as big of a faux pas here as it was in other cities. There wasn't much else to do in Joshua Tree.

The moment I walked in, I felt ridiculous. Everyone else in the bar was wearing long denim jeans, T-shirts with holes in them, and plaid jackets. I was *very* overdressed, and I felt about three dozen eyes land on me the second I realized this was a *very* bad idea. I rolled my shoulders back in mock confidence. Nicole taught me that you can never be overdressed or overeducated, so I strutted my stuff to the bar and tried to sit down on the tall stool without flashing everyone my vagina. I didn't want to be here. I wanted to drive home and lick my wounds. I wanted to start getting over Hunter Hammond, because I didn't want to let my obsession rule my life for an unworthy man. But Gavriel wasn't giving me much of a choice.

"You must be a tourist," the bartender said with a smile. I stopped looking around to meet his stare. He was handsome with his freshly shaven face, warm amber eyes, and a buzz cut. I noted the ink sprawled along his bulging biceps, and the veins popping out of his forearms.

"Is it that obvious?" I replied with the tilt of my head and a wry smile.

"Pretty things don't stay here for long. People come and go like the seasons in Joshua Tree. Only people that stay are trying to escape from something, and you don't look like a girl on the run. Did you come for the glamping compound? I hear that's really big with the Gen Z-ers these days." For some reason, my heart warmed at his words. I guess I *did* stop being the girl that ran. I almost reverted back to her when Hunter told me he wanted me gone. But I chased things now.

I glanced at his calloused hands as he poured me a drink. He hadn't even asked what I wanted, so I was curious about his assumptions of me. "Glamping compound?" I asked.

"Yep. It's all the rage these days. Fancy tents that'll look good on your Instagram feed. Mr. Lock charges four hundred dollars a night for people to sleep outside on a shitty mattress with no running water or air conditioning. But it's pretty and has a certain aesthetic people cream their pants for," he said with a chuckle before sliding the drink over to me. I wasn't paying attention to what mixes he was pouring in my glass, but I bravely picked it up and took a sip.

It was sweet and hard. Heat hit the back of my throat with a slamming punch, and I knew that whatever he poured me was fucking potent. I let out a hiss and set the cup down. "That sounds awful," I rasped. Whatever drink he'd given me had affected my speech momentarily, sucking the moisture out of my throat. I was ready for another. "I'm staying at the motel off the highway."

"That motel is disgusting. The mattresses are hard from all the middle-aged cum coating the sheets."

I shivered and cringed, curling my lip in disgust. "That's nasty. Maybe I should sleep in my car."

"Or find someone nice, strong, and handsome to go home with," he added with a wink.

I forced a smile. The last thing I wanted was to go home with someone else while I had Hunter on the brain. I'd be comparing every movement to my stalker. But some harmless flirting never hurt. "I'll keep that in mind," I replied before taking another sip.

"So what brings you here, then?" he asked. I looked around the bar and noticed a couple of people reaching over and grabbing their own drinks. This place was definitely low-key, so I didn't feel too bad about monopolizing the bartender's time. Hell, maybe he could give me some information about Hunter.

"I'm seeing an old friend that wants nothing to do with me. Figured I'd come to drink away my sorrow and figure out what to do from here," I replied. It seemed better to tell the truth than to lie. "I'm Roe, by the way," I greeted with a nod before taking another sip of my deadly drink.

"I'm Manny," the bartender replied with a nod. A man next to me asked for a beer, but Manny served him without breaking eye contact with me. His stare was heavy and assessing. "Is this *friend* the reason you stink of heartbreak?"

"I wouldn't call it heartbreak," I offered lightly. It was more like a tragic, disastrous catastrophe. "Maybe you know him? His name is Hunter Hammond. We were friends five years ago, and I finally tracked him down."

Manny's eyes widened, as if shocked to hear Hunter's name on my lips. "No shit?" he asked. "That fucker is in my bar almost every night. In fact, I'm pretty sure he's keeping me in business right now."

So Hunter had become quite the drinker now? Wasn't it just yesterday that we bonded outside Nicole Knight's house over our mutual distaste for parties? Was he searching for something or running? "I guess I should leave if I want to avoid him," I replied. I wouldn't be leaving; I was prodding Manny for more information.

"He's got an entire entourage of territorial women you definitely need to avoid," Manny said while nodding toward a corner of women giggling and slamming back cheap beer.

"They look like fun," I murmured while popping a twenty-dollar bill on the counter.

"They're bored women that like to fuck their way through town to make up for their mediocre lives."

Maybe I didn't like Manny after all. He sounded almost jealous, and judgmental men with opinions about a woman's sex life were usually overcompensating for their tiny dicks. "I'll keep that in mind," I replied with a curt smile. "Wish me luck." I threw back the rest of my drink with a hiss and a wink.

"You're going to need it, girl. Come back when you need more liquid relief."

Other women didn't intimidate me. I wasn't the sort of person to compare myself to someone else just because we both touched the same dick. I didn't fight for attention. I didn't take sides. I introduced myself.

Sex was a great cure for boredom, and if Hunter recycled through these women to pass the time, then they were my new best friends.

I stared at the group of them while wondering which one went home with Hunter last night. One had yellow-blond hair and ripped jeans that were barely hanging onto her thin frame.

The other woman wore smeared red lipstick and an oversized black shirt that made it look like she wasn't wearing any pants. I decided immediately that I wanted to be friends with them.

"Hello," I greeted with a half grin that felt uncertain. "I'm Roe."

Slowly, the two women turned to face me, both of them flushed from the alcohol and swaying in their seats. If there was anything that Nicole taught me, it was that drunk girls were the best girls. We just had to compliment one another and we were in. "Oh my gosh, I love your lipstick," I said to the girl with dark hair.

She impulsively licked her lips at my compliment, then looked me up and down. I gave her what I hoped was a convincing smile, and she returned it with equal enthusiasm. "Thanks," she replied. "I got it at Walmart. One of my fuck buddies likes how it looks wrapped around his dick," she cackled, making the blond woman giggle, too.

"Can't blame him," I joked. "It's hot. I struggle pulling off red shades, but I still try."

"Red looks great on you! You've got those plump lips," the brunette said with a wink. I puckered my pout playfully at her.

"I'm Butterfly," the blonde greeted while thrusting out her soft hand for a limp noodle handshake.

"And I'm Luna," the other said with a fist bump. "We work at the local glamping compound. I'm a massage therapist, and Butterfly teaches yoga."

How...appropriate, I thought to myself.

"Are you just passing through?" Butterfly asked.

"Kind of. I came here to find someone. Now I'm kind of finding myself. Then I saw the two of you and figured we could find the bottom of a margarita glass together."

Luna held her hands up and squealed. "Hell yes!"

Butterfly joined in. "Did we just become best friends?"

I closed my eyes and silently thanked Nicole for helping me navigate the secret language of drunk girls before ordering another round of drinks from Manny.

Within the hour, we were all shooting the shit and talking about the benefits of having a vagina. The more we drank, the looser my lips got, and pretty soon I was asking them about Hunter Hammond.

"You know Hunter?" Luna asked while giving Butterfly a conspiratorial side-eye. "Do you know him in the biblical sense or..."

"You're not even religious, Luna," Butterfly replied with an eye roll.

"I guess you could say I've known him my entire life," I interjected. "But I came here, and he wanted nothing to do with me."

"That's because he's dick deep in Roxanne's hot pocket," Luna said with a snort.

My drunken ears perked up. "Roxanne?" I asked.

"They aren't really dating. No offense, but Hunter has made his way around town. Even I've drank from the river, ya dig?" My heart panged, but Luna was being honest and sincere. I nodded to encourage her to keep going. "She's just his most consistent fuck around here, mostly because she scared everyone off. Sorry to break it to you, but we've all had a taste of the mysterious Hunter. She's the only one he's gone to for seconds," Luna said while waving her hand at Manny for another drink. "In fact, you kind of look alike. If you weren't dressed like a hooker, I'd say you were twins."

"I'm not dressed like a hooker," I sputtered drunkenly with a giggle.

"You're sure as fuck not dressed like a nun, either," Luna teased. She was definitely the sassy one in the group. Butterfly was the motherly hippie.

"Don't shame her for showing skin, Luna. The patriarchy has us all convinced that our clothes are for men," Butterfly said in a singsong voice. "Our body is not for their viewing pleasure. We are nothing more than sculptures in Mother Earth's garden."

Butterfly was definitely out there.

"So," I began, trying to bring the conversation back on track. "Do you know Roxanne?"

Luna let out a dark laugh. "Know her? We work with the bitch. She runs the music therapy class, and Hunter works with the horses."

"Wait," I said, holding my hands up. "Hunter works with horses?" I asked in disbelief.

"He manages the stalls and leads groups on trail rides. Lock wants to keep him forever. Ever since he hired him, everyone wants a ride."

Butterfly snorted. "Everyone wants a ride. That's funny."

The picture of Hunter's life here in Joshua Tree was starting to make sense. He slept around and lived in a trailer in the middle of nowhere. He worked at a hippie resort, taking care of horses and fucked with some girl named Roxanne. In less than two hours, I knew more about Hunter than I ever did. He really was building a life for himself here. A life without his obsession with me. A life free from Gavriel. Could I seriously bring him back to that?

Would Gavriel actually hurt Nicole if I didn't?

Why did it hurt so much to think of him moving on while I'd been stuck in his orbit?

There was a spark of pain thudding against my rib cage, reminding me that Hunter wasn't mine. Maybe he never was.

"Speak of the devil," Butterfly sang in a high-pitched voice.

I felt his presence before I even turned around. Dark, hungry and furious. I could sense his eyes on my back and his anger boiling in my chest. "Wow, his aura is sending all kinds of messages," Butterfly exclaimed while fanning herself. "I can't tell if he's pissed off or horny." "That's just the way I like my men. Walking that tight rope of murder and fucking," Luna replied with a moan. "Damn, Roxanne is with him. We have to be nice. No hard feelings, Roe. Her dad owns the compound where we work."

I shrugged, these women didn't really owe me anything. We were just bonding over a few drinks, but I immediately liked them more for wanting to reassure me. "No worries," I replied. "I can handle it."

Hunter Hammond had already broken my heart past repair. I was here for a job now. I'd have to separate feelings if I wanted out of this in one piece. "Damn girl, he looks hella pissed to see you. It's not too late to run," Luna offered while forcing a smile. Her bright red lips were stretched in an awkward pout.

"I don't run from a challenge," I replied.

"I'm loving her energy, Loony, can we keep her?" Butterfly said with a sigh.

"Stop fucking calling me Loony! It's Luna," Luna argued.

"Your real name is Megan, so you can just drop that argument at the door like you did your Dallas suburb roots," Butterfly snickered. "I know your hair is blond under that box dye job."

"I'm a fucking witch from the desert, and I will hex you if you say otherwise."

I focused on my two new friends' bickering as Hunter walked over to us. I didn't even have to turn and face him to know that he was stomping closer, with cruelty brewing on his tongue. I knew it was coming, but I wasn't expecting the prod of cool metal pressed into my back. Was that a fucking gun? He had it hidden by the way our bodies were positioned, but I couldn't ignore the threat.

"Roxanne, go get me a beer, Babe," Hunter said. Still, I hadn't turned to look at him. That sweet pet name sounded foreign on his lips, like sentimental bullshit wasn't the norm.

"Babe?" the woman scoffed. "You never call me Babe."

I kept my eyes trained on Butterfly and Luna. Their brows were raised, and their heavy drunken eyes seemed more awake somehow.

"I said get me a drink, Roxanne," Hunter demanded.

"Fine, whatever. I just wanted a nice night with the girls, and you just *had* to go all caveman on me. Save it for the bedroom, *Babe*."

I heard heels stomp off but still didn't turn. "Come with me, Roe," Hunter growled his demand.

Luna leaned forward, like she was prepared to yank me across the table and save me if necessary. Yeah, these bitches were joining my girl gang. I gave her and Butterfly a look of confidence, telling them without words that I could handle my shit. Then finally, I slowly turned around and faced him.

My heart did a little squeeze the moment my eyes landed on his. Hunter looked damn good. His arms were tanned and accentuated by the short-sleeved shirt he was wearing. The denim jeans he wore had holes at the knees that looked natural and rustic. He even had boots on. I knew he liked his seclusion in Denver, but he was embracing the hippie cowboy lifestyle here.

"I'm not going anywhere with you," I replied calmly.

"You tell him girl!" Luna interjected.

"Mind your own business, Luna," Hunter replied with a scathing look. "How do you even know each other?" he then asked, as if just realizing that we were all sitting together.

"I think we knew one another in a past life, but I'll need to ask my spirit guide during my evening meditation to know for sure," Butterfly sang.

"We shared a pitcher of margaritas and commiserated on all the shitty men in this world," Luna added.

"I got them drunk so I could ask them questions about you," I added in honesty as Hunter dug the gun deeper into my back. He was pressing so hard I was certain it would leave a nasty bruise. "That's awesome you get to work with horses now," I added before seeking out a chunk of strawberry at the bottom of my margarita glass.

"Get up right now," Hunter insisted. I gave him a stern look and a shrug before leaning closer to speak to him in a tone low enough that Butterfly and Luna couldn't hear.

"And let you shoot me in the parking lot? No thank you. I'll stay where there are witnesses."

A few bottles of beers were slammed down on the tabletop, effectively ending my stare down with my smoldering ex stalker. "Who's this?" a sultry voice asked. Dragging my eyes away from Hunter, I looked at the girl currently suction cupping herself to his side.

I nearly gasped. It was like looking in the mirror. Roxanne was like a more sun-kissed version of me. She wore ripped jeans, had a soft face, and...she looked perfect standing next to Hunter. "Hello, I'm Roe," I said while stretching my hand out to shake hers. She seemed hesitant to greet me but did anyway.

"I'm Roxanne," she replied with a firm handshake that squeezed my fingers. Even her greeting was territorial. The moment I drew my hand back, she wiped it on her jeans. I didn't take it personally. "You passing through?"

"Roe was just leaving," Hunter growled.

"No, she wasn't!" Butterfly interrupted in her soft voice. "She's going to my sunrise yoga class in the morning."

I grimaced. This was a drunk decision I'd likely regret in the morning. I was looking forward to the workout, but sunrise wasn't my thing. I always went to the gym late at night. Hunter scoffed, and everyone turned to look at him.

"What?" I asked.

"You hate mornings and exercise," he replied with an eye roll. My pride was wounded, but I preened at his remembrance of me. His assumptions and stalker tendencies once scared me, but now they had me glowing.

"I'll have you know that I box six days a week. I train with some pretty strong men," I added pointedly. Hunter's eyes turned dark.

"That sounds hotttt," Luna slurred.

"Wait, you know her?" Roxanne asked while squinting her eyes at me. My eyes zeroed in on her grip on Hunter's arm, and I watched her fingers turn white from squeezing him territorially. Hunter shrugged out of her hold while keeping the gun strategically at my back, making her grin dip even lower.

"We're old friends. I've been on a bit of a soul searching trip and stopped here. I'm working on my poetry," I replied, lying easily.

"You've come to the right place," Luna replied with a lazy grin. "Joshua Tree is where all the creatives find themselves."

Butterfly clapped. "Joshua Tree is the center of an energy vortex. I just charged my citrine stone at the full moon. I'll be sure to bring it out for you tomorrow. It attracts abundance, you know. How exciting! I love soul journeys!"

I eyed Hunter. These people seemed completely different than him.

Hunter stared back at me incredulously. I didn't want to participate in this standoff any more.

"I better get going. I've got an early morning," I said while winking at Butterfly and slapping a couple of twenties on the table. "It was nice meeting you."

The moment I stood up, Roxanne slid in my seat and gave me the sort of fake, forced smile you tossed strangers out of obligation. "It was… meeting you," she said with a grin.

"I'll walk you out," Hunter growled while wrapping his hand around my bicep and squeezing. I barely had time to grab my purse before he was dragging me through the bar. I didn't want to be in the parking lot alone with him, so I jerked out of his grip and jogged toward a side hallway leading to a back room. Hunter was hot on my heels, so I opened the door and slipped inside, thanking the small town gods for trustworthy bar owners.

It was a small room surrounded by bottles of liquor and cases of beer. I searched for an exit, and the moment I found it, the door to the stock room opened and Hunter stalked through the threshold. I tugged at the doorknob, but it didn't budge. I guess the bar owner wasn't *that* trusting.

I faced the door and steadied my breathing, curling my rough hands into fists so I could protect myself. I didn't have but a moment before he was shoving me against the door. My cheek dug into the wood, and his hot breath traveled down my neck. I refused to grunt or whimper. Though I felt at the mercy of Hunter's anger, it wasn't something I wasn't used to. "Pretty Debt, I told you to leave," he said in a deadly calm voice. It was so controlled that I was caught off guard.

His hand gripped my shoulder, and he spun me around, slamming my back into the door. A searing shock spiked my skull as pain reverberated through my brain at the impact. His hand wrapped around my neck, and he squeezed.

Hunter was no longer affected by my pain. In fact, now he wanted to cause it.

"I told you to leave," he said again. "What the fuck are you wearing? Were you hoping to entice me?" He ran his finger under the strap of my bralette.

"Hardly. I'm not some weak child you can intimidate anymore,

Hunter." I was proud of myself for keeping my voice so steady. "A lot can happen in five years. I might have been a scared little girl when you left, but I'm now a woman that knows what she wants."

Hunter laughed as if I had said the funniest thing he'd ever heard. "Do you know what I think? I think you're too stupid to be scared. I think I did you a disservice by making your life easier. I think your mom sheltered you—"

"Don't you fucking talk about my mother," I interrupted. His face froze for a fraction of a second, and I watched an indescribable expression cross his features. As quickly as it came, it disappeared.

"I'll say whatever the fuck I want," Hunter yelled before rearing back and punching the door. I let out a yelp when I heard his fist connect with the wood. And when he pulled back, there was blood seeping from his knuckles. I couldn't get my breathing under control, and I stared up at Hunter with fear in my soul. Maybe he was right. Maybe I took his protectiveness for granted all those years ago. Hunter Hammond was a seasoned killer, and I was no longer on his good side.

"Why are you here? Are you trying to fuck with me?" he asked before slapping the sides of his head with both his palms. I flinched at the loud smacking sounds and threw my hands up to protect my face. Hunter stopped hitting himself and grabbed my wrists. "Was this morning not enough for you? Do you need to get off? Is that what's keeping you here?"

Hunter slammed my wrists against the door and shoved his knee between my legs. "You dick!" I shouted.

Hunter started moving his leg against my sex. Up and down. Up and down. "No panties? You're soaking wet," he stated. It somehow sounded like a deranged insult.

"Get off of me," I said while squirming against his strong hold. I didn't want him off of me. I wanted him to keep going. Every movement made my clit throb against his leg. I felt trapped and embarrassed and yet somehow turned on. I looked around, as if searching for someone to intervene. But we were locked and alone in the liquor storage closet.

"Is that what you really want?" Hunter asked in a low voice.

I kept my mouth closed to keep the shameful truth from escaping. Yes. I really wanted him. I wanted this. All of this.

Hunter pulled me away from the door and dragged me over to a desk on the opposite side of the room. With his palm on my back, he slammed me down until my cheek hit the tabletop. I was staring back in shock when he placed his gun beside my head on the table. With one hand, he pinned my arms behind my back. His boots kicked my legs into a wide stance, and I whimpered. "Fuck you," I growled. It wasn't that I didn't want him to touch me. I craved him on a visceral level. I didn't care that he was using my body against me. I cared that I could feel the hate in his touch and hear his anger in every word. I cared that this wasn't an expression of long-lost love. Hunter fucked me like it was revenge.

"Look at those long, shaky legs," Hunter said before sliding his free hand up my inner thigh. I quivered at the touch. "Did you miss my hands on you?" He didn't wait for me to respond, though we both knew the answer was *yes.* "I'm gonna give you what you want. Then you're gonna get the fuck out of here. I'm not the sort of man to repeat myself."

I tried to disassociate the man cupping my cunt from the man that protected me my entire life. I breathed in and out, focusing on the dusty air and the buzz in my veins instead of the way his fingers circled my clit. My legs shook.

"I'm not going anywhere," I asserted. He plunged his index finger inside of me and curled it until it was stroking that special spot within me that bloomed with pleasure.

"Yes, you are," Hunter growled. He slipped another finger inside of me and started fucking me relentlessly. He was harsh and fast, pinning me down with one hand and ruining me with the other. My legs were like jelly, and if it weren't for his heavy body weighing me against the tabletop, I would've collapsed on the ground.

"I'm not leaving," I said, my voice strong and lusty.

I was so fucking close; my body betrayed me in a way. Hunter could command my pleasure like no other. Even when I was mad at him. Even when I was scared of him. There was no one that could touch me like he could. He snapped his hand away.

"Is this not enough?" he asked. I heard the distinct sound of his zipper lowering.

"You can fuck me all you want, Hunter Hammond. But it's not going to scare me out of your life. Go ahead and convince yourself that you're doing this to push me away, because I know the truth. You've been craving me just as much as I've been craving you," I snapped.

"Fuckkk," Hunter whispered before slamming inside of me. "I love it when you get angry. Scream at me again, Pretty Debt. It makes fucking you so much more fun." My cheek scraped against the top of the desk as he pounded my body. My skirt was lifted well above my waist, and I could hear the filthy sounds of our skin slapping with every quick, hard thrust.

"I'll clean my dick with your tears when I'm done."

"Go ahead and break me, Hunter. I want it," I replied. I wasn't the helpless girl he left five years ago. I wasn't intimidated by his hold over me. It was like each painful thrust was reminding me that I was a strong capable woman. I wanted this. He might be okay with lying to himself, but I owned his cock and mind.

"Why can't I get rid of you?" Hunter asked between grunts. I wasn't sure what he meant. He'd gotten rid of me for five fucking years.

His hands dug into my hips, squeezing so hard that I felt my bones ache. My legs trembled, and whimpers escaped my lips. This felt too familiar, like the time he fucked me before running away. But I wasn't the same girl. I didn't silently accept his goodbye. "Wherever you go," I began. He slapped my ass, his open palm leaving a red stain against my cheek that I reveled in. "I will find you. I will chase you down. You can never escape me."

Hunter moaned and groaned as he punished me with every thrust. He wasn't worried about equal play. He didn't care if I got off. He was punishing me and using me, and I let him. I wanted him to. "Why do you have to feel so perfect?" he grunted. "You're clenching my cock so good, Pretty Debt."

My ears perked up, and I looked at him over my shoulder. His face had turned tender. His movements, more languid and rhythmic.

"You missed me," I whispered, too afraid to speak it out loud and ruin our moment.

"Why can't I get you out of my fucking head?" he asked. I wasn't even sure if he knew he was saying this out loud. "Why was I fucking thrilled when you showed up, huh? How come your name makes my heart pound?"

The moment he came and I felt his body go stiff behind me, I took advantage of his pleasure, stood up, and spun around. He wasn't done yet, so I was gifted with the view of him finishing his load on the concrete floor, with his face relaxed and blissed out. "Because this means something," I said, answering his questions. "Because you and I are fucking inevitable. No matter what guilt you're still harboring. No matter the age difference, our past, our future, and your job. This"—I gestured between us—"fucking *means* something. Obsessions have purpose."

Hunter looked stunned, with his dick hanging out and his mouth propped open. His eyes were heavy with lust, but he also was filled with dangerous anger. I watched his hand tremble like he wanted to reach for a gun. "No. This can't happen. I'm going to make you regret coming here," he said before putting his dick away and buckling his pants. Running a hand through his hair, he looked me up and down before continuing, "I'm gonna make you wish you had forgotten about me. I'm going to ruin you and send you running home."

"I look forward to it," I replied.

Chapter 8

ROE

I spent most of the night tossing and turning at the motel. I only had one more day to convince Hunter to go back to Gavriel, and I had no idea how I was going to do that. My head was a mess of options. Last night felt like a declaration, but it felt like nothing, too. I felt like one of the girls he picked up from the bar and used to forget for a while. Why was Hunter so determined to forget me? Did something else happen? Maybe there was more to the story he wasn't telling me.

"You look well-rested. Your svadhisthana chakra is practically glowing!" Butterfly sang. Every time she spoke, it was like a melodic song of happiness. I didn't know what a *svadhisthana* chakra was, but the mischievous look the blond-headed hippie was giving me gave me a bit of an idea. I had the post-hate-sex glow, and Butterfly knew it.

Sunrise yoga on the compound wasn't exactly my idea of fun, but I wanted to prove a point to Hunter. I also needed the time to clear my mind and figure out what the fuck I was going to do. *And* a small part of me wanted to see what I was asking Hunter to give up.

The compound where Hunter worked was one hundred acres of beautiful wilderness with sporadic oases strategically placed on various trails. The main house was an all-glass, air-conditioned building surrounded by succulents and cacti. The multipurpose room was currently covered in yoga mats, and Reiki music was playing on a Bluetooth speaker.

It was beautiful. I understood why people spent ridiculous amounts of money to be here. It was calm and quiet. The world seemed to move slower here. The air was dry and crisp. The sand painted a beautiful landscape with curled Joshua trees planted proudly everywhere. It felt secluded and picturesque. No wonder he put roots here.

"I don't know what you're talking about," I said while wiping my face with a towel. Butterfly had three students in her sunrise class, two of them were an older lesbian couple named Eileen and Kaylee. They were staying in one of the tents on the compound for their second anniversary and talked a lot about being one with nature but also complained about the lack of cell phone signal. Butterfly took her job very seriously. One hour was spent in meditation, and the rest of the time we all attempted to mimic her difficult moves. She was the only one who could successfully achieve the side plank, and I spent more time laughing with Kaylee and Eileen and trying not to fall over than anything else.

It was just what I needed. I felt lighter and free. The heaviness of the last few days and the stress of Gavriel's threats were weighing me down. I felt bad for relaxing when I should have been figuring out a way to get Hunter to work again, but I needed to clear my head.

"Hunter had that freshly fucked look about him when he came back to our table last night," Butterfly prodded. I grabbed the water bottle and took a swig, swishing it around my mouth and swallowing before thinking about how to answer her. Luna had said they'd both slept with him, and I wasn't sure if Butterfly would be jealous or not. I already knew Roxanne was the territorial one of the bunch.

"Did he give you angry sex? God, I love Hunter's angry sex. He has such a red aura, and it just comes alive in the bedroom—or in the horse stalls," she said before nudging me with a giggle. She started walking outside, and I followed after her, letting out a sigh when the warm sun hit my shoulders. I refused to feel jealous, though that green envious feeling still burst with an electric shock through my chest. I wasn't saving myself for him and had a few romps of my own, but it still hurt.

"Do you sleep together often?" I asked. My voice sounded forced.

"When he first moved here, yes. He just seemed so angry and alone. I'm an empath, so I sensed his need for intimacy and human connection," Butterfly explained. She sounded like sex with Hunter was a selfless mission, and the idea made me want to laugh. Sex with Hunter made me *selfish*. All I could think of was more, more, more.

"But I stopped sleeping with him when I realized he was just trying to forget someone..." I listened to the way her voice trailed off, and slumped my shoulders. "Hunter came here damaged, and he'll continue to be damaged until he fills that void," Butterfly then explained. "He has so much guilt."

I let out a slow exhale and turned to face her. Butterfly was ridiculously gorgeous. In the early morning light, her pale blond hair practically glowed.

She had crystals around her neck and wore a burnt orange sports bra and tight yoga pants. Sex last night was rough and violent, but it left me feeling so empty and devoid of satisfaction. I didn't come. I felt used. My standards where Hunter was concerned always seemed to falter. The only enjoyment I got out of it was his confessions at the end.

"Last night was the most alive I've seen him in ages. His aura was very confusing, but I saw healing lavender. Who are you, Roe Palmer?" she asked with a teasing grin.

I decided right then to trust Butterfly. "I think I'm the girl Hunter was running from. I think I'm the void he's been trying to fill."

Butterfly tilted her head back and laughed, the sound like wind chimes. "Oh, I already knew that," she said with a giggle. "My spirit guides visited me last night and informed me all about your history. You'll be able to celebrate your birthday again. I promise. Don't let your mother's death stop you from enjoying life."

I dropped my mouth open in shock. Butterfly was legit. "Seems like you already know who I am."

Butterfly let out a sigh, then wrapped her arm around me. I felt self-conscious from all the sweat from our morning workout. She guided me over to a picnic table overlooking the desert landscape, with a gazebo blocking the sun, and sat me down. "You've been chasing Hunter for five years. You came here looking for him, but maybe you really do need to find yourself. So I'll ask again, who are you, Roe Palmer?"

"I-I don't know. Somewhere I started wrapping my identity up in my obsession," I whispered. Butterfly nodded politely, encouraging me to continue. "How can I find out who I am when he's been a part of my life since the day I was born? Even if I didn't know it, his presence was still there."

In many ways, I felt like I had found myself. I was stronger. More determined. The girl Hunter knew would've never fought back the way I did last night. And yet I still felt lost. I went to college because it just felt like something to do. I moved in with Nicole because I have no one else. My only unique and defining quality was that I could write, but even that was something I didn't know what I would do with. I lost myself during the time I was supposed to be free.

"Last night you said you are a poet," Butterfly said while digging through her backpack. "Why don't you just sit here and write? A lot has happened since you arrived. Take some time to process."

I took the notepad and pen from her hands and placed it on the picnic table. "Thank you," I replied lamely.

"See that trail over there," Butterfly said while nodding in the distance. I followed her line of sight and stared at a path of sand. "Hunter takes the horses there every day at noon. If you wait here, you'll see him. He's really good with the horses," she added in a dreamy voice.

Butterfly squeezed my shoulder and spun around to head back toward one of the main buildings. I watched her back for a moment, then drug my eyes to the notepad she'd handed me. She was right. It was time I found myself.

———

Citrine

Abundance.
Your heart is like a muddy puddle drought, and I'm drowning
in the idea that a little more rain could clear the dirt away.

I'll sell self-respect for a kiss,
My life for a quick fuck in a public parking lot.
You'll toss threats in my outstretched palm.

More, please.

My sense of self is like a foggy night with bright headlights reflecting
off the water molecules in the air.
I'm just trying to see. Trying to drive my car to wherever you are.
With your muddy puddles and your more.

And when I get there? I'll wear a necklace of citrine so I can tell you
how a rock brought us together. How I manifested
an ocean with a pulse by casting a single stone. I'll be so fucking proud.

And you'll look at me, frown, and shake your head.

More, please.

You need more than me.

Chapter 9

ROE

"What are you writing?" a gruff voice asked at my back. I was so lost in my words and the beautiful setting surrounding me that I hadn't noticed Hunter strutting over to me. I covered the lined paper, filled to the brim with my scrawled words, with my sweaty palm and turned around to face him, a blush of embarrassment coating my cheeks. Despite group critiques and getting a degree in English, I still turned bashful any time someone read my work. *Especially* when that someone was the subject of most of my poems. Hunter was the most devastating muse. They say artists have to experience pain in order to be profound, and there's something to be said for the dozens of notebooks filled with his name.

I nearly dropped my fucking jaw on the sandy ground when I saw his shirtless torso glistening with sweat, and his denim jeans hanging low on his hips. His skin was tanned and freckled from working in the sun so much, and the dust clinging to his pants made it look like he spent all morning rolling around on the ground. He looked hot and golden. Bright.

I swallowed before answering, not sure what side of Hunter I was going to get today. Would he be the ruthless asshole who hurt me last night? Would he be the man in awe that I was standing before him? Would he be the careless, crass, indifferent acquaintance? I least liked that version of him.

"You know," I began with a shaky voice. I wanted to sound playful and hopefully dispel the awkward, angry tension between us. "There was once a time that you didn't ask. You just watched me or picked up my journal to find what you were looking for." It was such a vulnerable thing to have the option of sharing your work taken away from you. He took the guesswork out of courage.

Hunter looked around while running a hand through his shaggy hair. I watched him debate what to say. Everything about his body language and stare seemed uncertain, as if he was just as curious as I was where we went from here. I'd never seen him so unsure. It was jarring. Thrusting his hands in his pockets, he then rocked on his feet for a bit before closing the short distance between us. "I've been trying to tell you this, Roe. That's not me anymore."

"I know," I whispered before looking out over the large stretch of desert. The Joshua trees for which the small town was named cast crooked shadows on the sand, and there was a slight October chill to the dry air. Pretty soon, the mountains in the distance would be capped with snow, a stark contradiction to the vast nothing in the valley.

"Last night was a mistake," Hunter said. I knew he'd say this, and he wasn't wrong. I craved a tender intimacy from him that I wasn't sure I'd ever get. He stared me down with his bright blue eyes. Though his words echoed regret, there was no remorse in his expression. I thought about last night, the invasion of his hard cock punishing me against the tabletop. I drove home with his cum dripping down my thigh and my eyes leaking with regret. Once was a mistake. Twice, a tragedy. Our pattern of fucking and leaving was getting on my nerves.

"Which part of it?" I challenged.

"All of it. You and I both know that I don't want to hurt you, Roe. But I don't want you here either. I will do whatever it takes to get you to leave. I can't…" He paused to look up at the sky in contemplation, then back at me. "It's too much to have you here."

"And why is that? Why is it too painful to look me in the eye, Hunter? I'm not the one that left you. I'm not the one that…h-hurt you," I croaked, my voice lingering on the word *hurt*.

Hunter clenched his teeth and curled his fist at his side. I feared our brief, civil conversation would soon be over. "I don't have to explain myself to you. You're not entitled to a fucking reason," he growled. "Why do you think you are owed an explanation? If I don't want you, I don't want you."

My mind lingered on those four little words.

I don't want you.

I don't want you.

I don't want you.

He kicked at the dust, and I watched his rambling tantrum in amusement. He was deflecting. "You're right," I replied with a yawn. Balling my poem in my fist, I stood up and sauntered over to him. "I'm not entitled to your reasons. I just hoped that our history would have meant enough to you to at least gift me with a little bit of closure."

"Maybe I don't want to think about our intertwined pasts!" Hunter yelled. "I paid my debt. I already fucking paid my debt. I want to live a life where I don't have to think about you or your mom."

I drew my eyebrows together. "Or my dad?" I asked. It was curious that he didn't mention Lake Palmer.

"Yes, *and* your dad," he sputtered. "Thank you for the fucking reminder." This man killed people for a living? So why couldn't he just let this one go? "I just want to be done, Roe."

"Then be done!" I exclaimed. "You paid your debt, so why can't you just let this fucking go?"

I sensed that the truth was on the tip of his tongue. Hunter fumed in front of me, his strong chest heaving up and down. I matched him breath for breath while daring him to speak, daring him to tell me why he was holding back.

"Fuck this," he gritted before spinning on his boots and heading back toward the trail he came from. I followed after him, determination pounding through my sandals. We both kicked up dust in fury.

"You keep running from me, Hunter. The mixed signals are exhausting," I yelled at his back. "You're my stalker. You want to protect me, but you hate me. You want to love me but also escape me. What is it, huh?" I pressed.

He kept walking. His steps became faster and harsher. I breathlessly followed after him. The buzz of anger mixed with lust made my sweaty skin turn flushed. Would I piss him off? Would he turn around and kiss me? Kill me? Fuck me?

"Why do you feel so goddamn guilty, huh? You saved me! And I might have been pissed at the time, but Mack is probably the second best thing to ever happen to me. He really loves me, you know?"

Hunter's steps faltered for a beat, but he recovered quickly. In the distance, I could see a large wooden structure with a fence surrounding it. Horses were playing in front of it. "You wanna know the first best thing, Hunter? It might surprise you," I continued to press. The thing about pressure was it demanded more. You couldn't expect anything to come to a head if you weren't willing to *press*. "It's you," I said softly. "I know you don't want it to be you, but it is."

Hunter finally stopped just outside of the fence. I watched him grab a shirt that was draped over the splintered, worn wood and shrug it on. I didn't think it was possible for a man to look sexy putting clothes *on*, but he pulled it off.

Hunter continued to ignore me, scaling the wooden posts and hiking his leg over so he could be inside with two white and brown horses.

They were beautiful beasts. I didn't know a single thing about caring for them, but Hunter seemed skilled. They were massive, with tall legs, round muscular chests and white noses. Their manes were perfectly brushed, and their large brown eyes stared assentingly at Hunter.

Within seconds he was clicking his tongue, encouraging them to follow him to the barn. Not wanting to hop over the fence, I spotted a gate and let myself inside.

I wasn't through talking to Hunter, but I also wanted to see this side of his life. It was hard to picture him in a gentle setting, caring for horses under the desert sun. He didn't glance over his shoulder to check if I was still following, but the stress in his shoulders made me think that he knew I hadn't given up just yet.

The barn was large and looked fairly new. Each stall was clean and organized. Various gear lined the walls, and stacks of hay were on the far west end. Hunter guided one of the horses into a stall and let the other one roam. "You seem happy here," I commented. There was less anger in my tone. "Do you like working here? Do you ever miss Denver?"

At the mention of Denver, his lip flinched, the only sign that he could hear me. I kept talking. It was like approaching a wild animal. If you keep speaking, eventually the sound of your voice won't startle it so much. "Not much has changed. I sometimes go to your old cabin." I paused, waiting for a reaction. He simply grabbed a water bottle and gulped some of the refreshing liquid down. I hungrily watched his throat bob. "The grass is overgrown. It's falling apart. Some kids even graffitied the outside."

His brow furrowed, and his eyes flashed to mine for a brief moment. "But I went out there and painted over it. I found a bright shade of pink and covered the entire cabin with it." Hunter flexed. I could play this game all freaking day. "It's bright. You'd like it."

And that's how the majority of our day went. I sat in the barn as he worked, swinging my legs back and forth and occasionally getting up to help him. I shoveled shit for a couple of hours, and I talked about Nicole's stripping job. He brushed their manes, and I told him about my favorite professor. I worked until my body was slick with sweat and my muscles burned. I didn't ask his permission to help, nor did I have any idea what I was doing, but I followed his lead and told him about everything that had happened over the last five years until my voice was so hoarse I couldn't speak.

I wasn't sure if I was doing this for my sake or his. Gavriel's threats seemed like a whisper as I updated him on my life. I mostly wanted him to know. I couldn't explain it, but there was a certain comfort in sharing my life with him. Hunter was this secret force—a consistent presence in my life. I wanted that feeling again. I wanted to involve him in the day-to-day aspects of my existence.

When the sun began to set and Hunter was done for the day, I followed him to his truck and got inside the passenger seat without permission. "I'm staying at the motel off Highway 10," I rasped while rubbing my throat. I needed some fucking water.

Hunter stared at me for a moment, determined not to break his vow of silence. I swallowed and tried to wet my tongue until a full water bottle was thrust in my face. "Thanks," I whispered before grabbing it from him and drinking the entire thing. He hadn't turned the car on, nor had he asked what the fuck I was doing. He just stared at me as rivulets of water traveled down my chin. And when I was done, I wiped it away with a satisfied hiss.

Hunter rested his chin on his fist and stoically stared at me. We sat in silence for a long while before he finally spoke.

"You worked hard today."

"Worth it. I got to watch a sexy, shirtless man pet horses all day. I'm filing this day in my spank bank for all eternity."

Hunter chuckled, and I felt thankful for the brief reprieve in angst and anger. Silence stretched for a moment before he spoke again. "It wasn't all bad, you know. I don't hate our time together. I just..."

I wanted him to finish his sentence, but he never did. "I know this is crazy. A lot of time has passed. I mean, it's been five years…"

"Not enough time," Hunter grumbled. "I wanted more for you, Roe. I wanted you to find a nice guy. Settle down. Move on."

"That's our problem," I said with a sigh. "You're more concerned with what you want for me, and all I want is you."

Hunter looked at me, licking his lips while scratching his veiny forearm. The moment stretched on. I wanted to lean in and rub my cheek against his scruff. "Why did you come back after last night? I thought I'd for sure scared you," he then asked, breaking the spell.

I debated on lying to Hunter. I probably should have. But I didn't want this momentary truce to be ruined with lies. "Something scarier sent me back," I murmured.

Hunter straightened in his seat and turned to face me. His face was shadowed with determination, and I saw hints of the man I once knew break through the cracks of my declaration.

"What are you talking about?"

"Gavriel Moretti does nothing for free," I replied with a shrug.

Hunter shook his head in annoyance and stared up at the roof of his truck. "Of course," he began. "He told you where I was. What deal did you make?"

"He said he'd give me your location if I get you to go back to work for him. He has Nicole as leverage."

Hunter absorbed my words for a moment. I waited for the ball to drop. I waited for him to lose his mind and curse me for involving him in the Bullets' affairs once more. "So you aren't here for me? You're here because someone is threatening you to be." Hunter punched the steering wheel, a look of disgust on his face.

I could have throttled him. "Oh no you don't," I replied before leaning over the center console and shoving his chest. "I didn't come here because of some threat, Hunter Hammond." I leaned over to hover my lips over his, not caring about the sweat or my frizzy hair and the horse shit on my shoes. "I came here because, since the moment I met you, I've felt like I was meant to have you in my life." Hunter's eyes widened in surprise, but he kept quiet, allowing me to continue. "I'm here because I felt stuck in this crazy limbo for the last five years. It was like I couldn't move on unless I knew you were okay. I wanted to look you in the eyes and feel this thing between us be over. I've been stuck needing you and needing closure. I made a deal with the devil because I crave you, Hunter. I ache for you. Even after five years. Even after you hurt me."

Hunter stared at my lips while gnawing on his own. Time lingered. It was like this beautiful moment where I sensed that the old Hunter was still here. "I came here, and I saw that you've moved on," I continued. "I respect that. I know that I romanticized what we had. I want to understand why you feel so much guilt. I need to know why it has to be all or nothing with us—why I can't even have your friendship."

"And you stayed because once again you need me," he whispered.

"I don't expect you to clean up my mess, Hunter. I can handle myself. I wanted to tell you the truth about what led me here, but I don't want you to go back to working for Gavriel. You're happy here. I'm just worried about Nicole. I don't know what to do."

"I will handle Gavriel," Hunter gritted. His voice was unyielding, as if there was no room for discussion.

"I made the deal, and I can handle the consequences," I replied. "I'm the one that wanted to see you."

My response made Hunter chuckle. "You're weak, Roe. The kind of consequences Gavriel Moretti is known for will keep you up at night. I know what it's like to have death on your conscience, and you aren't cut out for it. I will handle this shit with Gavriel so you can leave. How much time did he give you?"

A sense of relief filled me, but it was short-lived. If Hunter was going to fix the situation with Gavriel, then that meant I had no reason to stay here. "Two days," I blurted out in relief. I was thankful that he would help with Nicole.

Hunter stroked his jaw while simmering over my words. I knew that he wanted me gone, and the moment he spoke with Gavriel, I'd be out of here.

"You can stay here while I figure this shit out with Gavriel. But what happened last night can't happen again," he said. I nodded my head while averting my eyes from his heavy stare.

"Agreed. I'm not going to be able to move on if we keep doing things like that. It sends mixed messages when you tell me how much you hate me, then fuck me into oblivion."

"Agreed," Hunter began. He dug his fingers into my upper thigh, and I hadn't even realized he was holding me there. I was sitting in the passenger seat of his truck, staring at his hand and wiggling in my seat. Here we were talking about not taking things too far, and I was already sucked into his orbit. Hunter looked down, realizing what he was doing. Snapping his hand back, I whimpered at the loss of his touch.

"Besides," I chuckled darkly, trying to play off the moment with humor. I leaned back until I was pressed against the door. Every inch of space between us felt like a deeper breath. "I don't think your harem of pussy would appreciate sharing."

Hunter rolled his eyes. "There's not a lot of options in the desert, and I don't do exclusivity."

I patted my lips with my index finger in contemplation. "That bartender—Manny, was it? He seems kind of cute," I teased.

Hunter's eyes flashed with darkness for the briefest of seconds, but I caught it. It looked like furious jealousy and hate with one single glance. And then it disappeared. He fixed his face into a soft, easy-going expression like nothing was wrong.

We went quiet again for a lingering moment. "Thank you again for talking to Gavriel," I whispered. "I'm so sorry I got you involved in that again."

"You never really leave the Bullets," Hunter replied. "Only way out is death or jail."

"Then why did you leave?"

Hunter chuckled. "Just because I can't escape it doesn't mean I don't want to." Hunter stared at my sports bra and the way my stomach dripped with sweat for a moment before dragging his eyes back up to me. "It's crazy how easily I want to slip back into that role," he murmured.

I cocked my head to the side quizzically. "And what role is that?" I asked.

Hunter ran his hands down his stomach and stared at the center console for a moment before looking back up at me. I breathed in, expecting another hurtful thing to spew from his lips, but instead all that hit my nose was the smell of rosewood. Rosewood. He still smelled the same. "It's so easy to want to protect you, Roe. It's so easy to want to take care of you.

You're far more dangerous than Gavriel, Roe."

"What do you mean?" The back and forth was so fucking confusing and was driving me crazy. I just wanted answers. "I'd kill for him, sure. But I'd die for you."

I swallowed, absorbing his declaration while looking out the passenger window at the hazy pink sunset. Maybe Hunter didn't hate me. Maybe he was terrified of what his obsession did to him. I knew the feeling. It's what made me fly across the country to meet with Gavriel. It's what made me forgo pride, self-respect, and a sense of self-preservation, all for the *hope* that he'd love me again. My obsession terrified me, so I could understand why he needed space. It was like neither of us could breathe when we were around one another.

But there was something else, too. Another factor I missed. Hunter was filled with guilt, and it felt like he had more sins he wanted to atone for. I knew about our intertwined past, but maybe there was something I missed. Either way, I hoped I got to the bottom of it.

"You don't have to take care of me anymore. I take care of myself now," I whispered, though we both knew that in this instance, it was a bald-faced lie. I couldn't handle the Bullets and Gavriel. I should have never gotten involved. But I *could* handle Hunter Hammond. I could take his hate. Take his pain. I could take the abuse, because my obsession was like a sponge, and every cruel moment helped me understand him better.

Chapter 10

HUNTER

I was going to kill Gavriel Moretti, and I sure as fuck wouldn't do it efficiently. A single shot through the skull wasn't enough. I'd need to draw it out, make it painful. I imagined myself wrapping my hands around his neck and squeezing until his devilish brown eyes popped out of his head. Maybe a slow-burning poison. Maybe I'd snap his neck just so I could hear the satisfying crack of his bones. It had been a while since I'd daydreamed about murder. I hadn't wished to spill blood in ages. But the asshole deserved it, and I had a lot of reasons to be pissed right now.

He was probably smirking at his desk, thinking he had me right where he wanted me just because Roe delivered herself to him on a silver platter. We had a deal. She was always meant to be off-limits. She was a boundary he knew not to cross. I guess all bets were off when I went off the grid and disappeared here to get her out of my head. I wasn't foolish enough to think that Gavriel would let me off the hook so easily. I always knew the job would one day catch up to me.

I just wanted more time.

More time to get Roe out of my fucking head. More time to enjoy my job and the horses. More time in my airstream trailer. More time at the bar. More time finding the sins of my past at the bottom of an empty bottle. Hell, maybe even more time with Roxanne. I didn't love her, but maybe I could have settled down and possibly liked her eventually. I was older now. I wanted different things. I craved the simplicity my childhood didn't offer me. I'd never felt settled before. I never had a consistent home with a foundation that wasn't drenched in blood, drugs, and debts.

But now I was back to being the man hopelessly in love with a girl— no, *woman*—I didn't deserve.

I dropped her off at the motel and drove back to my airstream, gritting my teeth the entire way. She wouldn't look at me when she got out of the car. I wanted to follow her inside. I wanted to pry apart her thighs and bury my face there. I wanted to taste the memory of us on my tongue and punish myself with her pleasure.

But I sped off and didn't look back. If last night taught me anything, it's that one taste wasn't enough. I'd relapsed big time, and it terrified me.

I distracted myself by weighing all of my options and figuring out how I wanted to play this. If I agreed to work for Gavriel, he'd always hold Roe over me. He'd know that he has easy bait to get me to cooperate, and I didn't like that for a multitude of reasons. I wanted to be my own man. I didn't want to be tied to any person, debt, or...Roe. I couldn't be tied to her. Gavriel would happily stitch our skin together if it meant he could control me.

And the worst part was, I liked the idea of being tied to Roe. I wanted to blame Gavriel for my weaknesses. Use him as an excuse to give in—but I couldn't. She definitely wasn't making my job easy, either. Fuck if she didn't look sexy as hell in the barn, shoveling shit and updating me on her life. Every time I swallowed, I could feel her lusty screams traveling down my throat. Every time she spoke, I could feel her digging under my skin, tempting me with memories I'd worked fucking hard to forget. We'd changed, but the attraction was still the same. The *obsession* was still the same, too. It felt like I'd been walking on solid ground for the last five years, and now I was drowning in sinking sand. She was going to pull me under. She knew it, I knew it.

And Gavriel Fucking Moretti knew it, too.

Speak of the devil, my phone started ringing. I stared at the caller ID in annoyance. I wanted a bit more time to come up with my plan of action. He who made the first move always had the upper hand. The fact that he was calling me just proved he was armed and ready for mind games.

I let it ring and ring and ring until it went to voicemail. Gavriel liked his employees at the ready, always standing with their dick in their hands and willing to jack off at his command. I stared at my phone while getting out of my truck. I wanted to pace in the sand but figured I could trick my body into being calm if I sat in the lawn chair, so I settled into the metal seat with rusted legs and bright orange paint. Ten minutes passed until he called again, and like a bad habit, I answered on the first ring. Maybe it wasn't so bad if he thought he had the upper hand.

"Did you like the gift I sent you?" Gavriel asked without greeting. I ground my teeth, my jaw aching from the fury flowing through my jaw.

"Not particularly," I replied.

"Such a shame. I wrapped it in a pretty bow and everything."

"I didn't ask for this, Gavriel. In fact, I figured you'd understand that when I disappeared for five fucking years." I clenched my fist and stared at a lizard crawling under a rock near my foot.

"I see five years on that hippie compound hasn't improved your temper," he replied coolly. "A gift is a gift. You'll take what I give you with a fucking smile."

I let out a sigh. "What do you want, Gavriel? It's been five years."

"You haven't even asked how I'm doing. Business is booming, by the way."

"Isn't it always? Spit it out, Gavriel. I don't have time for your bullshit. Tell me what you *need*, and I'll consider helping you." I knew that would piss him off. Gavriel didn't like needing anything, let alone *needing* to rely on anyone else. He liked control. He wanted the world to spin on his fucking command.

"I have a job for you."

"Obviously." Gavriel wasn't calling to catch up. We weren't friends. Weren't the family he liked to preach about, either.

"It's the kind of high-profile target that needs your expertise. He's heavily guarded. In the public eye…"

I let out a sigh. He was probably a fucking politician. I had a certain knack for making hard to kill people disappear. "No," I replied, not waiting to hear the reward for this kill.

Gavriel went quiet. I heard him shuffling through papers on his desk, and I waited for the pen to drop, for the threat to spill from his lips. "Roe was a nice girl," he began. I didn't like how he said *was*. "Her friend Nicole is a pain in the ass. It would be no skin off my dick to kill them both."

Nicole was Roe's problem, not mine. I didn't give two shits about her. But if he thought for one second he could threaten *my girl*, then he needed to check his ego. He was definitely bluffing. I could too. "Go ahead." The words turned to ash on my tongue. It was a dangerous game of dares and power.

Gavriel chuckled darkly. "Springs Motel? Right off the highway. She's in room seventeen. She's taking a shower right now, actually."

My blood boiled, and my vision turned red. Standing up, I grabbed my truck keys from my pocket and jogged over to where I was parked. "You act like you don't care, Hunter. But I know why you ran. You don't want to be responsible for killing another person in her life, do you? First her father—"

"Don't say another fucking word." I couldn't hear it. I'd worked too hard to forget that—to move past those old memories. Old guilts. Old debts.

"Don't tell me what to do. I gave you a break, but vacation is over," Gavriel began. His tone was unyielding. "Take the gift I gave you and get to work. I need this job done in two days, and if you aren't headed here by then, I'll personally take my gift back and bury her six feet under."

I started the truck and peeled away from my airstream, barreling down the road and back toward the motel as fast as I could. I shouldn't care, but old habits die hard.

"If you hurt a hair on her fucking head. . ."

"Don't bother threatening me. I'm not intimidated by a man not courageous enough to be with the woman he loves."

Loves? What the fuck did Gavriel Moretti know about love? He *possessed.* I didn't know how Sunshine put up with him.

If I had to describe this thing between Roe and me, it would be more along the lines of:

Disastrous

Dangerous

Inevitable

Tragic

Toxic

Beautiful

Profound

Love

Love. Love. Love.

Love made people do deplorable things. "And yet you hire me to kill. I'm the best of the best, Gavriel. You might have an empire, but I have a knack for killing."

Gavriel went quiet again, trying to regain the upper hand with strategic silence. "You have two days, Hunter. Don't disappoint me."

He hung up, and I threw my phone in the passenger seat. "Fuck!" I screamed. Speeding down the highway, I raced toward Roe. Toward the sinking sand. Toward my greatest weakness.

Chapter 11

ROE

I let the steady stream of water fall down my shoulders. I breathed in the hot steam, letting it open up my choked throat. The bathroom smelled like bleach and my vanilla body wash. Today was exhausting. I was emotionally drained but hyped up, too. My body ached from helping Hunter in the barn, and my heart ached from our conversation in his truck. I closed my eyes and tilted my head up and against the steamy stream, blowing water out of my mouth as words for a new poem hit me like a freight train. I loved it when this happened. I loved the serendipities of language and the way they greeted me at random times.

I spun around and faced the fogged up glass door of the shower. Dragging my finger along it, I carved temporary words with my finger in the moisture.

Loving you is delicate.

Nothing about Hunter was delicate. He was all hard. His cut muscles.

His heart. His cruel words. He was like concrete, and I was a crack in the pavement that grew with time. My obsession stretched out during hot summers. It burrowed deeper and deeper until the road was split in two. Even the timelessly durable things could crumble. It was such a delicate thing, to be so hard. It made you break even harder.

I started writing more words, twisting letters and meaning with lazy assuredness.

Loving you is like dipping your toes in wet concrete. You're tempted by the idea of permanence, then get stuck when it hardens.

I loved taking showers. There was something beautiful about the vulnerability of being naked and the process of washing away the grit of the day. It felt like a baptism, and I needed to feel new again after seeing Hunter. I wanted to be a shiny, polished little doll that wasn't cut and scarred by the man I was hopelessly in love with.

I always came up with my best poetry in the shower, and today I was feeling inspired. I closed my eyes and took the finger I used to write the now fading words and trailed it down my body, thinking of the thin line of his lips. I sunk lower and lower, dipping my hand between my thighs and sinking into the pleading heat. I thought of his broad shoulders and strong arms. I thought of how gentle he was with the horses, the sweat dripping down his muscular back and abs.

I thought about his cold eyes and how devastatingly beautiful he was. I let out a sigh while writing poetry about Hunter on my clit with the tip of my finger. My soaking wet hair fell down my back, my hands trembled, and his name escaped my lips.

I imagined him at my back in the shower, bracing his hand against the tile and pressing into me. I imagined heated words.

Your pussy is so fucking wet, Roe.

I want to taste your come. Drown in your pleasure.

I imagined him pushing me against the wall with water streaming down his back. I imagined our bodies aligning, his thick, hard cock pressing at my entrance.

A loud knocking on the door made me jump, jarring me out of the moment. I'd put the Do Not Disturb sign on my door, so it couldn't have been housekeeping. The only person who knew that I was here was…

Hunter.

I quickly shut off the water and stepped out of the shower, letting droplets of water travel down my thighs. I grabbed a towel and wrapped it around myself. Running to the door, I peeked out the peephole then unlocked the deadbolt, opening it just a crack. Sure enough, Hunter was brooding on the other side, with his arms crossed at his chest and a frown on his face. I furrowed my brow in confusion at the sight of him.

He didn't wait for me to greet him nor did he wait for me to properly open the door. Hunter braced his hand against the wood and pressed, nearly knocking me back as he let himself inside. I gripped the towel tighter against my chest. "What are you doing here?" I asked. Hunter ignored my question. He simply started walking the perimeter of the room, checking the windows, doors, and furniture. I watched in confusion as he ran his coarse hands over every available surface. I asked him again. "What are you doing here?"

Once Hunter had touched nearly every available inch of space in the motel bedroom, he turned to face me. "I had a little chat with Gavriel today."

"I'm assuming you aren't on my doorstep because your conversation with Gavriel went well," I deadpanned.

"Has anyone stopped by?" he asked. "Any suspicious men?"

I rolled my eyes and dropped my towel, not caring about my nakedness. It wasn't anything he hadn't seen before. Bending over to grab the pair of yoga pants and a crop top from my suitcase, I let out a little groan as my muscles stretched to accommodate the movement. Fuck, today was a lot of work.

The moment I stood back up, my eyes connected with Hunter's cold blue gaze, heavy and sinking with heat as they traveled up and down my lean frame. I covered my breasts with my arms to hide the tattoo there. I wasn't ready for him to see that. I swallowed as we drank in the appearance of one another for a moment. His tongue poked at the inside of his cheek, and I remembered that he had asked me a question.

"Strange men?" I clarified. "None other than you. Careful, Hunter. If you keep worrying about my safety, I'll start to think you care."

My words seemed to break the spell, casting a dark look of annoyance on Hunter's face. "I do care, Roe," he whispered. "The problem is, I need to *stop*."

I wanted to ask why and slap him across the cheek, but refrained. "So what's the plan?" I asked while slipping on my shirt without a bra and working the tight pants up my thighs.

"There is no plan. I'm not going to work for Gavriel again." Hunter looked around the room. "And I don't care if he knows it either," he added loudly. "You hear that, Gav? I don't care." He was practically shouting now. If the room was bugged, Gavriel definitely got the message. I was worried about Nicole. This wasn't the news I was hoping for, and the Bullets leader didn't seem like the type to take no for an answer.

"And how does Gavriel feel about that?" I asked.

Hunter clenched his jaw and balled his hands into fists. "He threatened to kill you and Nicole."

I figured that would be Gavriel's next move, but hearing Hunter say it so plainly sent a chill up my spine. "And are you going to let him?" I asked.

"I haven't decided yet," he growled in response.

I walked up to Hunter, approaching him with a sense of caution. Once we were toe to toe, I gently placed my hand on his chest. I reveled in the feel of his pounding heart. "You made the decision when you came here to check on me," I whispered, too scared that my cocky words would trigger his fight-or-flight response. Hunter Hammond was repelled by the idea of showing he cared. "Thank you."

"Don't thank me yet," he rasped. I took a step closer and breathed him in. Hunter still smelled of sweat from working in the barn all day. I briefly wondered what it would be like to live out here with him. With him working with horses, and me selling poetry by the moonlight. I envisioned us in a tiny house with a view of the mountains. I imagined him coming home every day and us standing just like this.

"Stop looking at me like I'm your hero. I don't want trouble in Joshua Tree. I've built a life here, and it would look bad if you turned up dead."

He had a point, but I still clung to the hope that he cared. "Until I can figure out what to do, you're staying with me." He grunted before taking a step back and stripping out of his clothes.

My mouth watered at the sight of him. "W-what are you doing?" I asked.

"Taking a shower. We need to be in a public space, so we're going to the bar tonight."

"It's Sunday," I stammered as he shrugged off his boxers and proudly made his way over to the bathroom.

"That hasn't stopped me before. Grab my clothes from my truck, will ya?" he asked playfully while gripping the door handle. "I want to look good for Roxanne." Fucking bastard. "And try not to get killed during your walk to the parking lot. I'd hate for a sniper to get you."

I marched outside to his truck and grabbed what looked like an overnight duffel bag he kept under the passenger seat for such occasions. Grabbing it, I cursed him all the way down the pavement, through my motel door and into the bathroom. My anger and jealousy stalled the moment I saw the outline of his tanned body in the frosted shower glass.

"Have trouble finding it?" he asked, his voice teetering the line between playfulness and breathy annoyance. I grabbed the shower door and opened it, licking my lips at the sight of his rock-hard dick covered in soap suds. He was breathing deeply, and his heated eyes drank me in.

I dumped the entire contents of the duffel bag on the shower floor.

"You fucking brat," he growled. He didn't move for his clothes, now soaking wet. He was too taut and rigid.

"Were you stroking yourself just now?" I asked while stepping into the shower. His eyes went wide with shock, and he stepped away from me, his back hitting the cool glass. He almost seemed afraid of my touch.

"What are you doing?" he asked. I stepped under the stream of water, letting it soak my white shirt, turning it see-through. I could feel my hair sticking to my back. My nipples were pointed peaks cutting through my shirt. Everything within me ached for a sense of intimacy or connection with him. It wasn't even purely physical.

He watched me with twitching fingers. I could tell he wanted to fist his cock at the sight of me. It was time for me to take some of my power back.

I reached out and wrapped my tiny hand around his large, hard dick. My thumb and index finger barely connected. He was so thick. I stared at the veined prize in my hand and bit my lip. "No one can touch you like I can, Hunter," I whispered while pumping him. The soapy suds made my movements slick and smooth. "Five long years, and I still think about how you moan when you come. The only time you let go is when you're balls deep in my pussy, Hunter."

His eyes rolled back. Lips parted. His head slammed against the tile as his rippled muscles flexed. Each heaving breath was long slow and exaggerated by lust. I wanted to get off so damn bad. My sex was practically begging for release against the friction of my soaking wet yoga pants. "You feel this?" I asked. "Feel the way I command your cock? Remember how good my soft hand feels sliding up and down."

Hunter groaned in response while reaching up to wrap my long, wet hair around his fist. I felt the tension against my scalp and welcomed it. "You can try fucking everything that moves to get me out of your memory, but no one will ever feel the way I do."

He tugged me closer and kissed me. Our tongues caressed and fought, and our mouths fucked. His sharp teeth bruised my lip. His hot breath feathered over my skin. I closed my eyes, though I wanted to watch him relax against me. My wet clothes stuck to my skin as I ran my free hand up and down his body.

Up and down his cock.

I stroked him until his cum was shooting on my stomach.

I tasted his groans of pleasure and turned his release into sweet poetry.

Loving you is delicate.
Loving you is like dipping your toes in wet concrete.
You're tempted by the idea of permanence, then get stuck when it hardens.
Loving you is worth it.
Loving you is like greeting death with a handshake and a smile.
You know it's inevitable, so you let pride guide your journey.
Loving you is complex.
Loving you is like dancing barefoot on hot coals.
It's a beautiful serenade but burns you all the same.
Loving you is demanding.
Loving you is like holding your breath.
It's got you wondering if oxygen is really necessary.
Loving you is delicate. Strenuous. Unremitting. Tiring. Spirited.
Loving you is like this halfhearted thing.
Where I supply half the heart and you supply nothing.

Chapter 12

ROE

The bar was just as crowded on Sunday night as it was Saturday. I guess there really wasn't much else to do here. Hunter had his hand perched possessively on my hip, and I couldn't help but preen when we walked through the swinging front doors.

We hadn't spoken complete sentences since I got him off in my motel. He got dressed in his work clothes, and I put on jeans and a tank top in silence. It was both an awkward and satisfying feeling. Once again I had no idea what I was doing with Hunter, but at least I felt like I had the upper hand. He said we should try to stay in crowded places in case Gavriel tried anything, but I knew he just didn't trust himself alone in a motel room with me. I wasn't in the mood to go to the bar, but he wasn't giving me much of an option.

What I really wanted to do was stay in my room and get off. Once again, I was left wanting, and my clit was practically begging for a little TLC.

I saw Luna and Butterfly chatting with Roxanne in a corner booth, and even though I liked two-thirds of their girl gang, my stomach still dropped at the sight of all three of them sitting together. Gavriel warned me that jealousy was a weak woman's emotion, and even though I didn't think it was wise to take advice from a man that wanted me dead, I forced myself to remember that five years was a long time and whatever Hunter shared with them couldn't possibly compare to eighteen years of stalking.

"I'm getting a drink," Hunter said in a curt tone. "Don't leave the bar. Stay aware. If anyone seems suspicious, let me know." I didn't even get the chance to respond sarcastically before he was abandoning me for a drink. I watched his back as he left, then made my way over to the girls.

"Hey!" Luna greeted while scooting over in the booth to make room for me. "I heard you spent your day working at the barn with Hunter."

"Word travels fast," I sighed while avoiding Roxanne's eyes, which were trained on me.

"Oh sweetie," Butterfly said from across the table. Her nimble fingers reached across and took hold of my hands resting on the tabletop. "Your energy is all over the place. Do you want to talk about it?"

Did I want to talk about it? I didn't even know what to say. I was terrified, sexually frustrated, hurt, annoyed, confused and broken. The combination of her sweet voice, my exhaustion, and fear finally caught up to me. My eyes filled with hot tears that streamed steadily down my face, and the table jumped into a flurry of activity. "I've got tissues in my purse," Luna said while reaching under the table for her crocodile print handbag.

"I'll start projecting positive energy and light," Butterfly replied while closing her eyes and humming.

My teary eyes finally landed on Roxanne, and she let out a sigh while flipping her brown hair over her shoulder. "For fuck's sake. I'll order drinks."

Once I had a very strong Long Island in my clutches, Luna made us all do a toast with the exclamation that "men ain't shit." I didn't tell them about how confused I was or how I feared for my and Nicole's lives. I just drank. And once three empty glasses were lined up before me, I realized Roxanne wasn't so bad.

"Good dick is hard to find. Keeping it consistently, even harder," she said before fishing for the cherry at the bottom of her drink with her tongue. Now that I had more time to look at her, we didn't seem much alike at all. Her eyes were smaller. Her lips rounder. Her personality was more tenacious. "Why do you think I turned into a territorial bitch with Hunter? He commands orgasms like it's his job." I giggled bitterly at that comment while the other two enthusiastically agreed.

"Preach!" Luna slurred while caressing the air. She'd gotten hot and taken off her black shirt about thirty minutes ago. Now, she was only wearing her sports bra. "I just want orgasms on the daily."

"Then you'll need to practice the beautiful expression of self-love," Butterfly replied. Her cheeks were flushed and her eyes hazy. "The only person that can make me come every time is myself."

The four of us started laughing loudly, probably gaining the attention of everyone in the bar. I grabbed a cube of ice from my drink and started running it over my neck and chest, sighing at the cool relief. I was burning up, probably from the copious amounts of alcohol coursing through my veins. "The last two times I've been with Hunter, I didn't get off," I said with a hiccup.

Luna gasped.

Butterfly rubbed a crystal hanging by her neck while exclaiming, "Sweet Mother Earth have mercy."

"That's just fucking unacceptable," Roxanne slurred.

A large shadow started looming over me, and my good mood almost immediately dissipated. I felt the entire energy of our table turn sour. Who would have thought that I'd prefer the company of the women Hunter had been sleeping with these past five years over him?

"Be gone, evil spirit," Butterfly said with a lyrical wave of her hands.

The entire room seemed to sway as I tilted my chin up to look at him. He looked slightly buzzed and completely crazed. He massaged the scruff on his jaw while eyeing the scene before him. "You owe this poor girl two orgasms," Roxanne slurred. "Minimum."

"What kind of man doesn't reciprocate?" Luna added. If I weren't trashed, I'd probably be embarrassed about this entire situation, but I was gifted with the bliss of not giving a single fuck.

"Roe, get your ass up. We're leaving." His response made my stomach burn. Or maybe it was the alcohol. Or maybe I just finally hated him back.

"Oh hell no," Luna said while clutching my arm. "We started a girl gang. You can't have her."

"Oh really?" Hunter's dark voice replied, a hint of humor coloring his tone.

"Yep!" Butterfly answered. "We're officially the Hunter Hammond Harem."

"Triple H for short," Roxanne interjected with a hiccup.

Hunter leaned over the table to whisper in my ear. "We need to leave."

"No," I replied defiantly, making my friends whoop in support.

Hunter shook his head at my defiance and practically growled. "What the fuck is even happening right now?" he gritted to himself.

"Never underestimate the magic of drunk girl bonding!" Butterfly sang. "It's a connection no difference can sever."

"Or dick can separate," Luna added.

"Or…what they said," Roxanne added before slumping in her seat.

"Men ain't shit!" I yelled, holding up my glass.

"Men ain't shit!" they all responded, making Hunter pinch the bridge of his nose.

Apparently done with the camaraderie, Hunter grabbed my arm and yanked me out of the booth before tossing me over his shoulder. I landed against muscle with an *oomph*, and I waved at my table of…friends? I didn't know when I'd ever see them again, life was too unpredictable at the moment. But I waved as Hunter carried me off, feeling good about my time with them.

Once out of the bar, Hunter started complaining. "Drunk women," he growled in disgust. My stomach sloshed and twisted.

"I like them," I said sleepily while swinging against his back. Nausea rolled through me like a booming thunderstorm. "Put me down before I puke."

Hunter quickly set me down on the ground beside his truck. "Do not vomit in my truck," he warned.

"I can find a ride back. I don't want to be around you." Everything was a confusing mess. I had no filter over my words or actions and didn't want to do or say anything I couldn't take back. I felt disconnected from my brain and awareness. Where was I again? My feet hurt. My mouth was dry. I smacked my lips like I could pool moisture from the air and drink from it.

"Yeah, fuck that. I'm taking your drunk ass home, end of story."

Right. I nodded. "Hunter always gets what he wants," I screamed while ripping open the passenger side door. "It doesn't matter who he hurts or what anyone else needs. It's just like always: your way or the fucking highway, like, damn." Did that even make sense? Probably not. I didn't even care.

He had to help me into the seat. Bracing his hot palm against my ass, Hunter shoved me into his truck with more force than necessary before slamming the door shut. I waited as he circled the vehicle, then started yelling at him again when he got inside.

"Men ain't shit!" I yelped before cradling my head in my hands. "Why are you so cruel to me?" I scooted over until I was in the middle seat, then rested my head on his shoulder, my voice growing quieter. Softer. More tender. I couldn't tell if he liked having me there or not. I wasn't even sure if it mattered. "Did no one ever teach you how to be kind?" I asked.

Hunter paused for a moment before turning the car on and reaching for my thigh. He rubbed my leg while driving. "I suppose not," he whispered in a voice barely audible.

"That's okay," I slurred while closing my eyes. Everything felt so slow. My body was heavy and my throat dry. "I was taught to love too much. All I want to do is love you," I said before placing my hand over his. "I just want to love you."

Hunter continued to drive us to the motel as I started dozing off. The last words I heard him say were, "I know, Pretty Debt. I know."

Chapter 13

HUNTER

I watched her sleep.

She was twisted up in the thick sheets, sweat sticking to her brow and a frown on her face. She was naked and reeked of alcohol. Her hair matted.

But the steady way she breathed in and out transfixed me. I watched her like I had never stopped.

I found myself matching my inhales to hers just for the opportunity to feel in sync.

I just want to love you.

Her words haunted me all night. If I were being honest with myself, I just wanted the chance to love her back. I wanted it more than anything. But she only knew half the truth—the half that was easier to swallow. The forgivable half. If she knew the rest, she'd never look at me again, no matter what my reasons were.

Her brown eyes popped open, and I watched her lick at her cracked lips with a dry tongue. She scrunched up her nose and rolled out of bed, marching toward the bathroom on unsteady feet. She hadn't even noticed that she was lying next to me. I wouldn't be surprised if she was still drunk.

I listened as she brushed her teeth and washed her face. With my hands propped behind my head as I lay on the bed, I waited for her to come back out and realize I was here. Would she be mad that I stayed the night? Would she wonder why I stayed? What excuse did I have for being here? The doorknob turned, and she strutted out in all her naked glory.

"Shit!" she gasped. "You scared me!"

I smiled as she massaged her temples, forcing my wandering gaze not to look at her toned body. She used to be so soft. She'd trained her muscles over the last few years, and I wanted nothing more than to run my tongue over every inch of her. I had a feeling I would want Roe Palmer in every way. Soft. Hard. Plush. Round with my ch—no. I couldn't even finish that thought.

"What happened last night?" she asked before finding an oversized T-shirt on the floor and putting it on. The hem hit mid-thigh, and I both cursed how fucking sexy she looked with the wrinkled cotton tee slipping off her shoulder and thanked God that she wasn't fully naked anymore.

"You joined my harem, apparently."

"Excuse me?" she asked while sifting through her suitcase for underwear. I had to choke back a groan when she found a lavender thong made of lace.

"You got very drunk," I explained in annoyance. It actually really pissed me off. She went and made a deal concerning my life with Gavriel Moretti, and instead of being panicked like she should have been, she got completely drunk off her ass with my rotation of pussy. I hadn't really dipped my dick in a while, but it was still uncomfortable to see them all together joking. Not because I was embarrassed. No, it was uncomfortable because seeing them all together just affirmed that Butterfly, Luna, and Roxanne paled in comparison to Roe. She was all I could see, and that terrified me.

Roe sat at the edge of the bed with her back to me. I watched her piece through the puzzle of her night and stroke her brown hair with her nimble fingers. "You also complained about not getting off the last two times we were together," I began while sitting up. The sheets pooled at my waist, and I caught her looking at me from the corner of her eyes. I was probably going to hell for this, but I couldn't help but tease and take another opportunity to touch what wasn't mine.

I leaned closer and brushed her hair off of her neck before sucking her salty skin. My tongue hovered over a thudding vein just below her ear, and she gasped. "Apparently, I owe you two orgasms," I rasped.

Roe's breath hitched, and she kept her gaze forward, though I could feel every muscle in her body growing relaxed. Her thighs parted ever so slightly, and if I wanted to, I could reach around and sink my fingers into her slick cunt. But I didn't. Not yet.

"I won't hold my breath," she replied while forcing her trembling body to stand. "I'm used to everything concerning you being unreciprocated." Her voice was snappy, and I wasn't sure if it was the hangover she was probably rocking or if that had just become her general tone with me. I couldn't blame her. I wasn't making this easy on either of us, but how could I have possibly known she was still thinking about me just as much as I thought about her? How could I have possibly prepared for this reunion?

It was easier to be strong when she was out of sight. But I almost forgot my reasoning for pushing her away when she was this close and in the flesh—and I had very good reason. If she knew the entire truth, she'd never look at me the same way again. I'd rather her indifference than her hate, I just didn't know how to make either of us unobsessed with the other. We were both in too deep, and it was getting harder and harder to play the part I was meant to play.

"Do you think I care if I leave you wanting?" I asked. To be honest, I did care. I cared so much that I'd spend the rest of my life with my head between her thighs, devouring her sweet pussy.

"You've already proven that you don't," she grumbled.

That didn't sit right with me. I stood up, clutching the sheets around my waist while approaching her. She stood her ground and eyed me warily. I couldn't blame her for not trusting my intentions. I probably seemed indecisive and overly cruel. She never knew which version of me she was going to get.

Dropping the sheets, I then reached out and grabbed her hips, her body tempting me in ways I couldn't even articulate. "You couldn't handle me caring, Roe," I said before pulling her close. She smelled like sweat, minty toothpaste, and alcohol. "If I cared about you getting off, I'd have you everywhere. I'd touch you in public. I'd wake you up every morning with my head between your thighs. And every night, I wouldn't rest until you were screaming my name."

Her breathing quickened. Her skin grew flushed. She tilted her head up, and I cupped her cheek, dragging my thumb along her bottom lip.

"You'd be surprised what I could handle, Hunter," she whispered before licking her lips. The tension was so thick in the room. My dick was hard as fucking stone.

And then my cell started ringing.

I took a step back, like being in her orbit burned me. Fucking hell. I reached for my phone while she disappeared back into the bathroom.

My phone was on the nightstand, and I grabbed it without looking at the caller ID. "Hello."

"I hope you had a good night, because shit just got messy," Gavriel answered. He didn't sound like his usual composed self.

"What do you want?"

"Check your messages."

I reluctantly pulled my phone from my ear and checked the screen just as a message from Gavriel came through. The image was dark and grainy, but I recognized the man tied to the chair. He had a broken nose and two black eyes. His busted lip had bright red blood streaming from it.

Mack.

"What the fuck did you do to him?" I asked before pulling the phone back up to my ear. I thought I had time to decide. I thought he'd let me choose. I thought Gavriel's threats were flexible. Not to mention, Mack had been working for the Bullets for years. Gavriel respected loyalty. What happened that made him turn his back on Mack?

"I didn't do this. If anything, you're to blame."

What was that supposed to mean? "Explain. Now," I commanded.

I heard the bathroom door open but didn't turn to face Roe. "Mack heard about Roe's deal with me. He figured if he could kill the target, I wouldn't make you come back."

I cursed while pacing the motel room. That sounded exactly like something Mack would do. But he wasn't as skilled of a killer as me. Sure, he was smart and could use a gun, but it took a unique sense of precision to be an assassin. I glanced at Roe, who was staring at me with concern. "How long ago?" I asked.

"I got the picture this morning," Gavriel growled. "My fucking target now knows I'm after him. This isn't good. Not good at all." He sounded pissed off. Gavriel was a lot of things, but he did care about Mack. He cared about all of his loyal employees. It's why I wasn't taking his threats about Nicole all too seriously.

"Do you think he's still alive?"

Gavriel let out a sigh, and I waited with bated breath for his answer. "I don't know. We need to take care of this. Mack is Bullet family, but I don't know how long he can last being tortured. What if he leads them to you? He already led them to me. What about Roe? These assholes will use anyone and anything as leverage."

Shit. I didn't want another situation where Gavriel's enemies tracked down the people I cared about. And if I couldn't get Mack out, I'd have to kill him before he could put anyone at risk. It was a tricky situation. I found my jeans on the ground, and while holding my phone between my ear and shoulder, I put them on. "No shit. Send me the details, and I'll be out within the hour."

"You have to go ghost," Gavriel rushed out before I could hang up. "This is high-profile. No planes. No public places. You can't leave a single trace. This isn't the kind of target my connections can help cover-up. I can send some help, but the situation has escalated. Don't call me until it's done. Don't talk to anyone. You can use some of my safe houses and vehicles along the way."

Gavriel hung up, and I was immediately emailed details of the target. The moment I saw the name, my chest constricted. This would be fucking hard.

Mayor Bloomington. He was a crooked man that ran the city like a crime boss. It came as no surprise that he was involved in shit with Gavriel. But making someone this public disappear would take a miracle. And saving Mack just became infinitely more difficult.

"What's going on?" Roe asked. I put on a T-shirt and opened my phone back up to the picture of Mack before handing it over to her. There was no use in lying or hiding. She needed to know what the stakes were. Roe gasped the moment she saw his broken and battered face on the screen.

"How—oh my God. Did Gavriel do this to him?" Her voice was shrill and full of vengeance. "I'll end him."

"No. The target he wants me to kill did. Mack tried taking him out and failed. It's up to me to save him now." I didn't mention that I didn't think there was anything to save, but I wasn't willing to admit that to Roe just yet. I didn't want to be the one to tell her that we were the reason the only father figure she knew was probably dead.

Roe processed the information for about ten seconds before frantically packing her suitcase. I knew she'd want to go but was proud of her for pulling herself together so quickly. She was always such a fighter. "You're not going," I said.

Roe stood up and straightened her spine, casting me a murderous glare. "Hell yes I am."

I saw the determination in her stance. There was no question in her expression, either. Roe had already made up her mind that she was going with me. But where I was going wasn't safe for her.

"You can't, Roe. It's not safe."

"He's the only family I have," she replied incredulously. "You can't seriously expect me to just stay here and wait patiently while you travel across the country to save him."

That was exactly what I was expecting her to do. It suddenly hit me that I had a choice to make. Roe wasn't strong enough to take on this job at my side, and I couldn't leave her anywhere, because I couldn't trust that she wouldn't follow after me.

"You're not going," I said again, this time more sternly.

"Yes. I am. Mack is the only family I have." Roe was standing with her arms crossed over her chest. She looked unyielding and powerful just then. It nearly killed me to know I'd have to break her to keep her safe. I had to do what I'd been running from. I had to tell her something that would make her hate me so much she would refuse this journey.

"You can't come with me."

Her eyebrows rose. "And why not?" she asked.

"Because I'm ruthless," I began while taking a step toward her. "Because this is the kind of mission that will require me to do whatever is necessary. Because I don't need you as a distraction. Because if it comes down to saving Mack or killing this man, I'll choose the latter. Gavriel gave me a job, and I am the only one that can get it done. Mack's been tortured probably past his limits. We don't know what he's said or if you'll become the target again—"

"Mack would never give me up. And even if he did, I'm not that important," Roe argued.

"You don't know that. They could have already gone through his phone. Learned about his history. About me. These people leave no loose ends and will grab hold of anything they think will give them an advantage. And if it comes down to it, I will kill Mack to save the rest of us."

Roe shook her head. "You don't mean that. You have to save Mack. No matter what happened between us, you know how important he is to me. You wouldn't kill him."

She sounded so confident. So sure.

If only she knew.

"Your safety will always trump your happiness for me. I killed your own mother. What makes you think I won't kill Mac to save you, too?"

I blurted it. It was out there now. My mind and mouth and determination to keep her safe released the one secret I still had.

She stalled. Gasped. Stilled. Then trembled. I saw the light dim from her eyes. It was 9:24 in the morning when she stopped loving me.

Chapter 14

ROE

Mom

Wake up, little dove.
Stiff wings of cotton and red, lifeless eyes.
You built a cage for yourself. Wood painted a dull shade of gold.
You sat on your perch and stared through the bars,
watching the world but never participating in it.

Wake up, little dove.
Sandpaper veins and foamy mouth.
I never knew of your taste for poisoned needles.
I never knew you wanted to trade your cage for a tomb.

Buried deep, little dove.
Bed of roses and a ceremony for one.
From ashes and dust to clouds and sun.
Fly away, little dove.
Fly away, Mom.

I absorbed his words. "I killed your own mother." Why did Hunter like to drop bombs in my lap with such simplicity and grace? He didn't handle my feelings with sensitivity. He destroyed me with calm truths. It was devastating. Who was this man? How did I not know this?

I couldn't quite make sense of what he was saying. "Excuse me?" I asked, seeking clarification. "Did you just admit to killing my mother?"

Hunter looked at the ground, then back at me. Swallowing, he replied, "Yes."

"Why?" I choked.

Hunter closed his cold eyes, like looking at me was too difficult for him. "I had my reasons."

He had reasons? What reasons could he possibly have? Maybe he was crazy. Maybe he wanted more accessibility to my life so he could control me. It all made sense now. Hunter killed my mother so he could insert himself in my life. "Did Mack know?"

I saw the lie flash across Hunter's expression. He *wanted* to tell me that Mack was a part of this deadly deed, but he couldn't bring himself to say it. He wanted me to think Mack was guilty in this so I wouldn't want to save him. "No. He didn't."

My relief was short-lived. Hunter killed my mother. He fucking *killed* her.

There weren't any sufficient words to describe the pain I felt. It all made sense now. This was the final piece of the puzzle. This was the driving guilt that forced Hunter into seclusion from me. This was why we would never be together. I wasn't just a debt to him. I wasn't even an obsession. Guilt and ruin lined the roads that brought us together.

I wanted off this path. I wanted to make him suffer. Hunter Hammond deserved the loneliness Joshua Tree offered him, and I would starve him of my empathy. I no longer cared about the little boy that watched my father die. The image of his sunken, boyish cheeks and my mother's willowy arm wrapped around his shoulder assaulted my memory.

How could he?

A series of realizations dawned on me as I stood in the middle of my motel room. She didn't kill herself. She didn't willingly leave me. Mom didn't *abandon* me. My mother's murderer had been inside of me. Hunter buried his cock and affections within my body. I became a home for his evil. He owned my body and mind. He'd corrupted my thoughts. He sparked a love in my soul. I'd coaxed undeserved pleasure from his cock, not knowing that he was the root of my loneliness. All this time, I'd been trying to find a sense of understanding in him, while he had been hiding the truth.

Murderer.

My. mind felt. Like.

Disjointed.

Rushing.

T

  H

   O

U

  G

   H

T

  S.

Thoughts about the woman that raised me. A mother born of grief. I thought she loved my father more than me. I thought she left because being terrified of living was stronger than the love of a daughter. Contemporary poetry streamlined my inner monologue so I could make sense of the painted pain across my soul. Death was such a fickle thing. Grief convinced me that I was capable of moving on, then peeled the scab off my wound.

She was such a lovely dove, my mother.

Would she have healed eventually? Could we have moved on E V E N T U A L L Y?

Or would we still be sitting in a cold apartment with the deadbolt locked and her tears mopping the floor?

She was a lot like a cactus, my mother. Lone. Prickly.

My obsession and love for Hunter shriveled up on the spot. What was once a beautiful bed of thorny flowers became a desert drought. I didn't want him anymore. I couldn't stand to even look at him, though I knew I needed to. I needed to stare him in the eye and let him see the pain there. Hunter Hammond had been running from the guilt, but it was fucking time to finish this chase. He felt pushed to admit what he did because he wanted me to run away. Everything Hunter did had a purpose. He wanted me to give up and leave, but I wouldn't give him the satisfaction of my fear.

I wasn't giving him what he wanted anymore. I was going with him. No matter what. Mack was too important to me to let him use this to keep me away.

A plan took root in my mind. I realized that he would need a reason to take me with him. Calmly, I walked over to my backpack on the floor and sifted through it. "You going to say anything, Pretty Debt?" he asked. How dare he call me that right now. Did he expect me to cry? Was he getting off on causing me pain?

My fingers hit the cool, heavy metal of my gun, and I pulled it out to aim at Hunter. One of the first things I did after leaving Gavriel's home was buy bullets. You couldn't own a gun unless you were prepared to shoot it, and now felt as good a time as ever to lose my sense of right and wrong. I was prepared to pull the trigger now. I just had to find the right source of anger to pull from, and Hunter was a bottomless pit of fury.

"You bastard," I said before pulling the slide back and loading a bullet in the chamber.

"You won't shoot me," he replied confidently. He was so damn cocky. He was so convinced that I cared enough to keep him alive. If I didn't need him to save Mack, I probably would kill him in this dirty motel room. I would happily go to jail and pay the price of avenging my mother's death.

But there was timing in everything. I needed him right now. So I aimed a little to the left and pulled the trigger. A hanging mirror beside him shattered, and splintered glass exploded around him. Naturally, Hunter didn't flinch. He didn't move. He stared me down as people screamed in the room next door.

"What the fuck are you doing?" he asked as I picked up my cellphone and dialed 911. I ignored his question the same way he'd been ignoring the truth between us.

The operator answered. "911, what's your emergency?"

"My ex-boyfriend is stalking me. He showed up at my motel, I had to shoot—"

Hunter stomped up to me and ripped my phone out of my hands.

Hanging up, he gave me an incredulous look. "What the fuck are you doing? Why are you calling the police when Mack needs me?"

"Because you need the incentive to bring me. Congratulations, Hunter. I don't trust you. That's what you wanted, isn't it?" He seemed to realize that I was trapping him, and he threw my cellphone on the ground, then crushed it under his boot. I continued speaking as he huffed. "I sure as hell am not trusting you to save Mack. I have a lot of questions, and you're going to answer them. And if you leave me here, I will send the cops after you. We have probably six minutes before they'll arrive." I raised my gun up and aimed at his chest. Instead of answering me, he walked closer and pressed his muscles against the barrel of it.

"You crazy bitch," he growled.

"You murderous stalker."

I killed your mother.

Fly away, little dove.

Fly away.

Little dove in eternal sleep.
Devil walking in clothing of sheep.
It wasn't a cage under lock and key.
It was poison and rage that did the deed.

He glanced at the gun. Both of us knew he could disarm me if he wanted to. But Hunter would have to lodge a bullet in my brain before I let him leave here without me. This wasn't another abandonment scenario. He was going to tell me everything. He was going to save Mack. And at the end of this journey, it would be *me* leaving him. I was done.

"You're not coming. You'd only get in the way," Hunter argued.

"I'm more capable than you think."

He wrapped his hand around mine, squeezing as hard as he could. I clutched the gun in my grip and refused to break eye contact with him. "You're going to have to shoot me. Are you capable of that, Roe? Can you do what needs to be done? Watch someone die and know it was your hand that pulled the trigger?" he asked. "Because I can."

Sirens in the distance sounded faint, but I knew it was only a matter of time before the loud wails were clawing up my skin. "Is that what you did to my mother?" I asked through clenched teeth.

Hunter squeezed my hand harder while looming over me. His morning breath slapped me in the face. "I poisoned her while you were watching television in the next room. I crawled through her bedroom window. She didn't even see me coming, and no one thought twice about a crazy woman ending her life."

His words cut and stung and bruised. It was validating in a way but also made me sick. "You won't change my mind. Let's go," I growled.

Our standoff lasted a few seconds longer, but Hunter finally relented. "Fine." I relaxed as he pried my weapon from my fingertips. "Grab your shit, and let's go before the cops arrive asking questions. We don't have time. The drive will take us three days minimum, and Gavriel doesn't want the paper trail or security cameras associated with flying. You'll listen and do what I say."

I bit the inside of my cheek while gathering up my things. "We can split up the drive," I offered in an emotionless tone. Now that he'd agreed to let me come, a sense of numbness had taken over.

"Hurry," he demanded.

The sirens were louder by the time we got in his truck. He peeled out of the parking lot, leaving nothing but dust behind. I pressed my body against the door, determined to be as far away from him as possible while peering out the window.

Chapter 15

ROE

Silent Treatment

Lips shut with concrete pain.
You prod with silent stares.
We play the games we were taught to play.
There's power in silence, and I am
the queen of my own catastrophe.

Screams like wind on a dull day. Unmoving branches answer me. Strong like a statue, you wait for the concrete to crack, and for my lips to fold into a frown. I am unmoving and Herculean.

Never let them see your smile slip. Never part your lips for ears that don't deserve your honey tongue. Never cry for evil too stuck in their own observation of you to notice the crushed skulls beneath their boots.

Keep quiet, pretty queen. Save your energy for revenge.

I didn't dare open my mouth. For seven straight hours, not a single word escaped my lips. I didn't turn to face Hunter as he drove, and when we stopped at gas stations to fill up, I stole his keys and took them with me to the bathroom.

I realized on the drive that Hunter and I had developed a pattern of sorts. I spent the majority of our fucked up relationship asking him questions and trying to make sense of everything. He was used to my inquisitive demands. I knew he was expecting me to plead for answers. He seemed to sit on the edge of his seat, words hovering over his velvet tongue as he waited with bated breath for the inevitable fight that would boom from my chest and ruin us.

But I liked the power of doing the unexpected. I loved withholding my questions because it confused him. He liked having control of a situation. He prided himself on having me figured out. I wanted to knock his ego down a peg and bring him to the brink of exasperation before finally releasing my demons.

It wasn't until we were in Holbrook, Arizona, that he broke. I smiled when the rough tone and clumsy words escaped his lips. It felt like a win, despite the condescending thing he chose to say.

"Are you seriously going to give me the silent treatment the entire way?" he asked. You'd have to truly understand Hunter to hear the pleading undertones in his voice. He was sitting up tall and proud while nervously spitting sunflower seeds into a cup. His salty mouth was ready for a fight, and I refused to give it to him.

"Didn't you fight to come with me? You made all that fuss in Joshua Tree, and now you're sitting there digging into your skin with your nails and ignoring me." I hadn't even realized I was hurting myself. Sure enough, there were bloody marks in my arm from where I was pinching myself.

It sucked, didn't it? I thought to myself. Knowledge was power, and there was something to be said about being the quietest one in the room. It was nice sealing your mouth shut when the world expected you to scream. "You found *me*, by the way," Hunter argued. I listened, waiting for something to use against him. "I was perfectly fine leaving you alone. I had a life. You were no longer my responsibility. If you hadn't come, you would have never had to find out. If you hadn't come, Mack wouldn't be in this situation."

There was no use in pointing fingers and placing blame. He was gaslighting. We both knew it. This was a classic example of the chicken and the egg. None of this would have happened if my mother hadn't loaned his mother two thousand dollars. None of this would have ever happened if he had been a normal boy with normal coping mechanisms, not some ten-year-old with a guilty conscience, trying to work through the trauma he'd seen.

Maybe it was my fault for opening old wounds, but I spent five years with my damage breathing, and I needed closure before I bled out.

More time passed. Hunter fluctuated between fuming and softening. I could practically feel the energy in the car twisting and turning as his thoughts progressed. Man, what I wouldn't give to crawl up inside his mind. But the longer I stayed quiet, the more the walls of his filter shattered at my feet.

"I never wanted you to find out like this," Hunter whispered. I scoffed. He never wanted me to find out at all. "She was sick, Roe. Very sick."

I closed my eyes and then opened them again, this time my vision blurred from the hushed tears in my eyes. It was dark outside. The only thing I could see was what the truck headlights illuminated on the pavement.

"I was twenty. I had been working with the Bullets for a couple years. I had a couple kills under my belt. I liked the freedom the gang offered me. I had more resources to...watch you."

I refused to look at Hunter. I refused to turn in my seat and cock my head to the side to better hear him. Inside I was begging him.

Keep talking.

Please, keep talking.

Let your damage breathe, citrine lover.

"I also had access to your mother's computer. I learned a few things, like how to track her searches." Why was he tracking her searches? I wanted to ask. But again, I held my power close to my chest.

"She was getting worse. She started looking up remote places to live. I could have let you go, Roe. In fact, I would have gladly let you go. I thought that if she left, maybe I could feel normal. Maybe I could stop obsessing over your safety and release my debt."

She wanted to move? That was news to me. Occasionally mom talked about leaving the city, but I never took it seriously. She talked about a lot of things. She was always focused on running. She always thought it was safer somewhere else.

Why didn't you let us leave, Hunter? We could have avoided all of this. I could still have a mother...

But what kind of life would that have been? A homeschooled life of seclusion and fear? Would I ever have met friends? Kissed a boy? And despite it all, a life where Hunter didn't exist didn't feel right. I knew it was wrong on a carnal level to have thoughts like that, but I couldn't help it.

"But then…" Hunter's voice trailed off. I forced myself not to hang on the edge of every word. "Roe, listen to me."

My eyes flickered over to him of their own volition. I couldn't really see him in the dark car; the lights from the center console cast a neon blue light across his shadowed jaw. His eyes were dark, his entire presence haunted. "You're going to have to tell me if you want me to keep talking. What I'm going to say could change how you view your mother. Could change your memory of her."

I wanted to scream. Didn't Hunter know? Answers and clarity were all I ever wanted. "Tell me," I whispered.

Hunter jumped at the sound of my voice. "She was looking up murder-suicides, Roe. She was researching the most humane way to kill someone."

No. Certainly he was wrong. Maybe she was just focusing on another obsession. She found ways to die and feared them, becoming consumed with them. I cracked my knuckles and furrowed my brow. Swallowing the protests, I continued to listen.

"She bought poison, Roe. She wrote a note. It wasn't just for her. She wanted you both—"

"You're lying. How can I believe a single thing you're saying, Hunter?" I could have bit my tongue off for betraying me. Silence, he deserved silence. But this was so absurd I couldn't help myself. He was lying. He had to be. My mother feared death. She was terrified of it. Her entire existence was committed to keeping me safe. She'd never hurt me. She just couldn't. She wasn't capable of it. She. Was. Not. capable. Of. killing. Me.

My mind.

Had become a.

Choppy, disjointed.

Mess.

Of declarations and understanding and trying to feel the truth in his words. Hunter Hammond had a sandpaper tongue, and he was grinding me down for his pleasure.

"I called CPS, do you remember, Roe? They came to your apartment. Your mom made you wear a yellow dress."

I shook my head and sifted through memories long forgotten. I remembered the dress, though. My birthday dress. I remembered the woman that came by. I remembered her clipboard and questions. As a child, I was just excited to speak to someone new. The yellow dress hit just below my knee. Mom tied my brown hair up in ribbons. The sleeves were ruffled and frilly. Mom never let me wear dresses, but she did that day. It felt special. I felt beautiful.

"They were going to take you away, Roe. Your mom got desperate. It was your birthday, remember? They gave her one more day because they didn't want upheaval on your birthday."

I closed my eyes. Most of the details of that day had been buried deep in my chest. I didn't want to think about the foam collected in her mouth or the way her lifeless eyes stared at me as I shook her frail body. Hunter pulled off the highway and parked at a motel. I sat frozen in my seat.

"Roe. Tell me you understand. I tried to get her help. I had therapists knocking on her door. She didn't want to get better."

"You didn't try hard enough."

"I didn't have to try at all, Roe."

"Convenient, huh? You get to pick and choose when your obsession is worth it to you. You get to care when it makes you feel better, but right now you get to pretend to be the hero. You killed her out of the kindness of your heart, right? Put her down like an old dog because you didn't want Mom to suffer?" I asked. My words were spewing from my mouth like vomit.

"She would have killed you eventually, Roe. I gave you a life. Freedom," Hunter began. He grabbed my arm, tugging me toward him. I shrugged out of his grip. "She was sick. She had a plan. She had the motive. She didn't want the state to take you away..."

I didn't listen to the rest of his excuses. I got out of the truck and slammed the door, shouldering my duffel bag and a frown. Hunter followed after me, and I felt his eyes scanning the parking lot like the predator he was. I had half a mind to make a scene. "Roe," he called at my back. I spun around and pinned my lips closed. "I didn't want you to know."

"Well, I know now, Hunter. I'm not the same girl you left behind in Denver. I'm not even the same girl that showed up at your door a few days ago," I began while stepping forward. Hunter looked down at me, his eyes soft and swimming with emotion. "We keep doing this. You keep hurting me. You don't deserve me, Hunter. You can spend the rest of your life feeling good about the debt you paid. You can sit up on your high horse and pat yourself on the back for saving me from my crazy mother. You can smile when you think of Mack. You can pad my bank. You can save me from the enemies you've made. You can kill everyone I know and sleep well at night, thinking you're my savior." His mouth dropped open. "But you'll never have me. You'll always be forced to watch from the outside. You'll never be a part of my life, Hunter. You got what you wanted. I'm going with you to save the only family I have, then I'm done."

I marched up to the lobby, leaving Hunter standing there with my cruel words. My chest constricted, and I wanted nothing more than to scream. I should have just given him my silence.

Those words didn't feel true. Even as I spoke them, I knew that this wasn't done.

She wanted to kill me? I squeezed my eyes shut, then opened them again.

"Just one night?" I bounced on my feet as he gave the woman a fake ID to check us in.

"Yep," he replied. She stared at the pretty murderer in awe, disarmed by his beauty as she swiped his credit card and explained the amenities. She was gnawing on her plump lip, running her hands over the smooth dark skin of her arm while asking him if he needed anything.

"Do you have a gym?" I interjected.

She turned to look at me, as if just realizing Hunter wasn't alone. "Yes," she said with a cough. "On the third floor."

Good. I needed to run until I vomited.

Chapter 16

HUNTER

J ust as she predicted, I watched her. I stared until my eyes burned, unwilling to even blink. I'd slipped back into my obsession and compulsively locked my eyes on the broken woman before me. It was late, and I wanted nothing more than to sleep, but I refused to leave her side. Roe Palmer wanted to work out her frustrations, so I sat on a nearby bench and watched her slowly fall apart. Patiently. Painfully.

Her tight gray leggings moved with every deep stride of her legs on the treadmill. She had the speed turned up high. Sweat dripped down between her breasts, her bare abs flexing as she moved. She wasn't graceful. She ran like a machine, effortlessly working her frustrations out through each thundering step. Though she was stationary on the treadmill, it felt like she was running from me. There was symbolism in this moment. I could feel the poetry rolling off of her as she worked out. Running as hard and fast as she could yet never going anywhere. Our relationship was the same.

I was always pushing her away, yet we kept colliding. I kept destroying her.

I didn't know what to say. I kept chewing on my tongue, wishing I could further explain my motives or why I thought it was the best way. My relationship with Roe back then was flat and one dimensional. I saw a problem and acted out the solution that made the most sense to me. I was thinking like a robot, fueled by the logic my job as an assassin had thrust upon me.

Mrs. Palmer wanted to kill the girl I felt responsible for; I had to kill Mrs. Palmer.

I was kicking myself for fucking this up so epically. Roe was never meant to know. Not just because I couldn't handle her looking at me like the murderer I was, but because the truth about her mother would likely ruin her already skewed perceptions about their relationship. It was bad enough I killed the woman, but now I killed her memory of her, too. Roe wasn't disillusioned about her mother's mental health, but she still loved her. She loved her *deeply*. And I was so desperate for forgiveness I shoved the truth in her face the first chance I got. I hadn't even lasted eight hours before I was begging her to understand why.

I killed for Gavriel without conscience. I didn't need backstories or motive. If I was given a job, I didn't ask any questions. I acted on duty and responsibility, pulled the trigger as if it meant nothing. I battered bodies and commanded blood without a second thought. Some assassins thought of their kills before bed, but I slept soundly.

But not this kill. Mrs. Palmer's ghost stuck with me. I still stood by my decision, but the repercussions were something I'd be forced to live with for the rest of my life. Roe was right. I found comfort in the knowledge that it was the right thing to do. But I couldn't pretend anymore. I had been pushing down her death since falling for Roe, pretending that chasm between us didn't exist. But now that the truth was out, I was consumed with what I'd done.

Roe kept running. The rhythmic pounding of her worn sneakers on the treadmill thudded through my ears. Boom, boom, boom. Each step was loud. Like a pattern of thunder and force. I think I always knew I'd tell Roe. I was a weak man, confessing my sins the first chance I got with ridiculous reason. We both knew I'd bring her with me to save Mack. Not only because he was her only family, but because I was in too deep to say goodbye.

Roe grunted, then turned off the treadmill. I couldn't help but feel relief that she was finished. Her legs shook with exhaustion, and her chest heaved in and out, those beautiful lungs of hers gasping at life as she punished her body for the pain she felt. She'd been running for an hour and a half, and we'd been traveling all day. Emotions were high. How much more could she take?

I stood up from my spot on the bench, prepared to go back to our room when she went to the free weights. "How much longer are you going to be?" I asked. It was nearing one a.m., and I needed to sleep for at least four hours before we hit the road again. I waited. And waited.

And

Fucking

Waited

...for her to respond, but the only sounds coming from her were harsh breaths and the clanging of metal from her systematically lifting and setting down the heavy weights. She was giving me the silent treatment again. I fucking *hated* the silent treatment. I spent our entire lives stuck in the silent treatment. She didn't speak to me directly. She didn't touch me with her words. I sat in this quiet little box of observation, watching her live her life while struggling to live my own. When we were together, I craved the fire she spat out.

"You're going to make yourself sick," I added. "You won't be much help to Mack if you're too sore to move."

She paused, gripping the bar until her knuckles turned white. Her salty skin, slick with sweat, taunted me. "You're more than welcome to go to bed. You don't have to wait here for me."

I knew I could. She wasn't going to leave without me. She didn't know where Mack was or how to get him back. Logically, I understood that she wouldn't and couldn't leave. But fear still kept me firmly planted wherever she was. I was terrified by the fleeting nature of this journey. If time wasn't of the essence, I would draw out every mile and circle the globe six times for just a chance to be with her longer.

I'd pushed her away. Out of guilt. Out of fear. Out of necessity.

She deserved better than someone who not only put her in danger by his mere existence, but also played a part in the death of her entire family. It was fucked up.

"I'll stay," I replied quietly.

She scoffed and dropped her weights. "You're about five years too late." Ouch. I fucking deserved it.

I opened my mouth, then closed it, not sure what to say. I was completely exhausted and strung out. I couldn't trust myself to say or do the right thing in the best conditions, so I sure as hell couldn't say anything now. Not to mention, my mind was still focused on the logistics of my kill. I thought I'd be rusty or that it would be difficult to step back into the lifestyle of a killer, but already I was working through a plan to kill the highly public mayor of New York. I had an idea, though, and there was a good chance I'd be killed.

"Please go," Roe whimpered. I could hear the crack of her breaking point. All those walls she'd precariously built when she found out what I'd done were crumbling with a single plea.

My eyes snapped to her. She was wiping a mixture of sweat and tears from her face. She was falling apart, and it was all my fucking fault. I walked over to her with the caution of a predator. One wrong move could spark a chase. She was skittish of me now.

"Was she really going to kill me?" she sniffled. The question broke my heart. *This* was what I wanted to avoid. I held my hand out for her to take, a peace offering of support and...love.

I loved her. I really loved her.

She grabbed my hand, and I pulled her in for a hug, wrapping my arms around her small, shaking body as she pressed her forehead against my chest. "The signs were there, yes. But who knows what she would have done in the moment?"

My words felt like a hybrid of the truth and a lie. I recognized the murderous intent in her mother. It was the same sort of determination I felt when I got an assignment. I saw it. I knew in my gut that she was unhinged and prepared to end both of their lives. I'll never forget the way she didn't fight when I wrapped my arm around her head and covered her mouth with my hand. I was trying to stop her from screaming before injecting her with the drugs she wanted to pump through her own daughter's veins. It was like I'd validated her in a way—as if she'd always known this would happen and she was relieved that her fears were warranted. She knew the world was out to destroy her, and I confirmed that knowledge. I was the monster that kept her up at night.

"It's easier to blame you," Roe sniffled.

At that point, I would have given her anything, and that desire wasn't driven by guilt. It was fueled by compassion and care. I wanted to take away her pain. Now that there weren't any secrets between us, I was able to let myself feel the things I wanted to feel. I still didn't deserve her, though. But what else was new? "You can blame me, Pretty Debt," I whispered while stroking her sweaty back. I didn't even care. I wanted to hold her as long as she'd let me.

"Okay," she replied before pulling away.

We went upstairs in silence, and I made her a PB&J from supplies I'd gotten from a gas station outside of Phoenix. When she emerged from the steamy bathroom, wrapped in a fluffy towel, I openly observed the bags under her eyes and the way her legs wobbled with every step. I itched to get up and carry her to bed, but even when breaking apart, Roe Palmer was strong and prideful. It was one of the many things I loved about her.

God, I loved her.

She sat down on the bed, and I handed her the food and a bottle of water. She stared at a blank space on the wall. Her body seemed vacant, and her mind was time traveling through all the memories. I knew with complete certainty that she was overanalyzing every moment leading up to her mother's death, searching for an explanation. This was what I wanted to avoid. *Why did I fucking tell her?*

"You were tired of keeping the secret," she answered me. I hadn't even realized I'd said that out loud. It was like I'd completely lost control of my mouth. "You told me because you were tired of it keeping us apart."

She nibbled her sandwich while continuing to stare at the wall. I wanted her golden brown eyes focused on me. I wanted to find and dissect her thoughts. Once half the sandwich was gone and the entire water bottle was empty, she went to brush her teeth and change into pajamas. When she came back, she slipped under the covers, and I turned off the lights. I'd gotten us a single room so I could have a thinly veiled excuse to sleep by her again.

In the darkness, I spooned her under the motivation of providing comfort. She didn't relax against my chest, but she didn't pull away, either. With our synched breaths and wide eyes, the both of us lay there in silence for what felt like hours. Even though exhaustion pulled at my eyes, I didn't dare fall asleep until she did.

"She could have gotten better," Roe whispered.

I lied back. "She could have."

"But we'll never know."

"We won't."

I watched her body shake as silent sobs escaped her. "I believe you. I—I remember the yellow dress. And CPS." I held her tighter. "I remember mom saying she'd make it all better."

"I'm so fucking sorry, Roe."

"Did she suffer?"

It was the most humane kill of my life. "No."

"Did you?" she asked.

Every day of my fucking life. "Yes."

"Good." My chest constricted. "Why me?" she then asked. "Why didn't you feel a debt for my mother? She was the one that paid the two grand. She was the one your mother betrayed. Why didn't you save her like you saved me?"

I had asked myself that question plenty of times over the years and had come up with a reason after leaving Roe. "Because she died when your father died," I answered. "I felt like it was already too late."

Roe wiped her tears on her arm. "She was alive, Hunter. People change all the time. Even you. Just because we change for the worse, doesn't mean we don't deserve to live."

I didn't have the heart to tell Roe that it wasn't just change that afflicted her mother. She'd become a shell. There was nothing left to save. "You're right."

I played over her words in my mind.

It's easier to blame you. It's easier to blame you.

I'd take the blame if it prevented Roe from becoming the shell her mother was.

Chapter 17

ROE

Yellow Dress.
I forget how to breathe.
The fabric so tight it feels like hands plastered to my body.
You say it's supposed to feel that way.
Our love is stitched together with your rules.

Yellow Dress.
Just above my polished knees.
No concrete scrapes or scars from the playground.
I'm a pretty, porcelain doll for you to dress up.
Your lies are tied together by the crisp apron around your waist.

Yellow Dress.
Bury me in soft silk.
Fabric the color of sunshine.
Mourning feels like cotton ruffles and chapped smiles.

My life is held together by the ribbon in my hair.

The next morning, we woke up and awkwardly untangled our limbs. It both disgusted and comforted me to know that I slept in Hunter's arms. Things had changed so quickly. One moment I was willing to cross the country for him, now I craved distance. And yet, he comforted me last night. I wasn't sure what to think of the way he held me and stroked my back with his steady hands. At the time, I just needed someone to hold me together, but in the light of day and in the cramped cab of his truck, I was thinking about every moment.

There was this little voice in the back of my mind, a dirty, nasty voice that I hated. She wanted to celebrate. She wanted to feel triumphant. She was whispering, *He saved you, Roe. There's no more secrets to keep you apart now.*

How on earth could I find something positive in such a disastrous revelation? And why did I seek his comfort again?

The truth was like ripping open my grief once more. I felt like the little girl that had to bury her mother alone, once more. I could almost taste the birthday cake on my tongue. I'd moved past my trauma, but it still stuck with me. Waiting. Watching. Anxiously prepared for the right moment to strike me with despair.

We were back on the road long before the sun had risen. The truck had a full tank of gas, and we had a couple day's drive ahead of us. I spent most of the time breathing in the rosewood scent that saturated his seats. We kept moving and moving, time a slow passing of excruciating worry. It gave me a lot of time to think. About everything. I hated it.

We had a lot of ground to cover, both literally and metaphorically. I still didn't understand why we were driving and not flying, but I trusted Hunter's expertise. *He was the skilled assassin*, after all, I thought bitterly. I didn't really have a choice but to go with him. He was the only person that could get Mack back. He was also the only person with enough information to find him. I was a strong, independent woman, but I knew my limits. I needed Hunter Hammond.

During the long yet empty hours of driving, I let my mind wander and work up scenarios. The pavement stretched endlessly before us, but I was completely consumed and trapped in my thoughts of Mack. Was he still alive? Would I lose yet another person I loved? I felt so incredibly helpless but at the same time hopeful. Even though Hunter's involvement in my mother's death brought out a deep conflict within my soul, I held onto the hope that he would help save the man that raised me.

"Have you heard anything from Gavriel?" I asked while massaging my thighs. I was sore from my workout last night. Sitting in the car had made my bones grow stiff. I wanted to rest my feet on the dash, but Hunter gave me a murderous glare every time I inched my legs up to prop them against the console.

"Nope," Hunter replied. "And I won't hear from him until the job is done, either. I've gone ghost."

Gone ghost? What did that even mean?

It was then that I realized I'd never really had the opportunity to talk to Hunter about his work for the Bullets. He was gone before I had time to comprehend it all. Maybe part of the allure was his mystery. I think I was subconsciously transfixed by his life because it felt like a giant puzzle I needed to figure out. His job was like the last little corner piece to the bigger picture. If I could understand his role as an assassin, there would be nothing left to make sense of. *There would be nothing left to hold on to.*

"What does going ghost mean?"

Hunter passed an eighteen-wheeler before answering me. I listened to the angry groan of his truck as he accelerated. "It's what I do when my target is very public. High-profile kills require a certain amount of sensitivity. No traffic cams. No airports. Basically, anything where my presence can be detected is off-limits. Gavriel won't call me because he doesn't want it on record that we spoke. On the off chance I'm caught, he needs plausible deniability. And I need to be able to hide my tracks. You notice I'm picky about where we stop?"

He made sure to stop at tiny mom-and-pop gas stations, and even last night's motel seemed to be family-owned. Every time we got out of the truck, he scanned the building, as if looking for cameras. "So what? Are you going to slip in, kill him, then slip out?"

Hunter flashed me a smile, probably the first one he'd given me since I arrived in Joshua Tree. "That's an extreme oversimplification of what I do, but it's probably better you don't know the details."

I bounced my leg as he continued to drive. Tall trees that cast shadows over the road passed by in a blur of brown and green. "Why does Gavriel want Mayor Bloomington dead?" I asked.

"You should probably forget that name if you know what's good for you. And I don't know," Hunter replied easily. "Unless the reasons affect my ability to do my job, I typically don't ask."

That answer shocked me. How could Hunter so flippantly murder someone without knowing the reason why? "You don't know?" I asked incredulously.

"Nope. I'm not the judge or jury, Pretty Debt. I'm just the executioner."

His smooth voice rolled over that familiar nickname effortlessly, making my chest constrict with a familiar pain. I ignored the way I wanted to hear it again. "That sounds like a cop-out. Shouldn't you want to know why you're killing these people?"

Hunter glanced at me for a brief moment before returning his gaze to the road. "People think the man that pulls the trigger is solely responsible. I guess you could say it helps me sleep at night to know that Gavriel Moretti is the one that calls the shots. It helps to know that I'm just an employee doing my job. He's the one with the vendettas and blackmail and goals."

"So you don't think you're responsible for any of their deaths?" I asked. I wanted to understand Hunter's thought process, because I thought it would help me connect the dots to our own relationship and what he had done. But it just felt so robotic.

"Maybe I'm fucked in the head," Hunter said. "I could blame it on my childhood, could blame it on Gavriel, or I could even blame it on my lack of empathy. I just do a job. A job I wanted to quit until you came back." I refused to feel guilty for my part in this, but shame still slapped me in the face. "I don't care about the people at the end of my gun. There's only one person I care about in this world, and that's you. And there's only one kill I regret, and that's your mother."

My traitorous heart panged at that statement. I didn't want to be the pathetic girl that gave in to pretty words despite his unforgivable actions. But there was power in the purpose and motivations of a man.

"What about Mack?" I asked. We were driving across the country to save him—or to fulfill Gavriel's job, whichever way you looked at it—but he had to care about Mack at least a little.

"Don't you see?" Hunter asked. Though we were both staring out the windshield, it felt like I was locked in a tension-filled staring contest with him, just waiting for the words that would follow. "I care about Mack, obviously. But I'm driving across the country and risking my life because he's important to *you*. I would have done the same for Nicole, but something told me Gavriel was bluffing."

Those words left a bitter taste in my life. His answer should have flattered me, but it didn't. "I guess that's just hard to believe. You've spent so long convincing me that you hated me, that any sort of compassion or care feels inauthentic."

Hunter immediately crossed three lanes of traffic to pull off the highway. I screeched in confusion as an old Honda honked its horn at us and zoomed past. Hunter put his truck in park, then turned to face me. "Listen," he said. I kept my gaze fixed on the window. His hand reached over to grab my chin, jerking my attention to him.

"I'm listening," I gritted.

"I spent a ridiculous amount of time being cruel to you. I twisted your mind. I convinced you that you meant nothing to me, because I was terrified by the idea of obsessing over you. I had a lot of guilt over the death of your mother, a feeling I wasn't used to. You make me...empathetic. You make me care. I know that this thing is over. I can feel it. There used to be this strong tether between us, and yesterday it snapped."

I could feel it too. Things did feel over between us. And even worse, I was saddened by it.

"But when you leave here to live the rest of your life, free of me, I want you to at least know that you're the only person I've ever truly felt something for."

I was? Having the validation of hearing what I meant to Hunter felt freeing. I'd been wanting those words for so fucking long. "I just wish you would have been honest with me in the beginning."

"I don't regret it," Hunter replied honestly, his thumb now stroking my cheek. I reveled in the warmth of his hand. "If you had known, you would have never let me kiss you. Touch you. L-love you. It might have been a lie, but I'm thankful for it."

Love me.

Me too, I thought. It felt sick, and dirty, and wrong. I hated how easily I melted at his kindness. It gave me such whiplash. Not enough time had passed for my damage to air out. And yet I was thankful for the lessons Hunter had taught me. I was thankful for the journey. And most of all, I was thankful for the truth in the end. This moment felt a lot like closure, so why did it hurt so fucking much?

"Thank you for being honest with me, Hunter. I wouldn't have changed it either." I wasn't planning on admitting the last part of that, but I did it anyway. He was right. I never would have fallen for him had I known. But now the lines were blurred. The loyalties were skewed. Would I align myself with the ghost of my mother?

Or would I forgive the living, breathing man that saved me?

Hunter was right. Mom died long before she took her last breath. I just felt like I was supposed to feel a sense of loyalty to her. I was supposed to be outraged.

But I wasn't.

I was just sad. So, so sad. Sad for the woman that died before she could heal, and sad for the relationship lost before it could start.

He leaned forward, staring at my lips for a lingering moment as more cars passed on the highway. His truck shook from the force of another passing eighteen-wheeler, and I pressed closer. "You're welcome, Pretty Debt," he whispered.

Chapter 18

HUNTER

Gracie Mansion mocked me. The yellow wooden house on the Upper East Side of Manhattan was surrounded by shrubs and thick trees that seemed immune to the incoming fall weather. Hardly any leaves had fallen, and the branches were covered in foliage. Mayor Bloomington's home looked over the East River, but the open water had no covering, so a boat was too obvious for long-term watching. I ended up finding a vacant Airbnb close by. It didn't have ideal views, but at least I could settle for a bit and observe the perimeter. When dealing with a high-profile kill, you had to be willing to get creative.

Guards walked the front lawn with guns holstered to their waist. They looked like the men Gavriel employed and nothing like the clean-cut suits a proper mayor would hire. Tats covered their tanned arms, and I caught a few of them smoking joints along the side of the house. They looked dangerous, but they were relaxed. This could play in my favor. But what they lacked in organization and clout, they made up for in numbers. Twenty men were stationed on the lawn, and there was no telling how many were kept inside. Was Bloomington always this heavily guarded? Or was he anticipating retaliation from Gavriel? Something told me the answer was a little bit of both.

I couldn't get close enough to do a proper stakeout, and my eyes were blurred from the exhaustion and staring into my binoculars for the last two hours. I watched for patterns. When shift change was. Who was coming and going. If there were any known criminals sneaking in through the back door.

It was like a miniature White House, hidden away from the center of the city, with enough security to protect the President. As a man familiar with death, I knew that this ancient home reeked of it. I read once that Alexander Hamilton was brought here to die after a duel. My exhaustion imagined ghosts fluttering across the lawn.

I struggled to keep awake. My mind was muddled with thoughts of Roe and stretched thin by our drive here. We made it in three days, switching off every six hours for the last day and a half so we could get here faster. I was thankful we could divide the ride. I wasn't sure how many more secluded nights in small motel rooms I could handle. It had been a long while since I had to go ghost, and I'd almost forgotten how exhausting it was. Adding Roe to the mix just made me confused, depressed, and sexually frustrated. I needed a good shower and a hot fuck. Not necessarily in that order. And then I needed to hold her. I needed to pulse forgiveness through her veins.

After rubbing my eyes, I continued to watch from my perch. Mayor Bloomington ran a tight ship, but with a little patience, I caught some important details. I saw Lorelei Brand, his rumored mistress, seamlessly stroll through the front door without care. She wore an easily detectable, bright red dress with her tits practically hanging out. No paparazzi sitting by the lawn dared take a picture, though their relationship was a well-known scandal in the city. My guess was, everyone feared the bastard and didn't want to put gossip about his sex life on a headline, because he had a habit of making people disappear.

So did I.

Seeing Lorelei made me realize that Bloomington was bold as hell. My preliminary research on the car ride here told me that during the election season, he sold himself as a bona fide family man. His wife and teenage twin daughters followed him on the campaign trail, boasting of ethics and values important for the city. His wife was a pretty woman. He had to either be pussy-whipped or egotistical to think the city wouldn't care about who he sneaks into his bedroom which was funded by taxpayers. Either he was good at controlling the narrative surrounding him or he was lucky to have enough influence and power to not care. Either way, it wasn't good for me.

I watched as more people filtered through. He must've been planning to host an event, because gardeners, caterers, florists, cleaners, and other random people started showing up in the afternoon. They loaded tables and chairs into the weathered yellow mansion. A gardener started wrapping the trees with twinkle lights.

A quick scan of the local news told me that the mayor would be celebrating his birthday tonight. Everyone was invited. Even President Gump would be making an appearance, which was bad news for me. There would be too much security here. Secret service. NYPD. There was no way in hell I'd be able to sneak in undetected and kill him. It was all too public.

But also, this reaffirmed my belief that Mack wasn't being held at the Gracie Mansion. Bloomington wouldn't want to risk someone finding him—that is if there was someone left to be found.

I put my binoculars away and climbed off the ledge where I was sitting. I refused to think that Mack was dead. My fucked up brain was fixated on the idea that I could make everything better with Roe if I just saved him. This was my path to redemption. I craved Roe's forgiveness like I craved her touch. I had to do this. For her. For Mack. And for me.

I checked my burner phone. Roe was at a motel outside of the city, waiting for me. I convinced her to stay behind and rest, but she was probably doing pushups and other shit to break a sweat and pass the time.

Roe: Are you done yet?

Hunter: Headed back now.

I was thankful that she didn't insist on coming. The long drive from Joshua Tree to here was mostly spent in silence. But what little talking we did was centered around my routine as a killer. I told her how I had to understand my target and watch their patterns. I told her about high-profile cases and the level of security I'd need to get around in order to make this happen. I shouldn't be proud of the fact that I was a good killer, but her faith in me to save Mack made me a bit proud. It was strange to speak so openly about my job. I was worried the flippant way I spoke of death would be triggering for her so close to the revelation about her mother. But she took in the information like a sponge. She didn't speak with judgment, mostly just surprise.

It was dangerous to tell her about my kills. Every word that spilled from my mouth could lock me away or land me at the bottom of the lake. But now that the truth was wholly out, I couldn't stop it. I wanted her to know everything about me. I wanted *someone* to know everything about me.

Roe: Hurry back

I focused back on my task. Where would Bloomington keep Mack?

I started researching the properties he owned, but all of them were too public. It was almost ridiculous how easy it was to find. Lorelei's smug face hit me like a ton of bricks. Maybe his mistress was helping him? I quickly looked her up and surprisingly found nothing about her. She had no school records but used to work as a waitress at a seedy bar in Harlem. There were no photos of her with Bloomington, either. A few gossip blogs mentioned her by name, but even those were watered down with ridiculous speculation that would be difficult to prove. It took some digging, but I found records of a house she bought in Muttontown. Paid with fucking *cash*—Bloomington's cash, no doubt. It looked like she stayed there regularly.

I mulled over the secluded house. Google Maps showed me that the lot was huge with shaded trees. It was a historic home, something the wealthy loved to buy and fix up so they could brag about the *original* wood, just to paint over it. A quick search of county records gave me blueprints with detailed information about a large basement—a large basement that would be perfect for housing and torturing someone.

Gavriel would probably be pissed if I spent my time looking for Mack, but I didn't really have a choice. The birthday bash tonight was a real bitch on my plans. I had to be a ghost, and that was impossible to do with Bloomington sitting under a gigantic spotlight. I needed more time.

I debated sending the elusive Bullets leader a message, but I knew the rules. Above all else, keep his name out of my dealings. He didn't mind micromanaging the deaths of those he deemed unimportant, but Bloomington was too well known to be caught with your dick in your hands. I looked at my burner phone and quickly typed a message to Roe while trying not to think of how fucking risky it was to have her in the know. It was weird doing this with someone. It was weird having someone I could report to. The entire situation was definitely fucked up, but I really liked having her to talk to. It made me feel human. It made me feel sick.

Hunter: I think I found Mack

I waited for her response, hating the ancient technology of the burner phone in my hands, because I couldn't see if she was typing or not.

Roe: Is he alive?

I chewed on my lip. The truth was a dangerous fucker, but I knew I needed to be cautious about getting her hopes up.

Hunter: If he's alive, he's in Muttontown.

Roe: And if he isn't?

I couldn't come up with a good response. There wasn't anything I could do if he wasn't. I was already planning on bringing Bloomington down, and if I could bring back the dead, I would have done that ages ago. Instead of answering her, I slipped the phone in my pocket and gathered my duffel bag full of supplies. I'd have to go tonight. Most of his guards would be at the party. It was my only chance. Now, I just had to convince Roe to stay home. I'd tie her down in the bathroom if I had to.

Hunter was gone for eight hours. I tried my best to understand his process as an assassin, but it made me anxious when he was gone. When he'd come back to the motel, every bone in my body ached to hug him for some ridiculous reason. I knew I had two choices today. One, I could cry and workout and burn through my energy with tears and regret. I could hate Hunter today. I could think of ways to get back at him. Or two, I could push it aside. I could wrap up what happened and put it in a nice little box in the back of my head. I could pretend it didn't happen and use my time to support the man that would save the only father figure I'd ever had.

I chose the second option.

"You found Mack?" I asked quickly while pulling myself up off the carpeted floor and walking toward him. Hunter set his duffel bag down on the bed and pulled the black shirt he was wearing off before tossing it on the floor.

"I think so," he replied while popping his neck.

"What does that mean?" I asked. Hunter made his way to the bathroom and pushed his black sweats over his thighs, revealing his tight, toned ass underneath. After turning on the hot water, he got into the motel's shower, then sighed in relief. "Are you okay?"

"I'm just tired. Long trip. Long day. I was on the balcony for hours trying to come up with a plan." A plan. Right. I ran over to my iPad and brought it into the steamy bathroom. Condensation started to fill the mirror up with fog. I sat on the toilet and scrolled through the information while trying not to watch the outline of Hunter's form washing his long, muscular body.

"I did some research on Gracie Mansion today," I said while scrolling through the websites I'd bookmarked. "Did you know it has tunnels underneath it? They lead to the East River. People used to smuggle goods, and it was used as a quick escape route for—"

"Where did you find this information?" Hunter asked before shutting off the water. I set my iPad down and quickly grabbed him a towel. I somehow managed to hand it to him without gawking before answering him.

"It was on a couple of sites," I answered excitedly. Maybe Hunter could sneak in through the tunnels. He wrapped the cotton towel around his waist and passed me to stand at the bathroom sink.

"I'm assuming you want me to sneak in through these tunnels?"

"It could work," I replied, hopeful I had actually contributed something.

"You want me to sneak in through the *novelty* tourist trap tunnels that every history buff with half a brain knows about?" Hunter asked sarcastically while placing his flat palm against the glass to wipe away the moisture.

I completely deflated. He was absolutely right. "I just figured—"

"You're not the assassin here," Hunter interrupted. "I am."

"I know that. I just feel helpless sitting here. I tried to find out information on Bloomington. I looked at his social media and looked at all the people he spends his time with. I just want to contribute something."

Hunter grabbed some shaving cream from the toiletry kit we'd picked up at a gas station in Virginia. After lathering it up in his hands, I watched as he meticulously applied the cream to his sharp jaw, which was covered in scruff. He rinsed his hands off, then grabbed a razor before leaning over the sink for a better angle. The towel looked like it was about to slip. All thoughts of the mission at hand fled my mind as I stared at the gorgeous man shaving his face. What was it about men shaving that was so fucking hot?

"You came here thinking we would be sidekicks. You practically blackmailed me into bringing you."

"After you threatened me away," I grumbled.

"The point is, this isn't you. You don't know how to read a situation the way I can. You don't know what you're getting yourself into. My mind hasn't miraculously changed just because we drove across the country together. You're not coming with me."

I knew in my boiling blood that Hunter was absolutely right. This wasn't me. I wasn't a murderer. An executioner. I couldn't analyze every aspect of a scene within seconds. It took a certain skill set to do what Hunter does. "So what can I do?" I asked as Hunter finished shaving and wiped his face clean.

As he turned to face me, I stared at his stacked body and tried to remember that we were nothing. We had to be fucking *nothing*. "You can stay here. You can stay safe. You can be ready for when Mack comes back. He's probably going to need medical attention."

"Right," I said while making a mental note of all the supplies I would need. I didn't know how intense his injuries were, but this was something I could focus on. This was something I could do. "Got it," I replied.

Hunter pursed his lips as if he wanted to say more. Instead, he simply nodded and spun around and strutted out of the bathroom, the towel firmly in his grip. I followed after him, clutching my iPad with a vice-like hold because the sight of Hunter had me feeling so hot and confused and disgusted with myself that I couldn't trust my fingers not to reach out and touch him.

And it wasn't just his cut abs and piercing blue eyes. Hunter Hammond was a beautiful human. There was no denying it. No, it was the way he handled the situation. He was so fucking sure of himself and had every step laid out. This was his domain, and even if many heads rolled in his kingdom, it was still sexy to watch him wield such surefire power.

"What else can I do?" I asked while looking up nearby pharmacies. I could walk a block and have a first aid kit ready and waiting.

"You can pack your bag. You can be ready to leave at a moment's notice. I'm not sure what tonight will bring, but if I don't come back, you have to promise me you'll get the hell out of here."

That request made me pause. I looked up from the iPad just as Hunter pulled his boxers up over his thighs. I caught a flash of his junk and had to swallow my tongue. "I'm not making that promise," I replied as he put on his jeans. The tight denim taunted me.

Hunter ran a hand through his hair. "Yes. You are. I can't guarantee I'll get Mack back. Hell, I can't even promise you that *I'll* make it back."

"What is that supposed to mean?" I asked. My feet moved of their own volition. I shuffled closer to him, my lips parted in a half-hearted combination of awe and concern.

"There's a reason Gavriel wants me involved. I'm expendable."

Expendable? Hunter was far from fucking expendable. Even if I was struggling with what he'd done, that didn't mean he was expendable. I said things in the height of my hurt, but Hunter was meant to be in my life for a long fucking time. "But you're not going after Bloomington tonight," I stammered. "You said Mack was being held somewhere else."

"Yeah. Somewhere that could very well have thirty guards waiting for me." Hunter must have seen the fear on my face, because he let out an exasperated sigh. "I'm not trying to scare you, Roe. I'm just trying to prepare you for the reality of the situation. Mack might already be dead. I might die too."

"You're the best of the best," I insisted. "That's what Gavriel said."

Hunter smiled and glided closer to me. "Your faith in me is really fucking nice. But I just want you prepared to run, okay?"

That wasn't good enough for me. I rested my hands on the waistband of his jeans and lifted up on my toes to brush my nose along his. "I don't like this. It's like I have to choose between leaving Mack there or risking you."

"I didn't realize you cared," Hunter replied, prodding for the confession he knew was already there. "Besides, you're not making this decision. I am. Gavriel is. He wants Mack saved and Bloomington six feet under."

I didn't realize you cared.

Hunter looked like he was about to back away from me, but I pulled him close. "Am I crazy for caring?" I whispered. "Are you just going to throw it back in my face? Am I wrong for...wanting you?" My dark mind answered for me: Yes. Yes, it was wrong. "I should hate you, right? I should want nothing to do with you. Part of me knows this. The rational part of me doesn't think any reason is good enough for killing her."

"But?" he asked.

"But the other part of me knows she wasn't healthy. The other part of me is slowly remembering the signs. The whispers she'd mutter under her breath. The promises she'd make. I rarely left the house. I...I'm not ready to think poorly of my mother, Hunter."

Hunter leaned down and kissed the top of my forehead. "If I could do it all over again, I wouldn't take this for granted. I wouldn't have run. I wouldn't have ruined us before we even started."

"Why does it sound like you're telling me goodbye?"

"Because I am. Because I usually have more time to prepare shit like this. Because this is a high-profile kill."

"No," I began. "You're the fucking best of the best. You're Hunter Hammond. I've *seen* you in action. You and I both know that you've got this under control. If you're just trying to make me scared so we can have goodbye sex, I'm not giving it to you."

At that, Hunter chuckled. "You caught me," he replied. Some of the tension in the room disappeared, but I still held onto him. My fingers dipped. Our breaths quickened. His hands wrapped around my waist and squeezed.

"Don't tell me goodbye. I...I'm not ready for this to end. I want to work through this. We just need more time. There's so much I wanted to do. So much we need to say…"

"I do owe you two orgasms," he said, trying to once again lighten the situation. "And you know how important debts are to me."

"We are not having goodbye sex, Hunter Hammond," I explained breathlessly while pressing against his chest. My fingers curled, as if aching to dig into his muscles.

"We don't have to have sex. I just want to get you off," he growled before picking me up. "You can't say things like that to me and not expect me to want to kiss the fuck out of you." I wrapped my legs around his waist and whimpered. His lips found my collarbone, and he kissed my soft skin while walking over to the bed before laying me down. What the fuck were we doing?

"You don't get off until you come back," I insisted. I wanted him to have a reason to return.

"Of course, Pretty Debt." He sucked on my collarbone after saying that, then started migrating down my body. He lifted my sweater up a few inches to kiss my stomach. The sight of him slipping down, down, down had me shaking.

"Call me that again," I whispered while sitting up. I grabbed the oversized burnt-orange knit sweater that covered my torso and took it off, my head getting clumsily caught in it. I was ruining the moment, and intrusive thoughts started creeping in as I struggled.

"Pretty Debt," Hunter began while helping me out of the tangled mess, "you're adorable."

I rolled my eyes and reached behind my back to unclasp my bra. The moment my breasts were free, Hunter's crisp blue eyes widened, and he licked his lips. "Call me that again," I whispered, suddenly nervous to show him the script I had permanently needled into my skin. Our previous fucks had been too quick, too rushed for him to see. I softly touched myself, tracing lines along my cleavage, drifting lower so he could see.

"What is that?" he asked as I lifted up my left breast to show him the artful curve there.

"Pretty Debt," I whispered. I'd had the name put there. Words were powerful. The name he picked for me felt permanent, and I wanted the reminder of Hunter on my skin long after he was gone.

"You're fucking crazy," Hunter whispered in astonishment before leaning forward to run his tongue over the cursive. "You barely knew me."

"I knew enough."

"Should I be getting a restraining order?" he teased before licking my nipple.

"It wouldn't keep me away."

Hunter sucked my skin while kneading my flesh. I threw my head back against the overstuffed pillows cushioning my body. Every cell in my body was on fire for his touch. He grabbed the band of my yoga pants and pushed the tight spandex material down, and he stopped fixating on my breasts and the tattoo that decorated the underside of them to look me in the eye.

"This isn't goodbye, Pretty Debt," he whispered. Fuck, I loved the nickname. I had missed it so much. "But promise me you'll leave if I don't come back."

"Never," I instantly replied. Hunter dipped his finger between my thighs and plunged it inside of me. He rubbed his palm along my clit. His lips devoured me as I moaned into his mouth. The pulse in my clit was *throbbing*. His other hand went back to my breast and squeezed it. My hair fell around us as he fucked my mouth with his tongue, and my cunt with his finger. I rolled my hips around his hand, whimpering demands as I went.

Faster and harder. I could feel my skin growing wet with sweat and the liquid heat pooling between my thighs. "Promise, Pretty Debt," Hunter groaned against my bottom lip before biting down on the bruised, plush skin. He tugged and tugged, like he could pull devotion out of me by his teeth.

"No." I could feel the crest of my orgasm coming on. "I'm so close," I whispered.

"Too fucking bad," Hunter said with way too much glee. Hunter stopped moving. I knew he would. I knew he'd hold my pleasure hostage until I agreed to keep myself safe.

"I promise," I lied. Hunter pulled his wet finger out of my cunt and licked it. Long, slow, and languid. He savored the taste of me with his eyes closed.

"Do you?" he asked.

"I do. Now pay your debt, Hunter Hammond." It was meant to be a teasing comment, in reference to the two orgasms he owed me, but there was more there. More to our story. More guilt and forgiveness and redemption shared between us than we could ever articulate.

His eyes flashed with an emotion I couldn't place. He stared at me for two breaths with his lips parted. "With pleasure," he replied before sinking down my body and plastering his lips to my pussy. He kept pushing and pushing. My legs fell apart. I loved his mouth. Hot and hard. He teased me with his tongue, flicking and brushing in ways that drove me absolutely insane.

My eyes wanted to flutter closed, but I stared at the beautiful, hardened man surrendering to my cunt. "You taste so fucking good," he rasped. "I just want to drown in your cum."

I shivered at his hot words. "Yes!" I screamed as he flicked against my hardened clit. I was squirming and arching my back, trying to get closer to his mouth, though it felt like too much. His tongue was commanding and sure. The rhythmic move of his mouth was driving me right back to that crest. "So close." Hunter sank against me, pinning my trembling legs down with his arms while eating me out. I came hard. It had been building up for so long that my body practically exploded from the sensation. I felt my muscles dip and relax. My eyes closed. I ground against his lips as my back arched and moans of pleasure escaped my mouth. "Fuck!"

"One more," Hunter said with pride before standing up. I felt limp lying on the bed but already greedy for more. I might have come, but I wasn't done. Not yet.

Hunter stripped off his pants and boxers as quickly as possible before hovering over me. "Pretty Debt, this isn't goodbye sex, okay?" I nodded as he positioned himself over me.

I flipped over on my stomach and rested my chin on my shoulder. "Make me come, Stalker," I moaned.

Not needing any more invitation, Hunter grabbed my hips and pulled my ass toward him. Hardness greeted my tight hole, and I whimpered at the idea of him thrusting inside of me there. "Not today," Hunter said, as if reading my mind. "I want to take my time when I fuck your sweet ass,

Pretty Debt."

He rubbed his dick along my slick folds, coating his cock with my cum and teasing my sensitive nub all the same. His hands threaded through my long hair, and I felt him tug. It was then that I realized we were in this position exactly five years ago—right before he drugged me and left me. Emotions clogged my throat, but I didn't want them to ruin this moment. "Fuck me already," I said, letting my dirty desires take over because I couldn't handle my emotions. This felt a lot like the last time he said goodbye to me.

Hunter stopped. "This feels like goodbye sex," he whispered.

"It's a little familiar," I agreed.

Hunter gently eased me back onto my back. He looked me right in the eye. "Pretty Debt," he whispered before thrusting inside of me. He held onto my thigh as he plunged deeper and deeper. I cried out at the invasion of his hard cock. I locked my eyes on his, not breaking with each punishing thrust or even when he pressed his forehead to mine.

Our breathing aligned. Our moans filled the motel room. In and out. In and out. Sweat covered both of our bodies, and hours seemed to pass in that moment. Both of us were lost in each other. Fucking and coming, over and over and over again, in the safety of our non-goodbye.

And when we were done, Hunter held me.

"Remember what you promised me," he said. He was determined to make me understand. Fleetingly, I wondered if he was planning on not coming back. Maybe he was worried I'd lock myself in this motel room waiting, drifting away to nothing but bones and grief.

"You're going to try your hardest to come back, right?" I asked.

"I promise."

Chapter 20

HUNTER

The mansion at Muttontown had stark white wooden walls covering the expansive exterior. It was an intimidating sort of influence. Pride bled from the large double doors of the entrance. Privilege and secrets could be seen from every carefully planted shrub. The luscious green lawn surrounded a long, winding driveway made of brick, and the perimeter of the mansion had a tall gate of black steel.

I felt like I was walking blind. Because I spent all day researching where Bloomington lived, I didn't have time to stake out the Muttontown mansion where his mistress stayed. A few Escalades with tinted windows were parked out front, and as I waited for the right moment to sneak inside, I noticed various men with tattoos crawling up their necks coming and going. They definitely didn't look like appointed security for the mayor.

At around ten p.m., Bloomington's mistress exited from the front door and was escorted to one of the Escalades by a large man. He didn't even glance up from his phone as he walked her to the car, which told me this was a *really* inexperienced security team. They might have looked big and intimidating to the untrained eye, but they were lazy and cocky. Anyone worth their salt would have found me already with a simple sweep of the perimeter. This was both good and bad. Good because I could slip in easily, bad because untrained idiots with guns somehow always managed to do the most damage.

I stared at his mistress. Unlike the red ensemble she wore before, she was now wearing an elegant black gown that was both sexy and classy. I guessed Bloomington had a dress code for his birthday party. I also guessed he wanted her showing up later to avoid confrontation with the missus.

I wore all black and was strapped with weapons from head to foot. I had a pistol on my hip, an assault rifle on my back, and a Glock on my ankle. There was also a metaphorical knife in my chest from thoughts of Roe. Today had been tragically perfect. Her body was this soft, beautiful thing that shivered and quaked when I touched it. Her cum on my tongue was the sweetest taste. I was a fucking goner.

But I had to focus.

I knew that the security system at the mansion would trip the moment I hopped the fence. Luckily, it wasn't located in a gated community with its own security, but the police station was only ten minutes away. I estimated that I only had seven minutes to get inside, find Mack, and get out. I had been in worse situations, but there was no guarantee that the blueprints I had were up-to-date or even accurate. And on the off chance a police officer was on patrol close by, I could have much less time.

In a pinch, I could disappear out the back and slip into the neighbor's yard. I had parked my truck inconspicuously up the road and changed my plates before coming here. Usually, I would have months to coordinate and plan out something like this. I had to think of every last detail on the fly.

Once I was confident I could break in, I took a steadying breath and pulled my ski mask down over my face before hopping the fence. Every exterior corner of this house had a security camera mounted to it. I didn't want anyone getting a glimpse of my face. An alarm didn't sound the moment my feet touched the ground, but I knew I had tripped a silent trigger.

I sprinted in the shadows up the drive, toward the house, and didn't bother approaching the front door. There was no way in hell I could kick down a deadbolt in the amount of time I had. I also didn't want to waste my energy on that shit. There was no telling how many people were inside, and I needed to diligently focus on conserving my time and strength.

Using the knife I had strapped to my thigh, I punched a first floor window, shattering the glass and creating a space for me to climb through. Once the excess shards were pushed out of the way and there was clearance for me to slip in, I hoisted myself up and entered the home. If the alarm hadn't gone off when I hopped the fence, it was definitely going off now. I had six minutes at best.

I quickly realized I was in the sitting room. I didn't take much time to look at the decor, but noted the oversized furniture and a ridiculous portrait of Lorelei petting a pretentious looking white cat. The pussy had a hot pink collar encrusted with diamonds. Once I had my bearings, I made my way down the hall to where I knew the basement was. I kept my ears open, listening for signs of anyone. There was still one Escalade parked out front, which meant there were still people on the premises.

An empty house would be ideal, but keeping those guards stationed here meant that Bloomington had something he needed watching. I could only hope it was Mack.

I inched down the hallway toward where I knew the basement was, but paused when I heard a loud TV in one of the rooms up ahead. My brain scanned my memory of the blueprints I saw, trying to locate the source of the sound in my mind. There was a game room toward the back of the house that neighbored the dining room. Laughter boomed in that direction, making me grow rigid. Who was here? How did they not know *I* was here?

I took a moment to direct the adrenaline coursing through my body. It was always the calm before the kill. I took a deep breath and willed stillness through my body. The greatest strength was being able to control your fight or flight response. Your instincts knew it was dangerous; you were prehistorically conditioned through years of evolution and primal preservation to respond to fear. If you could stay calm, you won.

I went still. I stepped closer.

In this sort of situation, I knew that it was better to ask questions later. I also knew that it was better to be on the offense instead of the defense, so I quickly traveled down the hallway while gripping my assault rifle in both hands.

Once at the entrance to the room, I craned my neck to look inside, freezing when I saw three men sitting on a couch. It didn't take me long to realize that they were drunk off their asses. One of them was snoring, and the other two were watching a terrible vintage porno on the television. Amateur lusty music filled the speakers. I literally caught them with their dicks out. The porno was in a foreign language, and the guards were jerking off and laughing at the eighties hair and terrible acting. I guess it distracted them from the awkwardness of wanking it together.

Beer bottles and white powder covered the coffee table, and the room smelled like stale farts. It was like walking into a frat house. I guess, while the boss was away, they wanted to play.

I continued to scan the room, then froze when I saw a fourth body tied up to a chair in the corner. Bruises and blood covered his face, making his features nearly impossible to make out. But I knew instantly who it was. Mack. Getting him out of here would be fucking impossible. From the looks of it, he wasn't even conscious.

His hair was greasy, like he hadn't been allowed to shower in days. His skin was pale and clammy, like he was feverish. I'd bet my left nut that one of the many wounds covering his face was infected. He needed to be cleaned up and put on some antibiotics as soon as possible. I checked my watch. Fuck. I didn't have time for this. Even if these drunk bastards weren't paying attention, I knew we wouldn't be alone for long. It wasn't safe to linger.

One of the guys let out a laughing, repetitive grunt. "He, he, he." It was timed to his meaty strokes, and I could see sweat dripping down his temple. Fucking gross. It felt similar to my last assignment back when I lived in Denver. Flashes of the hooker I shot in the motel echoed across my mind. I didn't want to stick around. I easily aimed at the one going to town on his dick. The other one had already shot his load into a napkin. I breathed in. Breathed out. Pressed my index finger over the trigger and released a silent bullet through the air.

Down. Blood. Gore.

Screams. I released another. And another.

The three guards were dead in exactly six seconds.

I was simple and efficient. One minute, I had three grown ass men with families, pasts, sins, kinks, and preferences alive. The next, I sent them flying into oblivion. I was completely calm. Blood stained the powder blue couch. My heart rate slowed. My eyes closed. I could almost smell my mother's perfume of cigarette smoke and disappointment.

To some, murder was this traumatic thing that scarred them for life.

My kills were anticlimactic and boring. *This* was why I hated it. It made me feel inhuman. It made me feel like my mother's shitty boyfriend, Forest.

I jumped into action and quickly jogged toward Mack. Dropping to my knees, I shook his thighs gently, spurring him awake. Mack's swollen eyes opened and widened as much as they could, taking in the sight of my mask-covered face in delirious confusion.

I ripped off the tape covering his mouth unceremoniously and winced when he groaned. "Stupid fuck," Mack moaned while shaking his head.

"You're welcome, dick breath," I replied while pulling my knife out and cutting at the ropes binding him.

"Why the hell are you here? You won't make it out alive. I've tried t-twice." His voice was shaky. He was feverish as fuck to the touch. Mack needed a doctor immediately. "None of this is worth it. Gavriel's blackmail isn't worth it."

I didn't understand a single word that he said, but I managed to cut him free while listening. I didn't usually like to know Gavriel's reasoning. One, because it made me even more involved than I already was. And two, because it just pissed me off. I didn't like knowing that all of this was for some petty gang shit.

I hauled Mack up to a standing position, and he looked around the room in confusion. "Is that a dead man with his dick out?" he asked while furrowing his brow.

"Yes."

"I think he broke my nose."

"Your entire fucking face is broken. Let's go."

I guided Mack out of the house, gripping his elbow and dragging him along. I kept my ears open for approaching cars and didn't hear anything. Mack was wheezing and using his free hand to grab his side. Every step seemed to pain him. Fucking hell. I might have to carry him.

We walked right out the front door, deciding the pomp and circumstance of a grand exit was better than forcing Mack's broken body through a busted window.

I was skeptical of how easy it was. Someone should have shown up by now. Mack was practically in the open. The three guards watching him were useless. This was a fourteen-and-a-half-million-dollar home, and not a single cop showed up to check it out. Something was up.

We exited the front gate, and I had to practically drag Mack down the road. His legs were shaking as he walked. The night moon illuminated the pavement in front of us, and crickets could be heard chirping in the grass. "We'll never make it. We'll never make it."

I ignored Mack's repeated musing as we made my way to my hidden truck parked off the road and covered by trees. I was just about to open the door and help Mack inside when I heard *it*.

I heard the deadly parade.

Three decked out Escalades barreled down the road. Some of them had their windows open and guns aimed at the woods. Their headlights cast shadows along the trees, and I knew with complete certainty that they'd either find us or we'd end up in a car chase we wouldn't win. "Fuck."

I opened the driver's side door and shoved Mack inside. He struggled and whimpered as I pushed his back to get him in. Fishing in my pockets, I handed him the keys. "You better fucking stay awake and survive this, old man. If we both die, I'll kick your ass in hell."

"I'd argue with you, but we don't have time, and we both know you always get your way. God's speed, asshole."

I patted his shoulder. "My phone is in the glovebox. Call Roe and get to her. I'm going to take their cars down. The second I get the first one, you haul ass out of here. The distraction will give me clearance for the other two and should give you enough time to make it out."

I slammed the door shut, not waiting for his response. I didn't have time for goodbyes. I didn't have time to even think.

I held my gun at the ready and crouched down. Slipping closer to the road, I watched the headlights as they drove up and down the asphalt, looking for us. I went to my knees, then my stomach. Looking through the sight, I followed the closest Escalade as it sped down the road. I aimed. I breathed in and prayed they didn't have bullet proof tires.

One.

Two.

Three.

I exhaled and pulled the trigger, hitting the front, driver's side tire. The

Escalade spun out of control and ran into a towering tree. Wood splintered and exploded at the impact, as a shower of leaves fell down from the branches.

Behind me, Mack shot out of the woods and passed me on my right before peeling out on the drive.

The other two cars stalled indecisively, and a few men stumbled out of the first car. Mack drove on, not giving them a chance to catch him, and I waited for one of them to jolt out of their stupor and chase after him. One second passed, and the second car sputtered to life, accelerating down the long road after Mack. I aimed. I breathed in and out.

Down. I hit the rear tire with ease, sending the car to flip round and round and round. I listened to the crunching of metal. The squealing of tires. It scraped along the pavement and didn't stop until it hit dirt.

Adrenaline and satisfaction made me smile as I watched through my scope. The first car had all its doors open, the men flooding from the seats like ants to help their friends. I aimed at one of the taller men. He was a large, broad target.

Down.

I scanned the night for another. "Got you," I whispered when I found a clear view of another suit-wearing ill-trained idiot.

I aimed.

I let thrill spike through me.

I breathed in the smell of burning rubber and death.

"Not so fast," a low growl said. I gasped, then twisted my neck to face the man that had found me. But the moment I looked, I was greeted with the bottom of a boot.

And the world went black.

Chapter 21

Mack was half dead by the time we found each other. He couldn't even tell me what had happened. He drove until he couldn't drive anymore, parked, and called me.

I answered the phone, expecting to hear Hunter's honey voice. I'd been pacing the floors of my motel room, anxiously waiting for his call. I was thankful that Mack was alive, but that relief was short-lived.

Hunter stayed behind.

I wanted to have a moment of panic, but time was of the essence. I took a cab to where he was parked at three in the morning. The mediocre first aid kit I'd grabbed at a local pharmacy wasn't nearly enough to help Mack. His face was so swollen he couldn't really make facial expressions. His nose was crooked and broken. His eyes so swollen I was shocked he could see the road. He moaned and argued as I drove him to the hospital. "Don't take me to a damn hospital. I need Advil." I knew I was breaking some gang rules by taking him there, but we didn't have much of a choice. He was feverish and bloodied. I was surprised he managed to drive away.

"You need antibiotics. Maybe even surgery. You're wheezing."

"Fuck," he groaned as I sped down the road. I was thankful it was the middle of the night. At least I didn't have to fight New York traffic.

"You have to run," Mack said. We were parked outside the hospital. I'd run inside to get help, and we both had to wait a couple of minutes for a few nurses to help me lift him out of the truck. "You have to get out of here."

Hunter's promise stood out in my mind as Mack was pulled onto a stretcher. *Run. If shit goes south, don't stick around.*

I wasn't going anywhere.

"Mack. You're going to be okay, right?" I asked while following the team of nurses walking into the hospital. They were barking orders to one another, assessing his damage in rapid-fire procession. I could barely keep up.

"I'll be fine," he grumbled. "I fucking hate hospitals."

I realized quickly that his aversion to this place had nothing to do with outing his gang and everything to do with his daughter. I wished we had more time for me to reassure him, but Mack wasn't the type to talk about his feelings. I honestly just hoped they pumped him with enough painkillers that he forgot where he was. I softened and followed the team toward a set of doors. "Only family past this point," one of the nurses that was holding a clipboard said.

I snapped my gaze to them and rolled my shoulders back. "He's my dad," I explained quickly. I glanced at Mack, and his battered face twisted into a half smile.

We barreled through the door, and they started hooking Mack up to IVs. I waited by the curtain, watching with fear. "That's my daughter," Mack said, pride seeping through his tone. "She's my daughter, guys," he then slurred again. Tears filled my eyes. Mack really was my father. He protected me. Loved me. He was the only constant in my life.

"He's delirious," one of the doctors said. "We need to get his fever down."

"I want a cath and blood sample now," another said.

At the mention of the catheter, I immediately slipped out. I absolutely refused to see that.

I stood in the waiting room for a minute, glancing at the door leading to where Mack was, then back at my feet. I wanted to be here for him, but Hunter needed me too. I couldn't take on Bloomington by myself. I wasn't stupid enough to get my*self* trapped and killed, too.

But I knew someone with the resources to save him. I knew someone strong enough to stop all of this.

"Ma'am," someone said, drawing me out of my thoughts. "Is that your truck parked out front? You need to move it."

I took a deep breath. Mack would understand. I had to do this.

"Yeah," I replied. "I'm leaving. Can you give this number to the charge nurse? Tell him to call it with updates on Mack McCrey."

"Ma'am, there are forms to fill out..." he called at my back. I ignored him and strode out of the waiting room before getting in Hunter's truck. After turning it on, I took a deep breath.

It was time to find Gavriel Moretti.

———————

I DIDN'T HAVE to knock on the door of Gavriel's building. I just stood outside and waited. Gavriel saw everything. He knew everything. Three minutes in the autumn chill was all it took before two guards were walking toward me. "I'm here for Gavriel," I said to them while cautiously raising my arms up for them to pat me down.

"If I were you, I'd leave," one of them replied before running his hands over my back and down my thighs. They led me inside, and my heart raced. Last time I came here, things were different. Hunter said Gavriel didn't want to be involved, but this was *his* kill. This was his mission. I wasn't about to let Hunter die because of stupid gang shit. It wasn't fair. Hunter wanted out, and even though I knew Gavriel would have brought him back regardless, it still made me feel like shit that we were in this position because I couldn't let him go. There were no regrets, and I wouldn't trade my new understanding of Hunter for the world, but that didn't mean I was going to let this ruin everything.

The posh building was dark, the shades drawn, blocking the early morning light. Despite this, everywhere was stirring with life. I could hear a shower running down the hall, and I smelled bacon cooking. "He's in the kitchen," one of the guards said.

"Lead the way." My voice was rough. Feet trudging across the carpeted hallways, I kept my eyes and ears open. I didn't exactly know what I was going to say to Gavriel. I was desperate for help and had nothing to bargain with. Gavriel *seemed* to care a lot about family and loyalty, but that didn't mean shit. He was in the business of looking out for himself.

A hint of sausage joined the smell of bacon, both the savory scents filling my nose when I entered the kitchen. Gavriel was wearing a thick burgundy robe and was flipping eggs on the stovetop. "You shouldn't have come," he said, his back facing me.

"You and I both know I had to."

Gavriel reached to his right and grabbed a handful of onion and bell pepper to add to his breakfast concoction. "You don't know the rules, but you'll learn soon enough." I swallowed as Gavriel glanced over his shoulder at the men flanking me. "Leave," he ordered calmly.

I waited patiently as the two men shuffled out of the kitchen. Even though I knew they worked for Gavriel, I felt even more afraid when they left. Being alone with the infamous Bullet leader was like walking into a lion's den. It was like standing out in an open Oklahoma field and waiting for the tornado to touchdown. He was deadly. It was just the vibe he gave off.

"Hunter was captured last night," Gavriel began. He still hadn't turned to look at me, which for some reason made me even more scared.

"He went to save Mack," I explained.

"He should have waited. Bloomington was the target." Gavriel's voice was cold and calm. His shoulders rolled back with confidence as he cooked.

I shook my head. "Mack would've been dead by then. He's barely alive now."

Gavriel meticulously grabbed a nearby navy blue porcelain plate and put his breakfast on it. I watched him fold a cloth napkin into the shape of a triangle and slip a silver fork inside of the crease. "There are always casualties in war, Roe Palmer."

"But this isn't even our war!" I wasn't planning on raising my voice to

Gavriel Moretti, but it was infuriating how calm he was. "None of this is Hunter's fault, and now he's been captured." Tears started to slowly stream down my face. I hated looking so weak, but the emotions of the last few days had finally caught up to me.

"You're right," a soft voice from behind me said. "It's not your war. It's mine." I spun around to look at Sunshine. She was wearing a black silk robe that hit midthigh. Her hair was wild and full-bodied, like she'd been rolling around in bed all night. I didn't know this woman from Adam, but a spike of anger surged through me at her words.

"I was going to bring you breakfast in bed," Gavriel said. I was still very confused about all of their dynamics.

"I wanted to come downstairs," she replied. "Let's all have a seat, hmm?" At her request, the three of us found chairs at the breakfast table and awkwardly sat down. I didn't know what to say, but I was restless. I didn't have time for any of this. We needed to get to Hunter now.

"My father was a very bad man," Sunshine said while picking up her fork. She daintily put the cloth napkin in her lap before looking at me. "I've made it my mission to tell the world about the sins of my father. It's been several years since he died, but more and more information is still coming out. I'm still finding victims. We're still discovering his associates."

I briefly wondered what it was her father had done, but it didn't feel right to ask. What did this have to do with Bloomington? Sunshine seemed almost fragile as she spoke. She paused for a moment to run her thumb over the edge of her fork, as if counting each point. "I came upon some evidence linking my father to Bloomington. There's a network of men in political positions who use their power to get away with very bad things."

Her father must've had to be pretty damn bad. She was determined to bring him down even after death. And yet…she married a mob boss. It almost felt hypocritical, but I wasn't one to judge.

"So you have evidence on Bloomington?" I was trying to understand what she was saying without pushing too far. "Why don't you just go to the police?"

"For starters, it's not enough evidence to incriminate him," Gavriel replied. "Besides, men like him have too many people on the inside. He's too powerful. Two influential. Hell, he parades his mistress right under his wife's nose and yet is portrayed as this huge family man. We even tried submitting the tapes to someone in the news just to put doubt in the public's eye, and our contact ended up dead."

"But you have the leverage," I replied in confusion.

"Not strong enough leverage. It's not enough to get him in jail."

"If he's so powerful, then why not just let it go? Forget the blackmail and leave it be. Revenge on a dead man isn't worth all of this," I spat out. Gavriel immediately slammed his fist on the table. I jumped, but Sunshine stayed completely still. Apparently, that was the wrong thing to say.

"I can't let it go," Sunshine said while gripping her fork. I felt bad for Sunshine. She was obviously tortured by whatever her father did. She seemed lost in revenge. Just because I didn't understand the details, didn't mean I didn't feel empathy for the woman. But at the end of the day, I was here for me and mine. I was here for Hunter.

Gavriel spoke up as she stared off at the wall. "We had hoped Hunter would get the job done quietly so we could get our revenge and move on. Then Mack tried to be the hero, and Bloomington found out who was trying to tarnish his image."

"So what now? He has Hunter," I said.

"He does," Gavriel agreed. I tried to stay patient. He sounded far too fucking calm for all of this.

"I'm still confused. If your evidence isn't enough to do anything, why does he even care?" I asked.

At that, Sunshine let out a dark laugh. "He knows someone has tried repeatedly leaking a video of him and Paul Bright to the press. But up until Mack went Rambo on Gracie Mansion, he didn't know *who* had the video. And right now, our only leverage is that he doesn't know what the video *is*. He just knows it exists."

"He's spinning plates," Gavriel added. "Hundreds of them. One is bound to drop."

Paul Bright? Why did that name sound so familiar? Was that Sunshine's father?

"What is on the tape you have?"

"It's a video of Bloomington meeting my father at a park. The camera is shaky, but you can hear him shouting at my father to delete some tape. He's saying it was just one time. He didn't want to do it again."

Clarity hit me. "Bloomington thinks you have your father's tape."

"And whatever is on it is incriminating enough that it won't matter what connections he has."

"But you don't have it?"

"No."

I stewed over all of this information. Sunshine had blackmail but not *enough* blackmail. Bloomington was searching for who had the *original* tape.

I smiled.

"You don't have to have the actual tape. You just have to convince him you do," I replied, an idea forming in my mind. "It's your father's tape, right? If you showed up threatening to out him, he'd have to believe you."

"What are you saying?" Sunshine asked.

"I'm saying. You go there with a wire. You get him talking. Convince him you have the tape, then get him to admit what's on it. A confession is far more valuable anyway. There's nothing that can cover that. And we can bargain for Hunter. Trade fake blackmail in exchange for him and a confession."

"I don't like that plan for obvious reasons. We could just storm Gracie Mansion and kill them all. Assassins are cleaner, but I'm not afraid of war," Gavriel replied dryly.

I rolled my eyes. "You seemed pretty afraid of it when you sent Hunter in to do the job for you," I retorted.

"I sent Hunter to do the job I pay him to do. Don't question my ability to get something done, Roe. You need my help, remember?"

"You can't just kill the mayor and have widespread casualties, then expect no one to notice or come knocking down your door."

Sunshine pinched the bridge of her nose while gnawing on her lip. "We should arrange a meeting," she whispered.

"Absolutely not. Blackmail trades never work. The trust is never there. Who's to say I didn't copy the video? Shit like that never ends well, and if I make a grand show of caring for Hunter, Bloomington will feel like he has leverage. He'll threaten his life like he did Mack. Acting like I'm indifferent about his life is the only thing *keeping* him alive."

"Then don't bargain for Hunter. Bargain for cash, or whatever else it is you think you could squeeze out of him," I offered.

"Once again," he continued in an annoyed tone, "trades like this never work." He spoke to me like I was a naive child.

"*Make* it work," Sunshine interrupted. She stood up and placed her plate in the sink. Gavriel and I waited for her to continue. "I'm not going to let another person die because of Paul Bright. Call Bloomington. Tell him to meet us, and we'll exchange the evidence for Hunter. We'll meet him with gunfire. I don't care about the odds against us."

"He'll fight back," Gavriel argued.

Sunshine sauntered over to Gavriel and bent over to kiss him on the cheek before speaking sternly to him. "Then I suggest we fight harder. I want to be done with this. Let's kill the bastard so we can move on."

My brows shot up in surprise.

Gavriel wrapped his hand around Sunshine's wrist, squeezing gently. "Are you sure about this?"

"Yes, sir," she replied with a tight smile. "You just better not die, or I'll make sure to find you in hell and drag you back to me."

He shook his head, then looked at me. "I'll arrange it."

We sat there for a moment, and then I shamefully remembered something I should have been thinking about all along. "Wait. Nicole is here. Can I see her?" I asked while shooting up out of my seat. I was seriously the worst friend in the world, but I hadn't had much time to worry.

"She's in the guest room down the hall," Sunshine said with a smile. The heaviness of our previous conversation was starting to wear off. "I really like her. She reminds me of an old friend of mine, Phoenix. I think

I've convinced her to move to New York and run our club!"

What the fuck had happened these last few days? "I'll go see her," I stammered while exiting the kitchen.

"Third door on your right," Sunshine said. "We'll come get you once things are ready."

I nodded while jogging down the hallway. Counting doors, I made my way to the guest room Sunshine had indicated and threw open the door. Sure enough, my best friend was sleeping butt ass naked on satin sheets with her tits out. The shades were drawn, and her light snores filled the room.

I sighed in relief at the sight of her, then felt the weight of this week and my worry for Mack and Hunter hit me like a train. Part of me wanted to go back to the hospital. Part of me felt drawn to Hunter. And the other part of me just wanted to crawl into bed with my best friend and have a good cry.

The latter part of me won. Slipping out of my shoes, I crept closer to Nicole, smiling at her cat-like snores and sprawled body. I lifted the sheets and curled next to her as tears streamed down my cheeks. She woke up almost instantly. "Roe?" she asked. "Is that you?"

"I missed you so much. I'm so sorry," I sobbed.

Nicole wrapped her arms around me and held me tightly. She didn't yell at me for running away or getting her into this mess—though by the sound of it, she and Sunshine hit it off. Something told me anyone Sunshine liked was off limits to Gavriel. He might wear the pants in their relationship, but she controlled the zipper.

"Honey, don't cry!" Nicole's sleepy voice said. She scratched my back with her long fingernails as I hugged her.

Nicole did what friends do. She held me as I cried. She didn't ask questions. And when the sobs had stopped and exhaustion took over, she cradled me as I started to fall asleep, brushing my hair with her fingers and murmuring words of encouragement. Though I felt guilty for giving in to my tiredness, my body felt heavy and lethargic. I hadn't rested in days, and it was all piling up on me.

"Sleep," she promised. "I'll wake you up and yell at you later, boo."

"Thank you," I whispered. I'd need the rest if I was going to save Hunter.

Chapter 22

HUNTER

My head felt like I'd experienced my own personal earthquake within the confines of my skull. The first thing I felt when I regained consciousness was complete and total pain. It was like my brain was too big for my body, swelling, swelling, swelling and spilling out through my nose and ears.

Blood tainted my tongue, the rusty taste coating my teeth with crimson evidence that something was very wrong with me. "Get him out of the truck," a voice said. The tone was muffled, as if he were speaking from the inside of a coffin. Or maybe it was me that was in the coffin. I couldn't be sure. My vision was black, and I felt fabric wrapped around my eyes. A blindfold, meant to hide where I was. It stifled my breath too. It was like my entire head was stuffed in a cloth bag.

Metal clicking clanged against my vibrating senses, and strong arms yanked me from the lying position I was in. I quickly grew to recognize the binding ropes wrapped around my wrist and ankles. I struggled to see how tightly they were tied, but they didn't budge. My skin burned from the friction. I was swiftly tossed on the concrete by whoever had pulled me from the car, and I choked on groans of pain at the impact.

"He's safe," a voice growled. I tried to place the Northern accent and familiarize myself with the tone. My survival was dependent on my ability to pick up the little details. But my brain was so damn confused from the agony swirling around my brain.

"I want to see his face," a voice replied. I knew that voice well. It belonged to the man who taught me how to fire a gun. It was the same voice that had both bullied me and built me into the man I was. Gavriel Moretti.

Harsh hands ripped the fabric from over my head, and I blinked at the bright lights that greeted me. I don't know why I was expecting the night sky and complete darkness; it felt like I had been sleeping for days only to wake up in the dead of night. But no, it was bright afternoon. The sun was unhindered by clouds and buildings. It beat down on all of us mercilessly.

"See?" the other voice replied. "He's fine." I blinked my eyes a few times, trying to focus on one thing—on anything. The world bounced, and my vision was so blurred it was like looking through a muddy river. I blinked again, then blinked a third time and swallowed the moan of pain that traveled up my throat and threatened to break past my teeth.

I needed to shut it down. Pain was temporary. Death was forever.

Slowly my vision cleared as I strained to focus. Mayor Bloomington's short stature stood in front of me, a Glock in his hand and two strong men flanking either side of him. It was almost humorous seeing him up close. He was short and stocky, with his dark hair combed over to hide the baldness in the middle of his head. He had a cocky sort of expression, as if he were convinced everything was under control. My fingers twitched against their bindings, and I ached to grab the gun from his palm and shove it in his mouth so I could pull the trigger and end his pathetic life. I'd never wanted to kill someone so venomously.

"I'm assuming you want to trade? The video for your assassin?"

I fixed my eyes on Gavriel, who was surrounded by his men. Blaise Bennett. Callum Mercer. And Ryker Hill.

"I'm not really good at trading," Gavriel replied coolly. I didn't know what game he was playing at, but having all of us here wasn't very good. I quickly counted at least forty men behind Gavriel and just as many behind Mayor Bloomington. We were in a large open space, it looked like a clearing of trees in upstate New York. A large concrete slab covered the ground, like a building used to be here. Escalades, Hummers, and Jeeps created a circle of massive vehicles around us. One glance behind me, and I was able to see that they pulled me from the trunk of a Range Rover.

I guess they didn't want to have the showdown in the public eye. A gang fight out in the open would look bad for the mayor, and Gavriel probably wanted to avoid getting arrested. Probably. I rolled my eyes.

Slowly, my brain started to piece together what was happening. The pain receded as I pulled my focus to my surroundings. It was like tugging the curtain back on my mind and letting clarity through. I didn't have time for suffering. "I'm not really good at that either," Mayor Bloomington replied.

"You're just good at kidnapping, fucking, and murdering innocent boys, huh? That's why you were hooked up with Paul Bright, after all," Gavriel replied.

Anger fumed through me. I didn't usually like to know the reasons for my kills, but I was thankful to hear this. So he was a sicko? I eyed the asshole up and down. He certainly looked like a disgusting fucker, and the careless way he paraded his mistress in front of his wife just furthered that point. He was selfish and entitled. It would make ending Mayor Bloomington's life that much more pleasurable.

I watched as the mayor's cheeks turned red. A split moment of terror flashed across his features. It lasted only a moment, but even my sluggish mind caught it. I saw in that brief moment that he was absolutely guilty. But then he opened his mouth and let out a dark laugh, as if the accusations were amusing to him. A couple of the guards standing by took small steps away, shifting to create distance between them and the murderous pedophile.

"Your accusations are bullshit," Mayor Bloomington said. "Killing boys was more Paul's thing. I don't think you actually have a video. If you did, you'd know that I was more into watching than participating."

What a sick motherfucker. Fucking hell.

An expression I couldn't place crossed Gavriel's features. It looked like a cross between determination and disgust. I was feeling the same thing. I had plenty of reasons to want to kill this man. It stopped being Gavriel's fight when he hurt Mack. But knowing this, simply validated the kill. Mayor Bloomington was breathing on borrowed time.

"Evidence is for cops," Gavriel replied. "I don't need proof to know you're a shitty human and even shittier mayor."

Mayor Bloomington clutched his chest in mock pain. "Ouch, Gavriel. That hurts. *Especially* coming from a washed up gangster. Your empire has slowed down over the years. I'm surprised you even had the resources to show up. And not to be rude, but your men could use some proper training." Fucking bastard. I had other shit to worry about, but that was definitely a hit to my pride. I didn't like sitting here on the floor tied up. I was Hunter Fucking Hammond. "I've always wondered why the Bullets took it upon themselves to ruin Paul Bright's legacy all those years ago. It wouldn't happen to be because of that sweet piece of ass you're married to, would it?"

I knew immediately that was the wrong thing to say. You could break every single bone in Gavriel Moretti's body, and he wouldn't give two fucks. You so much as breathed in Sunshine's direction, and you were a dead man. Blaise, Callum, and Ryker all wore equally murderous expressions. This little standoff was going to end soon, and there was a good chance that Bloomington wouldn't make it out alive.

"I'm bored. Let's end this."

Though he mock yawned for emphasis, I saw the quick snap of his hand and the rapid fire of his gun. Gavriel was the first to shoot, and flying bullets rained down like hellfire on the open space. I lifted my bound hands up to cover my head and rolled toward Gavriel, my head throbbing as I went. One bullet clipped my ear mid-roll with an echo of screams bouncing along my skull, but I continued until two hands lifted me up and a knife sliced through the ropes on my wrist and ankles.

"You'll have to teach me that rolling maneuver," Blaise Bennett, Gavriel's right hand man, said in a slight shout. "You looked like a cute little rolling pin."

Rolling pin? They were seriously fucking with my pride. "Fuck off and give me a gun. Where is Gavriel?"

"Already in the bulletproof van," Blaise said before shoving me behind a Hummer. Glass shattered to our right as a car sped off. "That bastard got the glory shot of nailing Bloomington between the eyes, then left. We had a bet that whoever made it home first gets to eat Sunshine out," he teased. Only Blaise would joke in the middle of a fucking shoot-out.

I peered over the hood of the Hummer and aimed at one of Bloomington's men as more cars sped by. Some of his guards were fleeing. Some of them were hiding. Only a handful were shooting back. His men definitely felt no loyalty. All of Gavriel's men stood like brick walls, making sure his car got out of there safely while firing at the mayor's men.

I aimed at a guy with blond hair and a tattoo of an eyeball on his jugular. I shot him quickly, hitting him in his left temple. "Ryker is gone— probably racing Gavriel home. Callum is dragging Bloomington's body to one of the trucks," Blaise said, giving a play-by-play while shooting down another guard. "Man, I haven't had fun like this in ages."

I spotted a man hiding behind a large slab of concrete. He wasn't even looking where he was shooting, just holding down the trigger of his automatic rifle and aiming blindly. He took down four of his own men before showering us with bullets.

"Shit. Fuck. Damn. These idiots have no idea what they're doing," Blaise said before tossing me another magazine. I reloaded my gun, then aimed at the idiot.

I breathed in and out, then shot him in the chest.

My head ached. My parched mouth was pursed. "Okay, the others are loaded in the car. Let's go," Blaise said before opening the back door to the Hummer and climbing inside. I joined him and had to duck and crawl across the passenger seat and the center console to get behind the wheel.

"Go!" Blaise demanded, his body hanging out the back window as he shot at the remaining guards. I sped off, kicking up dust as I went, leaving behind nothing but blood and bodies.

"That was a fucking mess," I said, shaking my head.

"Yeah, I don't envy the team that'll be on cleanup duty for that." The adrenaline and Blaise's nonchalant attitude made a wide grin cross my face. "Shit. We did it! Your girl was all worried for nothing," Blaise said with a wave of his hand.

My girl? "Roe? She's still here?"

"Yup. Probably braiding Sunshine's hair or some shit as we speak. Gavriel *might* have left while she was asleep. She seemed like the type to want to come, and none of us really wanted the risk of pissing you off—though I have to admit, you've lost your touch."

My mind ran with thoughts of Roe. I told her to leave, but she didn't. "Thanks for saving me," I said, feeling awkward as I accelerated and merged onto a highway.

A hand clasped my shoulder, and I glanced at Blaise from over my shoulder. "You might be this independent, recluse badass, but you're still a Bullet. Bullets forever, bro."

"Yeah," I replied incredulously. "Bullets forever."

But this entire ordeal helped me realize that now more than ever, I desperately wanted to leave the Bullets behind.

Chapter 23

ROE

Gavriel Moretti had a gym in his building. A *nice* gym, with fancy equipment, a steam room, and plenty of treadmills, ellipticals, bikes, and various weight machines. But I didn't want to use any of that. I missed my simple gym. I missed punching a faceless bag until my knuckles screamed. I was on the ground doing crunches. Up. Down. Up. Down. The repetitive movement was like rocking a baby to sleep.

"They're going to be okay," Nicole said from her corner of the room. She was sitting on a bench, munching a jelly donut and drinking orange juice.

Up. Down. Up. Down.

My core cramped with every movement. Sweat dripped down my abs.

"I can't believe that bastard left without me. I wanted to go," I gritted.

Nicole rolled her eyes. "You and I both know that you wouldn't have been helpful in that situation. And maybe I'm selfish, but I'd rather you not die. Any word on Mack? Should we go to the hospital?"

Mack. I probably *should* go to the hospital, but I felt glued here. I was desperate for updates and just wanted to know what was happening. "The nurse called an hour ago. He's on antibiotics. They stitched him up, and he's sleeping." I felt bad for not being there waiting for him, but I was only one person. One of the things my mother taught me was that you couldn't pour from an empty cup. Maybe that's why our relationship felt so calculated and strained. She had nothing left to give me, because all her energy was spent surviving. Besides, I knew that I wouldn't be much help there. Mack needed to sleep, and I needed to focus on not completely freaking the fuck out.

"That's good," Nicole said. Her voice was cautious. "Let's go there whenever you're done doing...whatever it is you're doing. Is this what your gym time is like? I feel like this is some hella toxic coping mechanism, girl."

"Can we do therapy some other time? You already spent the last hour yelling at me. I'm not saying I don't deserve it, but I'm about at my threshold of taking shit." I did another crunch. Up. Down. Up. Down.

"Fine," Nicole huffed.

I moved until my abs burned, and then decided that it was time to stand up and run until I puked. Wiping the sweat from my brow, I pulled myself up and was about to do just that when a commotion down the hall made me snap my attention to the door. "Hunter," I whispered.

My feet moved fast, pounding the tiled floor as I ran out of the gym and down the stairs to the entryway. I couldn't pick out any specific, individual voices. My feet shook as I moved. Drowning in anxiety, I didn't stop until I was running into the commotion. "Whoa, whoa," a tall man said as I collided with a hard chest. I looked up and stared at a man that was splattered with blood. "Slow down," he growled before wiping his forehead with the edge of his sleeve.

It looked like a war zone. Bodies entered the immaculate foyer, covered in blood. A few of them were limping. There was a too-still body lying on the tile in the far corner that I knew in my twisted, paranoid gut was dead with a capital *D*. Luckily, he had brown hair, so I surmised that it wasn't Hunter.

Sunshine was fluttering around, dividing people up by injury, with Gavriel at her side. The other men I met when I first visited with Gavriel strolled in, looking disheveled and annoyed. The moment she saw them, Sunshine let out a sigh of relief and wrapped them both in a hug before quickly unbuckling the blond's belt and using the thin leather strap as a tourniquet on a man bleeding out. Damn, she was a pro at this.

"Hunter?" I called out while picking through the various men, searching their faces for him. "Hunter?"

Someone else walked through the front door, Blaise. "Honey, I'm home," he shouted, obviously uncaring about the chaos going on. It really felt like soldiers coming back from war. Unlike everyone else, Blaise looked like he just got back from an afternoon stroll in the park. Not a gelled piece of hair was out of place, and he still wore his aviator sunglasses, with a smile on his face. Sunshine immediately went to him for a quick hug before returning to the writhing man on the floor.

I had just started to push through the crowd to get to the front door and ask Blaise if he had seen Hunter, when a second slumped body stepped through the threshold. My heart swore immediately. I knew who it was, despite the large blooming bruise on his forehead the size of a golf ball. Dried blood covered his swollen face, too. He staggered inside and searched the room, and I got the sense he was seeking me out just as I was looking for him. Our eyes collided, and it felt like the entire fucking world stopped spinning.

"Pretty Debt," he mouthed.

"Stalker," I mouthed back.

The broken men surrounding me slowed. Their groans of pain dimmed at the site of Hunter. My heart beat three achingly slow times as I stood there in a trance. A body bumped into me. Blood splattered on my calf. It was a brief, fleeting moment of relief—but it was ours. I savored it, I treasured it, and then I immediately jumped into helping Sunshine.

"This man is about to bleed out," I said.

"I've got a team of doctors that'll be here in five minutes. They've been on standby," Gavriel yelled over the noise. He had his phone stuck to his ear and was barking orders to whoever was on the other end of the line. "I want the cleanup crew to get rid of every body left on that scene. I don't want anyone linking it to me. If there is a single hair or drop of blood left behind, I'll personally cut your balls off." My brows rose at his threat.

"Hunter?" Gavriel then called. "On a scale of one to getting captured by Bloomington's men, how capable are you of making the mayor's body disappear?" the mob boss growled. Hunter exchanged a longing look with me before answering the angry Bullet leader. I knew what he wanted because I wanted a reunion too, but there was too much shit going on.

"I'm on it," he replied before following Callum outside.

"You," Gavriel said while pointing at Blaise. "Make every single bullet-holed vehicle parked in my underground garage disappear. Take it to Josi's junkyard. They don't ask questions."

"On it," Blaise pouted before blowing Sunshine a kiss.

On and on and on it went. Gavriel took control of the situation like he'd been doing it his entire life. I guess, in many ways, he had. He was born for this. If anything, this entire situation made me realize how unfit Hunter really was for the Bullet life. This wasn't him. The more I saw of the Bullets, I knew that on the surface he seemed like a perfect fit. Protective and kind. Brutal. Demanding. Smart, hardened by his past, and assessing, but also gentle when he wanted to be. I wasn't disillusioned about what he was *capable* of. But this life was chaotic. He needed the calm seclusion of Joshua Tree. He thrived in simplicity. I'd seen the evidence of it. This wasn't his life. Hunter wasn't a Bullet. Not really.

I stood there and helped where I could, eager to help while thinking, *what now?* We were safe, Bloomington was dead, Hunter looked okay, and Mack was stable. I pushed myself to be busy assisting Sunshine, because the alternative was thinking about my reunion with Hunter. I couldn't help but wonder if all of this would end with goodbye.

———————

Lovely

Waiting lips like lovely little dips of your hands.
I patiently admire the way you always have me at the edge of my seat.
I realized long ago that waiting doesn't feel like
waiting when it's for someone you love.
I also realized that love isn't as cruel as everyone thinks.
It takes work. It takes grit and forgiveness and grace and patience and…
Waiting lips.

"You're still up," Hunter said while slipping into my hotel room. I spent the afternoon mopping up blood on the Moretti foyer. I snuck away for dinner with Mack at the hospital and had been staring at the ceiling of my hotel room for the last hour. I didn't want to stay at Gavriel's home. Two men died there today, and it felt too familiar and triggering for me. I had grown a lot, fueled by the truth, but it didn't mean I felt like opening myself up to the fresh ghosts now living there.

"You're still alive," I croaked, emotion bubbling up my throat. He slipped under the covers and enveloped me in a hug. Pressing my head to his cheek, I breathed in his woodsy scent and grounded myself in the fact that he was here. He survived.

"Takes more than that to kill me," Hunter said. His tone sounded forced and playful all at the same time. We both knew this was a close call. He was lucky to be alive.

I looked up at his face, wincing at the golf ball sized bump there. "That looks awful."

"Some asshole kicked me." I reached up and hovered my fingers over the swollen wound. "Gavriel fired me today. He said I single-handedly started a war, and I should go back to Joshua Tree."

My mouth dropped open in shock. What? Did that mean… "You're free," I whispered in awe.

"I'm no longer an assassin," Hunter stated. He spoke as if the concept were foreign to him.

"What are you going to do?" Part of me wanted to know if he planned on going back to Joshua Tree, but most of me wanted to know if his plans would include me.

"I'm not sure," Hunter replied. "I guess that's something we should talk about."

I guess it was a good sign that he wanted to discuss it with me. Did this mean he wanted... I tried not to hope. "Is this the part where we have the *what now* conversation? It's been a long day. I'm not sure I can handle you deciding that it's better to leave me—or even worse—having a *define the relationship* talk," I murmured while closing my eyes. I couldn't handle the disappointment. Now that the danger was gone, would Hunter be willing to push past his bullshit and allow himself to love me?

"You're mine, Roe Palmer," Hunter replied. "I'm not going to risk another second without you in my life. Another moment. Another—"

My heart fucking soared. My chest swelled with a foreign sort of happiness I had buried down long ago when he first left me. "Hunter?" I interrupted. I was feeling bold. And I fucking wanted him. I didn't want him to make any plans or promises just yet. Things were still raw, and we had a lot to discuss. Just knowing that he *wanted* me in his life was enough for now. We could work out the details when things weren't as raw. "How about you show me what this thing between us is instead of telling me?"

"So impatient," he teased. "And yes, I plan on doing that. But first..." his voice trailed off, and he threaded his fingers through mine before kissing the back of my hand. "I love you. If I'm being honest, I've always loved a version of you. That love evolved and changed over time. I loved the innocent baby that made me feel like I could fix the sins of my parents. I loved the growing girl that had survived such a tragic childhood. I loved the teen girl that rolled with the punches and demanded answers from me. And I love the woman that didn't give up on me. I love the woman that tracked me down and demanded better of me. I love the woman willing to forgive me."

Willing was right. I wasn't quite there yet, but I also wasn't pushing him away either. I understood him. I also understood that I'd want Hunter forever. If I wanted a shot at happiness, I'd have to work through this grief. He was willing to help me walk through the trenches of that sadness, and even if he caused the fire in my soul, I knew he was the only person capable of helping me put it out.

His voice choked up, and I swallowed his emotion with a kiss. He responded to the feel of my lips in a devouring sort of way. We both tangled our tongues and our doubts up in a pretty little knot, then drowned in the sweet taste of our love. I kissed down his neck, stripped him out of his shirt, then groped for his cock. I didn't want to waste any more time. He dug his fingers in my hair before pressing me into the mattress, and I felt secure under his weight. "You smell so sweet, Pretty Debt," he whispered. The tiny pulse between my legs throbbed, and arousal painted my inner thighs with molten heat. He slid his hand lower and lower, grazing my breasts, circling my navel, then dipping inside my panties. I was breathing hard. *So fucking hard*. Panting. Sighing. I wanted. I craved. I ached.

He wrapped his free hand around me and squeezed me, pulling me hard against him while his other hand continued to tease my cunt. Hunter rubbed his middle finger over my clit in small, slow, teasing, miserably leisurely circles. Neither of us talked for a long while. We let our bodies move with the melody of our hopes and gratitude. It was just us. The truth was out. There was nothing left to say.

He rubbed faster, making me gasp and whimper. My nipples pebbled;

the hard little points poked through my bra. I needed something more. Something only Hunter could give me. I craved his solid dick pulsing inside of me. But not yet. My stalker would make this moment last. Everything he did was with intention, and this would be no different.

My clit continued to pulse at his command, and I felt my orgasm climb that summit. I wanted for him to make me scream and come, and for us to submerge one another in everything we'd been denying ourselves. I wanted to be breathless in an endless cycle of pleasure and reassurance. I stroked his cock with my trembling hand as he lavished my mouth with more kisses. His scruffy beard created a harsh and unforgiving friction against my cheek. I could feel him everywhere. And still I wanted more.

He broke our kiss to speak to me. "Do you feel that?" he asked. The thick, hard ridge of his cock nudged my palm, making me groan. "I've never wanted anyone as much as I want you."

I came at his words, bursting with bright, blinding bliss all over his hand. He was relentless, drawing out every ounce of pleasure with his middle finger. Rhythmic, tantric, he demanded an orgasm from me, and I was helpless to deny him.

Within seconds, we were both stripping out of our clothes, baring ourselves to one another completely. He hovered over me with while sucking on his finger, moaning and groaning and licking up my cum like it was fucking honey. "You're so fucking sweet," he promised. I lifted up to bite his cheek, drawing his attention back to me. My heart practically jumped out of my chest as he moved over me, taking my lips once more.

The heat of his tongue sent buzzing sensations right between my legs. I cried out, but it disappeared in his mouth. I tried to taste myself on his tongue, but it was all him. "Fuck," I groaned between kisses. I slid my hands up and took the back of his neck to lock him closer to me. I never wanted this to end. My blood was rushing under my flushed skin. "Fuck me," I begged.

Hunter positioned himself at my entrance. "Your sweet, tight pussy was made for my cock, Roe."

He slid inside of me with a groan. The invasion of him was hot and full. I gasped and arched my back to allow him deeper. Thighs parted, bodies molded perfectly together. He thrust again and again, harder and harder. All I could do was fall back and take what he had to give me. Take the man that challenged me. Hurt me. Broke me. Then loved me.

And when we came, it was fucking perfection. I wanted him again and again.

My lovely obsession.

Epilogue

ROE

OCTOBER FOURTH

T he dry desert air brushed against my cheeks as I bent over to blow out the candle on my cake. It felt like my entire life had been building up to this moment. I inhaled and tried to think of a wish, the birthday magic held captive in my lungs.

I didn't know how my life could get any more perfect. I had a quiet life full of poetry and love. I had friends. I had him.

I blew out the lone candle and wished for nothing new, just held hope that my life would stay this way. I'd grown into quite the optimist over the last year but couldn't help clinging to the wish that this would be the life I lived forever.

"Happy birthday, Roe!" everyone screamed. Luna was fist pumping the air and drinking something strong from a shot glass. Butterfly was praying and looking up at the moon, a serene glow on her face. Nicole was popping her ass in celebration to the low music playing from our jukebox. Roxanne just clapped politely.

Dad looked on, his eyes swimming in tears. He was proud of how far we'd come. He visited once every other month and was looking at moving closer. I guess he was finally ready to retire.

"What did you wish for?" Hunter whispered, his lips hovering over the shell of my ear. His arms were wrapped around my bare middle, and I caught him glancing down my black crop top from over my shoulder. There was one word that best described us: insatiable. Having one another didn't make our obsession end, it made it bloom.

"This," I croaked. "I want this forever."

Hunter shuddered behind me, moved by my words. I knew he wanted this forever, too. "Go sit down. I'll cut the cheesecake."

We decided to keep with the housewarming tradition for my first official birthday celebration since Mom's death. "Okay," I beamed.

Hunter and I had a tiny house built on the plot of land where his airstream was. It was eight hundred square feet and overlooked the mountains. The kitchen had a subway tile backsplash. Our sofa was the same color as the setting sun, and the sheets on our bed were rarely made up—mostly because we messed them up all the time. Hunter built a large wrap-around porch that fit a long enough dining room table to seat all the people we cared about when they visited. It was a simple life. We built it from the ground up. We lived cheaply, worked in the sun, and loved by the moon.

I guess I had become a little bit of a hippie since moving here.

Hunter worked at the compound, raising the horses and leading trail rides. I wrote poetry and shared it online. I'd actually grown quite a large following on Instagram and was currently in talks with some publishers.

"It's so freaking quiet out here," Nicole said while rolling her neck.

"She lives six months in the city and is already complaining when it's quiet," I replied with a laugh. Nicole took Sunshine up on her job offer, surprisingly. Now, she was getting her MBA online while running one of the most successful underground clubs in the country.

"I wanna visit your club, Nicole," Luna jumped in.

Butterfly chuckled. "Count me in too. Let's take a girls' trip to New York!"

"Maybe my father will shut the compound down for a weekend so we all can go," Roxanne said breezily. She and I only got along when we drank, but most of our gatherings involved alcohol, so it worked.

"That sounds awesome. I miss Sunshine," I replied.

Hunter growled at my back while placing my plate of cheesecake in front of me. I twisted to stare at him. "What's wrong, Stalker?"

"I'd have to come with you. I'd be a miserable, jealous fuck if you went to a sex club without me."

"Only if you put on a show, Lover Boy," Luna laughed, making everyone else join in.

Dad looked like he wanted to exit the conversation and fly back to New York. The look of pure discomfort on his face made me laugh.

"Everyone dig in!" Hunter shouted over the commotion, albeit a bit nervously. I directed my attention to the cheesecake in front of me and gasped at what I saw there. Sitting on top of the dessert was a ring. A motherfucking ring! It had a gold band with a black onyx pear-shaped stone on top. A halo of diamonds surrounded the centerpiece, creating a dramatic effect I loved.

"Roe?" Hunter asked. I spun around on my bench to find him kneeling before me. He grabbed my hands and peered up at me with his icy blue eyes.

"I've loved you for twenty-four years. You've seen me at my worst. You've loved me through the hurt. You took a chance on a life with me here in Joshua Tree. We've built a home together. Built a..." Hunter paused to quickly glance around at everyone and back at me. "A family, Roe. We have a family."

He choked up on that part. I did too. At the end of the day, both of us were broken people seeking consistency in the world from people who cared. We now had that in spades.

"You're my heart. My everything. You taught me to let my damage breathe. You ripped open my wounds and let truth and forgiveness flow through. You helped me let go of the past and gave me a future I'm unworthy of but am extremely thankful for. Please, Roe Palmer, will you marry me?"

I leaned forward awkwardly to wrap my hands around him and cry into his neck. I loved him so fucking much.

"Yes, Stalker. I'll marry the fuck out of you," I rasped.

When I pulled away, Hunter had a blinding smile on his face. He reached for the ring and put it on my finger, the gold band easily sliding on. Perfect fit.

"You're mine forever, Pretty Debt."

"I wouldn't have it any other way."

AUTHOR'S NOTE

Hey there! Thank you so much for reading!

We made it! I learned a lot from Hunter and Roe, and I hope you did too. I've always enjoyed poetry, and it was really fun to incorporate it into my writing. Thank you for letting me share that part of myself with you. If you enjoyed this book, please leave a review. Reviews are the lifeblood of an author's career, and it would mean so much to me.

xoxo,
CJ

ACKNOWLEDGEMENTS

This book would not have been possible without the support of my wonderful PA, Amy March, as well as Christine Estevez with Wildfire Marketing.

I would like to say a special thank you to Jane Washington, who always encourages me.

I am grateful to all of those with whom I have had the pleasure to work with during this book. I'd like to especially recognize my editor, Helayna Trask. She always takes the time to dive into the worlds I create and make sure they are perfect for you all. I would also like to thank all the dedicated members of my Facebook group, The Zone.

Nobody has been more important to me in the pursuit of this series than the members of my family. I would like to thank my parents, whose love and guidance are with me in whatever I pursue. Most importantly, I wish to thank my loving and supportive husband, Joshua. Thank you for working hard for our family.

And to my two wonderful children: Everything I do is for you. Everything.

Printed in Great Britain
by Amazon